"Yes, I pledge my hand to yours," Cara blurted out.

It was the wrong answer. She knew that immediately by the dark shuttering of Gordie's eyes. They went from deepest blue to tempest black.

"'Tis done." Clenching her hand in his, Gordie jerked his fist high so that all within the hall might see. "I take Cara Mulvaine as my wife. Be there any kinsman here that deny my right to make this claim?"

"Nay!" the men thundered in one voice.

"Be there any who denies hearing the Mulvaine swear her hand to mine?"

Again the thundering nay resounded and the swelling, shrill sound of Clan McKenna roaring into battle split the air. A sound like none other heard on earth. A battle cry of triumph, a sound so chilling, it would frighten the life out of anyone who was not Kenna born and bred....

Dear Reader,

When we ran our first March Madness promotion in 1992, we had no idea that we would be introducing such a successful venture. Our springtime showcase of brand-new authors has been such a hit, that it has become a priority at Harlequin Historicals to seek out talented new writers and introduce them to the field of historical romance.

This month's titles include *All that Matters,* a haunting medieval tale about an imprisoned woman and her unwitting rescuer, by Elizabeth Mayne; *Embrace the Dawn* by Jackie Summers, the story of a woman kidnapped by a highwayman and forced to play his bride; a Western from Linda Castle that features a blinded hero and the woman who helps him recover, *Fearless Hearts;* and *Love's Wild Wager* by Taylor Ryan, a Regency-era story about a penniless heiress and the rogue who wins her heart.

We hope you will enjoy all four of this month's books and keep an eye out for all our titles, wherever Harlequin Historicals are sold.

Sincerely,

Tracy Farrell
Senior Editor

Please address questions and book requests to:
Harlequin Reader Service
U.S.: 3010 Walden Ave., P.O. Box 1325, Buffalo, NY 14269
Canadian: P.O. Box 609, Fort Erie, Ont. L2A 5X3

All That Matters

Elizabeth Mayne

Harlequin Books

TORONTO • NEW YORK • LONDON
AMSTERDAM • PARIS • SYDNEY • HAMBURG
STOCKHOLM • ATHENS • TOKYO • MILAN
MADRID • WARSAW • BUDAPEST • AUCKLAND

ISBN 0-373-28859-X

ALL THAT MATTERS

This edition published by arrangement with Harlequin Enterprises B.V.

® and TM are trademarks of the publisher. Trademarks indicated with
® are registered in the United States Patent and Trademark Office, the
Canadian Trade Marks Office and in other countries.

Printed in U.S.A.

ELIZABETH MAYNE

is a native San Antonian, who knew by the age of eleven how to spin a good yarn according to every teacher she ever faced. She's spent the past twenty years making up for all her transgressions on the opposite side of the teacher's desk, and the last five working exclusively with troubled children. She particularly loves an ethnic hero and married one of her own eighteen years ago. But it wasn't until their youngest, a daughter, was two years old that life calmed down enough for this writer to fulfill the dream she'd always had of becoming a novelist.

For Gabriel, you are my rock and my foundation.
I love you always.
This one's for you, Spotty!
For Lois Maynard Wiegand, who taught me the
meaning of strength and the courage of
unconditional love.
And for Kathryn Donovan, who instilled in
all her children and grandchildren the art of
spinning a tale.

Book One

THE GHOST OF DUNLUCE

"Ill-gotten treasure profit nothing, but virture saves from death."

Proverbs of Solomon 10:2

Chapter One

Dunluce Castle
Antrim, Ireland
October 26, 1588

The wind howled savagely. The sky purpled and ran black from the north though it was two hours before sunset. Cara Mulvaine leaned into the wind, welcoming the storm's lash against the aches in her body.

Before her, white water swept up the causeway, obliterating rock after rock.

Neta whickered fearfully. Cara stroked her hand down the pure white star that marked the mare's head. In the distance, Mimms romped and howled like a frisky pup. Cara shook her head, but that did not clear it. Likewise, the penetrating cold did little to alleviate the stinging welts that crisscrossed her back.

"We don't any of us belong here," Cara said aloud. The horse perked its ears, straining to hear over the storm's crescendo. Cara searched futilely for a meaningful prayer.

God had long deserted the Mulvaines, and He held in contempt all O'Donnells. Like the enemy families from which she'd sprung, one Irish, the other, Scot, she was doomed and cursed.

So she waited for the storm tide to meet the cliff walls at her back and end her suffering. She could think of not one soul who knew of her despair. Nor one who cared. Her death would be a private matter between herself and God.

Mimms leaped onto a high rock, his long-legged, wire-haired body leaning into the wind. He barked, howled and snapped at the white spume, defying Neptune, daring the sea god to throw his trident all the way to the foundations of Dunluce once and for all.

Cara wished the sea would obliterate the fortress forever.

It would not happen. Dunluce stood firm, unmoved and unaffected by mere wind, pounding surf and gathering storm, while Cara bent against the wind and her horse shivered and trembled in fear of lightning and thunder. Only Mimms courageously defied the elements with the same vigor he used in going after the old man who tormented all of Cara's days. Had the dog not come to her rescue, the welts on Cara's back would be raw bloody cuts and her bones might be broken. The dog championed and protected her. No man in Ireland dared the same.

Mimms ran half a league away, barking ferociously, skidding on the shale to a stop nearest the surging water. His disturbed howl carried backward on the wind. Cara fixed upon that one distant point that on a clear day gave her the faintest glimpse of her never-forgotten homeland, Scotland. Against the encroaching storm, no land could be seen. Instead, a wall of high water raced toward the rocks whereon she stood.

A knot of fear twisted inside Cara's stomach. Her legs stiffened and she braced against the wind...holding her breath...as the water rose higher and higher.

The flap of an uncleated sail rose like a ghost out of the high, incoming wave. It was so unexpected a sight, Cara blinked. The sail snapped, a taut flag tearing away from a tall mast stripped of yardarms. Then the prow of a ship poked out of the crest of the wave. The wave broke and tumbled. The ship fell into the trough, out of sight.

Mimms nearly stood erect, leaping over breakers that washed his promontory rock. His deep, full-chested bark howled a warning, a caution.

Cara dashed her fingers across her eyes, clearing them, and stared hard into the roiling sea. Thunder cracked close and was deafening.

The ship appeared again on the next surge, up for a breathless moment riding the crest, then floundering sideways into the trough as the curl drove over it. It should have capsized. As one massive wave died on the rocky shore, another rose like a tower behind it.

Cara whirled about, striking her boot into the stirrup, hoisting herself astride Neta's back. Her old skirts dragged against the soggy saddle, wool and leather tugging against one another. Neta's warm flanks between her knees, Cara drew her cloak across her chest, glad for the tight weave that shed more water than it absorbed. Standing against her stirrups, she shielded her eyes from the lash of the rain.

The ship spun eastward, a child's toy, rushing toward the dangerous fingers of rock that flanked Chimney Tops, a peninsula of broken jagged stone that stretched far, far out into the sea, seeking Scotland, but not quite reaching it. From Chimney Tops, the legendary *Finn mac Coul* bridged the gap between Ireland and Scotland in the time of fairies and giants of ancient lore.

She walked the faceted stones often when the tide was low, as if that exercise could somehow provide escape from Dunluce. She knew the rocks as well as any. The curious outcrop of stone was no bridge. A dangerous trap waited under the surging water.

Clearly, the ship's pilots knew nothing of the coast. She had to warn them. Galvanized to action, Cara galloped across the slippery shale to join Mimms and shout a warning, hail the ship, alert them of the danger. Had she a light, a lantern, anything? There was nothing. She threw up both her hands, waving, screaming.

The ship surged onward. Closer.

Cara kicked Neta's sides, following the push of the wind eastward. With every surge the ship crept nearer the jaws of death. She thought they knew.

Another sheet of lightning gave Cara clear view of the struggle on the decks. She saw men hauling ropes, throwing baggage overboard. Oars flashed and stroked.

Cara inhaled sharply as the ship swept higher still on the next surging wave. She prayed as the crest washed across the underwater thrust of stone.

Urging Neta round the face of Chimney Tops, she sought higher ground, to see if the ship made it past the barrier reef.

The wind brought the sound of wood shattering. She turned in the saddle and saw oars splinter from the ship's sides. Spar and sail cracked and the thundering scream of the hull rendering asunder came all at once.

Then, Cara heard the scream of the banshee, the spirit that warned of coming death. The wail of pain and sorrow was so deep and poignant, so hopeless and dismal, she crossed herself in fear of it. She did not hear her own voice accompany it.

"Dear God, no."

Men flew from the decks, tumbled out of the riggings and poured from the split halves like seeds spilling from a ruptured melon. The water hungrily swallowed them with huge greedy tongues.

"God have mercy," Cara exclaimed. "No. Don't let this happen."

She blinked her eyes, as if that would clear away the horrifying maelstrom churning in the water below the jutting tors of Chimney Tops. It was real, too real, and she was as helpless against the sea as the men within it.

Mimms abruptly sank to his haunches and howled a lament. Neta whickered in concert, and reared as if to run.

Too late Cara realized Chimney Tops was unfit for man and beast. She reached down with a trembling, shaken hand to quiet her horse, but would not depart.

Drawn to the lowest rocks where Mimms howled his sorrow, she sat astride her horse, staring at the violent sea in silent powerless horror.

Beyond her reach one side of the split galleass stood impaled on Lacada Point. The other half churned in the surging water toward the mouth of the Bunboys. It listed, top-heavy and leaning, sweeping dizzily toward more perilous rocks and turbulent water. Each violent, churning wave wrenched more souls to their death, thrashing men like wheat between millstones.

There was nothing Cara could do. Too much water and treacherous waves separated her narrow swatch of land from the rocks of Lacada Point.

Abruptly, Cara dropped from her mare's back and knelt upon the shingle. A prayer came to her at last. She shivered as the banshee's scream swept landward on the wind, wailing and screeching. It would have its due.

Even as her salt-caked lips invoked the words of forgiveness, Cara felt the hand of God stir the ash-strewn embers of her heart. Life was too precious and too great a gift to carelessly throw away. Why had she thought of it? Because the pain of her grandfather's strap was too much for her shoulders to bear? No. It was not. She was stronger than that. Tears mingled with the rain and salty spray that wet her face. The horror and wanton destruction shook her to her very soul.

Raising her head, Cara wiped the rain and salt spume from her face. Mimms paced between the last jutting tors left uncovered on the causeway. Wild water steadily filled the last passages up the cliffs. Neta jerked again, wanting to be gone.

"All right." Cara came stiffly to her feet, soothing the horse. "Be calm, Neta. We'll go now. Mimms."

Cara looked at the surging tide.

"Mimms, come," Cara called as the wild incoming wave died upon the base of the prisms, obliterating the last shelf of stone beneath her feet.

The dog howled and danced in the crashing waves and would not come away.

"Mimms. Heel."

Mimms was too distraught to obey her command. Holding the reins fast, Cara picked her way carefully through water swirling round her boots and skirt. Her horse balked at crossing the wild, uneven and slippery passage.

Grievously agitated now, Mimms leaped from one incoming wave to another, barking at the foamy spume, tasting it, pausing to sniff the sodden air, then shaking from great head to straggly tail.

"Come back, you fool dog. There's naught we can do," Cara shouted. Neta sank to her haunches, refusing to traverse farther onto water-covered rocks. "Damn you. You will help me." Insisting, Cara yanked on the reins, pulling the mare to where Mimms growled and fussed. Ignoring the danger to herself and faithful horse, Cara had no intention of leaving her dog stranded on *Finn mac Coul*'s bridge.

Whining, his whole body shaking, Mimms leaped at Cara, slathering his great pink tongue across her face. Cara quickly fastened her lead onto his collar. "We must go."

Mimms bounded about the deepening water as Cara climbed onto the saddle. Another mighty wave overran the rocks underfoot, splashing, licking upward over the very top of the nearby tor then backwashed furiously, dragging Mimms into its undertow.

"Mimms!"

Pie-eyed with fear, the mare lurched landward as the dragging current swept under her belly. Cara fought to control the horse, afraid for herself, but more frightened of losing her treasured dog.

Mimms' head surfaced just as Cara dug her heels into Neta's sides and kicked. The leather strap fastened to the saddle tightened across Cara's thigh and cut deep against the drag of the current and Mimms' heavy body.

Neta's hooves sank deep into loosened shale and found solid rock. All of Cara's weight, fueled by fear of certain loss, went into the thrust upward to drier land even as she screamed against the pain biting into her skin. It was so intense, she knew instantly she should cut the line to save herself. Still she would gladly lose her leg before losing her dog.

Then, all at once, the lead went slack. Neta panted on higher rocks, shaking from head to sodden tail.

The great dog slumped in the shallows. His head bent peculiarly and his studded collar rode his ears. Spread out, humped in exhaustion, his strong legs lacked the wherewithal to stand clear of the swirling waters.

Cara shoved the lead off her thigh and, gasping in relief, slid it past her knee and dismounted. Gripping the lead betwixt horse and dog, she trailed by it to the crumpled animal.

She fell to her knees and tried to pick up Mimms' head. But she couldn't budge it. Two arms were fastened in a death grip round Mimms' bulky neck. Likewise, Mimms' jaws clamped upon a tattered garment. Beneath Cara Mulvaine's wolfhound, a man clung to life. Both choked the other as the seawater rushed away from them.

Cara touched fur, then hair, then skin and sodden cloth.

Another wave came at them. The man on the bottom struggled wildly to clear his bearded face from the water.

Mimms broke clear of it first.

Neta stood firm until the wave swirled under her; then she panicked and dragged both dog and man across the sharp rocks in one lunging retreat. Cara scrambled after, screaming, pulling on the leathers, her skirt swirling in the undertow. Cara held fast to the strap tethering dog and horse. She wound up being dragged just as rudely across the rocks. All were choking then. Dog, man, woman and horse panted, out of breath and exhausted. But Neta cleared them all of the treacherous water.

With labored efforts, each struggled to get air in their chests. Mimms recovered first, shaking saltwater from his coat. The shiver worked down his body to his tail, dislodging the weakened grip of two arms. Mimms barked a watery yelp of triumph. He shook his head and growled with fierce pleasure at the limp prize he'd stolen from the water.

"For pity's sake, Mimms, you haven't caught a rabbit," Cara said. Mimms acted as if he had, barking and thrusting his nose into the man's face to get his scent. Cara knelt beside the man, afraid to touch him. Did he still breathe? Mimms rudely jumped onto his chest, his paws striking with a heavy thud.

"Get off him, Mimms." Cara pushed the dog aside. The man choked and coughed. He wasn't dead. She pulled her courage up from her boots, hoisting head and heavy shoulders upright. He slumped against her. Seawater gushed from his mouth and nostrils. The spray from the crashing surf covered them both in a mist heavier than the unrelenting rain. "God be praised, you are alive."

"Mother of God, help me," he gasped, then choked, and more water streamed from his mouth.

Cara cradled his battered head. His lips were blue and his skin was unbelievably cold, so cold, he didn't shiver as she did. His weight bore heavily against her. His head lolled sideways, and blood ran down his neck. One side of his face was battered to a bloody pulp, the eye swollen shut.

His pantaloons ballooned with heavy water. He wore no boots. Had he been wearing high-topped boots, he'd have sunk like a stone. Her grip faltered and she lost hold of him, causing his head to bang against a rock. He groaned.

Mortified that she had caused him more injury, Cara hastily raised his head and shoulders, supporting him with her own body.

He lived, but would soon die if Cara tarried in getting him to safety and warmth. His uninjured eye opened, his fingers clutched at her cloak. "God bless you, God bless you and forgive me."

Dumbfounded by his English words, Cara muttered, "Are you English, mon?"

Her question received a groaned, indistinct response. He raised one shaking arm to wipe his hand across his face. The man looked at her from one startling dark blue eye, its mate too swollen to open. Like his English words, the color of his eyes unsettled Cara. His hand went limp across his chest and his eye closed.

Cara exhaled. He lived. She lifted his shoulders again, raising his upper body half-upright. She looked down at his chest and saw movement. He breathed.

He wore no weapons, no belt or scabbard. His face barely looked human. Blood seeped through his sleeveless jerkin. His bare arms were deeply cut and abraded. A black iron manacle encircled his thick wrist. Alerted to the one, Cara quickly noted iron manacles on each extremity.

For a long minute Cara just stared at those black irons. One hand lay palm open against his thigh. Peeling blisters and thick calluses padded his fingers and palm. His thumbnail was curiously black, ragged and broken. What he was, Spaniard, prisoner, convict, criminal or traitor, she knew not which. What was she to do with him?

She saw how painfully he struggled to breathe and rouse himself. Between spells of violent coughing, he came alert. His one uninjured eye focused upon Neta. He moved his hand as if to catch hold of the horse. Cara struggled to her feet, pulling the fearful mare close.

"Can you stand? Mount my horse? I will help you." She drew his arm across her shoulders, tugging on him urgently. He was in no condition to walk, much less stand, but he made a valiant effort to do just that, actually getting a hand upon the saddle of the skittish beast.

Between the mare's proximity and Cara's determination, the man fell clumsily across Neta's back. Cara slid his terribly cold, bare feet into the stirrups, lengthening them quickly to accommodate him. Then she took hold of the bridle and carefully led Neta up the twisting path to the cliff round Chimney Tops.

Mimms circled them, barking with a water-clogged throat.

Midway up the cliff's path, Cara rested and soothed her unhappy horse. The man barely clung to consciousness, and his seat was precarious at best. He dwarfed her saddle and his long legs hung well past Neta's sides. He was too large and heavy for both of them to ride the young and delicately boned palfrey. Cara removed the lead from Mimms' collar and tied the man securely to his person, hesitating only when she noticed a single ornament to his person. A gold signet of curious design, seated with a brilliant, faceted diamond cradled between calipers and rule fitted tightly round the swollen ring finger of his left hand.

No sooner did Cara touch a curious finger to the ring itself, than she felt the swelling sensation of her gift of second sight rising inside her. The moment stretched, freezing as Cara's fingertips lingered upon the signet and the heel of her hand rested on the iron manacle.

The swift vision assaulted her. A ceremony wherein the signet had been fitted to his hand. Pungent incense flared Cara's nostrils. Sandalwood and myrrh smoked round a high altar. Chants and prayers drummed above the pound of the storm and the wind whistling in her ears. A church rang to the very rafters with jubilant shouts, cheers and happy laughter; then the sweet incense burned acrid and bitter and mixed with the smell of the sea. There was a fire, a ship...many ships burning, torched and exploding. Her ears rang with the boom of cannon, screams of agony as flesh seared and burned...a battle upon seas.

Cara recoiled; her fingers drew sharply away, as if touching the man had burned her, too.

She shook her head, freeing it of unnatural sight and stepped back, holding tight to Neta's bit and bridle. She licked her lips, tasted salt and stared hard at the unconscious man limp on the back of her horse. Who was he? What was he? Why had nature moved so mysteriously this evening to place her here and this man into her care? She did not even try to formulate any answers.

Again her eyes roved to the signet then upward to the man's barely human face. His ring told Cara he was a knight, true. She couldn't guess which order. Sir Almoy would know. As for the rest of him, she didn't know what to make of him.

First, she must get the man out of the elements. But where in all of English-ruled Ireland would any Spaniard be safe? Where in ever-rebellious Antrim would any Englishman be hidden?

Mimms yelped and bounded to her side. Neta poked her weary, exhausted nose into Cara's belly. All wanted the comfort of home.

Dunluce, Cara thought. How, in the name of all the saints, would she explain having found a man to any at Dunluce?

Chapter Two

The solution to his safety was so simple that afterward, when the exhausted survivor lay safe upon a pallet, Cara wondered why she had ever thought of anything else. The dungeon.

Beneath Dunluce a network of caves honeycombed the cliff that supported the black fortress. Cara knew all the secret passageways better than anyone who lived at Dunluce in a hundred years. A dozen tunnels led from the fortress down inside the forgotten dungeons then out through the caves to the sea gate. The maze would confound a stranger, but not Cara Mulvaine. Had she not spent fifteen years hiding from Sorely's wrath? Aye, she had.

From the sea gate itself, a full view of the wreck could be had when lightning struck through sky. By the time she had the survivor settled and a fire lit, one half of the sinking hull was gone.

These days, no one came to the sea gate. The burned wharf was proof of a holocaust. Scorch marks licked up the cliff. When the water calmed, a graveyard of sunken ships could be seen in its depths.

No more than an occasional fisherman plied the cove. Those who fished never put foot to Sorely's land. Not that there was aught to steal. The Mac Donnell was as poor as he was bitter.

The Mac Donnell's retainers were all as ancient as he. They said nothing as Cara made trips in and out of Dunluce's many halls. Likewise, her sojourn into the kitchen to take food went without comment from all save Brenna, the cook.

"You've been out in the storm."

"Aye," Cara answered true. She had no reason to lie to Brenna and it was obvious she had been wet through.

"You be daft to do such a thing. You'll pay for it in your bones should you live to my age. Best take the soup, and plenty of it."

"Ta." Cara ladled a generous helping into a Wexford bowl. She took bread and cheese and, while Brenna's back was turned, tucked a flask of whiskey in the fold of her tunic. Cara customarily ate in her solitary tower. None would look for her, or miss her for the rest of the night. She held no consequence in her grandfather's home and as such, remained overlooked for days at a time.

In the dry niche where the sailor lay close to a warming fire, Cara set her provisions down and eyed the man. He did not waken when she called to him. Nor had he roused enough to do the sensible thing and remove his soaked garments, such as they were. Gently she touched his brow, smoothing back his lank, tangled hair. His skin still felt chilled, sapped of all heat by the cold, unforgiving sea.

Abruptly, his uninjured eye flew open. Fingers snaked round her wrist. "Where am I?"

Mimms took exception, bared his fangs and growled deeply. Surprised at the man's Gaelic question, Cara answered cautiously. "You are safe."

"The others . . . the ship?"

Cara shook her head, her tight-lipped silence answer enough.

"God help the pur bastards," he moaned. A wash of what looked like guilt shut his eyes. "Forgive me, forgive me."

Cara inhaled sharply. "'Twas no your fault, mon. 'Twas an act of God."

Tears escaped the constricted squeeze of his eyes and his mouth clamped in a white-lipped grimace. Neither effort prevented Cara from witnessing the trembling of his bearded chin, nor the anguished bob of his larynx as he fought to retain a man's control.

Cara laid her other hand over his, sensing his grip loosening. "You'll be fine, now. I promise."

"Do you, me wee lassie?"

Cara's eyes widened. Was that not the rolling brogue of a Scot? Was she wrong about the identity of the ship? It was

Spanish. She'd stake her father's claymore on that, but this man was no Spaniard. Could she trust his accented tongue? He spoke freely in dangerous English, and Gaelic. Uncertain, Cara bent her head till her lips nearly touched the reddened shell of his right ear and whispered in Gaelic. His good eye flickered open no more than a slit, but his gaze caught hers and held fast for a moment. His fingers tightened briefly on her wrist in answer, but the only sound his throat could make was a strangled whisper that sounded like "ayagh" to her ears.

Mimms still growled, even when the man's fleeting grip fell away. Cara turned his callused hand on his chest, knowing he'd slipped out of conscious. "He canna hurt me, Mimms."

The dog paced round the inert male, snuffling as Cara set to work. Snipping at the laces of a sleeveless doublet, Cara pondered about the iron manacles fitted to his wrists and ankles. So, he was a prisoner of the Spaniards. If his brogue were true, he was no Sassenach. The Scots were allies of Spain. Why would he be a prisoner then? That was a puzzle.

Her shears made short work of frayed fastenings, but she cut with care, not speed. Cara laid the garment open. Doing so exposed a brawny, muscled chest lightly covered with coarse, curling hair. Cara hesitated, her hand hovering above him. He had curious flat nipples. Her hands sank to her lap and she could go no farther.

So this is what a man looked like beneath his clothing, she thought. He was banded by ridges, plump, hard curves and smooth stretched depressions. The most curious dimples decorated the inside of his elbows. His veins stood out in hard relief against the solidity of his muscles. There was no hint of fat to his lean, muscular form.

Amazed, she raised her hands and touched him. The hair on his chest ran coarse and damp beneath her fingertips. Gliding her hands down his ribs, she splayed her fingers across the hollows that formed with every breath he so laboriously sucked within his lungs. There was a fierce, powerful beauty to his body.

Mimms sniffed at his head, then followed a trail down to the man's toes. Satisfied, the dog settled nearby, watching, waiting, ever alert to any sign of danger.

The job of undressing the man had to be done whether Cara wanted to or not. He could not be left in wet clothing. His skin must be washed of the seawater, and his injuries treated. She had no choice but to do it herself.

Cara lifted his shoulders one at a time and removed the wet garment. Should she cut the ties of his pantaloons? As compelling as the urge to help him was, she could not forget that he was a man. That truth impeded her. She had never touched a man—ever. He was helpless, injured and ill. If she didn't help him, who would? Steeling her resolve, Cara tugged the soaked clothing from his legs. That was her undoing. Naked, exposed, the man's body, in particular the thick nest of hair surrounding his manhood, stopped her cold. Her resolve fled to where it had come. Pressing a hand to her flaming cheek, Cara took a deep breath. To her relief, he showed no signs of reviving.

Cara closed her eyes, trying to think what she should do. Hastily, she fetched her bowl of heated water from the fire, and soap and flannel to get on with the business of washing the seawater from him, saying over and over, If I do not do it, who will? Her hands trembled as she set the bowl of water on the stones beside him.

Swallowing her fear with her reluctance, Cara looked at the first bit of torn flesh she could manage to deal with properly— his swollen eyes and shapeless face. Long hair hid a deep gash behind his right ear. The skin there swelled so ferociously, the bleeding had stopped. Cuts and bruises marred his shoulders, marked his sinewy arms. One knee bled profusely, the other leg was mangled raw from calf to hip. His stomach sunk concave and his ribs stood apart with each bellowslike effort to draw his breath.

The rattle of wind in his chest made Cara frown with concern. He was deeply ill.

Beyond that, she had never studied a man at such close quarters. A man, it seemed, was a most oddly made and curious being. Inside his elbows and arms, his skin was as smooth and soft as her own. Elsewhere, her cloth made scratching noises as she scrubbed hair-bristled, weathered skin. As she wiped each limb dry, that hair sparkled redder and redder in the firelight. His skin, where he wasn't tanned by sun or blackened by bruising, shined quite pale and lightly freckled.

The cool water that she rinsed him with caused gooseflesh to erupt across his neck and shoulders, convincing Cara that she must finish quickly. And thinking of Jesus' scourged body taken down from the cross, she went ahead, washing all of him, patting the bruised skin dry, wrapping him in clean linens then warm wools.

The task completed, Cara sat back on her heels, conscious of a new respect for the opposite gender. His hands doubled hers in width. Were he possessed of the strength his body was capable of containing, he could crush her in the blink of an eye. She smoothed a healing balm into his damaged fingers, marveling at the thick callus pads that attested to active, daily use. No scholar or sophist, this was a man of deed and action.

She laid her ear to his chest and listened closely to his labored breathing and the slow steady beat of his heart.

Despite his injuries he contained a raw beauty unlike any men she knew. But then she knew of none who were not old and long past their prime, except the O'Neill. No one dared call the earl of Tyrone, Hugh O'Neill, anything but fearsome in both temperament and size. Cara had never thought a man could be pleasing to look upon. Even injured, this man was. He was an awesome sight to the eyes of a singularly lonely twenty-year-old maid.

What she knew of men was that they were harsh, cruel beings no matter what their age. Sick and weakened the survivor may be, but tomorrow his strength might return. Cara knew her limitations all too well. A woman had no strength against any man full grown.

Though a decade had passed since Dunluce had boasted of any prisoners in its dungeons, the necessary implements for confinement remained. Had not her own father languished for nearly a year in this very prison? Aye, he had.

In deeper cells, lengths of rusted chain testified to the true purpose of the dungeon. Cursed souls died here. Ghosts of Vikings and Danes, shades of monks and hermits roamed freely in these caves long before Dunluce had been erected. The sense of their spirits remained.

Thinking of her own safety, Cara considered fetching some chain and anchoring his manacles to the adjacent wall. His injuries were many, but none alone should debilitate him long. His cold skin had begun to warm from the nearby fire's heat and the whiskey she'd rubbed into his limbs. Laying her hand against his brow, she moved aside the dark, damp tangles of his hair.

Some inner voice appeased her fear of him. He was in no condition to harm her, and there was Mimms.

Cara covered the survivor well and stoked up the fire to provide more warmth against the chilling damp. He showed no signs of waking and the food she had brought had gone cold. At storm's end his condition worsened. A sick wheeze racked his laboring chest.

The night passed and Cara slept not. She paced the limits of the dungeons, her ears acute to any sound precluding discovery. No one must ever know she had hidden the man. She did not want to leave him, but he needed ointments, medicines and bandages. Only one person in all of Dunluce might give her aid.

"Mimms." Cara took the food the man could not eat and placed it near the entrance where she had left Neta tied to the gate. "You will guard him. See that no one enters the gate."

Mimms yapped an acknowledgement, then sank his muzzle into the cold bowl, devouring the food that was meant for the man. Cara took hold of Neta's reins, leading the mare outside.

The storm had abated, though it still rained. Guiding Neta the short route round the shingled beach, Cara came upon carnage of the wreck. A shudder whipped through her at the sight of many mangled bodies. Relentless waves washed clothing up and down limbs stiffened by death. The splatter of rain made the scene unreal, like the odd illuminated pages in Almoy's books—visions of Hell.

Turning from the dead, Cara spied several trunks awash in the ebb tide. Her survivor needed clothing.

Brown kelp trailed back into the sea from the first battered trunk she approached. The bottom was split open and the black shale beneath glittered unnaturally. Dropping from Neta's back, Cara struck her fingers into the earth and held up a fistful of coarse black sand and gold coins.

"Lord in Heaven," Cara whispered. The day's sunlight barely illuminated the narrow beach, yet, under the surf, glittering lights reflected the gold coinage. Her eyes grew larger as the enormity of the catastrophe sunk into her brain. "Why, there is gold enough here to buy the world."

It was true. Taking the reins in one hand, she hurried to another trunk. It was heavy, a solidly made wooden casket, strapped with leather and iron bands. Two more were still lashed to the boards that had held them in place on the ship. The trunks rocked on their makeshift raft, awash and in one piece.

Cara glanced to the misty horizon. The sun was a red orb rising. Soon there would be word of the wrecking, and all of Dunluce, Portballintrea and Bois would be scavenging on the shore. But she was the first to come upon it.

The Mac Donnell would claim it all. Gold would fill his coffers.

Though little peace ever reigned at Dunluce, the last few years had passed without war touching it. Sir Francis Drake had rendered the Mac Donnell impotent in one fell swoop. Spanish gold would change that.

"Well, not this time," Cara announced to her horse. She took Mimms' rawhide lead from the saddle and fastened a secure knot onto the first trunk, then used her horse to pull the trunk all the way to the sea gate. She made four trips in all and spent another half hour plucking coins from the shoreline. The more the tide ebbed, the more gold shimmered in the shallows.

Cara's harvesting ended abruptly. Her grandfather, Sorely Boy Mac Donnell, arrived himself, catching her on the beach. Cara was glad she was mounted on her horse and not caught kneeling on the shale gathering up gold coins.

"What do you here, gel?" Sorely Boy Mac Donnell did not speak until his horse drew abreast of hers. Despite the gout that plagued his leg, Sorely Mac Donnell could still ride and terrorize the countryside. He wagged his riding whip, demanding, "Why did you not come tell me of the wrecking?"

"I have just come upon it." Cara averted her face from a clump of lifeless bodies. "'Tis a horror."

"Aye." Sorely's eyes narrowed and he glared at her, not the carnage. Cara looked away to the cliff face lest he detect any lingering guilt in her eyes. She saw seven of her grandfather's most trusted men winding their way on foot down the twisted path from Dunluce. Loyal old Donovan and Sir Tom Arner led the pack.

"I've sent for the priest," Sorely continued. "Bodies are washing ashore from here to Ballintrae. It's no place for a gel to be. Lest you want another skelping, get you back to Dunluce. I've left letters for you to scribe and want a tally made of this. Go, I said."

He swung his crop in a deliberately harsh blow against Cara's unprotected back. Neta sidestepped nervously. Controlling her animal, Cara whirled the horse about and glared at her grandfather. He'd not have touched her if Mimms was at her side. But it was Mimms' defense of her that had sent him over the edge to violence the day before. She was damned if she did, damned if she didn't.

"I said get away." The Mac Donnell raised the crop again, though his voice never lifted above the cold, cutting depth of old hatred that ran bone deep. "You'll no touch what is mine, you damned witch. Get out of my sight. There will not be a coin wasted on you."

Cara stayed the urge to whistle for her dog. She did not want the man in the cave discovered and was twice certain she did not want her grandfather to have the gold. She turned Neta aside and galloped past the men-at-arms. Although two shouldered empty trunks, they managed to free a hand to make a hasty sign of the cross to ward against the evil eye as she passed them. That was a gesture she had grown inured to over the years, but hated none the less. The Irish hated and feared her. It mattered not that she was half-Irish herself.

All along the shoreline betwixt Chimney Tops and Dunluce, Cara saw more and more bodies rolled in the surf. Living beings sifted amongst the dead. Near the village, servants and crofters alike waded hip-deep in the water, using reed and woven rakes to glean the golden harvest. Six small caskets had also been found. Boats plied the now-calm water.

Disgusted, Cara realized the gold she'd hidden was nothing to the fortune being claimed by Sorely Mac Donnell. His men guarded five Spaniards bound together by hand and foot. To

Cara's discerning eye they appeared nearly half-dead. No English skulked about that Cara could see.

Away from shore on the road from Dunluce to Bushmills, she came upon her uncle James, riding hell for leather with Hugh O'Neill and a massive squadron of Irish warriors. She yielded the twisting road, averting her face from the flying mud and sod churned by their horses' pounding hooves.

At Dunluce the whole castle seethed in an uproar. Sorely's old retainers were hard-pressed to get the hall aired and opened, and the trestles in place. In the kitchen Brenna had been joined by a dozen women from the village, all conscripted to work. If the O'Neill was about, the standards of Dunluce had to quickly muster up to par to serve an earl.

Tired now, Cara put away her saddle, fed the weary mare a good measure of oats and staggered up the winding staircase into the east tower. Her own quarters in the cold north tower beckoned, but she could not stop to sleep just yet.

The heavy door at the top of the twisting stairs stood ajar. A good thing it was, for Cara thought she lacked the wherewithal to open it on her own. A white-faced cat groomed her mewling kittens on the rush-strewn floor of the high chamber. Peeking past the door, Cara spied Sir Almoy at his windows. The mullioned glass faceted the daylight, sparkling on his white hair and beard.

"Good morn, Sir Almoy," Cara called out, making her presence known. It did not do to sneak up behind Almoy. Ancient he might be, yes, but he was never without his sword.

"What do you?"

Cara stepped past the cats and into the dust-mote-filled sunbeam. "I've come for a poultice."

"Ha. That's not all you seek." The old man slowly put the window to his back. His tunic caught the breeze, and the cross emblazoned over his chest moved like a pennant.

"Perhaps." Cara let her eyes wander with unabashed curiosity.

There was a wonder of contraptions scattered about—miniature arbalists, catapults and machines with all manners of gears and wheels that could propel a man through space and time. The walls were lined with shelves cluttered with glowing pots, stoppered flasks and glass flagons. Fancy iron spigots plumed with golden light provided by flames. For Sir Almoy, the air itself would burn and yield light and heat. Magical devices, potions, medicines, books, tablatures and glittering crystals occupied every nook and cranny.

The warrior-monk was quite mad by the castlefolks' estimation. Cara knew him as the oldest resident of Dunluce, older even than her grandfather's hallowed four score.

"Where did you put him?"

"Beg pardon?"

"Don't play the idiot with me. I know what a sly brain you possess. The gold is cursed. Better to drop it into the sea than to put your store upon it rescuing you."

Had she thought of that? Perhaps, Cara mused as she wandered to the long table where Sir Almoy's latest experiment was laid out. His art was alchemy, and he knew things that no one was ever supposed to know. What held her strongest fascination was his amethyst crystal ball. It sat upon a gold filigree ring and was cloudy, reflecting the bank of mullioned windows and the sun. But she had not come to look at that.

Instead she turned to the deep hearth, above which was hung his coat of arms, calipers, rule and all-seeing eye shared with the Templar patte cross.

"Well, state your purpose, gel," the old man barked.

"I need a medicine for water in the lungs," Cara said.

"You do not look to be ill." He moved to the tall shelves that banked the inner wall, his shuffle-gaited step telling of his age and old wounds.

Cara cocked her head and gazed at the suit of tarnished armor that stood in one spare corner. Though the years had turned the silver black, the gold inlays retained their shine. "Not all gold is cursed."

"Think you not?" Sir Almoy sputtered. "Gold—want of it—is the root of all evil."

Her grandfather claimed Almoy was the last Master of Ireland, the titular head of the fabled Order of the Temple. The Grand Knights Templar had been disbanded by Philip the Fair of France in the Avignon Captivity in the year of Our Lord 1314. Almoy had come from France, though in what year, Cara would not even try to guess.

The Sir Almoy she knew looked as if he could never have supported the weight of the armored suit standing erect in the corner. Except the suit was all long of limb, as he was. Despite his withered muscle, he had no difficulty mounting a slanted, roll-about ladder to take jars of medicants from high shelves. He did it slowly, though, at a pace that maddened one her age.

"What else?"

"Poultices for joints, broken skin, cuts."

The ancient man cast her a penetrating look.

"'Tis not for me," Cara explained.

"I know it isn't. You've found a man. And I know you've hidden him, below."

Sir Almoy waved in the direction of his crystal and Cara stuck her tongue to the front of her teeth, sucking upon an incisor as she considered the knight's words. He knew things, saw things, divined all sorts of things. But his was not the gift of second sight that she was cursed with; his was by different means, magic and otherworldly.

His white brows wrinkled together and he laughed gleefully. "Do not even think it."

"Think what?"

"To compare a gift to learned knowledge. There is no match from one to the other. One takes effort to acquire, the other a fluke of nature, like being born with ears that protrude from yer head."

Automatically Cara touched her ear to see if hers were peculiar. Almoy chuckled and she dropped her hand to her side. He puttered round to his table, setting down what he'd gathered. "Watch now. Always keep your eyes open. Listen. Even the sounds of what I do have meaning."

Cara watched in fascination as he ground a yellow lump with his mortar and pestle until it was a fine powder. He added pinches of herbs from other jars, crushed leaves between his fingers and carefully unstoppered a dark glass of smoking liquid, making certain the fumes did not enter his nose. Cara almost laughed. The old one quirked a brow at her and asked. "What do you plan to do with him?"

"I haven't decided. He is ill."

"Bah," Sir Almoy croaked, and swung about to take from a dark shelf a sheaf of what looked like parchment to Cara. He turned it over and scraped the blackened underside with a thin blade, sending sprinkles of what could have been dirt, lampblack or mold into the bowl. "Sell him. Ten pounds English, you'll get. You can buy yourself a kirtle and slippers—even a bauble or two for your hair."

"No." Cara answered flatly.

"You would keep him, like a pet, like your dog? Chained and fettered? What good will he do you?"

His hooded blue eyes seemed to bore through her layers of sins and secrets. He turned his gaze back to the concoction he was preparing. A thick green liquid adhered to the marble sides of the deep bowl.

Cara's nostrils flared at the rising scent that was potent, strange and noxious. "I mean to keep him safe from Kelly's ropes."

"Ah." Sir Almoy stood back, his arms folded across his bony chest. "He is not English, then? 'Twas not Drake's *Golden Hind,* was it?"

"Nay, the ship 'twas Spanish, but he is not. He wears a signet." Cara could not fathom why that bit of fact made her feel proud. Her man was a Scot, she was sure of that.

"A family crest? What markings?" Almoy's interest sparked anew.

"Nay, no family crest that I recognize. 'Twas calipers and rule, and an all-seeing eye, like yon shield there, but different. I thought it might be the order of St. John, but it is not that, either." Cara pointed to the Templars' patte cross mounted on the wall above Almoy's hearth right next to the aging shield of the Knights of St. John's Hospitalers. She lifted her shoulders in a gesture of dismay. "None exactly so."

"What is different about it?" Almoy asked impatiently, "Think. What did you see?"

"Flowers. Leaves and flowers twined round about the rule, encircling it."

"The House of Ross. The Green man, the vines and roses? Do you ken?"

"Perhaps," Cara could barely suppress her eagerness now. "You could come and see for yourself."

"Nay, I cannot leave my work even if the brotherhood grows bold again," he ruminated, working his jaw back and forth, his eyes considering a distant thought. "He could be a spy or a traitor. Many a man would risk his soul to claim what I have here."

"'Twas an accident that brought him to Dunluce," Cara returned. "Mimms saved him. He would have drowned or been battered to death on the rocks if not for my dog."

"Stranger things have happened in my time. I would not trust him, were I you. Countless are the ways to explore the universe."

Disappointed, Cara scoffed softly, "Yet, there be no way except by ship to get off the rocks of Ireland."

"Ireland is a fine place to be, a sanctuary from shore to shore. Do not trust the man. Tell him nothing."

"He may not live to be trusted. Salt water weakened his lungs and his injuries are many."

Sir Almoy thought upon that.

"Do not feed him the elixir all at once. Better to dilute it with tea or broth over several days' time. 'Twill clear the chest and bring on a healing cough. If not, the waters have gone too deep and only prayer will ease his suffering. A lingering death does no man good and torments his faith."

With incredibly steady hands, the old man poured the elixir into a flask and stoppered it. "Now, be there anything else?"

Cara cast a longing glance at Almoy's crystal and was caught by an impulsive urge to ask him to look into her future, but the selfishness of that impulse held her back. She shook her head no, and stroked her fingers across her brow. Taking the flask to hand, she stuck it inside her sleeve, which was still wet and clammy from the morning rain.

Almoy smoothed his palm down the wild tangle of his beard, separating it across the faded red cross that decorated his tunic. "Perhaps you will bring me a sample of the Spanish gold. I wish to test its origins, to see if they have learned the art of changing lead. I see the gleaners work upon the beach. If it is possible, you might look about for a casket of gunpowder. A galleass would have plenty in its stores. 'Twill have to dry, of course, but once done, my experiments can begin afresh."

"I will see what I can find," Cara promised.

"And do not forget your lessons. I will excuse you today, but that is all. Go now."

* * *

The north tower reeked of damp. Cara's fire had burned out and she was in no mood to fetch wood or water. She stripped off her sodden clothing and scrubbed hastily with what water remained in her standing pitcher. She bathed unassisted. The north tower was forbidden to all in Dunluce except Cara. The rule had hardened down the years. Cara Mulvaine fended for herself.

Daylight faded as Cara dressed in warm wools, thick breeches and stockings, then wound leggings fast around her feet and went down to the kitchen, taking her meal from the scraps that were left from the evening's supper.

Brenna looked frazzled, having worked hard over the hot fires all the day, for the hall was full of hungry men, shouting and demanding more food and ale. She cast no more than a cursory glance at Cara's clothing. The women from the crofts had curious eyes for her, though they said naught to her. That also was forbidden. The Mac Donnell's Irish did not speak to Cara, a Scot, who was known as the Mulvaine.

"Ach, there ya be." Brenna dragged her hands across a stained apron spread over her broad belly. "Good thing, too. There be another storm abrewing."

"I know." Cara let her eyes stray to the door that overlooked the sea. Already, lightning and thunder rumbled close. She filled a bread trencher and sat near the roaring fire on a bench. The roasted venison was good and she felt guilty sinking her teeth into it. Brenna's potatoes fried in butter and onions and scrambled with milk and egg were the best she'd ever tasted. Was her captive starving for lack of her providing him nothing better than cold broth? Cara cocked her head to the side and stared at the roaring fire wondering silently why she thought of him as *her captive*. Was he?

"How's yer cough?" Brenna asked.

"Better," Cara said, and sputtered on a morsel of bread, her hunger abated by her guilty conscience. Brenna wasn't asking about congestion in Cara's lungs. Cara had never been sick a day in her life. But she'd been laid low by beatings more times than she could count. It was to her condition today that Brenna inquired.

"You'll catch yer death. Don't think I don't know you're watching the gleaning of that Spanish gold." Brenna crossed herself and spat in the fire. "Poor devils. May God bless them, dashed to death upon the rocks. 'Tis no place for the Mulvaine to be. Mind what I say, gel."

That was as close to a scolding as Brenna would give her. Cara gathered more food to her trencher, piling it on to feed the man, guiltily casting side glances at Brenna as she did so.

"Go on, take the pudding, too. 'Tis for you."

Cara looked at the linen tied with string—a boiled pudding. Beside it sat a small jar.

"The pot, as well. Make sure you rub your chest well with it. Put camphor in it. I did. Mint and a touch of camomile. Use it all, and the morrow will see you yerself again, God willing."

"Ta, Brenna," Cara said gratefully. The salve was an unguent for healing sore and aching flesh. It was a boon to have as a present. Cara's survivor had much need of it.

"Go on, be off wit' ya. No man here needs the Mulvaine underfoot. Go on."

Shooed out of the smoky kitchen, Cara eased through a door that opened directly onto the cobblestone bailey. A high wall blocked the wind that might have cooled the hot kitchens. Rain again lashed Dunluce's dark, moss-covered walls.

Cara threaded her way into the dungeons, passing empty cells, working down treacherous steps to the lowest level. There, she set the tray of warm food on the rock floor. The lantern she'd lit earlier still burned, but the fire had burned to gray embers. Even in her heavy wools, she was unable to ward off the chill.

The man stretched upon the pallet had sickened. He had thrown off his coverings and his body shook with chills. He fought her efforts to re-cover him. She prevailed, but not without a struggle. Even sick, his strength astonished her. She asked herself what she had expected. He was more than twice her weight. Swaddling his brawny arms under a turn of the blankets, she shuddered, imagining what a blow from his great fist might do.

Why, looking at him now, she realized he was nearly the same size as the O'Neill, and everyone called the earl of Tyrone a giant, for that is what he was. She thought of shackling the survivor again for her own protection.

Harboring the knowledge that it would be cruelly unnecessary to shackle a sick, unconscious man, she was still tempted to take the key and fasten his manacles to the lengths of available chain. He may be injured and spent with no weaponry, but he was a man none the less.

A man who could harm her just as grievously as any other ever had, save ancient Sir Almoy.

She couldn't do it. Nor could she go to her own bed knowing he lay on the cold stone of a cave, starving, perhaps shivering his life away. She gathered straw from the stables and brought it below, making a thicker pallet, which she covered with her good wool cloak. She huffed and puffed to move his inert body onto it, straining her back and arms to do the task with as little injury to him as possible. But moving him had jarred his head wound and blood seeped anew from it. He would not be roused from his delirious sleep to eat the meal she'd brought him. Mimms made short work of it, starving for sustenance himself.

Cara trickled a dosage of Almoy's elixir down the man's throat, then wrapped the sides of her woolen cloak across his exposed arms and shoulders. He coughed and threw off the wool, fitful and restless, muttering loudly in his delirium.

He needed more than she had provided him, that was clear. She would go up to the hall and take what he needed.

Chapter Three

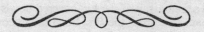

Gordie Mckenna woke with a start. A slathering muzzle fanned his face with foul-smelling breath. Gordie froze, recognizing the deep-throated growl of some hellish beast.

"Stay, Mimms," a brisk voice commanded from the darkness. The beast's claws clicked as it obeyed the command. Gordie could see its glowing, dangerous eyes. Then a wraithlike figure came into Gordie's view, and the tension inside him immediately lessened. It was the woman who had saved him.

He recognized her voice. She knelt beyond his reach, feeding bits of fluff into a tiny flame upon the stones. Carefully, with one hand guarding it, the other brought scraps of peat to enlarge the fire. The light flickered on features cast in shadows by a cowl encircling her head.

She touched a straw to the fire and lit a punched tin lantern, tending the wick with care to yield the greatest light. Elsewhere, inky blackness enshrouded her.

The peat burned yellow and blue. The smoke flavored the air with smoldering earth.

Gordie struggled to sit up. A rough wool slid down his chest. His skin burned despite the chill of cold, damp air. Sharp pains cost what strength he had. He fell back against the hard pallet.

"I have brought you food and drink." Her voice came so softly, it strained his ears to decipher the Gaelic lilt that brought to mind music of a pleasant, cheery timbre.

"Aye." His nostrils flared with familiar scents, damp earth, camphor and burning peat.

"And I washed your clothes and mended them. There are more in yon trunk, but I do not think the shirts will fit you. Your arms are very long."

Gordie blinked his dry, crusty eyes. More speech was beyond him. It took effort to moisten his cracked lips.

"You've been very ill," she explained further, coming closer with a wicker basket to kneel beside him. Her skirts spread about her, folding and bunching at her knees as she unpacked her basket and set an array of napkin-covered bowls about her. Tantalizing steam rose from the first bowl she uncovered.

"It's been three days since the ship was wrecked. Nights, I mean." She raised a wooden spoon and brought a measure of heated broth to Gordie's mouth. "Oh, here. Let me lift your head." She put bowl and spoon aside and scooted closer. Gentle hands maneuvered his shoulders until his head rested on the warm firmness of her lap.

Gordie's head swam. He closed his eyes. A trickle of the broth made it inside his mouth and she scrubbed a napkin against the tangled beard on his chin. The thin broth could not nourish a healthy man's appetite, but it was warm and wet and he could make no protest.

"Only five others survived the storm. They are Spaniards one and all and do not speak our language. A Jesuit priest came from Killybegs to talk for them. He is an odd duck, the Jesuit, that is. His eyes are as black as granite and wicked to behold. He sees sin in everyone, especially my grandfather for swearing and claiming the Spanish gold."

Cara paused to take up another bowl, this one of cool mashed berries mixed with sweet cream. Gordie swallowed what tasted like jelly, sweet and tart at the same time. She followed that with a spoonful of vile and bitter oil, which made him cough and choke.

Cara quickly brought a small cup of fresh water to his lips, hoping to wash the taste of Almoy's elixir down his throat. She massaged his throat with a soothing hand, all the while chewing the corner of her lip. His skin scorched her palm.

Worse, the rattle in his chest had deepened over the days. It took ages to get water down him. Mimms stared at her with ful eyes.

"You mustn't give up, sir," Cara said urgently as she moved his head back to the pallet. He rolled, upending a shoulder from his covers. "Really, you mustn't. I know it hurts you to breathe, but you must keep breathing."

She looked about her for something that might help, give him interest, spark some flame of life inside him. He was fading so quickly, seeming to shrink in upon himself. "Did you know that your ship has sunk into the Bunboys? There is naught left of it. There were so many bodies that it was feared they would spoil the fishing. So the priests ordered the bodies burned and prayers said for all the men that were lost. You must have been a special favorite of some saint.... Sir?"

Cara caressed his brow, her own deeply creased in concern. "Sir?"

Mimms yawned and looked hungrily at the bowl of stew. Cara slid the bowl over to him then meticulously inspected the survivor's bandages. None festered.

"So." A voice spoke out of the gloom. "This is the man you saved and hoard to yourself like treasure."

Cara's head snapped round to the inky blackness from whence the words had come. Sir Almoy stooped to enter from the west tunnel. What little light there was reflected from his garments and snowy beard.

"Ah, Almoy, my lord, you've come at last."

"Humph," the elder grunted. He squinted through one eye, showing displeasure. "You avoid your lessons to tend a worthless man."

"Nay, my lord. He needs the care I give him."

"So you say," Almoy complained in an injured tone.

"Oh, but he does," Cara justified. "Yesterday, I bathed and tended to him with diligence, heating water on yon fire. It must be kept alight to ward away the chill. I've put healing balm to all his wounds and bound the worst of them with clean cottons. While I've ministered to him, I've thought of only Jesus' body scourged and beaten, taken from the cross."

Almoy did not deign to remark upon that. "Well, then, let me see him."

Cara spread open the cloths that covered the survivor. Almoy grimaced. "The man should be dead, battered like that. You say he survived the tors of Lacada Point?"

"Aye." Cara's hand lingered protectively over the auburn hair neatly brushed back from the survivor's brow.

"He must have been a strong, healthy man. No broken bones? Ah, I see his limbs are straight and true. The bruises will fade, aye, but he will bear the scars all his days."

"I canna change that." Cara stroked the long hair she had so carefully washed. "He is cut here, behind his ear."

Almoy bent closer so that his gnarled finger could probe the wound. "You must stitch it up."

"It will hurt him more."

"He will not feel it. You have needle and thread?"

"Aye."

"Fetch them. Boil both, then sew the wound closed."

"I don't think I can."

"Then who will?" Almoy asked as he straightened. "Give him up to the Mac Donnell. Let his servants tend the man. Come back to your lessons. They plague me in my chambers. Twice the earl's men have searched from cellar to parapet. They seek you, Mulvaine. 'Tis a dire warning I give you. There is trouble afoot."

"I will heed your warning," Cara assured the elder.

"You must do more than heed it. Here." From within his tunic, Almoy produced a talisman. "Wear this if you are to evade the laird's inquisition. The English have come to plague Sorely's soul. That Jesuit snoops like a cat round my sanctuary. 'Tis dangerous times. I must protect the Temple's knowledge. Take heed, Mulvaine."

Gordon Mckenna struggled with the befuddling effects of increasing fever. If necessary, he could open both eyes. The only thing he could truly bear doing was to lie as still as possible.

He knew his mind was confused. Rational thought was not part of his present state. He was aware that the girl hovered over him and her care kept him alive, just as he knew they were alone. Certain he heard another voice, he forced both eyes open to slits.

That is how he saw the gaunt, ancient man. Then he knew how sick he truly was. The old one could have passed for a ghost. Gordie was disproved of that notion when the man put tremulous fingers to his head where the greater portion of his numbing headache originated.

Gordie slammed his eyes shut, nearly fainting from the renewed ache and the agony of an unwanted probe. His fevered mind played tricks on him. Instead of a harmless, withered old man, it was the Grim Reaper reaching down to take him. Gordie had no strength to outwit him.

Fever overwhelmed him. His mind began slipping away. His last conscious thought was, *Temple's treasures... what temple... what treasures?*

Cara settled the talisman around her neck. The medallion lay heavily between her breasts, seeming warm from newly cast spells, a potent amulet. She got her threads and needle and boiled both, then did the required stitching. Her hands trembled badly, but the stitches were as neat and small as she could make.

Despite the huge lump that surrounded the wound, the man did not groan nor move nor even seem conscious of the needle that passed through his skin. If he did not jar himself greatly, the stitches would hold.

He subsided facedown against the lambs wools, unable to remain on his side without support.

"You know you are safe here. I've hidden you well, you see."

She uncovered his back and dipped her fingers inside a small crock of camphor cream and slowly massaged his burning skin. The ointment melted at once, becoming slick against her hands, allowing her fingers to glide without friction. He coughed deeply, but did not rouse.

"'Tis John Kelly that Almoy mentioned, an Englishman," Cara said aloud. "He claims to be of import to the harlot. We spoke yesterday, when I dug the clams for the chowder for you. His governor demands all survivors be surrendered. Kelly's a damned fool, or so the Irish say. My grandfather told him to go to hell. That made the Jesuit turn as pale as cheese. You needn't worry that anyone will discover you or that you'll be hanged. No one knows you've survived. Besides, Mimms is very loyal. He must like you, too. He hasn't bitten you. If he didn't like you, he would have."

Cara paused to shift his arm from underneath his chest so that he lay flat upon his stomach. Again he coughed, but that was all he ever did. The tight, constricting cough sent waves of pain washing across his unconscious face. His eyes looked better, less swollen, though the bruising had gone to purple. She rose upon her knees and coated her hands again with the camphorate cream, starting the deep massage again from the curve of his spine up to his neck.

"I heard talk of one man, an Englishman, who was spared from hanging. He claimed to be someone of import, a nephew to the great harlot's paramour, Leicester. What were you, sir?"

Cara's brows flexed. She continued rubbing his back. "I suppose you might think it odd that I have helped you. 'Tis because you are a man of the plaid. Well, 'tis more than that, too, but I know you are a Scot."

Cara touched his clenched left hand, where the signet ring was embedded in his swollen flesh. "I am half-Scot and know the oral genealogies. We might be related somehow. You could be a Kyntyre or a Sterling. My great-great grandmother was born a MacGregor." Cara took her hand from his and stared at the empty shadows.

"It has been told to me that my mother, Leah Mac Donnell, disgraced the Mac Donnells. My grandfather held my father, Brodie Mulvaine, captive in this very cell until he agreed to marry my mother. I was the third child born to them, though my mother died soon after and my father was lost in a storm at sea. My brothers died young. I am not sure I would like it if you were a Malcom or McTavish. They are foresworn enemies of the Mulvaines and the Kyntyres."

Cara paused to lay a small log on the glowing fire. The cavern was deep and high and the smoke was absorbed within it. A good thing for him, otherwise he would have no fire, no matter how sick he was.

Her expression remained thoughtful. "It is possible I might be able to send word to the Kyntyre. We keep pigeons for such duty in a dovecote upon the roof of the south tower. Donovan tends them. He will not gainsay me if I open a cage or two."

That said, she resumed the slow, steady massage. She was certain the massage helped, but it was a mistake to stop chattering. Silence opened her mind to too many sensations. Like the supple, heated feel of his flesh beneath her fingertips. That was disturbing, but not as disturbing as the visions that filled her head.

Images flooded inside her mind, views into his past and future made manifest by her cursed second sight. He laughed at a wondrous court. Smiled as he pranced to outlandish dance steps with women whose gowns of silk and velvet twinkled with gems and jewels. Washing and bandaging his hands, she'd felt the weight of his sword resting easily in his grip, felt the shudder of a ship's wheel as it plowed the sea, caught her breath in fright as he'd deftly laid charges to powder kegs and set the sea and a flotilla of ships to blaze with Greek fire.

Cara tasted secondhand his bitter agony at capture, and knew his rage when he had been chained to an oar in the bowels of a Spanish ship. She keenly knew his relief when, at each juncture of his adventurous life, he'd outwitted death and survived.

All that mattered to him was to defeat his enemies.

All that escaped Cara was his name. She knew that he'd left his home after some great argument, an argument between thundering father and stubborn, wayward son. Oh, and he was loved, loved and adored in ways that Cara had never known. By her gift of second sight, she knew that the filial love he'd abandoned was waiting for him tenfold. And she knew that his heart was true. That he was a good man, beset by a cruel fate, but not cruel or mean-spirited within himself.

He would return the prodigal son, a hero much lauded and feted, even more so for his long absence. He was a lucky man, favored by God.

So, Cara talked endlessly when she came to tend him, fearing the unhindered views silence allowed. Were he conscious, his own active mind could block her gift.

Mimms was used to her rambling and sometimes cocked his head and groaned or yawned or yipped if he saw the need to comment. When she finished soothing and smoothing the healing cream onto the survivor's back, she brought the soft linen and warm wools carefully up to cover his shoulders. She moved quickly to his other side to straighten the pallet and smooth the crumpled lambskins under his arm.

As she tugged upon one that was bunched beneath his left shoulder, that arm suddenly flexed and moved.

"What?" Cara gasped as his iron grip encircled her waist and swept her down beside him.

"Wench, where's my ale?" Gordie muttered in a hoarse voice. His throat ached miserably and he was tired of waiting to be served. "Gads, wot's this? Megan? Since when did you eat like a sparrow?"

Against his heated flesh, the woman in his grip felt as frail as a shadow. Gordie rolled onto his back, drawing her across his chest, freeing his other hand to stroke across her small breasts. "Megan, where's my ale, damn my eyes? What's it take to get service? A kiss?"

Cara blinked in astonishment, not at his words, but at the quick movements of his hands. One tugged on her laces and pushed aside the warm wool. The other caught the back of her head, drawing it downward as his lips smacked on her throat.

"Sir." Cara pushed at his chest, straining to hold her distance.

"That wasn't a kiss. You can do better, hmm?"

A heated trail of kisses snaked up her chin. His whiskers grazed her lips with startling determination.

"Umph!" Cara exclaimed a muffled protest as his mouth focused accurately on the target he sought.

He turned again, rolling both of them over. "Ach, so sweet, so sweet. Kiss me, love. Don't be shy."

"You don't know what you are doing," Cara said, wiggling in containment, shocked by the touch of his fevered hand on her breast. Then she couldn't say a word as his mouth fused over her own. He radiated heat throughout, covering her with a weight that might have been dreadful if it wasn't so utterly comforting. A flash of thought told her the comfort was illusory. He dreamed, awash in his own fevered fantasy.

Still, it was her first kiss, ever. And it was nice. Oh, so very nice. She did nothing to stop his most pleasant assault, allowing and accepting his continued touch because he was ill. He really didn't know what he was doing or that it was she he was doing it to. His touch did not frighten her in any way. In truth, it felt very good to be held so close against him.

His mouth left hers abruptly. Grasping her to him, he rolled her on top of him, turning his head against her shoulder, and coughed. From somewhere deep in the shadows, Cara caught the ominous threat of Mimms' most dangerous growl.

The spasm racked him so deeply, it shook the both of them.

"Oh, God, I am dying," he moaned, and his arms fell away. His body rolled to his side, exhausted.

Fearing she had hurt him, Cara scrambled off of him, snatching her skirts out from beneath his legs. She jerked the rumpled covers back over his bare chest. Rattled, she looked about to find Mimms hovering, his fangs bared and gleaming.

"Hush, Mimms," Cara scolded, ashamed she had allowed the embrace to continue. "He's a sick man. Don't be so bad tempered."

What was she thinking of? Cara wasted not a moment putting more distance between herself and the survivor. It was unconscionable to take pleasure from one so sick. Heat rushed into her face. She blinked again and swallowed. "Oh, dear."

She brought the lantern closer and peered at his face. "Sir?"

She risked touching his brow. It singed her. Hot. God in His merciful heavens, the poor man was on fire.

"Oh, no." Cara stroked her hands down his cheeks, tenderly cupping the soft fullness of his beard. It was so different from the silky auburn hair that covered his head. His beard fascinated her greatly. He fascinated her completely. She touched his neck and felt his racing pulse.

She pulled aside the wools and linens, removing the blanketing covers that only intensified his inner fires. Then she sat abruptly back on her heels, shocked by the thrust of his manhood, tall and erect from his body. Not once had he ever looked so. Thinking his fevers had driven him into terrible pains, Cara almost reached out to touch him. Mimms' warning bark stopped her.

"Be quiet, Mimms." Cara threw a light cloth over the survivor's hips. She did not know much about men, but she knew horses and other animals. Embarrassed, she hastily fetched a basin of cool water. She soaked a flannel in it, squeezed out the excess and laid it across the survivor's brow. She put another on his throat, and spread more on his chest trying to cool his heat. She ignored the awesome rod beneath the linen, trying vainly to remember the Christian thoughts that had allowed her to tend to his most basic needs without shame or fear.

His flesh shivered under her touch, like Neta's flanks did when Cara petted or soothed the animal. This wasn't a sign of appreciation, Cara knew that. He was so very, very hot.

"I cannot let him die," she whispered desperately when the water did nothing to abate his raging fever. "Praying for a miracle is not enough. Mimms, guard him well. I go to Almoy's tower."

Gordie wandered in and out of a nightmare. Sometimes his head was quite lucid and clear as he sat talking and laughing at his father's table...the queen's table...dancing attendance upon her majesty. Then Bess faded and he rode the lowland hills with young King James.

Rarely did he stride about the deck of the *Swiftshure* or stand at the quarterdeck holding the wheel, speaking to Templeton and Trews. He seemed to have lost all sense of the sea, the feel for it.

In his delirium, he thought himself caught in a dungeon where a gray mouselike girl tormented him.

Ah, but the shy little mouse interested him. She tiptoed about when he closed his eyes the tightest. In his dreams, she had the biggest rat ever conceived for a pet. Its yellow eyes glinted in the dark. Instead of having rat teeth, it had a wolf's fangs...fangs that it bared with the least provocation...like a rabid dog.

If he was sly, sometimes Gordie could catch his mouse. He liked to hear her squeal when he trapped her. But the oddest things happened to the mouse when she was caught.

She was a changeling.

Enchanted or bewitched, he knew not which...the stuff of his childhood fairy tales.

Beneath the gray covering there was soft, sweet flesh, as cool and as supple as silk. He thought it was Megan, caught in a spell, except the mouse's breasts were small and firm like autumn apples, and all the women Gordie knew were more than a lusty handful.

Ah, but Megan had her own accomplishments. Legs that fastened strongly round his hips and clung for the wildest ride until every ounce of pleasure was wrung from him. The gray mouse could have been very like her, with those small and delicate hands that cooled and soothed his burning flesh.

That's when the rabid rat-wolf-dog would howl so fiercely, it caused his ears to throb. Naught relieved the pain in his ears, the hard rasping in his chest or the poison burning his throat. It was just more pain to add to a season of pain.

Gordie would sleep then.

Sometimes his vision was so clear that, despite the gloom, he saw the girl who had saved him. He had fought and fought with the sea, knowing he was dying, tumbling over and over in the violent waves, bashing against the rocks. Then he'd caught hold of a furred log and next he knew the sea rushed away from him.

There she had been. A wet little thing not much bigger than his sister Becca. She fought the sea to save him. He wasn't worth saving, not when the blood of hundreds of men lay on his hands.

Dear God, but she annoyed him with her neverending insistence that he live. Poor little thing, she crept up to him with miserable food, horrible soups, vile broths and heaven only knew what else—slithering bowls of leeches, fetid-smelling concoctions that no man could stomach....

Not that he was much of a man anymore. What scrap of humanity he had retained after the firestorm at Calais was beaten out of him by the lash of a Spanish whip. Condemned and chained to a galley oar, starved and beaten until only the animal in him survived. He hadn't the strength to squash a fly. Why was she so shy of him? He'd never harmed a hair on a single woman's head, ever.

Why couldn't she bring him an ale to quench his burning thirst, or something stronger? Whiskey would do. He would give his left arm for a joint of beef dripping with juices. But no. She had no idea what to feed a starving man.

And she chattered incessantly, talking, talking in that soft lilting voice, sweet as spring honey. Nonsense...she talked to herself. A mad mouse that talked to the empty air.

His wild fevers sent her scurrying back to the mouse's hideyhole. She flinched when he flung out his arms to catch her.

The rat-wolf-dog growled more viciously. Gordie howled back, but his growls ended in spasms. Racking, burning coughs that choked the life out of him. The yellow-eyed beast won those contests.

The girl won the others. Rail as Gordie might, she always came back . . . her soft, caring hands a lifeline in turbulent water.

Gordie wanted the struggle to end. The endless pain, the empty belly, the bones that ached and throbbed and, worse, the fire that ate his breath away.

It had to stop.

His breath came slow and shallow. It hurt too much to suck in another breath.

"He is dying." Cara whispered. The weight of failure cast a heavy gloom around her.

Sir Almoy sighed, laid a ribbon across his page and closed the volume he studied. The book's leather binding creaked. Parchment crackled. Powdery dust shot airborne into the sunbeams.

"What did you expect? No man's life is yours to direct. He has outlived his time. All but five were fated to leave the earth when the ship struck rock. You cheated the reaper."

"Nay." Cara shook her head, tears escaping from her eyes. "I didn't. He is the prodigal. I have seen his future. They wait for him at his home. He will live for years beyond this, and will do many good things for his people."

Almoy brought a bony finger to his lip and studiously rubbed his mustache. He meditated. When his eyes met Cara's they were crystal clear, despite his age and spent energy. His gaze penetrated Cara's, seeing her faults, her vanities, her flaws and her innate goodness. It shined out of her eyes in quiet desperation. "Perhaps it be someone else's future you see."

"No. 'Tis his. I am sure of it."

Almoy shrugged. "Go to your tower, then. The man will live without your aid."

"How dare you say that? That I aid him thus far and do nothing more? I must help him."

Almoy's shoulders drooped, and Cara was unaware of the tremor in his spine. "You ask the impossible. Such magic as you seek consumes all the forces that surround it."

Cara reverently turned full circle, examining every treasure she had come to love in this tower. It had been her refuge for years and years. She looked to the old, old man and asked solemnly. "Are you certain?"

Sir Almoy just looked at her obliquely. "Does the banshee scream?"

"Aye," her solemn nod confirmed, "the banshee screams."

"Well, then? You know the laws of all forces, to every action, there is equal reaction."

"Aye," Cara agreed, "and each spirit has its tasks, its duties to perform."

Almoy's mood changed abruptly. He shuffled back to his worktable, arranging and rearranging his assorted treasures. "As do all mortals. The trick, Mulvaine, is to know one's duty. You are an apprentice, decades from the skill you crave."

Disheartened, Cara walked past the crowded, cluttered shelves. She sat on a stool before the glowing fire and took a black-eared kitten onto her lap. Her hands smoothed down the animal's fur unconsciously. The kitten purred loudly and contentedly. Cara frowned at nothing in particular and thought very hard. Then all at once her brow smoothed and she looked back to Almoy.

"It is his spirit that is dying?"

"Ah, I see, you learn despite the thickness of your skull," Almoy said, and continued sifting powders.

"What man can live without his spirit?"

"Oh, there have been many that have. A Roman named Caligula. Others—there are always others. One you know."

"The Mac Donnell," Cara deduced.

"Aye, aye. His spirit died years and years ago."

Cara's head moved slowly back and forth. "No, no. This isn't to be. I know I'm right." She stroked the kitten's fur. Her eyes shifted to the open windows where the sun glowed on the western horizon but she didn't see the splendid sunset. Nor was it the kitten's fur her senses detected. It was the hard, cold manacles encircling the survivor's extremities that her fingers stroked.

Each band of Spanish iron disturbed and haunted her. Evil radiated from the metal. No key in Dunluce could open them. Nor had she access to a smith's tools or the skill to use them.

The iron bands remained fixed to the survivor's wrists and ankles. They poisoned him. They affected her. Each brush of a wayward finger against them filled Cara's head with the most horrible visions.

Not a one of Dunluce's Irish shades, mad monks or berserker Vikings of yore were as horrible.

The iron was forged in the pits of hell. She could see the red hot furnace glowing . . . hear the ring of the hammer pounding the iron into shape . . . smell the fetid wind of the bellows . . . taste the acrid sulphur steaming from the anvil.

The ironmonger sweated . . . a twisted, wicked demon, steeped in cruelty to the extreme. His victims wore the manacles, their bodies chained by pairs to the galleass oars, their souls condemned to death by the whip. A slow, tortuous death that came only after all hope of salvation was robbed from them, pounded ruthlessly out of them with the same cruel, vicious vigor the metal was shaped.

Without compassion to their humanity, without a care for their souls, their failing, hurting bodies starved and tormented until the moment they died.

Many—too many—such souls had worn those cuffs.

The survivor wasn't the only one whose spirit was trapped within the strangling, evil iron.

"I must do it," Cara spoke aloud.

"Do?" Almoy's voice cracked rudely. "You presumptuous pup. Think you to counter what is written in the *Book of Life?*"

He held up a long hand that was nearly transparent in the waning day's light. "'Tis preordained those men should perish. The gold 'twas stolen from a heathen land. The piece you gave me was not created by an alchemist. Brown-skinned savages dug it from the earth and fashioned it into likeness of a sun god. 'Tis pure, soft and malleable. A raw, base element of unnatural power, never meant to be in the hands of man. Blasphemy caused that ship to be doomed. I saw ten times ten the number of condemned souls perish in the making of one Spanish coin as those drowned in the ship transporting it."

"The gold is cursed."

"No good will ever come of it."

Cara considered that she had come to that very conclusion the moment she'd spied the gold. "I will take care of that, as well, my friend."

Her resolve strengthened, Cara stood abruptly. The kitten bounded from its warm perch on her lap.

"Ah, ah, ah," Almoy grated. "You cannot go casting spells and conjuring spirits to do your bidding without protections. Have you forgotten all I've taught you?"

"Not a lesson." Cara smiled then, and her face was so beautiful it arrested Almoy's breath. "I have just remembered the *Second Pentacle of Mars.*"

Almoy pursed his withered lips together and sputtered and blustered to his shelves. "Virgin parchment."

Cara continued to smile as he pulled item after item from his precious stores and thrust them into her arms—vellum paper made of the skin of newborn lambs, mastic, frankincense, charcoal, silk, exorcised knives and quills, blessed ink, until she could hardly hold the bounty of precious things.

He tapped the silver medallion hung from a strand of silk around her throat. "Heed my warning, gel. You must be clean of mind, soul, body and spirit. Make certain your circle is perfect and that the names of God are written properly."

Sir Almoy did not need to say what would happen if she cast the wrong spell or lost her wits. "Remember this, whomever you summon you must give license to depart, and if they do not come when you bid them, demand a messenger to explain why they cannot. Bind the spirits to you. Remain in control always, or do not interfere with that you cannot contain."

Very solemnly Cara promised to do exactly what she should. "Sir Almoy..."

The old one turned his back to her.

"Sir Almoy..."

"What is it now?" He swept round, his tunic swirling about him.

"Thank you, my lord."

"Hmph." The old one wavered, then slipped back into the shadow of his library's shelves. "Go...go to your man. It's him you want. All is done here. Go, Mulvaine, go."

* * *

Cara put all of Sir Almoy's precious gifts inside a sturdy pouch and took herself to the north tower to prepare. She bathed completely, immersing her entire person in blessed water. She put on a simple shift of pure white linen, fastened her cloak securely at her throat and went to the chapel in her grandfather's hall to attend evening mass and confession. Last, she gathered blessed water and pure beeswax candles, then slowly descended the twisting corridors deep into the dungeon.

The survivor had quit thrashing. His once-strong arms and powerful legs no longer fought the weights bearing down upon them. His chest moved hardly at all. The sleek muscles between his ribs barely stirred.

Cara froze in midstep. Terror slid down her spine. She blinked, once, twice, unable to believe what her eyes beheld.

On his chest sat a harbinger of death, a black and ugly spirit that sucked the vapors from the survivor's slackened mouth. It hovered with avaricious gleaming eyes, waiting for the man's unshriven soul to rise unfettered from his weakened, mortal body. The devil's hour was nearly at hand.

Shaken, Cara closed her eyes, trembling as she made the sign of the cross, then whispered the Lord's Prayer. Only when the last amen was spoken did Cara have the courage to look again.

Mimms whined hungrily, digging a paw at her cloak. For a moment Cara stared slack-jawed at her dog, then looked back to the shadowy darkness above the sick man. There was nothing there. Whatever the nature of the thing Cara had glimpsed, she could not see or sense it now. Cautiously, Cara unpacked the magical provisions and bent to the task she'd set herself to do. An eerie silence, punctuated by the survivor's shallow gasps for air, kept her company as her charcoal completed the first diagram.

Shadowing her every footstep, Mimms growled and grumbled uneasily.

One by one, Cara lit the candles and placed each in the proper position inside the pentagram. With each added light, she intoned the hidden names of the Creator saying her prayers in a clear, pure voice. *"In the name of Adonai Elohim Tzabaoth Shaddai, Lord God of Armies Almighty, may we suc-*

cessfully perform the works of our hands and may the Lord be present with us in our heart and in our lips.''

The candles burned without flickering, for the night was calm and quiet. The sea gate stood open, yet no breeze stirred out of the calm waters.

The moon rose, high, bright and full, though none of its light penetrated the caves.

Cara called Mimms to her side within the holy circle and poured blessed water over his head so that it ran down his coat to his paws and tail. "I command you, my companion, to befriend and protect me from every evil."

Mimms shook his head and drops of the blessed water sprinkled over the dying man. Mimms' growl deepened.

"Little can hurt me while I am awake, Mimms." Cara softly scratched her dog's ears, comforting and calming him. "Guard me well when the spell is cast, for then my talismans will not be the protection I need to guard my spirit. You must do it, Mimms."

Cara removed her tunic, laying it outside of the circle, and unbound her hair. It flowed down her like a silken cloth, its dark, rich color a complete contrast against the pale white of her skin. She settled seven pentacles of protection round about her shoulders, each a precious scapula, and knelt in the center of the pentagram beside the dying man. She stretched her arms over his prone body and began to pray.

Chapter Four

Gordie Mckenna's eyes shot open. All pain had left him. The killing weight upon his chest had evaporated. Reflexively, he sucked in a great gulp of phosphorescent air. It glittered and shimmered, a blinding wash of brilliant yellow pinpricks of light.

The taste that coated his parched tongue was as sweet as honeysuckle and pure as spring water.

The cold, heavy iron weighting each of his extremities throbbed with the beat of the earth beneath his spine.

Earth, wind and fire, which forged all metals, separated and softened, each into its own unique element. Flesh and bone seemed apart and away from all previously known realities. He felt his body strain against the earth-bound weights on each extremity. The manacles bore him downward into hell, doom and oblivion. His spine arched and the weighted limbs stretched, muscles lengthening out of his control, tendons pulling and being pulled. Upward, upward, he rose into warm, welcome healing lights. The iron cuffs, so cruelly solid and secure, took on the texture of heated sand and melting wax as his body levitated, higher, higher.

He opened wide his unfocused eyes, conscious, not conscious, sane yet mad. Hazy shapes rushed at him—fireflies, butterflies, things with transparent wings. The manacles ran into rusted dust, sand in a broken hourglass, spilling onto the floor. The bolts gave, the shackles broke.

Gordie's skin tingled, each nerve sharp and aware. His ears rang with a throbbing, strong and comforting pulse akin to a mother's heartbeat learned before birth, forgotten since.

Minutes, hours, days might have passed. He knew nothing more than the most elemental level of being. He breathed and savored the pleasure of it. No cough caused him to double. No razors tore between his spine and his sternum. No fire burned or constricted his throat.

The relief was so complete he opened his eyes, amazed by the sensations flooding him. He could see to the high, cavernous ceiling of the cave-dungeon.

The very air within it pulsed. His mind, reclaimed from delirium, recognized the phenomenon, a curious phosphorescence that the sea occasionally harbored in certain climes and strange waters.

It did not alarm him. That he could identify the eerie light told him his mind was whole, rational and intact. He could find no reason for his unearthly sense of lightness.

Slowly his true senses returned and the odd tingling in his hands and feet abated. He could feel the matted sheepskins against his back. His eyes focused on real things, not weird lights. He could smell the damp, the oily wicks of beeswax candles, the earthy peat-fueled fire, hear the drip of water oozing through the rocks and the pound of the sea against the stone. He turned his head sideways, his eyes open and wide, searching his surroundings.

Beyond the circlet of candlelight, the foul dog lay with its head up, its yellowish gaze fixed upon Gordie. The animal watched him, alert, waiting for what, Gordie could not imagine. Within the circle of candles, the girl was prone upon the stone floor.

She slept without aid of blanket or cloak to cover her bare arms. The black, silken curtain of her hair pooled about her sides.

Shadows formed under the sweep of her lashes on her cheeks. Her mouth was parted slightly, a sensuous, inviting sight to behold—sweet, pink and moist.

He thought he dreamed again, but somehow knew he didn't when his body moved upon the simple command of his will. Sitting, he rubbed his wrists, astonished that the heavy manacles no longer abraded his skin.

He stared at his wrists. Raw, red marks proved the irons had been there. Likewise, his ankles had been mangled. The irons were gone. Four piles of rust-scented dust marked the sheep-skins beneath him. He searched his muddled mind and found a hazy memory of the girl's efforts to try to pry them loose. He found another memory, that of the horrible moment when he'd been brutally restrained and the irons were plug-welded fast. He could not shake the sensation of feeling metal granulate. A preposterous thought, as irrational and foreign to his logical mind as that of floating on thin air.

The watchdog yawned and let escape a restless whine. Gordie fixed his attention on the beast. Beyond it, the door of the cell stood open. Swirls of fog curled off the cold stone floor.

Had he a stitch of clothing to wear? He half expected the sleeping girl to bolt and run if he moved and revealed how thoroughly naked he was. But neither she nor her dog made any movement as he rose unsteadily to his feet.

Weak. He was weak as a newborn foal. He flung his arms out, hands seeking something to grasp to steady himself. He tottered, arms floundering, knees buckling. Upright, his body lacked all sense of balance, and the dungeon spun round about him.

More brilliant, odd lights danced before his face with the curiously strange sensation of aiding his balance. He knew he imagined soft chuckles drifting past his ears. His skin prickled, and goose flesh rippled down his spine. The odd lights moved. The short guttering candles dipped and bowed.

He opened his eyes wide then squinted, trying to focus on just one candle stump. His stomach rumbled hollowly, his head spun merry cartwheels and his eyes played tricks upon him. Did the candle have another form? That of a miniscule person bathed and glittering in light? A fairy queen. In the back of his mind he heard laughter, happy and lighter than air. He shook his head to clear it of hallucinations and ran one hand roughly across his face.

His skin was dry. His beard scraped his palm. His fingers swept across his eyes, dislodging the crust of a long sleep. He felt weak in all his limbs, yet his strength was there, untested. Some other force held him upright, steady on his feet. Movement seemed beyond him.

"Lass." His voice croaked, the sound thick and rough. Not his voice, his true voice. He panicked, reaching for the sleeping woman, unable to bend or stretch the distance. He would fall flat on his face. "Lass."

A cushion of warm, living light held firm, bracing him. A cloud of phosphorescence that contained no shape yet had buoyancy kept him on his own two feet until the swimming lightness in his head steadied.

Finally he chanced a step. The chamber swam. The stone floor chilled his toes. His body creaked as lame, unused, untested joints bent. Putting his knee to the ground where the girl lay, Gordie placed one hand on her upturned shoulder. "Lass."

Name, name? Had she ever stated it? His fingers curved round living flesh. The wolfhound growled and stood.

The gray mouse-girl was boneless, limp as rags. Gordie's hand absorbed the chill in her bare arm. A cloak of hair covered her. Not even a kirtle sheathed her torso.

"What is this?" Gordie smoothed aside the thick blanket of hair. The candlelight flickered on milk-white skin. He traced the length of her arm, following marblelike smoothness down to a bare, cold-as-the-grave hip. "Ach, but yer a wee, pretty thing."

What was she thinking of to sleep unblanketed on a stone floor? It made no sense. But then nothing made sense in his head. Had they made love on the pallet and she rolled herself off to the cold floor? No. He had no recollection of that in his head. He remembered touching her, clutching at her warm, competent hands as if they were a lifeline, mistaking her in his delirium for Megan. Surely, he would remember doing more. He remembered thinking her a mouse.

His mind had enough to struggle with, explaining the dream sensation that he had somehow floated on air and the mystery of iron that had melted like wax. He didn't think about what he was doing as he gathered the young woman protectively into his arms. Her skin was cold and needed warming. She didn't seem to weigh anything. He didn't seem to have bulk or form, either. He cradled her against his chest and stared down into her sleeping face.

Dark lashes fanned in semicircles against her softly rounded cheeks. Her sweet, full-lipped mouth parted below a slightly upturned nose. Her chin was strong and firm, hinting slightly of stubbornness and strength, yet she felt so frail and delicate in his arms. Cool, yet warm and alive wherever his skin caressed hers.

That strange sensation of being given buoyancy by weird phosphorus light returned as he stood holding her in his arms. What to do? He eyed his pallet. It was soft and well laid with warm sheepskins. She needed warming and comforting. He could tell by the pale shadows beneath her eyes that she had exhausted herself caring for him. He had a nearly overwhelming desire to show his gratitude by kissing awake her sleep-slackened mouth.

He ached to sleep long and hard and wake feeling alive, well and real with a woman worthy of loving in his arms. He had much to thank her for. His life, possibly his soul.

The dog stood to its impressive height just beyond the candles. It growled menacingly, protective and territorial, but it remained outside the guttering circle of light. "Dinna fash yer beastie heart, dog. I'm no taking her anywhere."

Gordie laid the girl on his pallet. She shifted, turning her face toward him, her sleep undisturbed. One hand curled across her belly, drawing Gordie's attention away from her small, piquant face. Her breasts were well formed and full, and graced by rosy-tipped aureoles. The thatch at the juncture of her thighs proved her maturity, rich with dark inviting color as black as her flowing head of midnight-colored curls.

In his delirium he'd thought her immature, a woman-child. The lingering sweep of his eyes confirmed maturity. Now he saw that she was exquisite, as perfectly formed as Sandro Botticelli's painted *Venus,* hanging in the Florentine palace of his friend, the Count of Uffizi. Gordie remembered how he'd stood before that painting, awestruck by the artist's skill, and thought no mortal woman could ever equal the painter's idealization.

The clear memory of his past enabled him to see with more clarity than he had in weeks. His jolted mind examined the stark earth-chamber. He could not explain shimmering lights, unfathomable piles of rusty sand and the miracle of eased, unfevered breathing. He asked how, why?

"Lass." Gordie laid his hand on her smooth thigh. Tempted. God, he was tempted. Beneath her curtaining hair she wore a simple, peasant necklace of amber and lead beads strung on twisted threads. The largest medallion clung to her alabaster skin between her breasts. Gordie sighed. He'd not take advantage of a generous woman.

He felt the deep gnawing of hunger in his belly. Food—he'd give anything for a meal. He closed his eyes, his head too light to make sense of any of this. Gordie fingered his forehead and temple, pressing firmly, the gesture a purposeful one he hoped would clear the fog.

A little sleep and he would see to food. A little sleep, and he would find the words to thank her properly. He owed her his life. How would he ever repay her?

Sir Almoy paced the perimeter of the pentagram. His foolish apprentice did not stir. Now the man cuddled against her, asleep, as well.

Almoy grunted, sniffing the heavy-scented air, fragrant with incense and charged with power like that of a wild stormy night. All was calm, quiet and at peace. The fairy lights dimmed and faded. Cara had served her part well, her sacrifice had been accepted. The man was healed.

Morning wasn't long away. The dawn would bring Cara to her senses. Until then, her alert and ever-loyal dog would willingly guard her. Mimms lay outside the pentagram, his massive head cocked to the side, watching Almoy's slow and certain pacing of the diagram.

The old knight paused, stroking his withered hand down his white beard. He nodded and grunted again. All was well. Cara was safe, more protected now in the arms of the stranger than she had ever been since coming to Dunluce fifteen years ago. Satisfied, Sir Almoy raised a hand in salute to the elements and departed from the damp, throbbing cave.

Chapter Five

The smell of wood smoke layered underneath the dampness of the heavy fog. John Kelly's nostrils flared wide against his plain, pockmarked face. He leaned over his saddle, his cloak pulled tight around his chest, unable to shake the chill and the eternal wet from his bones.

The smoke came from the rocks, though there was no fire to be seen in any direction he looked. That was peculiar. It caused him to rein in his horse on the cliff facing the sea, puzzling out that peculiarity.

The sun was up, but it would be hours before it melted the fog away from the cursed Irish coast.

He yawned and wiggled a broad knuckle into the corner of his right eye. He had damn good eyesight, thank the Lord, otherwise he would have been found dead years ago for his proclivity to wander the cliffs near Dunluce.

When he removed the finger gouging his eye, he saw her. The Mulvaine picked her way up the stony path along the cliff face. His mount snorted, reacting to the minute compression of Kelly's tensing knees. Before the girl finished the steep climb, John Kelly had swept his damp cap off his head, flourishing its limp feather in a gallant greeting. "Good morn, Mistress Mulvaine."

Cara stopped just below the precipice where John Kelly blocked her path. "Squire Kelly." She returned his greeting and drew her cloak fast round her simple tunic. A stain crept into her cheeks at the memory of awakening naked in her survivor's arms, compressed tight against his warm, hard body. "Good day to you."

"You be out early."

"Aye." Cara held her place. The Englishman looked down upon her, tongue-tied, ever unable to state his words. He glanced to the burned wharf at the bottom of the cliff and wrinkled his large nose.

"'Tis most odd how the smell of burning wood lingers here."

"Aye. 'Tis true, the smell remains."

"Wouldn't think it would last so long."

Cara half turned toward the sea, taking a deep breath of the air. She smelled smoke, not the stain of it, but the fresh scent of a newly laid fire. A fire she'd just kindled to take away the morning's damp and chill within the cave. It was the least she could do for her survivor. He slept so peacefully now. Well and at ease. But John Kelly needed diverting from her doings. "Aye, 'tis been a long time, but the cliff bears the signs of Drake's power and his fire storm. 'Tis said he used Greek fire because it burns and burns. A frightful sight, it was. The smell lingers. I expect it always will."

"You were here then, Mistress Mulvaine? You saw the hell-fire?"

"Aye, Squire Kelly. I was here and I saw the fire. I'll no forget it."

The Englishman's brown eyes searched the gray depths of Cara's placid stare. "I expect you will never forgive the English, then."

"'Twas not your doing nor mine. Will you let me pass, now, John Kelly?"

"I would rather you stayed and talked a while longer."

"'Tis morning and the sun rises. The fog is lifting even as we speak from the edges of Dunluce. Another moment or more and the lookout from Dunluce might cock an arrow to his bow and fire it upon your unprotected back. You take chances no Englishman should."

"Do you care, Mistress Mulvaine?"

Cara wondered if she did. She met his questioning gaze levelly. The middle-aged man was the only resident of her grandfather's land that dared break custom and speak to her. He was oblivious to Sorely Mac Donnell's law only because he was above it.

Kelly's hand tightened on the sorrel's reins and the animal moved back to give the young woman access to the path. She did not answer his question, and he found that did not surprise him. He was content to study her piquant face and, as she moved past his mount, he saw that her hair was unbound. It flowed down her back like a black river, sleek and polished, unfettered and well past her knees.

"Mistress Mulvaine."

"Aye, Squire Kelly?" Cara paused, her hand upon a thrusting, broken tor at her side, and she cast a backward look at the Englishman.

Her direct look took John Kelly's tongue away. He blinked once, then a second time, and his mind went utterly devoid of thought. Cara smiled a little. He was a kind fellow, a man she might like a little more if her grandfather would but allow it. But he was English.

"Sir?" Cara prompted him.

"Would you come to Ballintrea on market day?"

Cara considered the invitation. She rarely went to market of her own accord as it was forbidden that she leave her grandfather's land. It was imperative that she go this week to make arrangements for her survivor to escape Ireland. But it would not do for this Englishman to think she was accommodating him. Her grandfather had made clear what he thought of Kelly's interest in her person, but then what better way to cover her tracks and take the dog off the scent, than to use John Kelly's infatuation?

"Aye, I go to market this week."

Kelly looked past her to the blanket of heavy fog that swirled round the base of Dunluce. The castle was enshrouded, indistinct and distant, though it was really very near and solid. "God be with you until then, Mistress Mulvaine."

"And you, as well, Squire Kelly." Cara drew her cloak away from her feet and turned back to the path. Her steps were quick and silent. A moment passed and she was out of the Englishman's sight completely, swallowed by the fog and the rocks. He remained on the promontory, wondering to himself how it was she came and went from the impregnable fortress with never so much as a creak from the portcullis.

* * *

Cara went carefully round the narrow, dangerous path skirting the cliff to the kitchen door and slipped inside the smoky room. Brenna was already stirring the porridge. The thickened, sweetened brew hissed and bubbled. There was bread hot from the first oven and sausages dripping grease into the fire.

"Good morn." Cara said, tightening her grip upon her cloak as Brenna wordlessly handed her a piece of bread and sausage.

Brenna's eyes bespoke a caution. Cara nodded and took the offered food and she quickly slipped out of the kitchen into the courtyard. The fog hung thick within the enclosure of the walls. She went quickly to the north tower, let herself within and slid the bolt across the door of her own chamber high in the upper levels.

Only then, when she was safe within her tower, did Cara think of the way she'd awakened that morn—naked in the survivor's arms. Her eyes had opened and she'd been fully aware of how she was not clothed, how she'd felt. Safe, as safe as she'd ever felt in her life, and naked.

It had pained her greatly to separate her arms from their grip around the survivor's wide chest and to untangle her legs from the cocooning warmth of his. She had never felt so right . . . so close against him.

Cara slowly removed her cloak. She looked down at her gown. It was no more than a night shift. She closed her eyes and tried to piece back together the long night. It would not come. Her mind remained blank. The spell had worked. The man lived.

Now she must get him free of Dunluce.

Exactly how long he slept, Gordie would never truly know. He woke to the cave's encompassing darkness, which was relieved only by a dying fire consumed to soot-crusted embers. He woke, reaching for the warm, scented body his arms had grown accustomed to holding in his sleep. His questing hands came up empty and bereft.

She was gone. Damn, she was always gone when his faculties were in their right places.

In the space where she had been, clothes were folded and waited his use. A clean, lavender-scented shirt of fine linen replaced the one he'd lost in a flogging aboard a Spanish ship. His doublet had been washed and mended. Its fine quilting was frayed, but it provided comforting familiarity as he drew the new laces taut. Neat, unblemished hose were folded beside his mended pantaloons. He drew up both, thankful for the gifts. But where was she?

The dog guarded a pair of boots. They were of fine quality, not new, but well polished. They fit his feet snugly.

He stood, slowly turning round, getting his bearings. He was famished. So hungry that his stomach felt concave. He could tell by the way his clothing hung, he'd lost a great deal of weight.

He assumed he was on his own. She hadn't come. He would find his own way out.

His chamber proved to be some central warren. On one wall a tunnel snaked out into obliterating darkness, behind him two more yawned, to his left the standing door. Ahead of him the stone wall was bricked and manacles dangled from rusted chains.

The chains set his teeth on edge.

Gordie lifted the tallest of the stumpy candles from its bed of pooled wax, uncovered a coal and lit the wick. Determined to find the exit, he searched the openings one at a time. The first led to a greater chamber that held rusting implements of torture. The next dropped to a cistern, a stone-bound pool of fresh water fed by a bubbling stream flowing through the rocks. He backed away from both, returning whence he'd come to search through another. The next was also a blind lead, for it chambered and diverged uncounted times into small fetid cells.

The worst rated as pits sunk into slime-covered stone. Those held whitened bones, rusted chain and unspeakable horrors. He had no interest in prodding upward on the slippery stairs and meeting the master of this hellish prison.

He went the way of the open door only to come to a small cave fitted with a fixed iron gate. The gate was locked and barred. The fresh wind that came through it blew off the sea and extinguished his candle. He didn't care. He could see past the rock and stone to the moon-bright sky. There, Orion glittered for him.

The taste of life and freedom was in his mouth. He inhaled deeply, coughed and cleared the last of the phlegm from his throat. His hands encircled the bars and his muscles flexed. He'd get out if he had to tear the gate from the solid stone with his bare hands. He would be free, unshackled, a man standing upright in the sun.

Chapter Six

"**Y**ou must come away from the sea gate—" a soft voice called to him from within the cave "—before you take a chill."

Gordie turned to find both girl and loyal dog behind him. He had seen too much in his short exploration. His teeth were on edge. His eyes narrowed and his voice roughened to match his mood, made dismal and foul by the sights he'd just seen.

"So, my benefactress presents herself? Have you slept well? The fetid air of your accommodations does not bother you, eh? Open the gate. I will leave this place now."

Cara swayed slightly, her grip upon Mimms' collar secure. The press of the dog's body against her legs gave her strength to stand. She stiffened as the survivor's bitter words and hard tone assaulted her. Yet, she had ached to see him thus, standing upright and strong, alive and well. She had given much to see it—her body had yet to recover from the emotional toll of casting the spell that had healed him.

"Not this night," Cara answered in a soft, barely audible voice. "When the moon is dark, yes, you may leave. Until then, you must rest and regain your strength. You have been very ill, my lord."

Perhaps it was the deference she showed with her last words that kept Gordie's flaring temper in check. "I have regained my strength," he replied. "I thank you for your care, but I will go now. You will not tell me that I won't."

He looked back to the sky beyond the locked gate and gripped the iron railings. It galled him that he still felt so weak, so vulnerable. Angry, he shook the blasted iron with what strength he did have. It held firm. "God. This is a horrible place. Where is the key? Give it to me."

His shout bounced off the stone and echoed back at him. Did he sound that desperate? Frustration tore at him.

He turned and squinted his eyes, trying to make sense of the shadows and the blackness. All it seemed he could find in the utter dark were the yellow eyes of her dog. Gordie had no words to describe the anger he felt when he realized she had deserted him again. Only her watchdog remained.

He fumbled in the dark, unable to trace her escape. "Girl. Girl. Come back here. Don't leave me, damn you. Don't leave me alone down here!"

He sank against the stones, crumpling, a wave of despair as black as the shadows hovering over his heart. The dog stuck its muzzle in his neck and whined.

"God forbid you start whining, too." Gordie wrapped his arms around its thick neck, hardly able to bear the animal's snuffling. "I'm the one God has forsaken."

Mimms barked and slicked his tongue across the man's chin. Gordie took that as comfort. It did little to ease the gloom and nothing to alleviate the utter blackness of this man-made hell. He was reduced to holding the dog's collar and letting the animal lead him back to the dungeon.

There, the fire and lantern had been tended and refueled. A tray of food, covered with a napkin, sat atop one of several sea trunks.

From then on, the girl showed herself with the irregularity of a ghost haunting the cursed place. Yet she was no ghost. He had felt her flesh and heard the reassuring beat of her heart beneath his head.

Oh, she came with food and provisions, simple enough fare. Sometimes it was hot, mostly it was not. Gordie made torches from the abundant rushes scattered round about the cell's floor. He bound them, soaked them with blobs of melted candle wax that adhered to the dungeon floor. Torchlight did little to abate the gloom. The odd sea-phosphorescence never came again.

Day by day, his appetite grew more intense. He paced in restless captivity, bored beyond his wildest imaginings. At least in the bowels of the Spanish ship he'd had companions. That hell did not compare with the isolation of being buried alive, trapped under a mountain of stone, unable to see the light of day.

His strength returned and with it came all of a man's needs and desires. Hour after hour he was tormented by the memory of waking to find a naked nymph lying like a gift from God on the floor beside him. He groaned and ached, remembering the press of her soft flesh against his. How long had it been since he'd been in control of his destiny?

He did not even know what day, month or year it was. His beard touched his collarbone. How long did it take for hair to grow that long? He didn't know. What he did know was he wanted out. He wanted a woman...not a frightened mouse-girl who ducked away and hid from her own shadow. He wanted a lusty wench to bury himself in, to feel the pounding of his heart as sweat broke out all over his body. He wanted the sun's heat, the wind, the rain. He wanted to feel alive. He wanted freedom.

He vowed to escape her prison, by any means he had to use. She wouldn't be reasonable. Wouldn't come to him and face him. Day by day his anger deepened.

He didn't want to waste another precious minute of his life spilling his soul to a dumb dog. It was the biggest animal of its kind Gordie had ever seen. It became a surly companion, he supposed, but its loyalty to him was temporary at best. It was devoted only to the girl.

Twice Gordie trapped her. Once by snatching her skirts and yanking her down onto the pallet beside him when she tiptoed past, thinking he was sleeping. The other time she blundered into his trap in an outer chamber. Both times he had no more than snared her than the dog reverted to kind and attacked. The first time its reaction had taken Gordie by surprise. But the second, he was prepared.

"Call off yer dog." Gordie demanded, and pressed his fingers against her soft throat, his meaning clear. He would snap her neck in two if she did not obey his command.

"Mimms, stay," Cara cried out. Immediately, Mimms sank to his haunches, snarling viciously, his teeth removed from the tasty leg he was about to puncture.

Satisfied the animal would not attack him, Gordie pressed the girl against the hard wall at her back. "Better." He spoke through gritted teeth, taking a breath to calm himself. He could tell by her trembling, he'd frightened her. "It's time we had a talk."

"Why are you doing this? I have brought you hot food."

"The hell with food. Do you think I am an animal you can keep in a cage? I want the key to the gate."

Gordie growled as viciously as the dog did. His hands swept down her person, searching in a most thorough manner. Today she wore wool skirts and whimpered at his harsh handling. She had no pockets, no ring of keys tucked beneath her skirts or stuffed inside her bodice.

"Damn you."

Gordie swung her into the large chamber where there was torchlight aplenty, but no sun. Released, Cara stumbled and fell to her knees, tripping over Mimms as he bolted to her side to protect and defend. Mimms faced the survivor and snarled a warning.

"*Grrrr*, yourself, you damned traitor," Gordie snarled back, outraged more by his wordless companion's instant defection than the woman's stupidity. Mimms snapped at the air, but made no contact. "I want the key, damn you. I want the sun on my face."

The volume of his voice set Cara back upon her heels, clutching Mimms' collar to stay the dog's attack. She gave ground quickly, letting the man advance into the cell. He spied the tray of steaming food and stomped to it, falling heavily onto the trunk that served as both seat and table. He grabbed the crusty rye bread in both his hands, tearing it apart like someone who had been starved for years.

Cara brushed dirt from her hands and saw that he was appeased. She signaled Mimms to lie down and the dog obeyed. Several minutes passed while the survivor ate and Cara waited for the escalated pounding of her heart to slow.

Gordie tore a mouthful of bread from the loaf and gnashed his teeth on that. He deliberately kept his back to her. Damn, he'd seen that horrible look pass across her face. As if he were some beastly creature that belonged in manacles and irons. He'd frightened her, and had meant to do more than that. He wanted out, now. He threw the bread on the platter, his appetite ruined. He wiped crumbs from his fingers on the napkin, folded it and laid it over the tray. Rising and facing her, he set his mind to forming an apology.

She beat him to it. "I apologize for what must seem to you a desertion. 'Tis difficult for me to move freely of late. I had not forgotten you."

"How kind of you," Gordie said with a sneer, his lip curling with surly, unvented temper. "Would it make any difference if I tell you a flesh-and-blood man takes care of his own destiny?"

"Aye, I know that. I am aware that I have interfered with yours."

Exasperated, Gordie ran his fingers through his wild, tangled hair. "For the love of God, woman, you saved my life. I am grateful. I stand eternally indebted to you. Now grant me the simplest request there is. Let me take care of myself. I will go and your burden of feeding me will end. Open the gate."

"'Tis not that simple. Please, finish your meal. I give you my word that I will no' slip away. I have a favor to ask of you."

A favor? Gordie's brow cocked above his left eye. "Join me." His hand swung in an arc that encompassed the trunk cum table-seat.

Cara almost refused. She sensed how he felt. The dungeon would make anyone's life a living hell. He was tetchy. She couldn't blame him. It was her fault he was still here, trapped. "All right, but I will tell you that I have already supped and I am no' hungry." She nodded with downcast eyes and moved past him, to the opposite side of the chest.

He gathered two sheepskins and tossed them onto the rocks behind her, a makeshift seat. Gordie caught her hand and held it. Without a chair or table, he could still see that a lady was seated first before a meal. It was a crude, awkward gesture, but he had not forgotten all of his manners and could make do with what was available. She folded herself rather stiffly. He clicked his heels, bowed and took the opposite seat on the rumpled sheepskins.

He uncovered the tray, reminded that she had little idea what foods to serve a starving man. He took the knife from the platter and carved meat from a whole fowl. Beef would have suited him better.

Cara took a deep breath, then launched into what she knew she must say. "I have made arrangements for you to leave."

"Have you now?" Gordie said mildly. He tossed a blackened piece of skin off to the dog and severed the legs from the small bird at their sockets while jadedly eyeing the tankard of foamy milk. Why she never brought ale or better spirits was beyond him. He grimaced, vowing inwardly that he would be pleasant to the last drop if that accomplished her remaining there, explaining herself and getting to the bottom of why she kept him locked inside this hellhole. "So? What be your fine arrangements?"

"A ship comes this night when the moon sets." Cara jerked a little when he pierced an apple quarter and held it out to her. Gingerly taking the fruit from the point of the eating dagger, she did not attempt to put the piece in her mouth. "That will be a few hours from now. Safe passage to Scotland is guaranteed."

"Why would I go to Scotland?"

Cara moistened her lips. She couldn't fathom his question. Where else would a Scot go? Finally she said, "There isn't any other way to leave here, except to go to Scotland."

"And what, pray tell, is your price for my freedom?" The edge in Gordie's voice was clear. He stared intently at her, wondering how much she knew about him. Had he babbled in delirious splendor? Compromised every loyal Stuart agent at the court of St. James?

"You must take all the gold with you."

"Gold?" Gordie cast his gaze to de Leyva's trunk, which held the tray. There weren't a hundred ducats in it. Two of the others had less. Did she think she had a fortune? The silks and the fabrics rotting underneath the coins were worth more than the little cache of gold. She hadn't the sense to know what was of value. "Your treasure was hardly worth the trouble of carting it from the sea."

Cara thought back to the visions she'd glimpsed when she'd first touched him . . . of his dancing at a sumptuous court. To her, the gold was a fortune, to him the chests were a nuisance.

He wanted to quit Dunluce and never look back. Could she blame him?

"There is more," Cara said plainly. "But I have no' the strength to move it. I need your help to do so."

"Why should I help you, wench? You have kept me trapped here, long ere I would gone. I am not an animal to be appeased by a stroke of your hand like yon dog there. I am a living, breathing man. I would find my own way out of the troubles I am in."

"I did not save you so that you could march out of this cave and be hung for a traitor by Lord Chichester's goons." Cara set her chin in a stubborn angle.

Gordie's brow cocked. "Chichester, you say? Perhaps the general would meet me with open arms. Did you ever think of that?"

"It just so happens that I did." Cara countered just as quickly. "And believe me, sir, if the English do welcome you, then the Irish will certainly kill you. The earl of Tyrone has his troops quartered within shouting distance of this cave."

"Oh, that's just dandy, then. I wouldn't suppose you'd have a few Spaniards lingering about, would you?"

"As a matter of truth, yes. A papal inquisitor."

"Bloody hell," Gordie snarled.

"And each plays his own game, holding survivors for ransom. There is a price on every man's head who had the misfortune to make it to shore—not just here, but all throughout Ireland." She looked directly at him, challenging his doubtful gaze. "If you do no' agree to help me, you will stay here in this dungeon until you rot."

Gordie's eyes flared, then narrowed. Her threat meant little. "Do you know what penalty you'd pay in Scotland for holding a king's man prisoner?"

Cara lifted her brow. "Are you a king's man?"

"Aye."

She made a sound that had no meaning in actual words, just a grunt of sorts. His contempt wasn't something new. She'd been told chapter and verse by her grandfather of how miserable she was. That had been echoed recently by her uncle James and the O'Neill. Both found her thoroughly lacking in all womanly virtues. But the proud angle of Cara's chin never wavered.

"Well, my lord, king's man or no, you will help me or I leave you with that tray as your last meal. I'll not ask again."

"Ha." Gordie rose to his feet.

She had the gall to stick out her chin at him. For a Scotch penny he'd snatch her off her high-and-mighty seat and blister her backside till it fairly glowed. She didn't know the meaning of arrogance. He was the heir to the Mckenna. He'd play her game if that was what it took to quit this foul place.

"Fine, wench. Lead me to your gold. What care I that you steal from the hand that feeds you? But I warn you, I am no thief."

"Nor am I," Cara answered. She was losing this argument. She had been losing ground every day since he had recovered. He grew stronger and she lost all trace of power. But in this she was determined to have her way. The Spanish gold was leaving Dunluce. "There is a king's ransom inside the castle proper. It came on the ship that you did. It does not belong to Dunluce. All I ask is that you take it with you."

"Dunluce?" Gordie scowled. "Is that where I am? This is the infamous citadel of Sorely Boy Mac Donnell?"

"Aye. These are his dungeons," Cara answered.

Should he believe her? Gordie wondered. "Why haven't I seen the old rebel?"

"My grandfather does not enter the dungeons anymore. He claims the ghosts haunt him, but more likely it is his gout that keeps him elsewhere. Besides, 'tis only the pleasure of torturing Englishmen that appeals to him. Scots run a poor second."

"Pur bastards." Gordie cast a backward glance to the maze of chambers, which all led to some unspeakable horror. "There's enough bones here to make one think of purgatory."

"Hell," Cara returned.

"Aye, hell. So, are you the next generation of Irish savages?"

"Perhaps. Though I am only half-Irish and therefore scorned because of my Scottish blood. That is why I chose to help you, my lord. Now, do we waste the whole night arguing, or do you agree to help me? I assure you, there is enough gold to make your efforts worthwhile.''

"You assume that I have need of it?''

"Why shouldn't I? A man who comes to Ireland with shackles on his hands must have need to get far, far away from the men that condemned him. For all I care, you may dump the gold into the sea. So long as it is away from Dunluce, I care not. I want the gold removed . . . and you gone, as well.''

Cara would not tell him that it was now impossible for her to sneak away unnoticed. He must leave this night with the gold, or not at all.

"We are agreed upon one thing, wench. I also want to be quit of you.''

"I am not a wench.'' Cara bucked against the insult. She'd had enough of men's disgust and abuse. "I have a name and a title, you miserable cur.''

"Oh, so the little mouse squeaks, does she?'' Gordie advanced toward her. Her eyes fairly glittered with temper. Pride made her straighten to her full height and gave her the power to stand up to him, most admirably. Small crinkles formed at the corners of his eyes, but he kept all show of amusement away from his mouth. "Are you a contessa, perhaps, a lady of some import fallen upon hard times?''

"Nay, you nameless bastard. I am the Mulvaine,'' Cara snapped.

Gordie arrested his forward movement, going rigid as the one name *Mulvaine* settled inside his brain.

"Mulvaine?'' he repeated. The name was synonymous with blood feuds, a cursed house and bloody death. "You are Cara Mulvaine, the child-bride kidnapped from the siege of Graham Keep, held for ransom by Sorely Mac Donnell?''

"Aye.'' Cara regarded him with hatred flashing from her eyes. So he knew her history. What Scot didn't? A clan doomed to murder and to be murdered. All Mulvaines were savages— every last one of them. Only there weren't any living Mulvaines in Scotland, not a one. Nor had King James the Sixth had the inclination to ransom the last Mulvaine from Ireland, and for that, Cara held his king in contempt.

"Now, do you ken why I want you gone?''

Chapter Seven

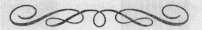

"Aye, you hit the mark at last. So where is this purse of gold too heavy for you to carry?"

"Come with me."

Cara whirled about, enraged beyond any anger she'd ever felt for her grandfather. She paused in the next chamber, waiting for the nameless cur to follow. He sauntered after her as if he had all the time in the world. She had already wasted too much of this night talking to him.

It was time for action, not words.

How she wanted to clobber him with a claymore. Instead she shoved aside a panel beneath the rack and dropped to a set of steps. She had lit torches earlier to light most of the way through this passage. It was the most treacherous, but provided the quickest access into the castle.

Gordie had to duck his head and twist his shoulders sideways to follow her. The steps were slick with moss and the stench was unbearable. The walls were so close, he almost refused to follow.

As small as she was, she had no difficulty ascending the narrow passage. She moved without faltering until the passageway twisted. The tunnel spiraled. His own breathing became labored in the dank, fetid air. Some of the steps were so steep, she had to kneel upon them and pull herself up to the next. There were no snakes, but there were toads.

She came to a stop. Craning his neck to see past her, Gordie saw a grill. It wasn't all that big or heavy, but she couldn't budge it, though she had hands and arms up and acted like she was going to lift the iron gate.

"Do you ken when to ask for help, lass?"

"I've lifted it before." Cara gritted her teeth. All it took was a shoulder placed in the right spot. She was damned if she was going to admit her shoulders were too raw to do the job proper.

Gordie shook his head. By the pace she'd set and her choice of exits, he knew good and well she was out to teach him a thing or two.

"Put your back to it or else admit that the wrong person is in the lead," Gordie said impatiently, wanting to be out of the earth at last.

"It's my passageway."

"Aye, but it is my freedom." Gordie took hold of her waist and lifted her off the higher step. Her hands dropped instantly to grip his wrists.

"Sir!"

"I won't drop you." Gordie held her fast, liking the neat feel of her nipped waist and the firm muscles that resisted the compression of his fingers. He lowered her with deliberate slowness, showing off a bit, settling her to the same narrow wedge of stone where he stood. It continued to irritate him that he could find no means to take the reins of power from her hands. Dependency rankled, and it rankled badly.

There was no room to turn. Her nose bumped his chest, but her breasts rubbed very nicely. He remembered exactly how they looked, what color her nipples were, how full and sweet they must be. He hadn't the faintest idea how she tasted. But he wanted to know.

"You made your point, sir," Cara said tightly.

"How old are you?" Gordie demanded.

"What difference?" Cara snapped. "Go up and lift off the grate."

"My, but you're a feisty little thing when you don't get your way. Answer my question, first."

"Twenty." Cara ground her teeth.

The number shocked Gordie. He'd have sworn she wasn't a day over five and ten. He muttered something nearly as vile as her tunnel and heaved his body up the last step. Pressed against the hard stone, Cara almost screamed when her sore back touched the wall. She bit her lip to prevent crying out loud. Still, her knees nearly buckled under her.

Gordie moved so quickly that he did not notice her strained expression of pain. A heartbeat later, he was free of the drain, outside in the clean air. He reached down, grasped her arms, and hauled her free of confinement.

Cara flew upward and landed on the stony earth seated beside him.

"I trust you will not order me to cart your king's ransom down that hellhole," Gordie said.

The air was crisp and cold, tainted by the scents of nearby animals. Getting his bearings, Gordie saw they'd emerged in a stable. He brushed his clothes, though why he bothered he didn't know. The smell wasn't likely to be brushed away. His lips curled in disgust. "I've smelled more fragrant sewers in London."

Cara was seeing too many stars whirl round her aching head to muster a scathing comment. He really was an odious man. She couldn't think of what had ever made her think she liked him.

While she summoned the effort necessary to regain her feet, he pushed the grate back into place, then struck off on his own. She ran after him, catching his arm just before he would have stumbled into a nest of slumbering trouble—O'Neill's snoring lackeys.

Gordie heard the snores before Cara laid her hand on his arm. His eyes were adjusting to the night. Perhaps his time in the dungeon had improved his eyesight. He saw the six men wrapped in green plaids as clearly as if they were stretched out in broad daylight.

It wouldn't do to go marching through a camp of armed men without a weapon to his name. He turned and nodded curtly to her and let her take the lead.

By the time they cleared the stable, her dog had joined them, proving to Gordie there was at least one other, less offensive way out of the dungeon. The dog smelled no more foul than it always did. She crept up wooden stairs against the northernmost wall, and traversed a stone catwalk overlooking the sea.

Gordie paused when the night wind struck his face. He was out of the earth. His chest expanded deeply. He smelled the sweet air, glorying in it, tasting the salt spray lingering in the mist. Cara waited impatiently at the end of the catwalk, hissing at him to hurry.

Dunluce's towers stood sentinel at each corner of the castle's walls. Its main buildings were apart from the battlements and the towers. She led the way into the north tower by dropping through a roof hatch and nimbly descending a rope ladder with the skill of a seasoned sailor. Gordie followed, enjoying the pleasure of dropping hand over hand to a solid floor below. He found himself standing in a round chamber, staring at her, rather amazed that she had the strength to do such a thing.

On the roof above them, Mimms barked a few times.

Gordie turned himself about, studying the odd room. There was no rhyme or reason to the scheme of it. A high bed dominated the chamber. Its millwork was adequate, but the mattress was a sagging uninviting thing. There were no drapes to block out wind or cold. It would be a chilly place to sleep come winter.

The Mulvaine strode to a trunk shoved against the wall. She knelt before it, holding the battered lid while she rifled the insides. From the bottom she withdrew a basket-handled claymore, scabbard and belt.

"I best give you this now. You might have need of it."

One punched-tin lantern sat alone and isolated on a jutting stone above her hearth, and a cheerless fire in the hearth below provided a minimum of light.

Gordie took the sword, gripped its handle and withdrew the blade from its sheath. The blade was well honed, sharp as a razor. He tested it in his hand, judging the balance.

"It is Damascened steel, the best there is. 'Twas my father's," Cara explained.

Gordie shot her a look. He held the sword point out from his side. "Brodie Mulvaine."

The way he said her father's name, Cara wondered if he was another enemy. Most likely he was. God be praised she hadn't pressed him for his clan's name. She would hate to discover him her enemy after going to all the trouble she had to save him.

He sheathed the blade and fitted the belt to his hips.

Cara saw that he knew what he was about, but then she knew he was a competent swordsman and more from her visions.

"Now where to?" he asked briskly as he adjusted the sword to his side.

Cara looked longingly at her bed, wishing she had nothing more to do than to collapse upon it. She hadn't slept in days.

Traveling to Portballintrae had been so dangerous. It was forbidden for her to cross her grandfather's boundaries. His serfs were duty-bound to report her flight. The *Avenger* had been easy enough to find at the docks. Convincing Grace O'Malley her survivor was a passenger worthy of transporting had taken all the skills Cara had in the art of persuasion.

Word of Cara's appearance in Portballintrae had preceded her return to Dunluce. Her grandfather waited with whip in hand. Cara knew the risk beforehand. She hadn't been quite so stoic when the O'Neill had intervened. He had his own charges, accusing her of consorting with the English by secretly meeting John Kelly. Which was all the Mac Donnell had to hear to be driven into a cold-blooded rage.

Not that a beating for her sins at this point mattered. There was no explaining anything she had done since the *Girona* was shipwrecked at *Port na Spaniagh* and she had looked into this stranger's compelling blue eyes.

"This way." Cara led the way out the door of her chamber. The stairs spiraled down three flights to the bailey yard. They both moved quietly now, taking care that their footfalls were silent.

In the hall, servant and lord sprawled across trestle tops, their heads and arms limp, their snores deep and resonant. No pallets were laid out. It looked like what it was: a room full of sleeping drunks. The oddest thing about the hall was that the dogs also wheezed and snored.

That was daunting. Gordie shivered at the eerie silence of the hall, punctuated by snorts and snores. Had some evil spell been cast upon the castle and dropped every man in his traces? A spell like the one Gordie had woken to, where candles bobbed and iron turned to sand? A glance to the woman enshrouded in a cowled cloak made him think that not all witches were old, ugly crones. They all started out young once, didn't they?

Outside her grandfather's chamber, no man guarded the threshold. Cara slipped inside to take Sorely's keys. They clanked as she returned to the shadowy corridor.

"What goes on here?" Gordie demanded softly.

Cara shot him a small, defiant glare that said much more of her mood than any words could have. "Dinna fash yerself. Come."

She was off and moving again, turning to a descending stair, her fingers trailing the wall to steady her passage. Not accustomed to having his commands ignored, Gordie took firm hold of her arm and whirled her about to face him.

"I asked what goes on here?" His voice echoed up and down the stairwell.

"Shh." Cara put her finger to her mouth.

"Dinna shush me, lassie. What has happened to the people of this keep? Are you a witch? Is this a spell?"

"A witch!" Cara's gray eyes widened. "Nay, no witch's spell put the snores in their heads. 'Tis a simple brew added to the ale. Come."

She pulled away again, descending to the bottom of the steps. There, a strong door was secured and another stood at the end of the converging stones.

Gordie stepped back up two steps to take a torch from the nearest holder. Below him, the ring of keys clanked as one was fitted into the keyhole.

She turned the lock and pushed the heavy door open. Gordie held the torch over his head and bent to clear the low lintel.

The glitter that flashed back at him stopped him in his tracks.

It was no grand treasury, just a storeroom, ten or fewer feet wide. Three strides from end to end and side to side. To the left were piled suits of armor and stacks of Spanish metal work. But to the right and before him, there gleamed a wealth of gold.

Not just gold, but polished silver, faceted jewels, cut glass and ceremonial crucifixes gleamed beneath the torch. Shields, pennants, saddles, swords and dirks were piled in each corner. Gold coin and stacked plates were strewn into careless abandon in the jumble of battered sea trunks.

He whistled soft and low.

Cara's tense gaze followed him. Gordie set the torch into a hook on the wall then pushed the door nearly closed. He sat down abruptly. The lid of the trunk that accepted his considerable build snapped apart a string of pearls. They went bouncing and rolling across the floor.

"All of this was on the *Girona?*"

"Aye." Cara's voice was soft, almost reverent. She heard the survivor suck wind past his lips; then his fingers clawed at his scalp.

"I canna take this."

"You will and you must."

"Nay." He shook his head fiercely, turning about, his hands agitated, his eyes black and fierce. Cara opened a closed lid, revealing an interior full of gold coins.

"You will be a rich man."

"I'm already a rich man. I've no need of this. Give it to the kirk."

"It belongs to Philip of Spain. That's where I want it to go. You told me you were King Jamie's mon. He and the king of Spain are allies. Take it to yer king and let him dispose of it. That is all I ask."

"You ask much." Gordie's fingers rifled through his hair, once again making it stand wildly about his head. There was too much. "I'd be hunted down, killed. I've no wish to spend the rest of my days in Dunluce dungeon."

"Who would hunt you? No one knows you exist except me. I'll no' tell."

Gordie grunted once. He pulled at his bushy beard and shook his head. "I know I exist, lassie. And I know a theft of this magnitude would be your downfall.... As to what you would do under the strain of questioning, well, Mulvaine, I've not met a woman yet that didn't break at the first sign of a fist raised against her."

Cara stiffened under his criticism. "I'm no' afraid of a beating." She closed the lid and glared at him, hard.

Gordie reached out his hand and caught the point of her chin, taking a good look at her face. She wasn't beautiful in the sense of the word, but she had character and that was more important. "No, maybe you aren't afraid. Or maybe the beatings you've had came from an old man whose arm wore out a long time ago. Tell me this, has the Mac Donnell ever told one of his vassals to give you the taste of the taws?"

Cara held her chin rigid in the grip of his thumb and forefinger. She matched him glare for glare. "No man has ever been allowed to touch me."

Gordie's thumb stroked upward on her chin, gliding just below the fullness of her lower lip. "Until now, eh? Well, lass, Scotland's a small country. You ken how there is no much to do except gossip in the winters. You're a legend, Cara Mulvaine. So is the Mac Donnell of the Far Isles. I'll take no part in the feud between you, not while I plan to live a long and trouble-free life."

Gordie bent his head, letting his lips go where his thumb paused, to taste the fullness of her defiant mouth.

"Coward," Cara muttered before his lips spread warmly over hers. The contact was startling. His head tilted and the grip of his fingers tightened on her chin.

"No, little one. You won't get me to do your bidding that way."

Cara's hands rose and pressed against the hard wall of his chest. The ring of keys slid to the bend in her elbow, rocking noisily in the scant inch of distance between their bodies. This time, she didn't doubt he knew exactly who he kissed. She welcomed the warm touch, amazed and wondered by it. It humbled her, brought her face-to-face with all the simple pleasures lacking in her life. Caring...she had never cared about anyone, but she had cared for and cared about him.

The kiss surprised Gordie nearly as much as the cache of gold had. He kissed her to prove his point, that she wasn't the un-touchable princess she thought she was. But her lips flowered beneath his and bloomed at the touch of his tongue. She had great promise and was more of a woman than she behaved. He drew back, smiling, still holding her chin in his grip. Her tongue made a lightning search round her mouth. Better was the soft-ened, wondering expression in her near-colorless gray eyes.

She needed kissing. She needed to be touched and well loved. He watched the question form on her lips.

"How?"

"How what, lassie?"

"Tell me how I get you to do my bidding."

Gordie chuckled softly, a smile creasing the corners of his mouth. "Well, Mulvaine, you could start by giving me that key and telling me how we get out of this dreaded castle. I've a mind to meet this ship you've summoned."

"It won't be here yet."

"Then you'll have time to give me the reasons you want this booty removed."

"But not time to see it done."

"That depends on you, Mulvaine." Gordie released her chin and held his palm between them. Cara looked at the cup formed by his curved fingers and crooked thumb. All his cuts had healed. He was whole again.

She surrendered the keys.

Satisfied, Gordie pulled back the door. Cara pointed down the short corridor to a heavy, iron-banded door at the end. It was the castle's sea gate. Taking firm hold of her upper arm, Gordie walked her to the door. He set her ahead of him, between his body and the cornered wall as he slotted keys one by one inside the lock.

Mercifully this door opened as easily as did the storeroom door. A strong wind rushed at them, flattening Cara's skirts against her legs as he hustled her down the granite steps cut into the cliff to the edge of the sea surging against the stones.

Gordie sat on the rocks hugging his knees, the ring of keys round his elbow. He scanned the water.

Cara stood for a moment staring openmouthedly at his calm, unruffled pose. She was anxious to empty the storeroom and clear all traces of his occupancy from the dungeons. Agitated, she glanced at the water, searching the cove. No ship approached.

"Sit down," Gordie ordered. "Dancing from foot to foot convinces me not. Talk, Mulvaine. I need reasons."

"You will take it, then?"

"I did not say that. I say I will listen."

Cara sat abruptly, her skirt fluttering as she crossed her legs and tucked the wool around her knees. What to say? She pressed her fingers to her brow, thinking. "There was no' even two days of masses said for the men who drowned."

"Thirteen hundred and fifty-two," Gordie said flatly.

Cara looked at his suddenly grim profile. He stared at the sea. "That's no...I mean, it is the point. The gold must go back to Spain. I don't want it on my conscience."

"Nor do I."

"I'm trying to explain. The gold must leave Dunluce. I saved your life. You owe me."

"We've no argument there. I own you fair ransom for my life. Rather than stealing from Dunluce, I would restore equal measure for my value."

"No. That is the very, very thing I don't want. You don't know what gold does here. My grandfather hates the English. He lives to hunt Drake, and to see the harlot's blood run like a river down her sagging breasts. He hates us all. That gold will enable him to buy ships, to outfit men and soldiers. The Mac Donnell's rebellion will go on and on. It will never end. Don't you understand? I am the last Mulvaine. I have spent my life imprisoned at Dunluce because of his hatred."

"'Tis no my quarrel, lass. I know nothing about that."

"No, you don't, but I do. God never meant for Sorely Mac Donnell to have another penny to his name. His vengeance dooms us all. This gold buys more killing. 'Twill go on and on down every generation until there isn't an English, a Scot nor an Irish family left that isn't cursed as the Mulvaines are. You don't have to keep the gold. Give it to your king. Maybe then he'll pay my ransom and I can leave this place."

That touched a raw nerve in Gordie. "What say you, Mulvaine?" he demanded. "Dare you boast of having such importance to a crown? Is King James your man?"

"Nay, I have no import to King James, nor doubt I ever did. It was his demand that I wed the Carlisle that started the war that killed my family. I hold him responsible."

Gordie glared at the girl. How in hell had he ever considered her a timid gray mouse? Her pride rivaled his own. He'd been knocked down a peg or two in the past three months since sailing to meet the Armada. She arrogantly courted the same humbling blow, but not from his hand. He returned his gaze to the cove and made his voice calm and reasonable. "You ask the impossible. One man alone would labor until noon to remove all that gold."

"So be it," Cara declared purposefully. "The castle folk will sleep past then. I drugged the ale. I took no chances that I would be found out this night. I made certain that every man among them drank full measure."

Cara did not think it was possible to sink any lower in the survivor's estimation, but she could tell by the hardening of his eyes that she had. Those cool blue-black orbs regarded her as a traitor to her own. He didn't know the half of it. She turned away from him, glaring across the water. Rounding the point were the black sails of Grace O'Malley's *Avenger.*

Gordie bolted to his feet, recognizing the black sails at once. *O'Malley.* "I'll be damned," he swore, "out of the kettle into the fire." What choices had he now? None. The witch of Dunluce had left him none.

"Pray, tell me, Mistress Mulvaine, is that your idea of safe passage to Scotland?"

His irony was wasted on the Mulvaine. What did she know of a privateer's battles? Gordie shook his head at the sheer outrageousness of his situation, saying aloud, "God assoil us all."

Chapter Eight

"Whose ship is that?" Gordie demanded because he wanted to hear from the Mulvaine what passage she thought she'd booked.

"Grace O'Malley's corsair. It is she who will take you back to Scotland."

"O'Malley. The woman pirate?" Gordie said flatly.

"Aye." Cara turned away. The chests in the cave must be brought out. She wanted nothing left that would prove this man had ever been to Ireland and that she had helped him.

The ship tacked into the wind, skillfully maneuvering the dangerous rocks protecting the deep water cove. Gordie clawed his fingers through his hair, torn between the coming ship and the girl. This odd adventure grew stranger by the moment.

The ship dropped anchor and a dory splashed into the water. Oars smacked into the waves as it hove to shore, coming for him.

Gordie ran down the cliff side after the Mulvaine. She had disappeared inside the cave. He caught her dragging a chest, huffing and straining against the burden.

"Stop that!" he ordered, and took the strap from her, setting her aside. "Leave it, I said."

"The gold came with you. It leaves with you."

Gordie swore an oath. "Cara Mulvaine, am I to trust you are not selling me as a galley slave for life?"

Straightening, insulted by his words, Cara declared, "Truly you know little of the Irish if you think that. 'Tis the Spanish who chain men to oars. In Ireland any man or woman who goes to the sea, goes freely. O'Malley promised me your passage in safety to my kinsman, Laird Kyntyre. From there you are on your own, sir.''

Cara stood stock-still, glaring at him, her face red with fury. "'Tis said O'Malley likes a randy fellow, but only on her terms. You'll do. I described you to her and she's come. That's all that matters.''

"I'm to stud for the lady pirate to earn my passage!''

Cara flinched as he raised his fisted hand.

"Be damned, we'll just see about that,'' Gordie said as he hoisted the chest to his shoulder that she could only drag. He strode down to the shingle and slammed it onto the ground, then went back for the others. Cara hurriedly tied sheepskins into bundles, then gathered blankets and all evidence of his tenure.

When he brought out the last trunk from the cave, the rowboat closed upon the shore. Five women plied it through the water, four at the oars, the fifth standing in the prow with her skirts hiked over a bent knee.

"Ahoy, Mulvaine, be you there?'' the standing woman cupped her hands and hollered ashore.

"Aye.'' Cara came to the water's edge. Mimms bounded round the cliff to join her, barking at the intruders.

"Be this your cargo?'' Grace O'Malley pointed to where Gordie stood beside four trunks.

"Aye.'' Cara splashed into the water, heedless of the cold and wet about her legs. "All to be delivered safe and whole to Laird Kyntyre as we agreed.''

Two of the women tossed a rope ashore. Gordie caught it easily, drawing the craft against the steep cliff face. O'Malley was the first off the boat, swinging a fleshy arm round Cara's shoulders.

"Damn me, that bastard never feeds you, does he?''

"Well enough, m'lady—you're twice the size I last saw you.'' Cara bantered back with a grin for O'Malley.

"Cor! Look at his arms, Jesse! What a fine figure of a man you be, handsome.'' Tess laughed with lusty relish as she and Jesse hopped ashore and hoisted a trunk between them.

"Here, now, Tess, there be none of that,'' Grace declared.

Shoving a trunk into the boat's keel, Gordie deliberately set the skiff rocking as he glared at O'Malley. "Am I to sail with a crew of puking women and mewling brats?''

O'Malley plunked her fists on her hips. She shot him a look that took his measure from head to toe. "Well, boy-o, we've also got a bawling cow, squawking chickens and a honking goose or two. But, then, we women have a hankering for meat and eggs and cream. If you prefer, yonder is Ballintrea. You can hike there and eat hardtack and suck on limes for all I give a damn."

"Grace, you promised me," Cara intervened. "He must leave, this night!"

"You have fresh eggs?" Gordie demanded, placing his booted foot on the top of the largest trunk, preventing O'Malley's girls from taking it.

"Eggs, bacon, a ham or two." O'Malley looked from the strapping man to the narrow-shouldered girl. The tension between him and the Mulvaine could be cut with a knife.

"And a fine cook," Tess said invitingly, twitching her knotted skirt to reveal a finely turned knee.

The five pirate women paraded before Gordie in blowsy shirts and shortened hems. All had more than ample meat upon their bodies, including full breasts and rolling hips. He was a starving man, too long denied his body's increasing needs. Without a glance at the will-of-the-wisp woman who was the source of his randy aches, he snatched up the heaviest trunk and heaved it into the craft.

Grace grinned boldly at Cara. "Want to come along, Mulvaine? Old Brian tells me there's a cottage or two vacant at Graham village. Ye could have your pick of the men there, handfast yerself to a bonnie laddie. 'Twould serve old Sorely right if ye did."

"Nay, I canna go." Cara shook her head, withdrawing to lead the way to the wide open sea gate in the castle proper.

"Bosh, ye can do anything you want." Grace studied Cara's bent shoulders as she preceded her up the steep climb. "Damn me, the bastard's done it again. That stinking tyrant, why ye don't shoot the old fool is beyond my ken. Get ye a knife, Cara, and the next time the Mac Donnell raises a strap to ya, cut his bloody heart out."

Grace's harsh words hit Gordie like a ten-pound cannon shot. He shouldered the middle-aged pirate out of his way and reached out to take hold of Cara's arm, a righteous fury brewing into an outburst.

"Hey, now, boy-o," Grace protested as he pushed between her and Cara and spun the girl to a standstill.

"Shut up, O'Malley," Gordie commanded as he gripped hold of the neckline of Cara's gown, ripping it down her back.

The assault happened so quickly, Cara hadn't time to snatch her elbow from his fist, much less bolt fast enough to prevent the destruction of her old gown. She tried to though, and got hauled right back by her hanging braid.

There was no moon, but even so, only a blind man could have missed the stark, angry welts crisscrossing Cara's back. Gordie's barely controlled temper intensified to a new level, into cold bloody outrage. Gripping both her slender arms, he demanded, "You have gone this whole night not telling me of this?" His eyes darkened, his grips tightened on her arms, and he shook her none too gently.

"Hold there, boy-o," Grace sputtered. The steel of her cutlass scraped.

"I said shut up, O'Malley!" Gordie snapped, outshouting Mimms' warning growl. "Why were you beaten?"

"Well, yer a damn fool, as well as an idiot." The point of O'Malley's blade dug into the soft tissue under Gordie's jaw. "Let her go! Or I'll cut yer heart out and feed it to the dog."

"Grace!" Cara appealed to the pirate. "Put down your sword. He won't hurt me."

"Cut away, O'Malley, I'll not let go until she damn well answers my question. Why were you flogged?"

"I went to Ballintrae."

"Was it the English that caught you?"

"Ha!" O'Malley interrupted needlessly. "That's Sorely's work. Had the English flogged her, blood would still be running to her toes."

Gordie's grip on Cara's upper arms lightened, but remained firm enough to contain her. He drew her up against his chest, his hands careful as he moved the two halves of her bodice back across her shoulders. She laid her head under his chin, taking a deep, calming breath to ease the fluttering of her heart. Gordie's eyes closed.

"I'm sorry," he whispered against her head, his voice hoarse and soft, for her ears only. "It was for me, wasn't it? You risked your grandfather's wrath to meet O'Malley and he caught you, didn't he?"

Cara swallowed the lump in her throat. Talking wasn't really possible. Never, in fifteen years of beatings had anyone offered her comfort. It was most odd, most strange. She nodded. He drew her shawl up, settling it loosely in place.

"God's blood, you could have told me. I feel like such a fool for manhandling you, saying the things I've said." Gordie's hands settled on her head, gripping it between his palms. He stared at her face. "Ach, lassie, what they say must be ever the truth. Sorely's a bitter, bitter old man, but you're his flesh and blood. The last of his line."

Cara had nothing to say.

"I don't like being beholden for more than what's fair, Mulvaine. Stand aside and keep that dog out of my way. I'll take the damned Spanish gold. I'll find some good use for it. No questions about where it came from, no regrets about where it went. Do you ken what I say, lass?"

"Aye." Cara nodded against the pressure of his hands. "But before you do, would you kiss me one more time? I like kissing better than shouting."

It was the last request Gordie expected to hear. A slow smile lightened the hardened set of his mouth and jaw. He stared at Cara's face, as if committing it to memory.

"A kiss, hmm?" A soft smile tugged at a dimple deep in his cheek. "Well, my lady, you had only to ask."

Gordie's head bent toward Cara's, and his mouth settled over her lips with warm, stirring intensity. He held her head fast as his tongue swept between her parted lips to plunder her sweetness.

"I don't believe yer letting that ruffian maul you." O'Malley snorted crankily, the blade of her cutlass scraping as she replaced it in her scabbard. "Lord Almighty! Where's the gold? Lass, we haven't got all night."

Waving at her crew, O'Malley stalked up the cliff.

"Cor, he can kiss me anytime," Tess muttered as she hurried after her grumbling captain.

Cara didn't really care where they went. Not until his persuasive lips separated from her own. Her eyes shone as she looked up at Gordie's somber face.

"You have repaid me well, my lord," she said gratefully. "My thanks and prayers for your health will always be with you."

Something that Gordie could not identify kept his hands fixed to her fine-boned head, holding her face still for the search of his eyes. "O'Malley's right. You've no need to stay in Ireland, lass. You belong in Scotland."

Cara pressed deeper into his strong, protecting embrace and shook her head. "'Tis no good. My grandfather has the O'Neill to send men to find me. I canna go to Scotland. I belong to Dunluce."

Inside the storeroom, O'Malley made a quick sweep of the valuables and pointed to three heavily laden chests. "We'll take those. Let Sorely keep the arms and petty jewels. Though the baubles be fair, I've no use for Venetian glass or Italian paste."

Her ladies hoisted a trunk between them. Gordie flipped the lid closed on the coinage and lifted it from the floor. Cara brought up the rear, toting a gunnysack full of chalices, gold crucifixes and medals. She locked the doors in their wake.

Mimms padded faithfully at Cara's side. They stood out of the way as the last trunk was loaded.

The women took their places at the oars, and Grace took hold of the stern rudder, settling herself amid the pile of trunks and caskets. Last, Gordie hoisted his body over the side. The skiff rocked dangerously, its load balanced but riding low in the water.

O'Malley's ladies wasted no time putting their backs to the oars. Water lapped over the edges of the craft as it shot away from the shore.

Gordie flexed his arm in a salute to the Mulvaine. He could barely see her against the black shale and dark stone. He couldn't tell if she responded, but he felt as if he took more than gold from Dunluce. He had the memory of a brave woman. She confused him, not being what he supposed any woman of her kind should be. A lady who wasn't a lady, an heiress who stood to inherit none of the properties her birthright entitled to her. The last of a clan.

He shook his head, changing his view from the now-empty wharf. O'Malley stared at him. He returned her measured glare. It was the oddest powered craft he'd ever ridden, with women pulling oars, and at the tiller. Fearless, loyal women who feared no man.

"Well, my fine boy-o," Grace O'Malley said. She lounged her ample hip against a coil of rope and chewed on a goose leg as the sun poked its golden head above the sloping mountain-top of Kyntyre, Scotland. "I'm dying with curiosity. How did the Mulvaine come to cherish you?"

"Cherish?" Gordie questioned her choice of words. He had his first good look at Grace O'Malley now that the sun rose. She strode about her ship on bare, callused feet, as nimble as a red doe, her windswept, black hair streaked with two furrows of silver against each temple. "Cherish is hardly the word, my lady pirate. Her mad dog pulled me from death. I was certain I was consigned to slow starvation at the Mulvaine's good and kind hands."

Sketching the young man with an earthy, appraising glance, Grace knew better than to believe his reply. If that was the way he wanted to play the game, so be it. She shrugged and bit into a plump breast of a roasted goose. "You look no worse for Cara's care. She did not take you to the Mac Donnell then?"

"Nay. I no met the old laird."

"Better for you. It costs a tongue in Dunluce for any to speak to the Mulvaine. Those who made the mistake of touching her have lost their hands or fingers."

"A fine inducement to stay clear of the chit," Gordie muttered.

"Ach, Cara's not so bad. Her mother, Leah—now, there was a wild one! Many a time I plied that young lassie between Dunluce and Kyntyre. She ran away from Dunluce every time the moon set, it seemed. 'Twas Sorely's fault."

"How so?" Gordie chewed on the plump breast of a goose they picked apart between them.

"By couching rebellion and treason and setting a wild example of his own. His sons were and are no different. Cara's timid by Dunluce standards. Sorely's raised her to be his final vengeance against the English. It surprises me to discover a man grown as her baggage-transport. She is supposed to hate all men, young and old. I cannot imagine why she aided you."

"Nor I." The fact remained he was alive because of her. "How then are you obligated to take me passenger?"

Grace settled more comfortably in the loop of ropes, a foot holding the wheel steady. The ship was on course in the deep channel between Jura and Kyntyre. "In truth, I've no obligation to Cara though I've an obligation or two to Kyntyre. One Sterling is deep in debt to me, as well. I've no love for Berwick, Lindsey or Ruthven. The rest of you Scots I'd as likely leave to battle amongst yourselves. And if that whelp King Jamie ever crosses my path, I'll slit his throat."

Gordie kept silent at her treasonous words. He wouldn't counter them. She wasn't a Scot and owed no allegiance to King James.

Grace gnawed the last scrap of meat from the bone and wiped her fingers on the red corset she wore laced outside her clothes. "I suppose in all truth, I'd add another to my list of unconscionable Scots. John Knox. Were I given the chance to send his sanctimonious bones to the briny bottom, I'd dispatch him in haste. It's curs like him that have the whole world in an uproar, seeing papist plots in everything, mounting witch hunts against the simplest folk, whose faith in God leaves his and mine in tatters."

"So you're a religious woman, Grace O'Malley?"

"Damned if I ain't. Was raised in a convent—what else would I be?"

Gordie threw back his head and laughed. "What else, indeed."

"Ho, did you think I came to be a sea captain and pirate by lying on my back, boy-o?"

"It seems an odd trade for a woman. Privateering is best left to the men."

Quick as a wink, the deadly cutlass on O'Malley's hip pointed levelly at Gordie's unprotected throat. "Think you so, my bearded youth? Need I skewer you and your tasty morsel of unchewed meat to prove how able and quick my blade is?"

"Nay." Gordie's face reddened. The woman had fast hands, but he had anticipated no threat from her. "Should I retract my opinion? I meant no insult on your unusual trade, my lady pirate."

"Retract it then." Grace allowed the point of the blade to swirl dangerously close to his chest in a calculated circle.

"I retract my impertinent suggestion. I am merely curious as to why you chose the risk."

"Chose or had it foisted on me, what is the difference? I am what I am. Enough of that. Who be you, young strapping youth?"

The blade withdrawn and sheathed, Gordie wiped his greasy fingers on his sleeves then bowed in as cavalier manner as he could affect without a cape or hat to flourish. "Sir Gordon Mckenna at your service, Mistress O'Malley."

"Ah." Grace smiled, her bright red cheeks dimpling. "So you do have manners, lout. Good of you to show them."

"Manners and courtly ways lost due to imprisonment like an animal, madame. My pardon."

"Granted. Are you related to the Kyntyre?"

"Nay, regrettably we Kennas are enemies of all papist Scots."

"Then why in the devil did the Mulvaine want you delivered to them? Better yet, what were you doing aboard the Spanish *Girona?*"

A good question, one that Gordie wouldn't answer. He was glad he had his wits about him. "I was a pilot, madame, hired to skate the fleeing ships round the rocks."

"Not much of a sailor then, are you?" Grace sharply assessed.

"Good enough for the purpose I was assigned to do, I assure you."

"And that weren't to see the Spanish safely home," the woman snorted knowingly. "Well, never mind." Grace turned to pull a chart from the rack behind her. "I sail no farther north than Dunaverty, which lies ahead a few leagues. Does that suit you, boy-o?"

"Admirably." Gordie grinned.

Casting a glance at her prodigious map, Grace squinted her eyes to read it. "There's English ships lurking 'bout Ayr everywhere. I'd rather skate those fellows." She put the map away and, in the next moment, fitted a telescope to her eye. "It is my fervent hope, young lord, that the *Golden Hind* remains a goodly distance away from my backside while I complete the business of delivering you safely to Scotland."

Sensing that she was saying less than she would to someone in her confidence, Gordie laid both his hands to the quarter-deck rail and scanned all quadrants of the open sea. "I've no relish in that thought, either, madame."

"The prospect of washing up on Ireland's coast another time pales, does it?" Grace chuckled. "Fear not, I haven't taken a dunk in the water in twenty years."

"Would that I could say the same," Gordie grumbled as he looked into the rigging where O'Malley's nimble-footed Amazons clambered about like monkeys born to the trees. Gordie laughed, amused. As one or two dropped to the deck with their skirts billowing about their shapely legs, he was more than amused. He was amazed. They were quite comely, too.

One bawd sauntered forward, her shoulder bared and half her full, luscious breasts exposed. "If you've no taste for the young lad, captain, I'd be more than happy to see to his base needs."

"Harlot," O'Malley snorted, and flipped a hand at the brazen woman. "You'll just saddle us all with another squalling babe, Pattie. He's a potent-looking specimen. Mind yer manners. These tight-lipped Scots care to do the pursuing themselves. Scat!"

The buxom woman gave a pouty moue at Gordie and he chuckled her brazen offer aside. He was not so randy that he would risk offending the captain of this particular vessel.

"Regrettably, madame, the captain knows my type well. Another time, perhaps," he declined with a charm that made both the women laugh, unoffended.

"You've the tongue of a courtier to you, boy-o. Mind, I might be tempted to break my vows myself. You've a handsome face and manly form to you. I'd say you've learned the art of diplomacy somewhere."

"I've spent a lifetime surrounded by women, Captain O'Malley. Mother, sisters too numerous to count, cousins and comely wenches all to be placated with a charming word. If that makes me courteous, so be it."

"Ah," Grace said with a sigh, "I'm tempted, boy-o. Yes, I am." She stroked her callused fingers across his bearded cheek, grinning as widely as the other woman had.

"Ho! Five sails port. English!" A shout from the crow's nest brought all on deck swinging round about.

"Blast it!" Grace stuck her telescope to her eye and released a curse as raw as any Gordie had ever heard. "I hope you're more than a pretty boy, Mckenna. I knew, damn my eyes, that there would be trouble with this passage. To arms, everyone, sound the alarm."

"Cap'n, it's the *Revenge!*" the lookout shouted.

"Battle stations!" O'Malley ordered. "Bring the guns about. Tack twenty degrees and prepare to attack!"

"Where do you keep your arms?" Gordie asked as the gangways disgorged more men and women than he'd ever guessed were on board such a craft. The last damn thing Gordie wanted was to face a sea battle against Drake's battleship, *Revenge.* Two months ago he'd attended the war council on its quarterdeck and been the man selected to pilot the fire ships into the heart of the Armada anchored in Calais. O'Malley couldn't beat Drake's *Revenge.*

"I've got the others. It's the *Aid,* the *Tiger* and I'm certain the *Swiftsure,* Captain!"

"I'll be damned!" Gordie muttered. He gripped the rail and strained his eyes to see the five sets of sails off in the distance. The *Swiftsure* was his own ship.

Grace lowered her brass telescope from her eye and said aloud. "Not a one of the bastards had turned to meet us. Now where do ye suppose they be going in such a hurry, boy-o?"

"Smerwick," Gordie answered.

"How would you be knowing that?" Grace wheeled about, her hands to her ample hips.

"I know Drake." Gordie shrugged, his eyes squinted on the distant ships, moving steadily away from O'Malley in the sitting duck position. "He would be after the last stronghold of the Spanish. Smerwick must be destroyed."

"I've mates in Smerwick who won't take kindly to that."

Gordie straightened to his naturally proud and arrogant stance and answered as honestly as he could. "Take care, my lady pirate. The English rule the seas. You can no more stop them than Sorely Mac Donnell could. Do you continue to go against them, you'll have no more than the old rebel does. Time, lady, marches relentlessly on. Old Bess bred no heir. The day comes that King James will rule the English."

"Bah!" O'Malley expressed her disgust at the notion. "A Scots king on the English throne? 'Twill never happen. He'll lose his head just like his mother did."

"No," Gordie said confidently. His singular purpose for the past six years had been to guarantee Scotland's young king's survival by uncovering English plots at their source. "A word of advice, madame. Heed it or ignore it as suits your purpose. Seek your letter of marque and let Drake go his own way. I know of no one who can stop him. Nor of any who can prevent England from its destiny."

"What kind of devil did Cara Mulvaine save from the sea?" Grace wondered aloud.

"Madame, I do not know." Gordie's head moved back and forth in slow motion. Off in the distance, the five ships were but specks on the hazy water. He was glad for that. He had no wish to see more blood, more death or hear more agony or pain caused by war or fighting.

Gordie Mckenna was a changed man from the youth that had left Scotland years ago at the behest of young King Jamie. As such, he'd wound carefully through Queen Elizabeth's many intrigues. He respected sly Walsingham and accepted missions assigned from him. He knew Essex and the power-mad Drake and thought John Dee the most impressive and intelligent man at court.

Power—the quest of it—drove them all. It no longer mattered to Gordon Mckenna. He could not put to words the sense of destiny that had come to him in his delirium. Perhaps he'd gone mad. How else could he explain his insight into the future? James would be king of all that Elizabeth now held in her iron grip. The future stood secure.

He was alive, and Scotland's shores were rapidly approaching. He was nearly home. Never had he felt such an ache in his heart. It knifed through him so painfully that tears sprang into his eyes.

Aye, Scotland lay ahead and, in any moment, his feet would touch the soil of it once again.

Dear God Almighty, he was alive. He was home!

* * *

The heavy trunks set at his feet on the soil of Scotland assured his future. King James would be grateful for the addition to his treasury. Scotland was not a land of wealth. Its needs were many, Gordie's were few.

He wanted a bed to lie his head on. A table adequate to his appetites and the daily affirmation of his faith in life. The sun rising, the sun setting, each season as it came flush and full with Scotland's beauty.

Gordie Mckenna was seven and twenty years old. He had changed from the callow youth that had left the Highlands to engage in the art of espionage. The hills of Scotland had never looked finer nor felt so dear. He longed to hear a soft brogue as sweet music in his ears. It was midnight and the small coastal village slept. Not even a tavern was open.

"Life," he said aloud to the empty quay, "was meant to be lived in peace. From this day onward, I shall live for its pleasures and enjoyments and its sweetest moments. To hell with war and power and position! Never will I leave Scotland. I am home!"

The words had no sooner left his mouth than he turned back toward the sea. Gazing to the unseen coast of Ireland, he remembered the girl that had saved, nursed and protected him.

She had kept nothing of the treasure for herself. Not cloth, nor coin nor even a treasured reliquary. Such an odd little person was Cara Mulvaine.

It bothered Gordie that no reward for her sacrifice could be paid. That increased his debt tenfold. She was not his worry, but when he gave the treasure to Jamie, he'd speak of the kidnapped Scottish maid. Mayhaps her ransom could be arranged.

Book Two

THE LAIRD OF THE CLAN MCKENNA

"Hear, my son, your father's instruction, and reject not your mother's teaching."

Proverbs of Solomon 1:8

Chapter Nine

Castle Kenna
April 1590

"**Y**ou will do it!" A massive fist sprinkled with red hair slammed on the trestle plank. Cups and pewter winked down the board. "It was bad enough that you defied me and went to fight with the English! Left your mother wailing, fearing for your life. Had you died serving England, there would be no son of mine to head the clan."

"Sit down, Father. This is no worth fighting over." Gordie placidly lifted his tankard of ale. He and his sire were much alike in build and coloring, save for the silver curling like wires around the Mckenna's temples. "None of the lassies interest me."

"You owe me another Kenna to inherit."

"Which, God willing, I will provide. But I'll have none of the lassies you've trotted before me."

"They are not fair?"

"They are all fair. Lovely maidens one and all. No doubt each has a generous dowry. Dinna you hear what I said? I want a woman of substance. A woman who knows something other than the colors of embroidery floss. Do you ken what I mean, father? I'll have one handfasted first and no the other way around."

"'Tis against God's rules."

"According to Knox, no other. The old kirk allows the Highland way. 'Tis the Puritans and the Reformers who seek to take all the pleasure from our lives."

"Pleasure!" Laird Mckenna threw up his hands. "You insult the fathers of the virgins offered to you."

"I do not. As the next Mckenna I claim the tradition. Mother handfasted. It is our way, as we have done for centuries, and John Knox or no, I'll have the same!"

John Mckenna sat abruptly, tossed his ale in one gulp then glared at his son. At last he said, "You are just being stubborn."

"I admit it, I am. You made me thus. A man of intractable will in the image of yourself. Will I be led by the whims of a half-mad churchman or that of a silly woman? Nay. What was good enough for you is good enough for me. Would you have me any other way, sire?"

"I would have a grandson before next summer and another each year thereafter."

Gordie smiled then and the look exchanged between father and son softened somewhat. "I, too, prefer to plow a fertile field. Pray you, not one littered with vapid English manners and affectations learned at court."

"You are impossible." The Mckenna's fist pounded against the trestle again, but not with the same force that had sent his guests lurching to grab tankards before they spilled into their laps. Gordie's point was valid. The Mckenna could see that the young women his wife brought to the hall lacked something.

As a group the four young maids rose from the end of the dais. Gordie looked to them, surveying the rising beauties hastened from the hall by his mother. Each had her delicate nose in the air, pointedly ignoring the high table where he and his father bluntly discussed the merits of marriage before one and all.

One of the young beauties cut Gordie a killing look, and audaciously stuck out her tongue only to realize he was watching. She colored red as a ripe apple and ducked out of sight. Gordie snorted. The last thing he wanted to be saddled with was a temperamental, undisciplined child-bride. Maybe the Irish had ruined him. A hazy memory of bold, courageous women put a wicked, devil-may-care smile on his face.

John Mckenna took that as a smirk. Tried sorely and out of patience, he rounded on his son when the ladies had departed. "If not one of those ladies . . . then name one you will have. I care not who she be, just that she be strong and of a good age to bear you sons."

"Father, this talk is tiresome. I haven't any one I fancy. I love all women, equally."

"Damn you! This is not a sport we are discussing."

"I've made my preferences clear."

"Can't you pick someone, Gordie?" The question came from the near right, from his sister Rose.

"What's the matter, imp? Do you grow long in the tooth waiting your own marriage?" Gordie never passed up a chance to tease. At nineteen, Rose was panting for the chance to marry. His other four sisters sat glued to their bench, watching and listening with avid interest.

"Mayhaps I tire of watching you wear out the servants." Rose was quick to lay into him and bring to his father's mind the two natural sons Gordie had sired. Kurt, the oldest, stood to the end of the table with a pitcher of ale, ready to serve at the slightest nod from any seated at the table.

"Mind your tongue, Rose." The laird cautioned his daughter and held his tankard up so that his grandson could fill it. Though the Mckenna admitted to no shame by Kurt's presence in the hall, the boy could not inherit over a true son or daughter. Laird Mckenna had no wish to see his lands fall into the hands of his daughters. They were as buffle-headed as the tender maids Gordie refused.

Motioning the boy from the hall, Gordie waited before saying. "I can oblige your desire for an immediate heir by recognizing Kurt. I am satisfied with the boy. He's as sturdy a lad as any his age."

"A bastard?" The McKenna's face hardened obdurately.

Gordie drew back, thinking he'd gone too far. He had, but there was no withdrawing what was said. He had two sons already well under the McKenna's feet. Kurt and a new one, born just months ago to Kurt's comely mother. Both were accepted by his family and well loved, for children were important to the clan—every last one of them.

As the color slowly receded from the Mckenna's face, he brought the discussion to a head. "You will make a selection, Gordon Mckenna, or I will make one for you."

There was a certain tone of voice that every clansman learned early and paid special heed to when the Mckenna used it. Gordie was no different from any man in the hall when it came to an order or ultimatum from Laird Mckenna. What followed if he did not choose to accept his father's last word was coercion.

"Do I make a choice will you respect that?" Gordie needed time, though he was not certain why. Maybe it was the feeling of having shackles fastened to his legs. His mouth went dry. He could hardly breathe.

With narrowed eyes and bushy eyebrows met, John Mckenna answered. "Provided the marriage can be done in a month's time, you may select the woman."

"I'll no relent on the handfasting, Father. That will be done first, a trial marriage as was done in your time. Only then will I take the sacraments over it."

"I will grant the handfasting. A trial of six weeks, no more. Name the woman."

"Cara Mulvaine."

John Mckenna exploded. His fist crashed onto the polished planks. A dozen tankards of ale clattered to the floorboards. "Be damned! She's held for ransom!"

"She's the woman I choose."

The Mckenna rose to his feet, furious. His face burned a swarthy red from neck to hairline. "Then choose you have. You will be handfasted within the month and I will have my true grandson by winter's end."

The Mckenna stormed out of the hall. Likewise, everyone else who'd witnessed the confrontation went flying out the doors to spread the news. Not a minute after the laird departed, Gordie was deserted by all except his fool of a cousin, Ulrich.

"Now you've done it."

"I think not, Ulrich." A slow smile contoured Gordie's neatly bearded face.

Ulrich propped an elbow on the trestle, inclining slightly away from Gordie as if to see him in better light. A puzzled twist wormed his brow. He slapped his free hand against his ear. "Beg pardon. I've gone deaf. Correct me if I'm wrong. Did you no tell the laird you'd handfast the Mulvaine?"

"Aye, I did." Gordie rubbed his fingers across his mouth, a wasted effort that did not remove his smirk.

"We are talking *the Mulvaine*."

"Aye."

"The one that has been held for ransom since God knows when. The one old Sorely Mac Donnell hied away to Dunluce and tossed in his dungeon?"

"The very one."

"Christ's blood. She must be ancient now."

"Not so very ancient." Gordie smiled. "Twenty and two to be exact."

"You know of her?"

"That matters not." Gordie's air of calm assurance rattled Ulrich. "The object is, cousin, to make my father cease making his demands I marry posthaste."

"When you have issued a challenge that set his blood to boil?"

"Aye, cease he will. The Mulvaine will never be allowed to wed a Scot. The Mac Donnell holds her for ransom so astonishingly high, it will never be paid."

"Ach." Ulrich shook his head. "Then why in the name of all that is holy did you name her? Is she some great beauty?"

Gordie looked into the shadows at the corner of the hall. His shoulders moved in a negligent gesture. "Beauty? No. Though she has something about her that draws a man. I could never figure what that was."

"You know her!" Ulrich concluded. "How? Where? You have said nothing about her in the past."

"Because there was no reason. Tomorrow my father will forget about her as well as his ultimatum that I marry now."

"Has she some great dowry?"

"Nay, nor patrons to sponsor her. James can find no lowlander willing to share the cost of ransoming her from the Irish."

"Nor any highlander willing to take the curse of the Mulvaines down on their own house," Ulrich added. "You think it will work?"

Gordie deliberated, grinning at his cousin's face. "What I want the challenge to do is end my father's tirade. I will find the woman I want sooner or later. There is no rush. The Mckenna is no sickly earl about to meet his maker, nor am I ready to have my leg shackled."

"Perhaps." Ulrich thought his cousin's reasoning flawed. "You issued a challenge, Gordie. The Mckenna will no rest until he's put you in your place. He must now produce the Mulvaine within the month. You should not have pushed him."

Gordie shook his head. "And when he cannot, that ends his interference. For now, let's ride to Aberdeen. A few days away will do us both good."

A few days turned into weeks, during which time Gordie Mckenna had plenty of opportunities to ride helter-skelter all over his beloved Scotland. Over a year at home had not reduced his pleasure at returning nor diminished his joy at being alive.

It was a time of peace and the troubles with England had lessened. His king made no demands for his time or service. Gordie was at ease with himself.

But with his father, the battles continued. The war of wills would never end.

"You have changed, Gordie," Ulrich said as they stopped their horses at a small inn on the Dee River near the firth of Bremen. There was a fair and games of contest, cabers to toss and wrestling—the local laird's boys against all comers. Bremen's women were fair and apple-cheeked, the lads robust and hardy. "You were never so fickle before."

"I dinna think I'm fickle." Gordie surveyed the decorated village green and the score of colorful tents set between displays of Bremen's finest stock. "You know, Ulrich, I've always thought that when I met the woman that I would truly love, I'd know it."

"The minute you lay eyes upon her?" Ulrich asked incredulously.

"Why not?" Gordie tipped his cockaded bonnet to a winsome lass with apple cheeks. "The search is every man's true quest, is it not? When the right woman stands before me, I'll know it."

Ulrich swung his leg over his horse and dropped to the ground. "How?"

"Oh, I just will. Lightning will strike me. I'll be struck dumb. I mean, I'll know. There'll be thunder rolling. I'll feel it here." Gordie's fist pounded in the center of his chest.

Ulrich laughed. "Then five minutes later you'll be counting the spots on the lady's face and gritting your teeth against the whine in her voice. I know you, Gordie. You wouldn't know love if it walked right up and kicked your arse."

"Christ's blood, it is useless talking to you. You haven't a sensible bone in your wastrel's head. I'm talking about love. Love that endures. Love that accepts all faults and lasts a lifetime."

"You've been listening to the minstrels again."

Gordie grinned. "Well, I guess I have."

"Ach!" Ulrich bounded off his horse, leaning close to Gordie as he pointed to the middle of the fairgrounds. "There's a lovely lassie. Hair the color of corn silk, and look at those huge blue eyes."

"No blue eyes," Gordie said, then walked along, leading his horse by the reins.

"Why not?"

"Blue eyes haunt me. The pur boy chained next to me on the *Girona* had blue eyes. He was ten and six, no more. Blue eyes make me hear the cadence of the drum and feel the lash bite my flesh. And will you nil you, desire flies out the window no matter how fair the maid. So blue-eyed maids are out."

"'Tis over, Gordie. Lay the past to rest."

"How? I think I was spared to bear the guilt to my grave."

"Aye, it haunts you, I won't argue there. But you were following orders and war bears different dispensations. All are agreed upon that."

"In other words, I'm the lucky bastard to be alive. I am not so certain."

"Come, Gordie, do not sink into your black despair. We are here to have fun, seize the day, the sunshine, the maids and the games."

"Would that I could. I canna, and this foolishness I indulge myself in is another waste of time. There has to be something more."

"Come, now, not so glum, cousin. No serious thoughts on this journey. We promised each other that. We are on a righteous quest, seeking the woman of your dreams. Perhaps you'll be struck here in Bremen by a thunderbolt."

Turning his eyes to a bustling crowd of merrymakers, Gordie managed what passed for half a smile. "Aye, so we are. Do you think it possible that herein lies a gentle, loyal maid, lovely and true as my own mother, kind, generous and sharp as a tack? A woman who can comfort and cajole and deal with the damned black heart I hide within?"

"A tall order, my friend. Look sharp about you. Here comes a fair damsel with eyes the color of violets and lips as red as berries. Yonder there stands another laughing at the jesters. I think I would love to dip my head to kiss those fair round globes that joggle to escape her bodice."

"Ah, to the fair, then." Gordie tugged his cap to a jaunty angle and strode forward into the merry crowd. Running after him, Ulrich couldn't resist another jibe.

"Don't look so sharp that you pick one to ride off with, lad. It will be to your chagrin to ride cross Kenna's drawbridge with one bride on your lap and your father standing on the steps of the hall with another, the Mulvaine."

"Bite your tongue, knave!" Gordie threw back his head and laughed. "That will never come to pass. Glib my father may be. Determined, another virtue he holds dear, but there's no reckoning with the Mac Donnell of the Far Isles. He'll no be turned from his vengeance against the English. His granddaughter is his queen in the last game of checkmate that he plays."

"How did you come to meet the wench? You talk of her too intimately not to know her."

"I told you how I was saved from the sea."

"The Mulvaine was the girl of the cave?"

"So she is."

"You are certain?"

"As certain as I can be."

"A child?"

"Nay, a woman formed, but small, you know what I mean."

Ulrich flattened both his palms across his chest and laughed deeply. "Flat, then?"

Gordie decided he'd said enough. He looked about the fair-grounds, measuring up the competition. "We best give our full attention to sport and games."

Ulrich slapped him hard on the back, chuckling. "Right you are then. I feel it in my bones there is trouble coming."

Chapter Ten

John Mckenna's hired galley lay to anchor in Portballintrae. He had his spies scour the town and the countryside for word of the English troops before taking the risk of coming into Ulster with his full complement of armed men. While other parts of Ireland might be trampled under English boots, Ulster, in particular, remained indomitable.

His scouts reported that the English were held back behind the River Erne. The O'Neill had everything north of the Pale under his control.

Before the Mckenna's feet touched Irish soil, word had spread to Dunluce and as far south as Dungannon that a powerful Scot had arrived. "What be their purpose?" the earl of Tyrone asked the Mac Donnell messenger.

"My lord James thinks it has to do with the old betrothal of his niece, Cara Mulvaine. Some say that a cousin of Brodie Mulvaine is on the ship, but no one knows what this Laird Mckenna wants."

"That old business." Hugh O'Neill shook his graying head. "Can't James handle this?"

"He begs me to remind you that the Mulvaine holds Dunluce and Glenarm since James was disowned by his own pa."

That brought Hugh's focus back to the forefront of the matter. His scowl deepened. Dunluce and the Mulvaine had been a thorn in his side since the day Sorely Mac Donnell died. "Tell your lord James that I'll be at Dunluce before sundown. And tell the blighter to have something decent to eat, and oats for my horse."

"Aye, m'lord."

It wasn't until the next morning that John Mckenna brought his regiment of highlanders inside the great portcullis gate of Dunluce Castle.

Castle the old battlement was. A true fortress of thick stone quarried from the native granite. Four round towers flanked a massive keep of impregnable rock. No moat was needed to make it less accessible. It stood surrounded on three sides by the sea itself; the one narrow fissure of land leading up to it, a twisting nightmare of treacherous rock.

John Mckenna dismounted uneasily. He had not expected the portcullis to be standing wide open. Looking sharply about as his men dismounted, Mckenna wondered if he hadn't ridden them all into a trap.

No stableman came to tend to their horses. No soldiers or squires lingered in the empty yard testing their arms. It was midmorning and full sun that day. He counted seven cannons on the battlements, two of which aimed directly at the lowered drawbridge. With shield up, sword drawn and visor closed, Mckenna dealt the door a stunning blow with the hilt of his claymore.

The awesome door of the hall stood ten feet across from beam to beam. Strapped with crossbars and studded with iron rosettes, it was engineered to deflect assault. From deep within he heard the clatter of only one pair of wooden shoes. The small wicket to the left pulled open. A bent, white-haired man poked out skinny shoulders and bobbing head.

"What is it? Who be ye?"

"Laird John Mckenna, come to parley with the laird of Dunluce, Sorely Boy Mac Donnell," John Mckenna roared.

"You be needing a devil to communicate with Laird Mac Donnell. He's dead since November last and cold in his grave, God assoil his soul."

The old servant's words put John Mckenna back a pace. He looked to his armed-and-ready men, still wary, still suspecting a trap. "Who runs Dunluce in his stead?"

"James Mac Donnell."

"Sorely's son?"

"Aye."

"He is within?"

"Within his cups, you mean. Aye, aye, put away your sword and I'll open the door, though to make my bones ache opening the blasted thing is work I'll regret for days. Could you not just bend your great head and stoop through the wicket, Mac Mckenna? I'm twice your age if a day."

"Where are the Mac Donnell's men-at-arms?"

"All five are within, drinking with his lordship. Will you come in the wicket?"

A stranger welcome John Mckenna had never had. Caution held him back. No Scot that he knew of outside of the clan Mulvaine could lay any slander on the steps of Dunluce. His gut feeling and the witness of his eyes to the unkept yard, unguarded portcullis and empty battlements told him there were not enough soldiers within to defend anything. But then, he asked himself, what was there to defend? A fortress atop a cliff that no man could level in a hundred years of war? What was there to take or claim? He felt foolish stooping to half his height to wedge his great armored body through a wicket gate.

Straightening, adjusting his visor with a gauntlet-covered hand, he stared at the gloomy interior of one of the finest halls ever built. The clatter of his men's sabatons on the flagstone floor rattled to the cobweb-shrouded, vaulted rafters. What light there was came from a stained glass window of breathtaking beauty, fitted to a high arch on the eastern interior wall. It wasn't clean, nor had the hall been aired in ages. Vermin and beasties had made a home of it.

"This way, Mckenna."

Bidden to follow, the Scots tagged behind the shuffle-gaited servant through the castle, past vast empty rooms and up a great stairwell to a gallery that ran lengthwise through the upper level. The floor above the gallery was in better condition. Air did flow through open shuttered windows, and years of dirt was occasionally swept aside.

At a set of fine carved oak doors bearing the Mac Donnell coat of arms and tree of life, the servant flung open both doors to a splendidly paneled room where seven men sat drinking at midday. One sallow-faced, pot-bellied sot of undistinguished proportions rose unsteadily to his feet. It was not the greeting John Mckenna had expected—not at all.

"Come, enter, sit down and join us. To what do we owe the honor of a visit from the renowned Mckenna?" James Mac Donnell said, managing to uncork his thick tongue. Before all twenty armed-and-dressed-for-battle Scots had filed inside the dining room, he'd collapsed back upon his seat. "We've no quarrel between us, have we?"

"Nay, unless you wish to make one." Mckenna gave signal to his men to stand at ease, and swords were sheathed. The Irishman's hospitality went to his table and he sent his doddering old servant after more rye and meat.

Mckenna's twenty soldiers stood while John Mckenna took the seat opposite James Mac Donnell. The ale presented tasted watery, but the whiskey kicked. James Mac Donnell's viands had the texture of saddle leather.

James Mac Donnell waved aside another drink for himself and shook his head to clear it. When word had come of the Scots' invasion, he and his last remaining vassals had set to frantic work to mount a third cannon aimed upon the only road up to Dunluce. No sooner had the hard, exhausting labor been done, than Hugh O'Neill, the hardest fighting man in the entire isle, had arrived and burst into laughter at their labor.

"Fool!" the earl had scoffed. "What good is a damn cannon when you're facing twenty men? The Mckenna hasn't come to lay a siege against you. He's come to bargain. Open your gates and let him enter."

Not knowing if he was relieved by that military genius's analysis or not, James relaxed and some of his new-fraught tension evaporated. Hugh O'Neill remained the night and was seated at the high table, on James' right at the end. Two of James' other men were Spaniards who chose to remain in Ireland.

Since his father's death, James Mac Donnell's sole interest and occupation had been the gleaning of Spanish gold from the rocks of Spaniagh Point and to that end, the Spaniards helped him. In Dunluce's warder was gold plate, coinage, jewels and other matter that would have astonished any outsider with its beauty and value.

Of course, there had been much more in the early days after the ship floundered on Dunluce's doorstep. They hadn't been very smart about that. Too many people had known of the salvaged gold. James Mac Donnell had always held John Kelly responsible for the daring robbery that had stripped Dunluce's storehouse once again.

But James was craftier than his father was. James Mac Donnell would rather be thought a dullard by the English governor than let the man know what a wily fox he truly was. It wouldn't do for the wrong person to learn there was gold at Dunluce. The earl of Tyrone knew of it, but that was different.

"What business brings you to Dunluce, Laird Mckenna?" James finally brought the light talk to a head after the Scots had been served a meal and seemed less likely to jump up and slit his throat.

"I come on behalf of King James of Scotland to parley with Sorely Boy Mac Donnell. Seeing that he is now dead is news to me. What happened to him?"

James' sallow face clouded. The days after the *Girona* had caused much change in Dunluce Castle. "A ship wrecked upon our coast in October of '88. My father went to the wrecking every day while we went about salvaging what we could. He took a chill that never quite left him. He died this winter past of a violent cough."

"You have my sympathies, Mac Donnell."

"Nay, I am James. I'm not the man my father was and there's no Mac Donnell to rule Dunluce anymore," James said without rancor. "He was an old man, and in many ways, a brave and defiant defender of Ireland to his death. He battles foes greater than the English now."

"Aye." John Mckenna sensed a bitter disappointment that filled the man before him. A loss perhaps, caused by what, he could not fathom. Surely James' fortune had changed. "The lady Cara Mulvaine, what of her?"

"Cara?" James raised his head and looked straight into the Scot's alert eyes. "What would you have of her? 'Tis my understanding the border baron whose son she was pledged to is no longer alive. What could you possibly want of Cara?"

"I have dispensation from my king to take her to Mount Kenna as a bride for my only son."

"Ireland is not a sovereign nation like Scotland," James replied. "I have been informed to hold her ready to send to England should the Queen command it. Chichester implies Her Royal Majesty may dispose of my niece as a reward to one of her favorites."

John Mckenna cocked his brow. "The queen's disposition? In good faith, mon, the queen never disposes of her favorites, she merely leads them along to that most dangerous of ends . . . the headsman's ax."

"Well said." Hugh O'Neill applauded, and Scots and Irishmen alike laughed in wry agreement.

"When was this offer tendered?" the Mckenna asked.

James ran his fingers down the heavy stubble on his cheek. "Before the Armada sailed. In June of '87, I believe."

"'87? That was three years ago. What has happened to the tender since?"

"You mean after my father spit in Chichester's face?" He chuckled softly. "Nothing. Though his adjutant Kelly swears the claim is under consideration."

"But no contract has been signed?"

James made the mistake of looking down the table to his liege lord before answering. The Mckenna saw the gesture and the younger, handsome man's silent nod for James to continue. All was not as the Irish would have him believe.

"None," James Mac Donnell answered.

"Then you are free to enter into agreement." Mckenna drew the obvious conclusion, the one they wanted him to make.

"Ah, but there's the rub." James sighed. "I am not free to negotiate the marriage of Lady Cara. She is a law unto herself, I am naught more than her lackey."

"You will have to explain further, James Mac Donnell. I do not follow you."

"But you should. In this age of queens it should be clear as a bell. I was passed over in my father's will, disowned, my lord Mckenna. The whole of Dunluce belongs to Cara Mulvaine, a chit of two and twenty with no more grace or manners to her than the wildest savage in the New World. I was left with nothing. So, you will understand when I tell you that there is naught I can do for you."

"Are you not the oldest living Mac Donnell?"

"I am the only living Mac Donnell, save for my niece, who is not a Mac Donnell and never will be."

"Therefore, you are her guardian?"

"Nay, sir, I am not. Her guardian is the earl of Tyrone."

"Do I take it, mon, that the earl is the bare-faced man at the end of your table?" Mckenna demanded without taking his eyes from the stare they held on James Mac Donnell.

"Aye."

The answer came from the right. John Mckenna shifted his focus to the scowling giant at the very end of the table. He could not help but wonder in silent admiration as the Irish giant rose to his feet and bowed.

"Your grace," the O'Neill intoned.

The Irishman's acknowledgment put them on equal footing. With a showing of true Scot's parsimony, John Mckenna said, "It appears I waste my breath speaking to the wrong man. Where may we meet in private, O'Neill? It is my intent to settle this quickly."

"I am empowered to act in Cara Mulvaine's best interest. She will honor any pledge I make."

"Were it your decision to pledge her to marriage, would that also be binding? Will the girl do as you bid her?"

At that question Hugh O'Neill paused. All this fuss over a girl he'd seen little and disliked intensely, but he knew full well what negotiations and concessions had to be made.

"Aye," he said at last. "Cara will do as she is told. But by pledging her we give possession of a fief. One that we can little afford to lose. There are men in service to Dunluce, though they are quartered in Glenarm, not here. We would not see Dunluce nor Glenarm go to the English. There is no other dowry to offer."

"I stated first, I came to ransom Lady Cara. By such payment, would not the right of chattel over her go to me?"

"Under those terms, yes, but I repeat, we will not relinquish Dunluce, nor fortress Glenarm from Irish control. As it sits now, in my full guardianship, should some ill befall the lady Cara, her properties consolidate with Dungannon."

John Mckenna cast a look about the room. Oh, this one was fine enough. Its ribbon paneling was well made and the room was satisfactorily furnished. But Dunluce was no prize. His son would not miss the burden of its care and upkeep. He could concede all Irish lands and demand full entitlement to all properties last held by the clan Mulvaine. "Suppose over and above the ransom I have brought with me, I am willing to relinquish back to James Mac Donnell the rights and entitlements of Dunluce and Glenarm?"

James' head jerked up and in one swoop he'd heard the Scottish laird hand back his birthright. Hope sprang in his heart for the first time in over a year. The decision to accept the offer had to come from O'Neill. Anxiously, trying to hold his emotions in check, he turned to look at the darkened face of the earl. It didn't look good.

"Why would you do that?" Hugh O'Neill demanded suspiciously. There was no disguising of his features now. He held the whole negotiation in contempt.

"What need have I of this fortress or its lands? I do not ply the seas with ships and need no harbor. My home and castle are well inland and free from the control of men like Chichester. I would not buy troubles. Nor have I any interest in the woes of an absent landlord. Nay, I came here for a bride for my son. Nothing more. I will take her with naught but the clothes on her back and she will not be shamed for it. I can well provide any of her needs. My lands are rich and fertile and we breed the finest horses in the isle. As far as continuing a quarrel with the English, it is a matter of time before the king of Scotland mounts the English throne. My son's future is as secure as it can ever be. He only lacks a wife."

Hugh O'Neill leaned on his powerful forearms, his broad hands clasped together on the scarred wood trestle. "Surely, there are maids aplenty in Scotland for this lucky son of yours."

"Aye, more than plenty. None that he will have. He was shipwrecked here, washed up on the ground you call *Port na Spaniagh*. A girl pulled him from the sea and hid him in a cave. When his injuries had healed enough that he could travel, she arranged safe transport for him back to Scotland. I believe that girl was the one called Cara Mulvaine."

"Your son has told you this?" O'Neill demanded more.

"No. My son has remained very closemouthed about his experiences here. I know that an Irish girl aided him. I believe the Mulvaine is that woman."

"And if she is not?"

The Mckenna met the earl's penetrating stare. "It matters not. I offer a contract of marriage. Do you accept it, or is the woman already taken?"

James dragged his fingers through his shaggy hair. O'Neill sat back, digesting the facts as he toyed with a wicked-looking dagger. "How much ransom do you offer?"

"Five thousand sovereigns English gold." Mckenna had brought ten times that when planning to bargain long and hard with the ironfisted Sorely Boy.

"English gold, you say?" That was a very healthy offer of ransom. Even the *Flail of Connaught* hadn't struck a bargain worth that in ransoming the *de Cordobas*. Hugh's brows rose. "Aye."

"We will put it in writing, swear upon it, and the girl's claim to Dunluce and Glenarm will end with her leaving. Neither her heirs nor her husband shall ever have claim to it."

A shrewd man, John Mckenna could see one codicil that needed to be added. "Contingent upon James Mac Donnell getting heirs of his own to continue the bloodline. Without that, the English have written laws to forfeit all entitled lands to the English crown. Best you think to your own house, young Mac Donnell. A man your age should have sons."

"I did," James said in the most controlled voice he had used yet. He rose to his feet, showing no sign of the heavy drinking that had appeared to cloud his focus in the beginning of this carefully staged interview. The Mckenna also stood. "Have your men make themselves to home and I will see to locating Lady Cara."

Chapter Eleven

Cara's cheeks were wind-whipped when she came in the old kitchen doorway and laid a basketful of clams on the table.

"Where, praise God, have you been?" Brenna whirled about from a sea of steaming, bubbling cooking pots, wagging a ladle at Cara. "The whole house is in an uproar. Sir James searched for you nigh the whole day long!"

"Who has?" Cara unfastened her shawl and hung it on a peg by the door.

"Everyone!" Brenna screeched. "The O'Neill is here and not one man less than twenty highlanders! We thought a war coming. Your uncle has roused himself from his stupor and is fair near apoplexy because you are naught to be found. Did you no hear them calling for you? 'Twas a noise to wake the dead."

"How could I hear anyone calling me when I have been to Mussenden Temple visiting Almoy in his new quarters? The two monks promise to take exceptional care of him. It does relieve my mind, greatly. He's too old to be climbing stairs and living in a tower."

"Ach, Almoy!" Brenna fussed. "The old bastard's a century older than God and will outlive us all! Did you no ken what I said? Go and put on yer best gown. There's visitors and they are to meet you."

"Visitors to meet me?" Brenna's news finally registered in Cara's distracted mind. "Who has come?"

"A clan of Scotsmen, strutting up in kilts and cockades, with green tartans slung across their shoulders and gleaming breastplates, bearing arms of the likes we have no seen in ages. They've been to your uncle's hall the whole day. I dinna ken their purpose, but maybe this time there will be a ransom with the old one dead not stopping it.''

Cara did not follow Brenna's rambling. "Who would be ransomed? We hold no prisoners and the Spaniards stay because they want the gold.''

"You, gel!''

"Me?''

"Yes, you! Have you forgotten that you are half-Scot? Go! Dinna argue with me. Put on your best gown and scrub your face and neck. Now go!''

Cara didn't go. She stood exactly where she was, frowning deeply. Oh, she was tempted to bolt the way she had come and hide in the caves until the disturbance settled, but her curiosity suddenly had the best of her. "Scots you say, Brenna?''

"Aye, a clan of great Scots.''

Cara took her shawl and drew it over her head, then went tiptoeing up the gallery stairs to peak in her uncle's hall and see these men for herself.

For once, she was not the invisible person she'd always been at Dunluce. She got no farther than the gallery before Kirk, Thomas and Old Arthur all saw her moving through the castle and hastened to give her the same scolding message Brenna had. Retreating to her tower, she met her uncle rushing down the winding steps.

"Where the devil do you get off to, gel?'' he shouted.

"Who wants to know?'' Cara asked, and tucked her stained fingers behind her back. "My time has always been my own, sir.''

"Your time!'' James rolled his eyes heavenward and threw up his hands. "Lost in the fairies' mist! Or galloping pell-mell over the surf on that half-wild animal. Look at you! You look like a wraith from the bogs. Come, come.'' James took hold of her arm and tugged her up the steps. Cara froze, her feet dug in to the lower level. Mimms cut loose with a horrific growl.

Abruptly James Mac Donnell dropped his hand from Cara's arm and backed away from her.

"Be still, Mimms,'' Cara ordered.

The dog barked and James still held his hands up and away, frozen. He had forgotten his father's orders of years ago. No one was to ever touch the Scottish girl. Old Sorely had touched her, but never with his hand. He'd had a cane right from the day she'd arrived and had laid it on her often enough—until the dog she'd rescued from the sea had grown to size enough to protect her from daily beatings. Maybe they were daily. James shrugged his shoulders. He didn't know. Caring for a bairn wasn't his responsibility or his interest, either. It hadn't mattered then. It was too late to matter now. He recovered his composure and moved his hand in a gesture that said she could precede him on the steps.

"Cara, 'tis time you were taken charge of. Henceforth, you will confine yourself to the castle walls. I'll not be tried spending a whole day looking about for you. Go and clean your face and do something about your dirty dress. You look like a beggar. Can you not comb your hair, as well?"

These were more words spoken to her by her uncle than he had ever said directly to her in her life. Cara turned on a step higher than he, her brow furrowed. She hardly knew how to address a question to him. As to her garments, she had little to choose from and it wouldn't do any good to tell him that. She wanted to say she did keep herself clean. She remembered what talking back had cost her in the past with her grandfather, and James had more the look about him to Sorely Boy by the day now.

Mimms' growl deepened. James turned away and fled from her, nothing more spoken between them until he reached the bottom of the stairs. He abruptly turned and ordered loudly, "And you're t' leave that dog in your quarters when you come t' me hall. You understand me, mistress?"

There was no mirror in the north tower of Dunluce. Cara diligently scrubbed and scrubbed her face and neck since twice she'd been told she was dirty. She parted her hair with a wooden pick and made two neat braids. She wound each carefully around until the long braids were completely turned and tucked. They were secured with the wooden pins Brenna had given her on her sixteenth birthday.

Done, Cara sat on the three-legged stool and idly rubbed Mimms' head. She neither wanted to leave the dog in her room, nor go across the keep to her uncle's hall.

"I will take you with me just in case." Cara said. No one had beaten her since her grandfather's death. Cara did not fear her uncle as she had feared her grandfather. They were not the same kind of man at all. Still, leaving Mimms behind when there was so much uproar didn't seem wise.

Thus decided, Cara went down.

Cara peeked around a marble column, very unsure of venturing inside James' hall. Brenna supervised four women who were lugging laden trays in from the kitchen. She turned and surprised Cara.

"Here ye be. Come on then. Don't act like a ninny. Go up t' the dais and join Master James. They all wait t' meet ye."

"I don't want to." Cara responded to Brenna's frantic attempt to shoo her out of hiding by flapping her apron.

"Here's Lady Cara, now, m'lord. And isn't she a beauty, too!" Brenna announced sotto voce. From out of the crowd, James Mac Donnell stepped forth and it was his hand that gripped Cara's arm, dragging her reluctantly forward into the melee. Mimms set to barking ferociously.

John Mckenna saw the wench dig in her heels and resist, and knew she would have run for the hills if she could have escaped her uncle's grip. A dog ran at both their heels, growling and snapping, while uncle and niece both fiercely ordered it to desist. Mckenna frowned, uncertain of what he'd expected to see in this girl.

Having heard her name from his son's lips as the only woman he would accept in marriage, John assumed her a striking beauty.

She wasn't that. Oh, she wasn't ugly or badly formed in any obvious way, but there was not an impact of instant beauty that would make a knight fall to his knees professing undying love.

As she was dragged before him, John Mckenna saw that her coloring was good. Her hair gleamed black as ebony, her skin the most desired white, pale and clear with healthy color to her cheeks. Most definitely she was not bold. Her eyes never once came up to challenge his when they were introduced. Even when Mckenna took the liberty of gripping her chin lightly and lifting her fair face up so he could see her eyes, she would not meet his gaze.

Her color receded to the healthy pink of a lass who was most commonly out of doors. She had few manners and no guile whatsoever. When her uncle commanded her to sit to the table with them, that's exactly what she did. She sat as rigidly as a puppet, back straight, hands folded in her lap. In fact, she was so stiff, she trembled.

John Mckenna knew the girl was as frightened as a doe flushed by hunters from the deep woods.

The laird of the Mckennas had a way with women. He liked them, for a start. Charm always worked to put men at ease; a genuine liking of other humans always won a lady's friendship. He had no luck beguiling Cara Mulvaine. Little by little she raised her chin of her own accord and began taking curious glances about the hall.

"Do you never come to supper in this hall, Lady Cara?"

A direct question demanded an answer. Cara looked hastily at this great, red-haired clansman. He wore a cap with a bright clutch of scarlet and blue feathers pinned to it by a gold broach. He had faint freckles under the fair skin beneath his dark blue eyes, and his lashes were pale. She liked the fact that his face was clean-shaven, adorned only by a trimmed red-and-gray mustache.

"No, m'lord." Cara returned her gaze to the plate of untouched food before her.

"I see. Then you and your maids must entertain yourselves upstairs. A quiet existence, hmm?"

Cara didn't think it wise to tell him there were no maids and the only woman at Dunluce was old Brenna, who cooked. That was too many words for her constricted throat to get out anyway.

"Do you sing?" Mckenna inquired lightly, determined to make some progress through her odd reserve. "My five daughters sing all the time. Sometimes they make such a racket it tries my patience."

The young lady shook her head, and for the moment that she looked at him again her pale gray eyes showed a hurt as deep as if she'd been wounded.

"Ah, I see," the Mckenna continued. "you are very shy. Perhaps I frighten you. As big as I am, with this wild red hair and a voice that shakes the rafters. You are not used to that, are you?''

Mutely, Cara shook her head. What was she supposed to say? She looked helplessly at her uncle and saw him jerk his head up and down, jabbing his finger at her in some strange signal. Talk to him, James Mac Donnell was imploring her. Talk to him? Cara blinked in utter shock. She was to do the forbidden.

Cara turned her face once again toward the clansman named Mckenna. She blinked her eyes then fired her one and only question. ''Why did you need to see me?''

Mckenna instantly made up his mind not to mince his words. The day had been long and well spent. The contracts were signed. The earl drove a harder bargain than James Mac Donnell ever would have. Mckenna parted with not five, but eight thousand crowns of queen's gold. Dunluce and Glenarm were the property of James Mac Donnell and his issue, but Cara Mulvaine was named as his rightful heir should no other live to inherit from aging James.

Before anyone in this poorly run, ruin-in-the-making castle could come up with the girl in question, John Mckenna drove a harder bargain home. Cara Mulvaine belonged to him completely. Should the handfasting with his son not work out, or should their union not produce his desired heir, he had the right to choose her next husband.

John Mckenna would not lie in answering any questions she laid before him, but then neither did he have to divulge everything he knew.

''I thought it best that you should meet me here within your home, first. Shortly, we will be leaving. You are coming with me to Scotland. There you will marry.''

Another wash of confusion swept over Cara. This was the border baron? Carlisle? No, he was named Mckenna. His name had never once been mentioned in Sorely's litany of curses. A flood of memories assaulted her, orders her grandfather had given her. Commands. Nay, oaths he'd sworn. He would haunt her all the days of her life. Distressed, she looked to James, then back to the large man at her side. ''You take me to England?''

"To England, no, no, my lady Cara. I would not take you to England. 'Tis Mount Kenna, Scotland, where I rule the land my son, Gordie, inherits from me and your son in his time."

"To Scotland?" Cara's mind went round about in a dizzying circle. "I canna go to Scotland. I belong to Dunluce and it to me. I have duties that none else will do. Sir Almoy needs me."

"Sir Almoy?" the Mckenna said. "Who would that be? You are not betrothed to another?"

"Betrothed? Nay, Almoy is my teacher. He needs me. I canna leave him."

Confused, Mckenna swung to face the O'Neill and demanded of him, "Who is this Almoy Lady Cara speaks of? Surely she is of age not to need further use of a tutor."

Hugh O'Neill cast a scowling look in Cara's direction, swallowed his ale and set his tankard down with a rattle. "Almoy? Christ's blood. The old man's tetched in the head, has been for decades. Dinna worry about him."

"I won't leave Sir Almoy," Cara declared. This was much more than she had bargained for when told to come downstairs to her uncle's hall.

"Well, he is far to old to go to Scotland," the earl countered. "He would catch his death on the sea passage, and we have need of him here. He is well cared for and respected at Mussenden Temple. There he will stay, lady. Cease your arguing."

"Aye, mistress, your liege has spoken," the Mckenna said more persuasively.

"I must go and think about this." Cara rose, Mimms steadfast at her side.

The tall Scot chieftain laid a firm hand upon her shoulder, staying her retreat, not even hearing the low growl that issued from the dog. "I have been told you have few possessions to put into a pack. The serving woman, Brenna, has been sent to do such duty for you, Lady Cara. I would prefer that you not wander far in your meditations. To see to your protection, two of my men will escort you. Kindly accept their service."

At a nod from the laird, two kilted Scots rose and fell into step, flanking Cara. She did not quite know what to do about that. "I was only going to walk a bit . . . across the battlement."

"We leave within the hour, Cara," the Mckenna told her.

"Within the hour?" Cara's startled expression turned from the Scot to her uncle. He smiled and bobbed his head like a cork in water. Confused, Cara looked to the O'Neill. At least his face held an expression she could understand.

"Is this true, my lord?" Cara asked him.

The O'Neill rose to his feet and Cara felt as if she was being overwhelmed by giants. "I have signed the marriage contract. It is done."

"But—"

"Done." The earl of Tyrone cut her off, his fierce expression silencing any further protest Cara might have made. She swallowed, dropped her gaze from his hardened expression. What was she to do? Her fingers knotted the cloth at her sides; then she dropped a hasty curtsy in the general direction of all the men and fled the hall.

Mimms trotted at her side. Within her room, she found Brenna folding her things and stuffing them willy-nilly inside a small pack.

"I am leaving," Cara announced, out of breath.

"Aye. You are. 'Tis a good thing for you."

"I don't want to go," Cara burst out. She collapsed on her stool, wild-eyed.

"Of course you want to go. You never belonged here in the first place."

"Sorely said I did. He left it all to me."

"Him!" Brenna grunted. "What kindness did he ever show you? Not a one. Until the day that dog turned on him, he beat you black-and-blue and twice on Sundays. And by the threat of death, he kept all within this cursed house from ever showing you the simplest courtesy. 'Tis a cold and hateful house you be leaving, Cara Mulvaine. God be praised your day has come. I'm glad for you."

"But what I know is here," Cara insisted. "The Mckenna set his men to watch and follow me, Brenna."

"As well he should. You're a beautiful lassie now, Cara Mulvaine, the image of your mother. A fine lady she was, too. You'll be just like her once you done some learning. This was never right. It was wrong of the old laird to make your life so solitary and forbid all friendship to you. He wanted you to turn bitter and hateful so that you would carry on his hatred. But he failed, Cara. He failed. You haven't in you what it takes to hate, but if you stayed here . . ."

Brenna held up her hand that lacked three fingers. "Aye, you'd learn to hate. Do you remember how I lost these fingers, gel? Nay, you were a child and children forget. I touched you. I buttoned your dress for you. For that he cut my fingers from my hand. Every one in this house saw his punishment. Every tenant learned of it. Nay, he had no right to do such a thing. You were a wee child, a baby. It was wrong. You'll go and forget you ever came to Dunluce, Cara Mulvaine."

Turning her back to the girl, Brenna snatched up the leather pack in an angry gesture. "Take yer dog and leave me, Cara Mulvaine. I was niver allowed t' serve your needs by more than cooking the food I made for one and all under this roof. Let me make amends for all the wrongs I've done ye by packing yer clothes in peace. Go."

"You've done me no wrong, Brenna. If I go, who will look out for you? Who will see that Almoy remembers to eat, or will remind him to take his medicants when his joints are in pain?"

"Ach! I will look after the old one as well as meself. Go, I say!" she repeated in the tone of voice that had sent Cara fleeing from the kitchen so many, many times.

Not at all at peace with what the old woman had said, Cara returned downstairs to find her escorts waiting.

"Ach, good." The one who was the talker of the two smiled in greeting. "The Mckenna is restless and bids you come. The tide is rising. It's time we leave."

"Her bag." Brenna thrust a satchel into the shorter one's grip as she came down the steps. Mimms pranced beside Cara, head up, sniffing warily at the friendly Scot.

"Your dog, mistress?"

"Y-yes." Cara stuttered, slowing, dragging her feet now with every step she had to take across the old closed and poorly lit great hall. Her mouth sagged open at the great doors. They had never been opened; only the wicket was ever used. They were propped wide. All of Sorely's old men stood on the steps holding flaming torches against the dark night.

"Ah, Lady Cara." The Mckenna grinned down at her from his lofty height. His men were mounted, as were the O'Neills'. "'Tis time we departed. I had not thought to bring an extra horse. You will ride with me."

He moved rapidly to touch her and Mimms cut loose with a fierce growl, causing John Mckenna to come to an instant halt. "Perhaps before we go farther, Mac Donnell, your man should pen the dog."

Old Tom Arner reached down and put a fierce grip on Mimms' leather collar to lead him away.

That was the last straw. To lose Almoy was pain enough, but to lose Mimms could not be borne.

"Mimms!" Cara shouted. "Nay, 'tis my dog. I won't go without him!"

"We have dogs aplenty at Kenna, Lady Cara." The Mckenna did not halt, taking hold of her by her waist and lifting her easily onto the tall, gigantic horse. "Gordie will give you the pick of any litter."

"But Mimms is my dog!" Cara cried out as the man came up behind her on the horse. She would have jumped down had not iron hands gripped her and kept her to her seat. "I won't leave Mimms here! He must go with me."

"Now, now! I have promised you another, lass." Mckenna dismissed her protest and spurred his horse across the cobbled stone, galloping forward to take the lead in the procession of mounted men next to Hugh O'Neill.

"I don't want another!" Cara insisted and was nearly driven to strike out at the man. But her small fists could do no damage to the Scot. If she struck him, his fist would cause her grievous harm. The act would be futile.

Something great, dark and dismal, flared in Cara's mind. An emptiness rose with the force of a violent storm, sweeping down, blinding her eyes. Potent fear took hold of her hammering heart. She screamed, "Mimms!"

Twisting far against the man's powerful restraining arms, Cara looked back to Dunluce as the horses galloped down the twisted path.

Dunluce receded in the darkening night, growing smaller and smaller. All at once Cara knew she'd done this before—been taken against her will from her home.

The full force of that long-ago night of terror rose up in images of clanging arms, hidden terror and fires that burned without and within Graham Keep.

"Mimms!"

It was the heartbreaking pitifulness of her wail that halted John Mckenna. Reining in his charger, he turned to the nearest vassal and ordered, "Go back, Jeffry, and get the dog. If it means that much to her, we will just have to bring the mangy thing."

Pausing a moment longer, the Mckenna looked down at the pinched face of the girl. Her eyes were wide and unfocused. Her every limb trembled.

"There, did you hear me? The dog will come. See that it doesn't bare its teeth to me again. Now will you be content? I dinna want to miss the tide."

"Aye," Cara forced herself to answer the huge Scot. Her head nodded loosely, like a broken doll's.

Satisfied, the McKenna signaled his men. His grip upon the bride tightened. He ignored her fear. She would adjust sooner if he gave no quarter. He spurred his mount back onto the road to Portballintrae.

Trapped in the brawny Scot's encompassing embrace, Cara pressed both her hands tight against her mouth. Mimms came running at full speed, yapping and howling as he loped alongside the destrier. Cara held back the sob rising from her chest. When had tears ever stopped what was meant to be? Not for her, ever. Her eyes went to the distant castle, searching for the lights that no longer burned in the north tower. She could see nothing of her past. It was gone. But try as she might, she could not stop the tears that flooded from her eyes.

She thought she heard the Scot make some noise in his throat. She rode with him, rigid and stiff. He took one hand from his reins and pulled his plaid from his armor-clad shoulder and threw it across her, tucking the cloth close against her body.

"Dinna weep, lassie. Ye can trust me when I say ye'll be fine as fine can be."

Chapter Twelve

"Careful, wench!" Gordie Mckenna yanked his foot from the basin of water. "You're burning me foot off!"

"It's no more than you deserve, Gordon Mckenna!" Rose kept pouring hot water from the kettle to the basin.

"What I deserve I'll not get from you, brat!" Gordie swung a broad hand soundly against Rose's hip.

"Mother!" Rose yelped and jumped clear of his range. Becca laughed from across the hall and Elaina came in from the hot kitchen, fluttering her apron at her reddened face.

"What is it now?" Elaina Mckenna took one look to encompass water seeping across the tiles, Gordie's smug face, Rose's hand to her backside and the steaming kettle.

"Gordie smacked Rose," Becca supplied unnecessarily, then launched herself into her brother's arms. Despite his foot, still held aloft, Gordie caught the wee sprite that was his youngest sister and hugged as she squealed, "I'm so happy you are home!"

"Why, then, are you womenfolk trying to roast me alive? You're strangling me, Rebecca!"

"Am not!" Becca kissed his neatly bearded chin. Her backside wound up on his lap and Gordie's injured foot settled into the basin of water once again. "'Tis you who's doing all the squeezing. Like a bear you are, Gordie!"

"He will not sit still and let anyone tend his foot, Mother," Rose announced. "'Twould serve the bounder right if his leg rots clear to his knee!"

Tickling the giggling girl squirming on his lap, Gordie said in mock severity, "'Tis lucky you are I can no run after you,

Rosie, else you'd pay dear for boiling the meat from my bones."

"Does it hurt?" Becca asked with concern. Gordie set the imp to her feet, leaned over his knees and scowled at the ugly, black-and-blue and bloody toe that was the root of all the commotion.

"'Tis a mortal wound, indeed."

"Well, it will never heal if you don't stick it in the herbal bath, you oaf!" Rose stalked away with kettle in hand and injured vanity showing. "You tend him, Mother. He's such a baby."

Lady Elaina tested the water then straightened and sternly addressed her son. "Will you keep your foot in the water? It will no kill you."

"'Tis too hot." Gordie grinned at his mother, offering her the same open arms that had accepted his youngest sister earlier after setting his injured foot back in the basin.

"What kind of welcome is this?" Gordie teased as his mother kissed his brow and smoothed his wet hair back from his forehead. "I am attacked, set upon, my clothes demanded from my back and here I can hardly walk. Where is my respect?"

"You're cursedly spoiled rotten, Gordon Mckenna." Lady Elaina encased his shaggy head in another affectionate hug. Now that he was clean and washed and dressed in a sweet-smelling shirt and tunic, it was bearable to embrace him. "Will you explain how you came by this injury?"

His answer was taken out of his mouth by his cousin, Ulrich, who came bounding in the open doors fresh from the bath and hungry as a bear just crawled out of a winter den. "Trouncing the devil out of Sterling's lads. 'Twas a fine fair and the purse one t' make any comer's eyes bulge. Only, Gordie was distracted by a buxom lass and dropped the caber."

"And if you believe that, Ulrich has a horse to sell you," Gordie added.

"I'll bet it wasn't a log at all." Rose stuck her head in through the open window, taunting. "I'll bet he was in his cups and his own horse stepped on his foot!"

"Rose," Elaina scolded.

Ulrich hooted with laughter and Gordie sent a wet cloth sailing toward his cousin's head.

Elaina Mckenna threw up her hands. The bedlam in her home hadn't changed in a score of years. The tone of the quarreling might concern a stranger, but she knew her children. None had a mean bone in their bodies, though the teasing never stopped. "Ach, Gordie, try to be a little patient. Rose is anxious over Ralph. And do keep your foot in the water."

"Aye, Mother." Gordie rolled his eyes behind her back and swung round to grin at Ulrich. "By God, it's clear they're glad to have us home, aren't they?"

Ulrich smoothed his palms across his cleanly shaved cheeks, grinning ear to ear. "Aye, the women are. Jeffry told me your father is out searching for us."

"Don't believe it. He'll be back afore supper—he always is." Gordie gingerly raised his foot from the basin and flexed it. "Damn, but this insignificant, useless wound hurts like hell."

"Right it should when the bone is smashed to pieces." Ulrich frowned at the injury. "You'll be laid up, waited on hand to foot, so stop complaining. Soak it. Then I'll cart your worthless body upstairs to bed."

"'Tis a toe that's busted, not my leg. Go have fresh horses saddled. We'll go inspect the crofts."

"You'll do nothing of the kind, Gordie Mckenna." Elaina roundly cut him off. "You're not to leave and that's orders from the Mckenna himself. He's been worried sick with no word from you in a month. And where have you been? Out riding from fair to fair, behaving as if you hadn't a care in the world."

"And well I haven't, Mother," Gordie injected in a serious voice. "I am completely at peace with myself, more than I have felt in the entire last year. I did my share of the labor, putting in the crops and culling the herds. You canna blame a man of my age for taking the challenge others give. I will be the Mckenna someday."

"No one questions your need to sow an oat or two or make your name renowned and respected as your father's is," Elaina countered, "but there's another season to plan. The Aberdeen auction comes soon. Horses must be selected for that. 'Tis way past time you were home. By the looks of your foot, you should have been back two days ago. You'll sit right there, soaking that injury or I'll send Rose in here to torment you!"

"I yield." Gordie raised his palms in defeat. Ulrich joined him, settling his lanky body in a high-backed chair.

"To a higher authority, the woman of the house. Wise move, mon." Swiveling his head about, Ulrich spied a golden-crusted pie advancing on the upraised hands of ten-year-old Becca Mckenna. "Now, there's a tasty morsel. Feast your eyes on that one."

"Ulrich, behave!" Becca flushed as pink as the berry juice oozing from the crust of the pie. She placed it on the table with a flourish.

Catching her apron ties, Gordie teased, "Dare we starving travelers hope that pie is for us?"

"I thought you'd never ask for food," Becca answered with a worshipful sigh.

"And who made this wondrous pie?" Gordie hugged the youngest girl to his massive chest.

"I canna tell." Becca's blush heightened even more. She was a bonny lass, bright-eyed and freckle-faced. Gordie tweaked her nose. "'Tis a wondrous pie, remarkable, for 'tis made with a sweet called sugar that tastes better than honey from a comb."

"Sugar?" Gordie's eyes widened in mock surprise. "Where did you get such a thing that only queens have tasted?"

"Ach, Gordie, ya know it came dear, a gift from the king himself. He sent us two caskets as a reward, with word that it came all the way from a place called Medina."

"A rare and tasty treat, then."

"Aye, like saffron and cloves, but better."

"Let's try it then, Ulrich." Taking a knife from the table, Gordie cut into the golden crust. Becca rushed to bring plates, silver forks and linens to each of the men, bringing last two frothing fresh tankards of milk. "Will you have a piece, little sister?"

"Oh, no!" Becca said ever so solemnly. "'Tis a special pie. Made only for Poppa and you. Ulrich, too."

Serving up two monstrous, juicy slices, Gordie winked slyly at his cousin. Becca hovered at the edge of the table as they both sank forks into the flaky crust and brought massive bites to mouth.

Gordie chewed with expectant relish. His jaw tightened. His gaze shot to Ulrich. Their eyes met, the lumps of pie held in their mouths like hot coals. The shock of tasting raspberry brine locked their jaws.

Achingly aware of the young girl anxiously waiting his praise, Gordie shot his cousin a warning look and swallowed with difficulty. He silently dared Ulrich to say a word to hurt Becca's feelings.

Swallowing the third bite whole, Gordie reached for the tankard of milk as Ulrich did the same.

"Is it too hot?" Becca gasped in a stricken voice.

"Not at all," Gordie lied.

"But how does it taste? Is is as good as Mother's?"

"Almost." Ulrich stabbed at the crust, demolishing what remained on his plate.

"Oh, absolutely." Gordie coughed, cleared his throat and washed the brine pickling his tongue and gums with more milk.

"Oh, praise the lord!" Becca clapped her hands. "Car—Cook will be so happy!" She stumbled over the name, correcting herself immediately.

The sisters had decided Cara Mulvaine's presence in Kenna House was to be a closely guarded secret. Dancing with joy, Becca dashed for the outer door.

"Cook made this pie?" Gordie hollered after her.

"Oh, most assuredly!" Becca paused in the doorway, her red head bobbing. "Don't eat it all, Gordie. Poppa must have some, too! 'Tis an important pie!"

"An important pie." Gordie shoved the plate away from him when the imp had run from the hall.

"God's toes, they're trying to poison us!" Ulrich choked. He raised his tankard and drained it of the milk, then sat with his head bent over his knees, gagging.

"I'll beat the daylights out of Grete Mckinsey!" Gordie also drained his milk, trying unsuccessfully to wash down the overwhelming taste of salt. "Wasting berries like that! It's a sin. I thought Becca made the pie, didn't you?"

"You know I did." Ulrich got control of his burning throat, but dropped his hand to grip his flat belly. "You'll have to do your own beating," he gasped as he lurched to his feet, "and no rely on me. I'm poisoned."

Any other time Gordie would have thrown back his head and roared as Ulrich bolted outdoors, choking so hard, his face turned green. But Gordie's own stomach took a turn for the worse, making a mighty complaint about the quantity of salt ingested with tart raspberries and fresh milk. None of the food mixed pleasantly.

Gordie lurched to his feet, hobbling barefoot after Ulrich in a race for the garderobe.

It was a good while before the spasms of retching ended and the two men sat on a bench beside the well, their hands wet with cool water, relieving their nausea. "Fetch me my boots, Ulrich," Gordie growled. "Grete Mckinsey's poisoned her last Mckenna."

Ulrich still spat repeatedly on the ground. "You wouldn't be doing anything rash, Gordie."

"Rash, my foot. Go and fetch my boots." The cold light in his eyes said he meant it.

"It would be better for all concerned," Ulrich argued diplomatically, "if I just helped you up to bed and went round myself to inform Cook of her error before your sire comes rolling in and is served the same poison. A thrashing the woman will live through. Dare anyone serve the Mckenna that poison, he'll have Grete's neck broken."

"Fetch me boots!" Gordie said unequivocally.

Chapter Thirteen

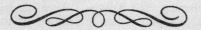

"We can go up now, Cara. They've gone to the bailey yard," Rose announced as she came inside the heated kitchen.

Rose had taken an immediate shine to the quiet, dark-haired lass her father had brought home two weeks ago. Once her brother Gordie married, then Rose could press her own match with her father more earnestly.

Rose wasn't getting any younger. Nor had she obtained the same concession Gordie had, that of handfasting with her true love, Ralph Stewart.

It was church vows and nothing less for the Mckenna's daughters. Rose championed any cause that would remove the last barrier to her own wedding. It was six weeks to the day before she could wed, now that Gordie was home. And wed she would, Rose determined.

Cara glanced into a kitchen yard that brimmed with raised beds, plants and herbs and vegetables, rows of strawberries bursting with fruit and the orderly patch of berry bushes that had yielded their best fruit for the pies. Only women and girls worked in the Mckenna's kitchens. Even the butchering was done by a great big woman of a size Cara had never seen until she came here.

No less than twenty attended all kinds of tasks, from little ones set to pulling weeds or minding the geese and chickens, to old women who spread white aprons across their laps and snapped beans or shucked peas from their pods. And in and out of this bevy of industry the laird's daughters came and went with regularity. They helped at baking or making bread or set their hands into tubs of steaming water and scrubbed plates and goblets and blackened pots. They carted trays or served in the hall and always, everywhere they went, they talked and laughed and chatted and giggled.

The Mckenna highlanders roamed in and out of the kitchens with the same ease. A hungry man thought nothing of striding into the three huge kitchens and parking himself at the nearest table to have whatever was at hand.

There were boys, as well, from littlest infant to proud strutting squires who dropped their work or games to come and snatch a cookie when the scent of them came fresh from the oven.

So many people! Cara was overwhelmed by them all.

She adjusted to this odd, new way of life with her eyes forever open wide, curious, yet as cautious as a cat on an icy pond.

"Come, Cara, let's go up."

Cara worried the corner of her lip, her hand idly stroking Mimms' golden head. His gold, black and white coat had never been so clean or glossy. "I think I'd rather stay here, Rose."

"Nonsense, 'tis perfectly safe. We'll take the back stairs. Gordie will never see you."

Nervously, Cara looked at the row of pies. The young lord's return had set off a flurry of activity. She had been given the task of making pies for the night's feast. The knowledge that this was her wedding day had kept Cara tense and distracted. Now she stared at the pies. They didn't smell right. She thought maybe Scottish berries were not as flavorful as those in Ireland. She didn't know and she wouldn't ask. Words still came very hard for her to speak.

Not that this sunny family of Mckenna folk hadn't gone out of their way to make her welcome.

Rose came within the quiet larder and sat to the bench beside Cara, instinctively dropping a friendly arm around the younger girl. "Don't be frightened, Cara. Gordie's a great big oaf just like Poppa, but he's a heart of gold inside him. Why, he'll take one look at you and fall head over heels in love!"

"There you go again, speaking of love." Cara's brow puckered as if she pondered a terrible puzzle. *Love*—now there was a word that tumbled off Rose's lips nearly every other time she spoke. "You love the berries. You love bonnie Ralph. You love a fine, clear day without a mist. Ach, Rose, I think you love most easily.''

Rose sighed ever so deeply, then grinned brightly. ''That's because I am in love. Dinna be shy. When you see Gordie, you'll know what I mean.''

''Will I?'' Cara had doubts. What love meant, Cara hadn't the slightest idea. She leaned forward across the trestle table, nudging her finger against the dripping, flaky crust of the nearest pie. Red juice oozed here and there along its joined golden crust. ''The pies don't smell like Brenna's do.''

''Ach!'' Rose stood up. ''Nonsense! They smell wonderful. Gordie and Ulrich took after the one Becca took them like the pigs that they are. They didn't leave a scrap for Poppa!''

Rose flipped her finger across the oozing crust and brought a smear of red juice back to her mouth and popped it inside. Immediately her eyes went round as saucers. She pulled her finger out and went for a second taste.

Cara's eyes narrowed apprehensively. ''They're not right.''

Rose had to clear her throat. No, the pies weren't right. Cara did what the girl had done and pulled a taste of the juice to her own mouth. Her mouth puckered, horrified at the taste.

''My lord, what did I do wrong?''

''Euch!'' Rose gasped, looking about the kitchen for what could possibly have ruined the berries. ''How much salt did you put in them, Cara?''

Cara turned round about the larder, to the huge earthenware bowl where the berries had been mixed with spice, and rare sugar, before she'd filled each shell and fluted the edges together. ''I measured just like Cook said to do, with the little spoons and the cups.''

Cara broke a piece of crust from the edge and put it to her mouth. It wasn't edible at all. She spit and wiped the taste from her tongue. The pies were as full of brine as pickled herrings.

''Oh, Rose, what did I do?''

Throwing open the doors of the dry stores, Rose immediately knew what Cara had done. Salt and sugar were kept in barrels side by side. Both were white and finely ground, precious commodities to obtain, not to even mention waste. They looked the same to measure. By taste they could be told from one or the other, or by reading the name neatly lettered on the barrels. But Cara Mulvaine couldn't read English, not even her own simply written name.

Hiding her pity, Rose turned about, briskly wiping her hands against her apron.

"I think we'd better start over."

Cara had snatched the two remaining pies from the counter. "Oh," she wailed. "I cannot even throw them in the scraps where the worms are dug. They'll kill them all!"

Rose deftly removed the pies from Cara's hands and put them in the burnable refuse outside the hot kitchen. She dusted off her hands as she returned to the larder. "'Tis not a problem, Cara. We'll start anew. There's plenty time afore supper."

"There's no more berries."

"We'll go pick more."

"I should stick to picking berries and not to cooking them," Cara said in a disappointed voice. Rose smiled to reassure her, but knew she didn't do a very good job of it.

The Irish lass was cut to the quick. Why, her heart was on her sleeve in everything she did. She knew absolutely nothing practical, not how to run a house or manage a kitchen or keep accounts. The only skill she seemed to have was that of plying a needle. Too late Rose realized it was a mistake to assume Cara could follow Cook's directions. She should have helped her.

But instead of bursting into tears as any of Rose's sisters might have done, the Irish girl stood rigid in the store, her face convulsed with shame, as if she'd committed some heinous crime.

"'Tis no serious offense, Cara," Rose insisted.

"Oh, aye, 'tis! 'Twas a foolish waste of salt and more. We could starve this winter for my carelessness."

"Starve? Don't be silly. 'Twas an honest mistake. You'll learn from it."

Rose could see that Cara was not convinced. She shook her head, standing between the larder and the storeroom door as a shadow fell across the floor behind her. She softly said, "No one can blame you."

The hackles on the fierce dog that never left Cara's side rose. He squared his huge, ugly face toward Rose, baring teeth as long as ten-penny nails.

Each time the dog did that, Rose backed up two steps. She liked Cara, but that dog was a damned dangerous beast.

"Be quiet, Mimms," Cara whispered to him.

"I want to know who is responsible for making that pie!" Gordie Mckenna roared in a much deeper growl than that the dog had issued. Rose whirled about, slamming the door between the rooms.

"Gordie Mckenna! What are you doing in the baker's kitchen! Were you not served to the table as your right? This is a woman's place, and well you know it!"

"Rose, that pie was laced with poison! Was it you that made it? Or Grete? Answer me!"

"Pie, what pie? We've no pies here, mon. There's sweet raisin bread, which, if you change your tone a wee bit, I might share with you." Rose's hands went to her hips in fists as she assumed a fighting position her brother knew well enough. He'd no find out who had made the pies, not even if Rose had to take his wrath herself.

"Pie, what pie?" Gordie mocked her. "The raspberry pie you sent my favorite sister bearing like 'twas a gift for the king. Who made it? I've been sick as a dog from it. Ulrich, too! Did you spice it with henbane or nightshade?"

"'Twas only a simple mistake of mixing sugar for salt, Gordie Mckenna. Now, get yourself out of this kitchen before I take a stick to you!"

"'Tis you who will get the skelping of your life if you don't tell me now who's responsible. 'Twas a waste of flour, salt and God's good berries. I'll no tolerate such and well you know it. Was it Becca or Grete that made it?"

Gordie's heels stomped on the kitchen's wooden floor. Inside the larder the dog growled deeper. Cara bent to shush him, terrified that the roaring man would find them.

Rose was not about to let Gordie meet his bride or find any fault with her before the wedding. She stepped before her brother, bravely blocking his advance.

"If you must know, I made the pies. Mother laid in new barrels of salt and sugar and they were unmarked this morning. I measured wrong, Gordie. It was a simple mistake, which I will correct immediately once you take your huge body out of my kitchen. I'll not have Poppa come home to find my error.

Won't you get satisfaction enough telling Ralph I've tried to poison you?''

"You deserve a stick put to you."

"Then go and get a stick," Rose suggested as she stood her ground. "You've no come with one in your hand and Poppa will break your neck if you lay your hand upon me. Poisoned or no, you're standing tall and twice my size. I'll no be beaten by your fist."

"Aye, I'll get a stick. Don't think I won't, careless lass. 'Twon't be the last one I take to you, either."

Cara held her breath, her hands tight round Mimms' muzzle as the shadow across the slatted door went away without another word.

Rose's final taunt came only after the sound of her brother's uneven tread had gone away. "You'll have to catch me first!"

The sister flung open the door to find Cara crouched upon the floor, holding the snarling animal at bay. Cara's grim-lipped face said more than enough to Rose.

"That was Gordie?" Cara whispered.

Brazening this crisis out, Rose bent and pulled Cara back to her feet. "Aye, that was Gordie. Don't be frightened. His bark is like your dog, much worse than his bite."

"Mimms bites very hard," Cara said. "You shouldn't have lied to him about the pies. 'Twas my fault."

"Don't be silly. The way I cook no one would think to blame it on anyone else. Come, let's go upstairs before the lord Mckenna comes back."

"He's going to beat you?"

"No, he's not, Cara. It's a game we've played since we were children. He growls and I snap right back. Gordie's never hurt me. Besides, I've already told you, he has a broken toe. I can outrun him."

Rose's teasing words were not having the effect they were supposed to have on Cara. The girl was supposed to laugh and be relieved. Instead, she looked about the larder and storeroom for a place to hide.

Rose was beginning to understand that Castle Mckenna was not at all like Dunluce.

"You really are frightened." Rose drew the smaller girl against her, wanting to kick the damn dog when it snarled its disapproval. Smoothing back a wisp of Cara's hair, she again tried to comfort her. "Don't be, sweetling. Nothing will come of it. I promise you. Gordie will be laughing by suppertime. It's no great error. You'll see."

There was no such thing as laughter over mistakes in Cara's past. She was unconvinced, and said, "I must go and tell your brother that it isn't you he should be angry with, but me."

"You will do nothing of the kind," Rose declared. "We will take ourselves upstairs and have our baths and swim in all the perfumes I can find. This evening when Poppa returns, you'll meet Gordie. Tonight, when you are in bed together, you can whisper to him about the pie if you must. But you will keep silent until then."

"Why should I tell him then, and what would I be doing in bed with him?"

Exasperated, Rose drew the girl out to the back stairs. On the way to their chamber, Rose asked. "Cara, do you know what marriage means? Handfasting?"

Before the question was completely out, Rose knew it was foolish to ask the girl such a thing. Perhaps there weren't two years between their ages, but there was a world of difference between them. "Come, silly, we need to have a serious chat."

Upstairs in the heavenly scented bathing chamber that all the Mckenna sisters used, Cara sat on a stool in a silk wrapper half listening to Rose's discourse on the birds and the bees. It was as frivolous a lecture as most any that came from Rose's lips. Her thoughts were quite peculiar, Cara decided.

"That explains everything, does it not?" Rose concluded as her busy hands worked Cara's dark tresses free of tangles. "Has your hair never been cut, either, Cara?"

"No. Is that done?"

"Well, of course 'tis done." Rose eyed the ends speculatively. "Mother always insists we girls trim our hair once a year." She tossed her red curls about her shoulders. "For healthy ends and shine, she says. It makes styling easier and curling, too."

"No one's ever touched my hair. My grandfather forbid anyone to touch me," Cara explained.

"Even to combing your hair?"

"Nay, no one ever did."

"What about when you were little?"

Cara tried to think. "I was never little. Small, yes. I could not reach things."

"How peculiar. I think we should cut it."

"No."

"But it is heavy and thick. See, there is curl here on the ends. I think if it were to your waist, at the most, that it would curl all the way from your crown to the ends. You would look beautiful."

"With my plain face?" Cara stared into Rose's cheval mirror. She was not quite certain that face belonged to her. Rose's glowing, freckled face appeared beside her own.

"You aren't plain."

"Sorely said I was. An ugly bitch, he always said."

"Cara!" Rose blinked. "Don't say that! 'Tis not proper. Besides, you aren't, not at all. Why, a bitch is a terrible woman, sometimes. Actually it's a dog's dame, do you ken?"

Cara stood, uncomfortable with the discussion, the grooming—the very presence of the other girl—even though she knew Rose's intentions were the best. Cara was also very, very confused. Castle Mckenna seemed all the more foreign and strange to her.

"You look very pale all of a sudden. Are you feeling ill?"

"I am fine." Cara searched for what she wanted to say. "You are just too . . . kind."

"Kind." Rose smiled and the two of them adjourned to her chamber.

As Rose began to select clothes to wear, she urged Cara to rest upon her bed. "A nap would do you a lot of good right now. It's been a hectic day. Why don't you lie down and rest? There will be much feasting this eve, celebrating, and it will tire you even more."

"I'm no tired. In truth, Rose, I am no much used to sitting about indoors. I'd prefer to go walking on the hills. I'm certain there would be much to see—animals, plants, things I've never seen before."

"You can't do that," Rose immediately countered.

"But I couldn't do it yesterday or the day before that. Rose, do you stay within these walls all the time? 'Tis confining, strangling like."

"There's always so much to do."

"I have to walk about awhile. Come, Mimms."

"No, Cara. Not today. Gordie's back and Poppa will be home any moment. Cara, could you do as I ask? It would please me greatly if you did."

"A nap is a waste of daylight. I sleep only at night, Rose."

"But you said you'd never been to a feast."

"That's true. I haven't."

"Well, then, you need to sleep now. You won't get the chance to do so again for a long time, believe me."

"Rose." Cara studied the Scottish girl intently. "You just explained that handfasted people sleep a lot of the time. Married people, too. I will sleep plenty from the sound of it."

Rose was suddenly completely beyond her depth explaining anything further about marriage or handfasting. Her pretty head bobbed up and down. "Maybe I haven't explained *sleeping* well. Trust me, Cara. Lie down, and for heaven's sake, don't go wandering anywhere outside my room. It's important. Promise me that you'll stay here."

"Very well. If I must," Cara said, and sighed. Rose seemed to know the way and means of everything. Cara did trust her. Cara lay down on the soft feather mattress and accepted the light covering Rose spread over her.

"You'll not leave my room, promise?"

"I promise."

"Good girl." Rose beamed happily, patted Cara's hand and left her to seek out her mother. She found Elaina in the weaving room. "Why on earth are you at the loom, now, Mama?"

"Because it soothes me." Lady Elaina's shuttlecock shot from right to left. She looked to her daughter as her feet moved on the pedals changing the heddles. "And what have you been doing other than tormenting poor injured Gordie?"

"Poor injured Gordie," Rose said, and laughed. Her laugh had no trace of sympathy for her brother. "Poor injured Gordie just frightened the wits out of Cara Mulvaine, Mama. I am more than a bit worried for her."

"Now, what is this about? I've already heard chapter and verse about your pies, Rose Marie, and Gordie did not once mention Lady Cara in the telling."

"He didn't see her, honestly, Mama. Give me due for having some sense. What I'm trying to explain is that Cara was in the storeroom when Gordie and I were in the larder shouting each other down. The great big oaf has given her completely the wrong impression of himself. He's all bluster. Unfortunately, Cara doesn't know that and will not believe me when I try to explain that Gordie's as soft as a kitten inside."

"Rose, don't mistake affection for softness. It would be better that you leave Lady Cara to form her own opinions about your brother."

"She's perfectly entitled to forming any opinion she wants about him, so long as it doesn't stop the wedding. What will stop the wedding is her innocence. She knows nothing of what is expected of her, Mama."

"Don't be so critical, Rose. 'Tis not like you."

"Mama, I am not disparaging her." Rose knelt at her mother's side and spoke low in great earnest. "She does not have the slightest concept of the ways of men and women, how to talk to a man, or look at one. Why, her face is like an open book. Everything she thinks appears upon it. The more I tried to explain what her duties could consist of, the less she comprehends. She's been sheltered, like a nun."

Understanding Rose's meaning, Lady Elaina let a few more passes of the shuttle go before she attempted any reply. "'Tis unlikely any girl would be completely ignorant, Rose. Even if she was not taught a great many things, she has been given good eyes to see around her."

Forced to be blunt, Rose replied. "Yes, but it will come to her as a great shock when Gordie takes her to his bed this night."

Lady Elaina's bent head came up straight at that bald statement made by her forward-speaking daughter. Her voice was sharp in reply. "Do you think your brother not man enough to realize that? You are much too bold, Rose Marie."

"Mama, Cara's a little treasure, so sweet and utterly lacking guile, and terrified of the way things happen so fast and quick here. I have not once heard her laugh, nor seen a true smile on her solemn little face. I truly think she is afraid of every one of us."

"Nonsense. You judge her by your own measure. Not every lass is as bold as you."

"Then you won't speak to Poppa?"

Shocked that Rose would ask such a thing, Lady Elaina's face turned fierce. "It is not my place, nor is it yours. Remember that and henceforth keep your tongue silent. Cara is in your father's keeping, and after tonight, she will be Gordie's charge. You will not interfere. You'll mix up trouble for yourself if you do not learn now to still your tongue."

"I thought my quick tongue was what endeared me to everyone," Rose quipped lightly, turning aside her mother's scolding with easy banter. "And yes, Mama, I will take your advice to heart."

"And so I will yours." Lady Elaina resumed her weaving and Rose went on to other duties.

Chapter Fourteen

All of the Mckenna sisters crowded into Rose's chamber when it came time to dress for the wedding feast. They eagerly advised and assisted in transforming Cara into a beauty.

Becca contributed a net of fine silver thread to encase Cara's raven locks. Margie had a strand of pearls that crowned her forehead. Bonnie offered her most treasured pots, secret oils that made Cara's lips glow as if they were wet by rain and the palest of powders that enhanced the whiteness of her skin. Janie shared the finest shift in the house, a wonder of lace and silk that had been hidden away from all her sisters for her own trousseau. Rose provided the matching jeweled broaches that held Cara's gossamer mantle in place across her shoulders.

Lady Elaina and her sister, Claire, furnished the wedding gown and all the necessaries that went beneath it. The skirt was heavy satin, overlaid with panels of gold cloth. Full deep sleeves stood away from the exposed slope of Cara's shoulders. A stomacher in the latest style circled Cara's waist and bust. It was heavily beaded with seed pearls in a floral pattern.

The gown shimmered and rustled as if it were alive. Standing before Rose's cheval glass, Cara stared at the figure of the woman in the glass before her, speechless.

"Tell us, Cara, what do you think?" Margie giggled.

"I think I shall collapse from the weight of this," she answered, and stuck the toe of her slipper before her, peering at the dainty satin worked with fine beads. "Am I this tall?"

"You're that tall," Rose assured her.

"'Tis much too fine a dress for me. Why, it looks fit for a queen. Sir Almoy would have a fine chuckle if he could see me now."

"If he is truly a knight, he would praise your beauty. It suits you, Cara Mulvaine," Jane Mckenna said, smiling. Of the sisters she was the quietest.

"Ach, I wish he were here," Cara murmured wistfully.

"Wait, that is not all." Bonnie produced one more vial, this one a decoction imported from France. When she removed the crystal stopper, the whole room seemed to flood with the fragrance of flowers, roses. Cara flinched when the cool liquid was touched to her throat, at the definite cleavage of her bosom and dabbed to each of her wrists. "Now you're ready."

"You are so beautiful," Becca crooned.

"Aye, a delicate beauty," Rose said with a sigh.

"Gordie won't know what has hit him!" That was from Margie.

"You are going to strike him?"

"No, Cara, you are." Jane laughed.

"No, I promise you, I will not do that."

"Never mind." Rose took charge and shooed her sisters out of the chamber. "Now turn around and tell me what you think."

"I don't know what to think. It's not as comfortable as my other clothes. . . ."

There was a knock on the chamber door. Cara spun to face it and Rose opened it to greet her father.

The Mckenna filled the doorframe, a startling dark green-and-red tartan belted round his body. It turned to form the swath of folded color streaking across one of his shoulders. A fine velvet jerkin, jeweled and embroidered, fitted his chest. Beneath the jerkin, the snowy linen of his shirting showed through deliberate slits in his sleeves. Cockade and cap and gold hasped sporran completed his elegant wear. The broad belt circling his trim waist was studded with jewels. His claymore, with an ornate filigree hilt, gleamed with lovingly polished sheen. Cara had never seen a more splendid-looking man, ever.

"Poppa!" Exuberant Rose attacked him, swinging loving arms around his neck. The laird swung her off her feet and smacked a kiss on her blushing cheek.

"Look at you," the Mckenna roared, his voice a teasing scold. "And who be the pur mon you are out to torment, looking as sparkling pretty as the morning dew?"

"You glib-tongued fox! 'Tis the same gown I've worn ten times." Rose laughingly slapped his brawny arms.

"Wicked girl." The Mckenna patted his daughter's hip affectionately. "You're no the one to have all eyes upon her tonight. I've come to bring the Lady Cara down. Where is she now?"

"Poppa, do not tease. Cara doesn't understand us when we tease each other. Look at her. Is she not the prettiest lassie in the land?"

Embarrassed, Cara had frozen when the Mckenna entered. She didn't feel any better when his eyes settled upon her. Rose was so beautiful, she looked like a fairy queen grown to human size. It did not surprise Cara that the laird had not even seen her.

"My sweet lord," John Mckenna murmured reverently. "Lady Cara? I think my daughters beauties, but they do not hold a candle to your flame. I would be honored if you would allow me the pleasure of escorting you to my hall."

Unable to utter a word, Cara came forward. She did not know how to take this blustery man, but she liked him. Hesitantly she placed her hand within the crook of his arm. He took it more firmly, patting away her nerves and smiling gently at her. "You wouldn't turn coward, would you?"

"No. No, uh, oh, yes, I could."

John laughed gently. "Don't. You have met every person in my household and they are already under your spell. 'Twill no take long and Gordie will be at your feet, as well. I'll wager before the night is over, his vassal Ulrich will be issuing a challenge to marry you himself. They are both rascals and deserve the comeuppance they will get this evening. I must ask you one thing, Lady Cara."

"What is that, my lord?"

"No matter what protests my son makes this evening, you will no take it to heart nor hold anything the fool might say against him."

"I don't understand," said Cara softly.

The Mckenna reassuringly patted her hand where it lay on his arm. "I should have explained this before . . . now, there isn't the time. You see before you a wily old fox, determined that his young whelp of a son sees to all our futures. He swore before the hall to be handfasted to none other than the Mulvaine. I know well what the scamp was doing—challenging me. You have my word before the evening is done, Mckenna honor will be satisfied and you will be my son's wife. Will you trust me on that?"

This was the oddest thing about all the Mckennas. Each asked for Cara's trust, time and time again. A foreboding sense that what she'd been told was to happen wasn't going to go the way it had all been planned made her want to deny the Scottish laird what he asked. She hadn't the nerve to deny him now.

"Yes, my lord, I will trust you."

"You are not quite sure of that."

Cara shook her head. "No, but thus far you have not let any harm befall me, Lord Mckenna. I will trust you. It is only that Dunluce was never like this. 'Twas quiet there. Here it isn't."

The Mckenna laughed at her soft words. "Quiet. The time to worry at Kenna House is when it all goes quiet. Then there is trouble brewing. Come, 'tis time to meet your husband."

As they started from the room, Mimms rose to his feet and padded silently behind his mistress. Where Cara went, Mimms followed.

Cara faltered on the gallery stairs when she saw how many people were crowded into the laird's great hall.

All eyes turned and focused on Laird Mckenna. She felt their stares. Blinking away the sting of smoke from the many torches, Cara peered into the hall, seeing ladies in their fine clothing, beauties, young maids and the incredibly wondrous assortment of men gathered about the massive room.

There were so many men! Elders like the laird whose heads of hair were the color of flame. More than double that had sunshine curls, flaxen hair the color of Mckenna's daughters Jane and Margie. She could not begin to guess which of them was Mckenna's son. A few she knew from the voyage and her short stay within the house, but it was impossible to sort one from another.

The plaids were of every weave imaginable. Some men wore hose and garters in the style of the English with flowing capes and jaunty feathers in their caps.

All along the gallery, children squeezed in between musicians and servants, the chatter of curious voices droning out the hum below.

The whole length of Laird Mckenna's hall was spread with long tables burdened with silver and gold plate and wondrous foods of every sort. The laird's family clustered upon the raised dais. Every daughter save Rose crowded round their smiling mother.

A silent hush fell over the hall. Laird Mckenna stepped off the last riser. The hall was standing, formally, facing their lord. One after another, the ladies dipped to the floor in deep abeyance, lowering their heads as Laird Mckenna swept Cara past. Men doffed their caps to the floor and bowed to the waist.

Here, Cara's mind completely faltered and she knew not what she was supposed to do. The laird's daughters curtsied to their father. Even Lady Elaina dropped deeply to her knee before her husband. Only one person in the hall did not bend his knee, remaining rigidly erect, staring at Laird Mckenna and Cara as they stopped before the dais.

"Good eve, wife," the Mckenna's voice boomed in the silence, startling Cara. He shifted his grip on her hand, raising her fingers from the crook of his arm to hold her hand aloft between them. "Good eve, friends and kinsmen, one and all. I present to you Lady Cara of the clan Mulvaine, sole surviving daughter of Lady Leah Mac Donnell and Laird Brodie Mulvaine. Remember you all the words of my son and heir, Gordon, that he would take Cara Mulvaine, none other, as his handfasted bride and wife. I give you the wife of the next laird of the clan Mckenna."

By the gentlest of pressure did the man convey to Cara that now was the time for her to make her abeyance. Wishing she had better practice at the skill Lady Elaina had just displayed so gracefully, Cara dropped slowly to her knee and bowed as low as she could go. All the while the laird's hand gripped her own, firm and secure. It was he who brought her back to her feet.

The hall vibrated with resounding applause and a swelling shriek like no other sound Cara had ever heard in her life. Or had she?

Beneath the awesome, unified cry, Mckenna coached her. "'Tis only the clan battle cry. A good sign to come so spontaneously." The Mckenna's eyes glittered with a sheen she had not seen before. "Remember, you promised to trust me completely."

"Aye, m'lord." Cara held her chin up firmly.

"Cara, darling." Lady Elaina took her in her arms and welcomed her with kisses to both her cheeks. From that greeting, Cara was turned to face Gordon Mckenna.

The deep-throated growl at her side warned Cara to look quick and hard. She raised her eyes to the tall auburn-haired man standing stiffly before her. His handsome face was completely healed. The wild beard and long hair had been sheared to trim order. Yet Cara would never ever have forgotten those dark, blue-black eyes. Laird McKenna's son and heir was the man of the cave. Her heart stopped dead within her.

"Lady Cara." Young Mckenna took her hand from his mother and Mimms' low growl turned vicious. Teeth snapped, but before they struck the bare skin of his knee, Cara's hand slapped across Mimms' nose. "No! Heel, Mimms!"

The controlling slap happened quick, but by the time Cara straightened and Mimms dropped obediently to the floor, six claymores pointed their deadly double-edged blades at the dog's head.

Loyal clansmen flanked the laird's heir, protecting him, prepared instantly to end any threat against him.

Frozen in fright, Cara swallowed convulsively. She couldn't hide the tremble that racked her as Gordon Mckenna slowly sheathed his dirk.

"A wise decision, Lady Cara," Gordon Mckenna said more evenly that he felt. He was stunned beyond belief at his father's gall. Clenching his teeth to hold his anger in check, he glared at the woman presented to him. "A better decision would have been to order your animal outside. Odo, remove the dog."

Mimms would not have gone peaceably with any of the Scots at that moment and Cara well knew it. "My lord," she blurted, "before your kinsman is bitten, allow me."

Cara snapped her fingers and evicted Mimms with one sharp command. How she wanted to escape with him! It was easier to watch her noble dog trot through the assemblage than to redirect her eyes to Gordie Mckenna. She wouldn't have looked back at him at all were it not for the fact that he still held her right hand firmly in his own grip. The tug that commanded her gaze back to his nearly pulled her up against his chest.

"Your looks have improved with the passage of time, Mulvaine." Gordie's teeth ground against the words he spoke. He knew what was expected of him, and the anger that caused simmered like a boiling cauldron in his belly. "I never thought to set eyes upon you again."

What was she to say to that? Cara flushed. "Nor I, you, m'lord."

"Aye, well, I can see my father's hand in this. You know the terms?"

"Terms?"

"That by holding hands, thus, before the assembly of my clan we become man and wife. Those are the terms."

"Aye, I was told we would be married this night."

"No. Not married, handfasted. Our customs differ in the highlands. We become man and wife, partners in all. You to my side will be, to my bed, to my hearth, to my needs. For six weeks' time. After that, 'tis the Mckenna's right to cast you off, mine to refuse you. There will be no church vows spoken until the trial is completed."

Cara tried to clear her stinging eyes and swimming head. She didn't want this at all. Hot color flooded her face. They stood on the raised dais, before all his assembled people. His hand gripped hers in a clench so fierce, she could not withdraw it. Did she have a choice? She didn't know.

"Do you so swear, Cara Mulvaine, under the ancient law and traditions of the clan Mckenna?"

She wanted to shout—no, scream it—in his face and rip her hand from his fierce grip. The cold fire blazing from his eyes frightened her wits from her. Not even the demon that had almost claimed his soul had frightened her more.

"Do you, Mulvaine?"

Cara shut her eyes. The pressure on her hand was unbearable. Either answer she might give would harm her.

"Your answer, yea or nay!"

Cara opened her eyes. She saw Laird Mckenna hovering behind the young lord. His wife and the sisters, all so eager and hopeful. Trust me, the laird had implored her. She could trust John Mckenna, but the survivor? Nay, she couldn't.

Then the most curious vision swam through Càra's mind. She saw the hall in a plainer occasion. Many of the same Kenna faces crowded round the single trestle. Father and son were fighting, shouting, arguing. The words of the scene were lost to her in the confusion of the hall.

The hush had ended. Voices whispered.

Gordie stirred in the restless shifting of the crowd of on-lookers. He wanted to roar a curse and turn to the first man that opened his mouth and slam his fist right through him. He wanted to spin round and wrap his fingers in the soft flesh beneath his father's arrogant chin.

The Mckenna had done the impossible!

The proof of his father's indomitable will trembled before Gordie's eyes. He knew without having to ask the ransom demanded had been paid and now the bride refused the pledge. He'd no ask again.

Cara's eyes widened. The survivor's skin flushed with high color. Were it possible, his eyes darkened more. Yet his facial expression remained utterly devoid of any telling emotion except that of the highest and most arrogant pride.

Pride! Cara made the connection between vision and reality. Did she deny the pledge, both laird and son lost stature before this assembly. So quick was the thought, Cara blurted out, "Yes, I pledge my hand to yours."

It was the wrong answer. She knew that immediately by the dark shuttering of his eyes. They went from deepest blue to tempest black.

"'Tis done." Clenching her hand in his, Gordie jerked his fist high so that all within the hall might see. "I take Cara Mulvaine as my wife. Be there any kinsman here that deny my right to make this claim?"

"Nay!" The men thundered in one voice.

"Be there any who denies hearing the Mulvaine swear her hand to mine?"

Again the thundering nay resounded and the swelling, shrill sound of clan Mckenna roaring into battle split the air. It was a sound like none other heard on earth. A battle cry of triumph, a sound so chilling, it would frighten the life out of anyone who was not Kenna born and bred.

Reeling from the shrieking cry, Cara stepped back a pace. As if her hand were hot coals, the young Mckenna dropped it, gave his back to her and strode out of the hall.

Cara's eyes unfocused and her unburned hand went to her throbbing temple. She'd have crumpled to the stone floor if not for John Mckenna's swift step to her side.

Sweeping the fainted bride into his arms, Laird Mckenna strode from the hall. He marched straight to his son's quarters and laid her unconscious form upon Gordie's bed for Lady Elaina to revive.

"Why on earth did she faint?" Elaina asked. "She's a strong lassie, not given to vapors."

"There is more to this than meets the eye, wife," the Mckenna decreed. "'Tis done, before witnesses, clansmen all. Loosen her stays and put a servant to watching over her, madame. I go to our guests. Our son married this night. That is all that matters. Leave her here and return to the hall forthwith. It will be up to them to sort out their pledge. Six weeks from this day, the church vows follow. Dinna fash yourself that else will come of this."

Mimms had joined the procession to Gordie's quarters. The moment the Mckenna left, Mimms leaped up beside his mistress, nuzzling Cara's pale face. At which affront, Lady Elaina ordered the dog put outside and chained.

For the minutes that followed, Elaina Mckenna thought she crossed the boundary into purgatory. The girl awoke and wailed. The dog howled. No sense could be made of either.

"'Tis him! 'Tis him!" Cara Mulvaine cried in terror. "I'll no marry him! Nay, I won't! Let me go! I'll go back to Dunluce, aye, I will!"

"Now, now, child." Elaina tried to soothe the young woman. Nothing the Mulvaine said made any sense. Nor did any of Elaina's entreaties bring Cara back to rational thought. She refused to return to the hall. Refused to remain in Gordie's chambers.

Lady Elaina forced herself to be blunt. "You have sworn to be my son's wife, Lady Cara. This is the only room within the castle where you may rest from this day forward. If the bed is not to your liking then you will have to request another from your husband. 'Tis as simple as that in all matters that concern you. Do you understand?"

"No, I don't!"

"From the moment Gordie raised your hand, you became his. Whatever you want, need or desire must come from Gordon Mckenna. Do you not ask him for the water you wish to drink, you may not be given it by any other. That is the bargain you have struck, the custom of the Mckenna clan."

"I canna do that," Cara whispered.

"Yes, you can. I did it and I have never regretted the day I pledged myself to John Mckenna."

Cara wanted to say that Gordie Mckenna was not the laird, not by any stretch of the imagination. She held her tongue; most of her reason had returned. It was the shock that had upset her. Aye, a shock it was, too. The survivor hated her.

"The feast will go on far into the night. Will you come and meet our kin and friends? Join the singing and the dancing and make this night one you will remember all the days of your life?"

"Madame, I shall never forget it," Cara said with deep foreboding.

"Then I leave you to the bed you've made."

Lady Elaina departed, leaving a sullen maid sitting just within the door. Cara turned to the open windows and sank to the floor, resting her brow upon the cool stone. She closed her eyes, swirling amid the terrible confusion. Why had this happened to her? Why?

Laying her brow on the cool sill, she could not discover a reason for God having played such a trick upon her. How she had hoped for a new life, away from that she had left behind. A place where no one called her a witch or knew one scrap of her history. It was not to be.

Looking out to the stars, Cara shook her head and whispered, "Ah, Almoy, what is to become of me?"

The magic of Kenna's peaceful home was as elusive as Sir Almoy's magic spells. Cara heard the young lord's threats to his sister repeat themselves in her ears. No refuge for her in Scotland. She remembered his unreasonable temper at Dunluce and had a strong glimpse of it here at Castle Kenna this very afternoon. Had she tied herself to a man who would beat her just as mercilessly as her grandfather had?

Another flush of shame swept over Cara. She wished herself across the Irish Sea, wished that the night had never come that she had seen a ship laboring on the shore by Dunluce Castle, and wished to God, Laird Mckenna had never asked her to trust him.

Chapter Fifteen

Though he knew better, Ulrich could not stop himself from perversely goading his furious cousin. "I told you so."

No sooner had Ulrich said those four words than Gordie's fist had him sprawling backward into the dirt.

"What the hell did you hit me for?" Ulrich roared.

"I've got to hit somebody," Gordie declared.

Sitting, Ulrich fingered his jaw, wincing. He waggled the joint back and forth then stood to his feet. "Damn yer black heart! Broken toe or no, take this, cousin!"

Ulrich kicked Gordie's feet right out from under him. "Ha!" Ulrich spat out, satisfied. "I wondered what you wore underneath that kilt that made you tougher than any other mon around!"

"Not a damn thing more than you." Gordie came up swinging from a most undignified pratfall that sent him rolling kilt over trews.

Ulrich met him halfway. Blows rained hard and serious between the combatants. Ulrich was good, but Gordie was better. They came apart, crouched low, circling one another, poised for the next onslaught.

"Why are we fighting, cousin?" Ulrich asked. "Is it your wish to die on your wedding night and see me hung on the morrow for killing the laird's son?"

"That will be the day." Gordie lunged forward. Ulrich sidestepped him. "Would that my father would come out of his hall and face me man to man. Instead he sends his lackey to try my temper!"

"I resent that!" Ulrich fought more coldly, more calculatedly, waiting for his opening, dodging and deflecting Gordie's strong fists as best he could. An undercut to his belly sent the air whooshing out of his lungs and sprawled him on his arse, kilt and legs flying just as Gordie had done. "Now *that* I really resent!"

Ulrich bolted upright, his fists planted on the wide leather belt that circled his hips. It should have protected him from the worst of the blow. It hadn't.

"You know what, cousin? I resent it, too!" Gordie planted his feet apart and stripped off his fine doublet and lawn shirt, casting both aside. "Come on then. You came out here to prattle me back within the hall. Come, kinsman. Make Gordon Mckenna do what he will not."

"The hell you say." Ulrich stiffened in outrage. "Ya damned fool, I came to offer my congratulations. No one else dares be the first."

Without further words, Ulrich stripped off his own tunic and threw his saffron-hued shirt upon the ground. Readjusting his wide belt to protect his stomach, he crouched in a fighting stance again. Circling Gordie, Ulrich took the offense, landing a solid jab in Gordie's jaw, staggering him.

"Then what are we fighting for?" Gordie asked, and punched right back, rapid blows, in one, two, three combinations that put Ulrich in the dirt again.

Wiping blood from his chin, Ulrich snapped. "Because, you dolt, you've got it in your head to murder someone, and I'm the pur bastard who stupidly walked into your fists."

Gordie put out his hand and raised his downed cousin to his feet. "You knew what you were doing when you shot yer mouth off."

"A mistake." Ulrich's fist sunk low in Gordie's belly.

"Mind where you hit me, curse you! I'm a married man this night!"

"Ach, forgive me." Ulrich let another fly.

"Rot!" Gordie groaned. "Let's stop." He dropped Ulrich a third time with an undercut to his chin.

"I've had enough." Ulrich stayed down, sprawled in the dirt, gingerly rubbing his battered jaw. "Where's a wench with some ale?"

"To the hall." Gordie dropped to the earth beside his kinsman and glared at the house. It was lit up like Twelfth Night. Music and merriment came from every portal.

"We are missing a feast of tremendous proportions."

"You can eat after the poison we were served today?"

"I can always eat."

Gordie picked up a stone and heaved it across the bailey wall, venting his frustration.

"Still angry?"

"Damn his eyes! He wasn't supposed to arrange this."

This time Ulrich kept his "I told you so" to himself. One beating was enough. Gordie swung his head and glared at him.

"Me thoughts are me own, Mckenna!" Ulrich warned.

"Not when I can hear them loud as church bells!"

"'Tis no my thoughts you are hearing, but your own. If the chit is so distasteful to you, why the devil did you ask for her?"

"I didn't ask for her. I gave my father an impossible quest."

"You misjudged the man."

"Aye, I can see that clearly."

"Tell me this. You ask for a woman you do not want. Then why do you accept her? Why did you force her to accept you?"

Gordie's sharp eyes turned on his cousin. So Ulrich had sense enough to notice how reluctantly the Mulvaine had responded to the vow, had he? If that lackwit had, then others might have noted the maid's hesitation, too. That stung his pride anew.

"What else could I do? Let her run screaming from the hall of the Mckennas? I'd no have the shame of that."

"So now what?"

"How the bloody hell should I know?"

"Do you ken that she fainted on the spot?"

"So what did you do? Rush to her aid, gallant knight?"

"Nay, 'twas your father who caught her and took her to your rooms."

"To my rooms!"

"Where else would a handfasted bride be laid except upon her husband's bed? How daft are you?"

Gordie turned his head to regard the west quadrant of the castle. His tower windows also glowed with light. He saw no movement, no shadows or figures wandering from room to room.

"She's got this wolf that slavers for my blood."

"So I noticed."

"I will have to kill it."

"A sure way to the lady's heart."

"A better solution than finding myself lying on the flagstones with my throat torn out."

"You could make friends with it."

"Humph!"

"What will you do, Gordie?"

"Renounce her at the end of the trial."

"What if she breeds well?"

"Then I have the heir my father demands. I dinna have to keep the woman."

"Aye, but a woman sent from your house in six weeks is no likely to hand over her infant willingly."

"Why do you hound me with details?"

"I don't know. 'Tis your problem, not mine." Ulrich rubbed his tender jaw then wiped the blood from his mouth and heaved his large body to his feet. He extended his hand to Gordie and assisted him to his feet. "You could give her the comfort of your bed and not touch her."

"I have already thought of that. By leaping out my window no one will be none the wiser. I'll sleep in the stables."

"Provided when you jump you land on your hard head, you mean," Ulrich taunted.

"Shut up, you fool. My foot is killing me. Give me your shoulder and let's go up to the hall and quench our thirst."

Returning unshirted, they both received killing looks from Lady Elaina, but admiring appraisals from the rest of the ladies. The Mckenna's stony expression should have dropped them both in their tracks. Ulrich was daunted by it. Not Gordie.

"I think I'll retrieve my shirt."

"Not I," Gordie said, and swaggered forward. "I've a wench to fetch it tomorrow, have I not?"

"Mind your temper, Gordie lad," Ulrich advised under his breath. "As I recall, the Mckenna's fists feel like a twelve-pound cannonade each time they land a blow."

"'Tis long overdue if he wants a battle." Gordie walked unstintingly across the hall and dropped to his seat beside his father's chair without further ado. Ulrich, who had reclaimed his shirt, pulled the laces to his jerkin before doing the same. His flanks had no sooner touched wood than Rose leaned over her smitten Ralphie and cooed.

"Been at it again like little boys, cousin?"

That one, Ulrich thought, needed her backside blistered. Lippy, Lord Almighty! He accepted a tankard of ale from a serving wench before turning to his cousin's beau and forming any reply.

"Stewart, do you know what kind of hell on earth a red-haired woman can make of your life?"

The blond youth between him and fiery-haired Rose choked on his ale.

"Bastard," Rose hissed, and launched herself upon Ulrich with her claws unsheathed.

She received, instead, a restraining hand from Ralph without his so much as even lowering the tankard of ale from his lips. Rose quieted immediately. Ulrich sat back, chuckling as he sipped his brew and thought to himself that perhaps there was hope for the lovesick pup, but he doubted it.

Gordie drank two tankards of whiskey-laced ale in stony silence, then slammed the drained tankard on the table. He stood with his hands on his hips, his feet planted squarely apart. He looked right, then left, sweeping his caustic gaze across every person within the hall, not finding the dark-haired woman anywhere in the sea of reds, browns and blondes. Abruptly, without a word, he stalked out of the hall.

Oh, brother, Ulrich thought, *here it comes.* He decided to eat while he could, knowing when Gordie came back, the Mulvaine a trophy slung across his shoulder—that the serious fighting would begin.

Chapter Sixteen

Dear Lord, whatever shall I do? That seemed to be the only coherent thought in Cara's brain after Lady Elaina returned to the feast. Cara moved by rote, knowing what she had to do could not be done in the strange garments she wore.

While the sullen maid stared at her, Cara began removing the fancy dress, sleeves first. She had to twist awkwardly to reach the ties of the stomacher. The stiffened brocade fell away, freeing her breasts, her ribs and her stomach, enabling her to take a deep and calming breath.

Megan came reluctantly to her feet, picking up the cloth of gold sleeves Cara had removed. The stiff fabric crackled in her roughened hands, but she touched it covetously, wishing it were hers to keep. "What do you, mistress?"

"I'm removing these clothes," Cara said simply.

Clothes the Irish didn't deserve to wear, Megan amended silently. She made no offer to assist, but merely watched as Cara pulled her hair to remove the veil and twisted knot of pearls that crowned her head. She tugged lose the ties on the farthingale and the heavy petticoats and stepped free of everything save her shift.

Cara's small trunk, which contained all the clothing she had in the world, had been moved to the young laird's quarters. Cara praised the providence of that as she opened it and removed a gown.

The maid bustled about, gathering up the many pieces of fine clothing Cara had shed, shaking wrinkles out before they could set in place.

"'Tis no finer gown in the whole world, mistress," the maid said plainly.

Cara raised her head and looked at the woman, but truly did not see her for the turmoil swimming in her thoughts. "Aye, so it is."

Cara knew the dress was the grandest she had ever worn, but she didn't want it. She ignored the blowsy servant as she dressed, unaided, in her own plain wool. Across her shoulders she fastened a mantle of fine embroidered Irish linen. It was the only treasured garment Cara had owned, and had once been her mother's. Inside there were stains where the linen had yellowed over time, but outside it was lovely, sun bleached and soft. The blue of her soft wool undergown contrasted well with the pale ivory linen.

Cara drew the mantle's crisscross laces tight down each of her sides. It was far out of date from the fancy gown Lady Elaina had insisted she be presented to her husband in. Cara smoothed the fitted sleeves at her wrists. Kicking aside the dainty leather slippers, she fastened soft kidskin boots upon her feet. The only other thing she took from her trunk was a soft leather girdle that held a small scabbard and her dirk. She was certain that she would need the knife on the long trek home. All she needed now was to find Mimms and her journey could begin.

"Where do you go, mistress?" Megan's eyes narrowed suspiciously as she asked her question.

"Dunluce," Cara answered.

Megan's eyes widened. The skinny Irish girl was obviously a fool. But then, Megan had seen the look of contempt on Gordie's face when he'd raised her hand aloft and declared the Mulvaine handfasted to him.

It was a forced match that wouldn't last a week, much less the six the laird declared. So there was no reason for Megan to do anything to stop the girl if she wanted to leave. That suited Megan fine. She had no intention of giving up her place in Gordie's bed. She watched the girl leave and held back a shout of triumph once she'd gone.

Then Megan turned and looked at the bed where she'd spent many a night keeping Gordie Mckenna satisfied and content. Her hatred festered and burned deeply for the woman who thought to take her place in that high bed. So the Irish thought nothing of the fine gift she'd been given. . . . Well, then, Megan would be happy to see that Gordie learned firsthand what value the Irish bitch gave to his possessions. The delicate cloth of gold Megan held in her hands, ripped in two.

Before returning to the hall, Megan looked in on her sleeping son. His angelic face reaffirmed Megan's place in Gordie's life. Eric slept, swaddled securely in his cradle. His rosy cheeks glowed bright. She smoothed her hand across his dark auburn hair, patted his bottom and felt the swell of possessive love fill her. All was right. Megan returned to her duties in the hall, her anxiety gone.

The girl had sworn false. The marriage was off. Megan's place as Gordie's mistress was secure.

Mimms barked only once as Cara unfastened the chain at his collar then walked straight through the portcullis gate. Cara would have liked to take a horse, but she had had no opportunity to get to know any of the Mckenna's animals. She would only ride one that she understood.

It was a boon that no soldiers were at the gate. Everyone had gone to the feast. It was the same in the village seated on the hillside below the castle. All were to the castle, even the stern minister who lived next to the kirk. The Kennas were Protestant, but that didn't matter a great deal to Cara. She had heard no more lectures on the perfidy of the reformation since her grandfather's death.

The road wound out of the village and into the hills. Cara had traversed it only once, on the journey to Mount Kenna. There would be Ben Nevis and other mountains to be climbed and circumvented. She knew it would take her days to walk across Scotland. She had traveled just a little ways down from the village, into a small woods, when she came to a brook intersecting the twisting road. No bridge crossed it. The water ran fast and deep.

That did not stop Mimms. He rushed ahead, lapping to quench his thirst then barked at a rabbit downstream and splashed after it. Cara did not call him back. He always returned when the chase ended.

She stood at the very edge of the water at an impasse. It was no river, but to cross it she would have to wade water no less than waist high.

It was bad enough that she had brought no cloak to protect her. Had she been home in Dunluce she would never have left her tower without her cloak's sure protection against the elements. Now she would be wet, too. That wouldn't do. Had she taken a horse, she wouldn't be stranded.

"I should have," she said aloud.

"Should have what?" a deep voice asked.

It was a sign of how distracted her thinking was, because instead of wondering who had spoken, Cara merely answered the question. "Stolen a horse."

"Why should you want to steal a horse?"

"To cross the mountains, as well."

"Where would that take you?"

"To Dunluce." Cara sighed, then she turned round to find out who the questioner was, fairly certain whom she would be facing. The survivor. Now he had a name.

Gordie Mckenna sat on a fallen tree trunk. It was back from the brook's edge by several feet. He scowled darkly at her. "You canna get to Dunluce on foot or on a horse."

"I know that."

Cara's fingers tightened in the linen at her sides. She cocked her head to the side and studied his kilted form. He wore leggings, as well as boots that protected his feet. His chest was bare, his arms exposed. He had the look of a man who had been in a brawl.

As was her way when confronted by someone stronger than she, Cara stood very rigid. She did not question how or why he was there.

"Your wolf deserted you."

"He will come back."

"And do you? Or do you leave Castle Kenna?"

"So, I have done."

Gordie's chin angled higher. What a confusing muddle she posed. "And you, of course, are ever intent upon following your own counsel."

"I have none other to guide me."

"You canna leave Kenna. Would you recant your pledge?" Cara swung her gaze to the sparkling water. Over the rocks, it splashed and raised a mist. She could see that if she went carefully, she could cross to the other side. She sighed and returned her attention to him.

"'Twas not my will to meet with you again, my lord."

"Nor mine," Gordie answered quick enough.

"Then how have we come to this?" Cara's confusion showed on her face in a twist of her brow and tight grimace about her mouth. "'Twas no my doing, my lord. I dinna know your name, nor your clan. I left it so."

Gordie thought, *because of my big mouth.* But he said, "You asked to be ransomed, did you not?"

Had she? Cara couldn't remember. She thought back to the trying time when he had been ensconced in Dunluce Castle. She had said a lot of things. She looked at the survivor in a new light, her eyes slowly widening with surprise.

"Was I?" Cara asked him.

That question exasperated Gordie. He hadn't the foggiest idea what his father had done. Nor did he want to own up to her his part in the matter. He'd asked for the match, but he couldn't put his finger on any specific reason why.

"Does it signify? Is your pride bound up in the matter of coin?"

Not exactly following his evasive response, Cara shook her head. "Nay, my pride is not offended. I only wish to know the truth."

The truth Gordie could not give her. He hadn't sorted it out for himself. "Then you have no objection to returning with me."

"It appears that my choices are few."

"Aye, you could have refused the pledge."

"And shamed Laird Mckenna? No, I think not."

"You said yes to spare my father? What of my pride, woman?"

Cara sensed a towering argument there and skirted round it. "It would have been no insult to you, my lord. The choice to refuse the match was equal, was it not?"

Cara's answer was so simplistic, Gordie's head cocked to the side; then he leaned back and laughed at the sheer irony of it all. He was hoisted on his own petard, did she but know it. She did not. She hadn't heard his oath of a month ago, his taunts that had brought this night upon him. *Woe unto him who tried to foil Laird Mckenna,* he thought.

"Aye." He finally spoke with laughter still in his tones. "But we both made our choice public. You can forget going back to Ireland. 'Tis a Scot you've chosen and in Scotland you'll remain."

So far, Scotland had been better than Ireland in recent times. Still Cara wavered at the edge of the brook, casting a longing glance at the stepping stones.

"Well, do you walk beside me willingly or do I toss you onto my shoulder?"

That question demanded an answer.

"I do not like to be touched," Cara said in her firmest voice, glad the moon had not risen and he could not see the color rising in her face.

Gordie quirked his head again. "Is that a challenge?"

"Nay, m'lord. I thought it best I tell you straight off so there be no mistake in the future as there was in the past."

"Come, then. Walk beside me."

"Very well." Cara nodded agreement and approached the stump where he sat. As he rose to his feet, Cara's eyes riveted to the thick stick he used to balance himself.

"What is it, Lady Cara? Now you fear me, but when I was seated, you did not."

Cara stayed her retreat, making every effort to control the urge to flinch. "I don't fear you."

"Good." Gordie saw that her eyes darted to his right hand, where he gripped the staff that steadied him. "I have not much use for chasing you farther, this night."

"You have hurt yourself." Cara astutely deducted.

"Broke my toe. 'Tis a small injury, more troublesome than serious. At the moment, it annoys me greatly."

"You were following me?"

The moon slid out from behind a cloud and bathed her upturned face in a glow of soft light. So serious, Gordie thought. Not a ghost of a smile shadowed her features.

"I was. Thankfully, you reached a natural barrier."

Cara swallowed the knot of fear clutching her throat. Her brow pleated lightly. "I dinna hear you following me."

"Your dog would make a good braying ass."

"Aye, he's a noisy creature and does not know how to go anywhere quietly."

"Come." Gordie waved his hand for her to step ahead of him. Cara watched him limp awkwardly, leaning heavily on the staff. A wash of relief flooded her as she realized the stick had a true purpose and wasn't intended to cudgel her.

"'Tis a short walk back to the castle. You can use my shoulder if that will help you."

"Ah, still generous to a fault, you are." Gordie slipped his arm across her shoulder and tossed the stick into the trees. They walked in silence through the village, where Mimms bounded out of the woods.

Gordie warily watched the dog approach. It sniffed at him, barked several objections before quieting at his mistress's signal. The animal fell into step beside Cara. Gordie kept an eye on it. In truth, alone he could probably tolerate the dog, but Mimms' single-minded devotion to his mistress posed no man good. Least of all, him.

Cara regarded the cottages clustered round the kirk. Their yards were neat as pins with bright flowers planted round the foundations. "The village looks prosperous," she said because she couldn't think of anything else to say.

"The life here is good," Gordie responded. "It shows in the way the people care for their homes. I have never properly thanked you for saving my life, have I?"

"I did not save you. God spared you. Mimms did the rest."

"Would you have me believe the dog also brought food, medicines, clothing to me?"

"No."

It was puzzling that she would not say more. Gordie deliberately limped more. Cara slipped her arm about his waist to help support him. Her palm against his side was cool to the touch. Gordie looked at her. A fleeting glance was all she gave him, but it was enough for him to sense her interest. She was shy of him, but not immune.

At the portcullis, Cara thought he could walk unassisted to the hall.

"No." Gordie clasped her hand as she began to withdraw. "I prefer you hold me so."

"'Tis unseemly to do so when we enter your father's hall."

"Yes, as I enter my father's hall." Gordie's grip remained firm.

"I am not going there."

"Aye, you are, Mulvaine."

"Nay, I am not dressed enough."

"You are dressed more than enough."

"But..."

"Come." Gordie purposefully drew Cara inside where the celebration continued with lively music, energetic dancing, laughter and talk. Poorly gowned in simple wool and linen, Cara balked at the archway. Too much splendor glittered in her eyes.

Determined, Gordie kept his pace and his grip, moving the young woman forward until they stood below the glow of the massive iron-and-glass chandelier. The Mckenna's guests moved warily back, yielding him room.

Gordon Mckenna stood perfectly straight and tall. He tightened his grip upon Cara, pressing her slender body firmly against his naked chest. He did that deliberately, to keep her from withdrawing from his embrace.

The laird of the Mckennas turned from his conversation. Both Mckennas formed a frozen tableau, each glaring at the other. Then the elder raised his chased goblet in a toast to the couple before him. The young lord nodded, accepting his due.

The wedding guests held their breath while this silent show played out. Then to their utter amazement and delight, Gordie Mckenna turned the woman in his arms and kissed her before one and all.

Cara hadn't an inkling of what Gordon Mckenna plotted. She sensed the pull of wills between him and his father, an ongoing battle she'd seen glimpses of through her gift of second sight. But now she was feeling the full force of the contest between both strong-willed, dominant men. She had never felt the like. No one had ever stood and openly defied her grandfather. Sorely Mac Donnell had ruled Dunluce and all within it with a heavy hand.

Before she could puzzle out the significance of that, Gordon's warm hands moved on her body.

Embraced, held fast against him, his lips slashed across her own and stayed there for an eternity. His fingers dug deep in the loose drape of hair that fell to her knees.

She didn't know anything after that, except that he gripped her firmly and then started spinning her wildly to the beat of the drum and the trill of the pipes and the deafening shouts of his clan.

Ulrich had watched the doors since his cousin departed. He'd expected Gordie back in minutes with the Mulvaine slung on his shoulder like a hunting trophy. The longer he was gone, the more anxiously Ulrich had watched the door. But the show he'd just witnessed was better than the one he'd imagined. Gordie spun the young lass, and her hair flashed like a silk pennant in her wake.

"I'll be damned," Ulrich muttered, and pushed away his platter of food. He stood, gave a nod to his uncle, the laird, another to his father, and went in search of a damsel of his own.

Chapter Seventeen

Until she'd come to Castle Kenna, Cara had never danced. Rose and her sisters had taken much time to teach Cara steps. She learned them, enjoyed the learning, too. But practicing such with five happy girls was not the same as moving in precision with a man. When she faltered, the giant gripped her and swung her aloft. Her feet hardly touched the floor until she miraculously found herself back upon the dais, seated on a backless stool placed between the tall chairs of the Mckennas.

"That was well-done." John Mckenna beamed approvingly. Whether his words were for her dancing or his son's, Cara wasn't certain. The mad, shirtless and sweaty man shouted for ale and meat and was rushed by a hoard of servants doing his bidding.

The food and drink waited while a bevy of ladies surrounded Gordie. They laughed, kissed him fondly, wound slender white arms around his shoulders and poutingly declared their adoration to him. Names failed to register on Cara when each, in turn, spoke to her. She was certain she would remember their faces.

One was most insistent, coy and enticing in her manner. Abruptly Gordie took that lady by the hand and joined the dancing. A man leaned across Gordie's vacated chair and touched Cara's arm. "You will have to learn our dances."

He was not one of the Mckenna clansmen Cara had met. Blond hair curled damply round his handsome face and his smile contained a gentle, encouraging warmth. The hall must have been too hot for him, as well, for he was stripped down to his sleeveless jerkin and that was barely laced, showing his fine chest to good advantage.

"You are very shy, Lady Cara. I am Ulrich, Gordie's cousin. Would you dance with me?"

It wasn't possible for Cara's spine to stiffen any more. She shook her head a hasty no, unable to muster the word. Then Gordie flashed past in the surging crowd of dancers.

"You won't let Gordie overwhelm you, will you? I understand you are half-Scot, half-Irish. The Irish are a fierce, lusty lot themselves. 'Tis a good mix to have the blood of both."

"That is not the way it has been explained to me." Cara found her voice, determined not to be a mouse in the midst of lions.

"It would be my wager that you have the best of two worlds. Scot courage and Irish tenacity."

"I was very young when I left Scotland."

"Aye, we've all heard the story told a time or two. The Mulvaines' fortunes fared no better than the Mac Donnells', but you've no need to worry about your future with the Mckennas. We're a fierce, proud people and no mon will put us under in this lifetime."

That was the deduction Cara had come to in the short time that she had been among the Mckennas. They were proud, brave and strong. She saw Gordie dancing, his blond partner beaming with joy. Again that intense feeling of dislike washed over her. It hit with a force that turned her hands into clenched fists.

This whole day she'd been buffeted by one powerful emotion after another. Here was another she didn't like.

Mimms moved restlessly at her side and Cara absently dropped her hand to stroke the dog's head. She froze, remembering the feeling of Gordie's hand stroking her own head as he'd kissed her. Her face flooded with color. She looked up quickly to see if anyone was watching her blush crimson. In all the revelry, she was mostly forgotten.

Then she leaned down and told Mimms to go outside. He barked and wagged his tail.

"I say go," Cara repeated. Mimms trotted dutifully outside and Cara turned to Ulrich. "I would dance with you now, Sir Ulrich."

"Indeed." Ulrich smiled, liking the shy girl, especially now that she'd sent that animal out of the hall.

The music changed tempo to a march. It still required care where Cara placed her foot, but it was not the wild fling that Gordie had spun her through.

"You are quick to learn." Ulrich's compliment made her smile. His hand grazed her waist and her shoulder, guiding her in the passes and turns. She did not find that alarming, which was odd, because Gordie's touch made her senses leap with alarm.

"I am enjoying this dancing."

"Are you now?" Ulrich teased, and grinned charmingly. Cara couldn't help responding with an equally light smile. The dance took them full circuit till they came face-to-face with Gordie Mckenna, barring their path. Ulrich burst out laughing at his cousin's fierce scowl. He bowed gallantly to Cara, handing her over at once.

"Pray, what was Ulrich telling you that was so amusing?" Gordie demanded as he spun Cara in the opposite direction.

Cara's tension returned full force. Her stomach lurched. Her palms felt clammy and wet. "We were not speaking of anything. I liked the dancing, but I do not like it now."

"No?" Gordie inquired coolly, drawing her closer to him. He hadn't liked seeing her in Ulrich's embrace. "You prefer Ulrich's stumbling to my skill?"

Cara slanted a glance up at his face. Was he angry? She couldn't tell. "He didn't stumble."

"Then he allowed you to, which is an unforgivable offense." Gordie swept her off her feet and spun her round full circle. Cara quickly put her hands to his bare shoulders, holding on. The man was so unpredictable.

Her expression showed total surprise and Gordie reveled in it. He took the pleasure of lowering her very slowly against his chest. She was an easy woman to lift or carry. It was nigh onto a scandalous act to do so before every guest in his father's hall, but he didn't care. The shocked look on Cara Mulvaine's face made any criticism to come later worth it. Before she was settled on her feet, he had to kiss her again.

Cara couldn't think how she came to be so intimately embraced again. The feel of his strong arms around her was unbelievable. His fingers rippled down her cheek, softly, softly, lifting her jaw with gentle pressure; then his lips touched hers.

It bemused her, that soft yet fierce contact. His tongue probed slowly, from corner to corner, lingering longest on the deep fullness of her lower lip. Beneath her hands his bare skin radiated cool heat. She could have stayed in that embrace forever.

She rocked dazedly as Gordie set her aside. His large hand clasped hers as he strode purposefully back to their places at the table.

There was food to be eaten. A ceremony to be completed. Gordie exchanged a jibe at his cousin, flirting as he turned away two other maids who begged him to dance with them and teased his sister Rose unmercifully. Then all at once his attention returned to Cara.

"Hand me my ale, wench," he shouted to the rafters.

Cara jumped, startled. Her senses reeled from being kissed mindless, ignored afterward and shouted at next.

"You have only to put your great big arm out and it will be in your grasp!"

Why she said that, Cara didn't know. It had to be because he smiled at the prettier-than-her women. The words were no sooner out than she wanted to retract them. Beside her the Mckenna suddenly turned about. The men and ladies dancing by the dais stared at her.

"You will not hand me my ale?" Gordie asked.

Pour it on you, Cara thought. He deserved it! No, she would hand it to him. No, she would not give him anything! Oh, what is happening to me? Cara snapped out of her thoughts, grabbing his heavy jeweled goblet with both trembling hands, half turning to offer the drink to him. Her eyes blazed, but the fire fixed no higher than the foamy surface of the brew.

Instead of taking the heavy goblet from her, both of Gordie's hands covered hers, pulling her and the goblet forward until his lips were to the rim.

What was he doing? Drinking? He could drink without her assistance! And drink he did, tilting the cup, the liquid pouring down his throat. It was more than half-empty when he lowered it. Cara tried to wiggle her hands loose. He gripped them tighter.

"Now you will drink, wife."

"Not ale." Cara refused. Relentlessly, Gordie guided the cup forward till its rim was at her lips.

"Drink," Gordie tilted the strong-smelling brew to her mouth. It was drink or be drenched.

The ale was strong and bitter. Cara nearly choked, as her mouth filled with brew that must be swallowed. Only then did Gordie lower the goblet. When it was set upon the table, he released her hands.

"The Mckenna's ale will be safe from that one, Gordie. She's no taste for it." Ulrich laughed.

"Ah, but will she have a taste for the Mckenna?" another taunted.

"That is a flavor that grows on one," Gordie bantered right back. "Am I not right, Lady Cara?"

Reeling from the strong brew, Cara pressed a hand to her burning throat and shook her head. Everyone laughed even harder.

"Would you drink buttermilk then?" Gordie shouted.

Jumping with fright, Cara found her voice and croaked, "Unquestionably."

"Then by all means, you shall have it. Bring milk for my lady. Bring wine, bring a bucket of water, whatever she desires to quench her thirst!"

"Do you have to shout it to the rafters?" Cara hissed in embarrassment.

"Aye, I do."

Gordie chuckled from some joke Cara did not understand. He pulled the platter of meats forward, removed his blade from his belt and pared a joint of venison to the bone. Stabbing the first slice, he put it in his mouth. While he chewed thoughtfully, he stabbed another and held it before Cara.

"A taste of meat? Try it. 'Tis well seasoned."

Cara glared at him, fearing he was making sport of her. She was fastidious, having taken meals alone the majority of her life. She raised her hand to take the morsel from his knife.

"Do not touch it with other than your lips," Gordie corrected. "You must eat as I eat, drink from the same font as I, the same fork, the same knife. It is part of the bonding. We are together, one to the other. As I am nourished, so are you. The knife in my hand will defend you, protect you, feed you. You have no need for a blade of your own, nor to touch one so long as I live and breathe."

Hearing such a pledge astonished Cara. She opened her mouth and he put the meat within, without the cold metal ever touching her lips. A slow smile spread across Gordie's lips as he laid down the knife, then boldly leaned forward and kissed her lips.

As he sat back, he remarked, "You are very quick, Lady Cara."

Cara touched two fingers to her mouth and could not take her eyes from his handsome, bearded face. He looked so different from the way she remembered him, yet still the same—eyes, mouth and coloring. He was less hardened; his lean flesh had lost its hungry look. The tasty morsel lay on her tongue unmoved for the sensation of his lips burning against her own in a caress that drove all thought away.

Gordie Mckenna slowly smiled, the creases in his cheeks forming deep dimples as the curve widened. He clucked Cara's chin. "Eat, sweetling."

He found it difficult to take his eyes from her face. Two slender fingers splayed across a fullness that palpated. Everything was new to her. Her eyes shone with the wide surprise of a girl that had never been kissed, yet he had kissed her and remembered how she had asked guilelessly to be kissed again. He wondered if she'd allowed any other to taste her mouth. His fingers lingered on her cheek, cupping the soft curve as he stroked his thumb across the deep, lower curve of her mouth. The warm tumescence of her lips against the press of his thumb shot like an arrow aimed straight for his heart.

"Chew," he advised. "Do not swallow it whole. I would not have you choke this night."

God, he had to withdraw his hand! To inhale sharply to tamp down the wave of desire that shot threw him—desire he had not wanted nor anticipated. She was no raving beauty who made a man's heart race, yet his shaft sprang instantly to life.

His father came to his rescue as a slow march played upon the pipes. "I would dance with my new daughter, provided her husband allows me the pleasure."

"Go and dance with the Mckenna," Gordie answered fiercely, handing his wife into his father's care. That, too, was a tradition that must be followed for a Mckenna bride to become part of the clan. He needed the break to quiet his body, to get control of his thoughts. What the devil was he doing? He didn't want the chit, did he?

But he was having a damned hard time taking his eyes from her. In simple wool and linen garments, her slender body was all but revealed in form. Cara stood out from all the rest of the ladies present. That sheet of black hair moving so powerfully with the sway of her hips made the curls and sweeps of the ladies gaudy by comparison. She had gained a sensuality to his eyes, a thing he'd been blind to until now.

No, she wasn't a beautiful woman, but she was desirable, and that made all the difference in the world.

Gordie motioned for his goblet to be refilled. Megan was quick with a pitcher, displaying her voluptuous breasts as she leaned toward him. Gordie's eyes flashed to Megan's pert face, catching her inviting smile.

His brow furrowed. "Don't do that again, Megan."

The maid stiffened. Her eyes blinked in astonishment at his rebuke; then she dipped him a hasty curtsy, filled Ulrich's raised cup and rushed away from the table.

Ulrich raised his tankard in a salute to Gordie. "You have handled yourself well this night, Mckenna."

Gordie put his goblet to his mouth and swallowed a mouthful. As he wiped the back of his hand across his mustache he looked straight at Ulrich and remembered their halfhearted fight earlier that evening. "Not as well as I could have from the looks of your face."

"Ha," Ulrich chuckled. "What's a few blows between cousins? Though you might not care for my opinion, I approve of your choice. But mind you, the hour is late and the ale is strong and you're a bloody ox when you're in your cups. I can forgive you most anything save the injury to an innocent."

"What the hell is your meaning by that?"

"None, hopefully. Mind you, there are fathers here who had hoped their daughter would have been the one you'd chosen."

"This is but the first night of forty. What I decide when the trial is up is what matters."

"Treat the Mulvaine fair, Gordie. If you don't, you'll answer to me. There is another that will champion her."

Ulrich's gaze transferred to the Mckenna. The dance ended. John Mckenna proudly escorted Lady Cara back to his son. Ulrich stood and shouted a toast. Servants ran with pitchers to fill every tankard.

Cara had barely regained her seat when jugglers and acrobats burst into the hall. It was the first such entertainment she had ever seen. She clapped her hands in delight, screaming with the rest of the audience as a man swallowed fire, then spat tongues of it toward the high rafters. Another troop came with rings and brightly colored balls, and dogs wearing colorful ruff collars round their necks.

The trained animals leaped through rings on command, hopped one over the other and balanced on bright balls while rolling them to and fro. Undaunted by fire, even the smallest of the pack dove fearlessly through flaming rings.

Next came jesters and fools doing the silliest things. The hall roared with laughter at their antics. Cara's face felt as if it was going to crack. She had never smiled so much in her life.

The feasting and the dancing resumed. Several times Cara's head took a spin, unused as she was to spirits. The milk that had been called for was never actually brought to the table, and she had only Gordie's cup to drink from. It stayed filled with foaming ale. Even the dancing came easier, as Cara recognized tempos and mastered the more simple steps. By far the liveliest dancer was Rose. She outshined all the women, dancing with nimble grace and lightness to her small feet.

Collapsing against Rose in a fit of giggles over her inability to master a competent fling, Cara laughed into her hands. "We are all so silly! What a sight we must make with me tripping and falling all about."

"We look ravishing," Rose said proudly. As she straightened, Gordie caught her eye and imparted a wordless command. Rose correctly interpreted his meaning. "Speaking of ravishing, 'tis time, Lady Cara."

"Time for what?" Cara spun about. "Oh, let's do try it again." She skipped a tipsy hop, wagging the wrong leg. Had she ever felt so happy? So giddy? No, not ever. The party could continue all night. She was willing for it to never end. Feeling thus, it came as a surprise to find Rose drawing her firmly away from the revelry. "Are we going to the necessary, Rose?"

Pulling Cara along with linked arms, Rose patted Cara's hand. "'Tis time you were to bed, Cara."

"Did the Mckenna say we had to? There are children all about the hall still. He seemed most happy to be dancing, as well. I never heard the likes of such singing. You've a wonderful family, Rose."

"Aye, we Mckennas are a law unto ourselves." Rose drew Cara through the moonlit garden toward Gordie's keep. The lights had been doused in the lower room. Rose led the way upstairs, swung the heavy door and halted abruptly.

"What happened here?" she exclaimed.

Cara came up short, bumping into Rose. She peeked around Rose's shoulder and blinked in surprise. "Oh, dear!"

"Oh, dear, is right," Rose said with great dismay. Gordie's heavy trunks had been overturned. Cara's beautiful gown spilled across the floor, pearls torn from the bodice, the cloth of gold sleeves torn to ribbons. "Who would do such a thing?"

Cara sobered immediately at the sight of the huge bed nearly turned over. When Rose turned to her, Cara immediately declared, "I didn't do it."

"Of course you didn't do it!" Rose quickly defended. "I have a good idea who did, and you can be sure she'll be punished!"

"Punished?" Cara swallowed.

"Aye, punished. I'll personally peel the skin from her back!" Rose declared furiously.

"Oh, Rose, you couldn't do that, could you?"

Instead of answering, Rose snatched up Gordie's garments, returning them by handfuls to his trunks. Cara hurried to help, gathering and folding.

"I told Mother to get rid of her."

"Get rid of whom?"

"Megan, that's who. She did this!"

"Megan?" Cara shook her head. "Oh, no, Rose. Why, Megan stayed with me and was ever so solicitous after I fainted. She wouldn't hurt anything of Gordie's. She adores him."

Exasperated by Cara's quick defense, Rose shook her head, her mouth grim as she struggled with the large mattress to return it to the bed. The job was too much for one alone. "I'm going to get Margaret and Janie. You stay here, Cara."

"Rose, don't tell anyone about this, please."

"Cara, the woman must be punished."

"I tell you, she didn't do it. Not Megan. I don't know who did it, but it couldn't have been her. Why, she has a baby. She wouldn't do anything that would cause harm to her baby."

"You know about that?" Rose asked incredulously.

"Aye, I'm quiet, yes, but I'm no blind."

"Well, I can't just let it go. Whoever did this must be found out and punished."

"But it would cause trouble and bad feelings. I've never had such a wonderful time in all my life as I've had tonight, Rose. Don't spoil it for me. We can put everything back the way it was. No one need ever know about it except you and I."

It went completely against Rose's grain to allow such a deed to go unpunished, but she could see Cara's point. The shy Irish girl was the intruder at Castle Kenna. Rose shook her head in defeat. "Cara Mulvaine, you are the most unusual person I've ever met in my life. Each time I think I know all about you, you surprise the daylights out of me. All right, it will be our secret for now."

"Thank you," Cara said gratefully. "Let's clean it up."

It took a half hour to right everything. Except for Cara's dress. Nothing could fix that. Cara put it in the standing wardrobe, out of sight. She would mend it as best she could. No one need ever learn of it.

Soon enough Rose had Cara changed into a night rail of fine lawn and lace. As she brushed the tangles from Cara's hair, she fussed, "We really should have cut your hair when I suggested it this afternoon."

"Why is that?" Cara asked.

"Because now it canna be done unless Gordie says it may." Rose had a practical answer for everything. "He'll probably forbid that. Men have awful silly ideas about a woman's hair."

"Do you think so?" Cara shook the heavy length free from her shoulders.

"Now all you need is a touch of perfume."

"Why? You will waste it. I can still smell the scent. See." Cara held up her wrist to Rose's inspection. The fragrance of flowers did linger. Rose shook her head, withdrawing a tiny vial from her sleeve.

"A little more won't hurt at all." Rose grinned coyly. She applied the scent, then inspected Cara critically, smoothing a crease from her gown, tugging the neckline a fraction lower to show off the girl's firm bosom. "There, you look stunning."

"There's no mirror here to see."

"Well, a small one." Rose turned Cara to a washstand where a small mirror could be tilted to Cara's view. "Someday you will have to tell me how my brother rates as a lover. 'Tis no likely he'd divulge the information I want to me."

"What information is that?" Cara asked blankly. The mirror showed her nothing more than her face or a square of her gown. It did not measure up to the tall, clear one in Rose's chamber.

Before Rose could respond to Cara's question, Lady Elaina and three other matrons entered Gordie's chamber. Lady Claire, the Mckenna's sister-in-law, bore a set of embroidered linens. Another brought toweling, the next a basin and the last a beautiful glazed pitcher of fresh water. They set their burdens aside, greeted Cara and Rose, then set to work stripping the bed and resheeting it.

"Why are they doing that?" Cara whispered.

"Shh! You don't want to sleep on dirty sheets," Rose said.

The linen hadn't looked soiled to Cara. She surveyed the strange, unfamiliar room and sighed. "I don't want to sleep here at all. Your room was just fine. Can't we go back to the hall?"

"Hush." Rose looped her arm through Cara's and pulled her to the open window. "Cara, there's not much time left. Maybe I should have explained things better this afternoon."

"Explained what?" Cara looked back to the bed-making operation where the four ladies had completed it to their satisfaction. Pillows were plumped, the heavy fur folded to the foot. Cara noticed the wide banding of crocheted lace. "Oh, such beautiful lace. Did you make it, Lady Elaina?"

"'Tis a gift from Lady Claire," Gordie's mother said proudly.

Cara left Rose to coo over the pillowcases and sheets. "Will you teach me to do work like that, Lady Claire? I can thread a needle, but fine work I've never had the chance to learn, much less admire."

"I would be most happy to teach you, Lady Cara," the silver-haired matron assured her. "It is time you were to bed."

"Most definitely," Lady Elaina concurred. Everyone said their good-nights, went overboard with kisses and embraces, and Cara found herself propped in the huge bed, her robe folded aside on a chest. All the ladies withdrew, leaving every single candle burning.

Well, that may be fine for them, but it isn't for me. Cara popped out of bed and trotted round, snuffing all the candles.

Now there was moonlight aplenty. She looked at the cloudy silvered sky. Despite her bare arms, it wasn't very cool. She wasn't sleepy, either.

The revelry in the hall continued. Cara thought it confusing that a family that was so open, happy and hospitable to their guests in general had sent her summarily to bed—like a little child. When she had children of her own this would be the way she sent them to bed, with embraces and kisses. She would never tell them *Go, get out of my sight. Stay to your chamber till you are sent for.*

Rare had been the time when Sorely had sent for her. He came looking for her with a stick in hand whenever the mood struck him to be cruel or vicious. These Mckennas were not like that, bearing grudges and holding hatred in their hearts to the grave. Sobered by the turn of her thoughts, Cara climbed back into the high bed.

Two pillows, such a luxury! She snuggled onto them, drawing crisp sheeting across her bare arms. One would have to be a very determined sleeper to do so while bagpipes and drums made such a racket in the hall. The tempo was maddeningly loud and strong. Cara's foot tapped beneath the covers. More pipes swelled into the barrage. Laughter and music spilled into the courtyard, and more voices joined in the song that she couldn't decipher.

"They're having a grand time," Cara said to the canopy. "I was, too! I don't like this room. It's lonely."

She knew that was the ale talking. It had loosened her tongue. The drumbeat kept getting louder and stronger, as if the clan Mckenna marched somewhere. They weren't winding down at all. The party was getting rowdier, lustier.

"How am I supposed to sleep?" Cara said aloud as she glared at the open windows. "'Tis too noisy here, and I can hear the horses. Tomorrow I'll tell Gordie I want to sleep in Rose's room again. She is good company."

Bagpipes screamed louder. Wanting to see what all the commotion was about, Cara jumped out of bed and ran to the windows. To her great surprise there wasn't a soul in the yard. Not even a servant.

"For the love of God." Cara whirled around, confused. The sudden movement almost unbalanced her. "Ale." She giggled, then surprised herself more as the room seemed to spin without her turning an inch. The floor vibrated under her feet. The drums boomed so loud, they should have been in the same room.

Below the bedchamber there was a hall. Gordie's public room was small compared to his father's. There were chambers above his, but the music wasn't coming from above.

"My God!" Cara yelped. "This tower is haunted!"

The revelation shocked her. She knew ghosts. Dunluce had scores of them. She thought she'd seen the last haunting. The hair on the back of her neck prickled. A shiver chased down her spine. Dread wrapped its fist round her heart. What if a ghost had torn the room to shambles?

What if that ghost was evil? As evil as the spirit she'd glimpsed coveting Gordie's soul? That one glimpse into hell was enough for a lifetime. Eyes widening with escalating fear, Cara stumbled about the darkened room seeking the candles she had put out. Her heart almost stopped when the door burst wide open.

A whole troop of Scottish ghosts burst through the portal! Each a wild specter, sporting kilt, plaid and furs. A silent scream strangled Cara's throat. Backing away from the intruders, frantic to find some means of escape, Cara stumbled over a stool. She fell backward in a dead faint, her head smacking hard against the wall.

Chapter Eighteen

"Put me down!" Gordie roared above the din and the rowdy merriment.

A dozen clansmen bore him aloft, roughly carting him to his marriage bed, a phalanx of torchbearers bringing up the rear. He caught a glimpse of Lady Cara, saw her eyes tumble back in her head. Then she crumpled out of sight. He roared a curse. That had the quelling effect he wanted. The lads dropped him, none too gently. One oaf stepped on his feet in the crush.

"Bring a light!"

"Ow! Mind yer feet!" Gordie tottered on one foot, grabbing the bedpost. "Don't lay a hand on her! You've scared the wee thing within an inch of her life! Get out, damn you! The shivaree is over!"

The idiots with the pipes and drums were the last to catch on to the state of things. The drum rat-a-tatted to a thunk. The bagpipes wheezed a dying shriek.

Ulrich caught his younger sibling, Bruce, by the back of his shirt, spinning him round before he touched the fallen lady. "Right, you go then, lads, you've had your fun. Go on out now. The Mckenna can handle it from here."

The men couldn't depart with their ribald jests unsaid, especially not when Gordie gathered a boneless woman in his arms.

"Ye can forget duty with that one, Gordie!"

"She'll be no giving you pleasure."

"An omen, aye, for the monk's life of a married man."

"Get out!" Gordie roared.

Ulrich shoved the last of the merrymakers through the door, then turned and asked, "Is she fainted?"

"That appears to be the case." Gordie laid Cara on the bed, hesitating before turning her face his direction, while he searched for signs of true injury. He stepped back and caught his foot in the trail of black hair that spilled onto the floor. "Lord!"

"What's wrong? What can I get you?" Ulrich asked.

"Fetch me some brandy in a small glass," Gordie snapped, looping the trail of silken hair across his hand as he brought the gleaming mass up to the pillows.

"Right then, brandy." Ulrich did as his cousin bid. He returned with a shot of brandy and saw that Gordie had not covered the Mulvaine. Ulrich grinned at the girl's winsome figure, clad in the sheerest of gowns. She was indeed a bonnie woman, full in the right places, small waisted and long of limb. He abruptly cleared his throat. "Anything else?"

"She's as wan as moonlight." Gordie hovered in indecision, glass in hand, as useless as two left feet.

"She's no going to drink."

"Right." Gordie bolted the shot down his own throat.

"Hell, cousin," Ulrich muttered, uncomfortable as a man could be. "You'll figure out what's to be done with her."

Abruptly, Ulrich about-faced and departed.

"Christ's blood," Gordie swore again.

As he put the glass to the nightstand he saw the crocheted linens, the intricate patterns of knots and roses. "Oh, for the love of God." He groaned, pushing aside the cascade of rich black hair to search under the pillow casing for the linen sheet. It was there, perfectly starched and pressed, tucked between the others—the bride's sheet. He shook his head, regretting not telling his mother to dispense with the custom. He could see his father's hand in this, as well.

Yes, indeed, the Mckenna was determined to see his will triumph over anyone else's!

His earlier fury at his father's sly machinations returned. Gordie hobbled to the nearest chair and dropped heavily into it. His foot was nigh well killing him. The injury had been abused in more ways than he could count. Groaning, he crossed ankle to knee, doing what had to be done to ease his throbbing great toe. As he worked the boot free of his limb, he cataloged all the consequences that could follow this night.

If he hadn't realized the totality of his father's triumph before, seeing the bride's sheet on his bed confirmed it now. Handfasted . . . soon to be married for life to . . . Cara Mulvaine.

Gordie's brows rose in sheer amazement.

With that damn sheet on his bed, Gordie was truly trapped by his own foolish words of a month ago. He must bed the wench. He raked his fingers across his jaw, the brandy burning in his stomach on top of heaven only knew how much other spirits. A few hours ago he'd been up to the duty, but now . . . now he wasn't up to anything.

If he did not bed the girl, come morning there would still be a houseful of guests to inspect the sheets. Bloodless sheets would ruin her. When it came to reading the banns, there could be protests lodged by any in the clan who claimed their marriageable daughters were virgins. She could be judged unworthy of the laird of the clan. Were the old laws strictly enforced, she could be publicly whipped, cast out or stoned to death.

Thinking logically only increased his dilemma. What if she wasn't a virgin? He tried to remember her age. Twenty . . . twenty and two, old for a virgin bride. If he did bed her and she not be innocent, it was expected that he not keep her, but cast her out himself. Yet, by his own knowledge and her admission, she'd had the freedom of her own counsel in Dunluce. He knew nothing about her except that she moved freely day or night in that dismal place. He had no proof that she was untouched.

Were she a virgin and he bedded her, he was committed to her. Unless . . . by some quirk of fate, she raised the ire of the entire clan. Only a betrayal would be serious enough to cause that—not a likely possibility in six weeks' time.

His boot off, Gordie exhaled a sigh of relief. He removed his other boot, as well as unbound his leggings. He stood and unfastened his belt, unhooked his kilt and threw it onto the chair. He poured water into the basin, splashed and scrubbed his face and neck. With a towel he blotted the moisture that trickled down his chest; then, with a grunt of self-disgust, he untied the laces to his trews and stripped them off.

He spread his fingers through his hair, tossed aside the towel and stared at the bed. The white-gowned figure groaned and curled into a fetal ball, her rounded bottom facing him. The tempting curves beckoned him.

A soft sigh escaped his lips. Tempting and inviting she was. He remembered another night when her pose had been just as artless. He couldn't take advantage of her then any more than he could now.

What a sorry day this had turned out to be! Gordie thought he might as well take a knife and cut his hand and smear the bridal sheet with his own blood. He wouldn't be waking the Mulvaine. Not to satisfy his father's schemes, nor to assuage his own manly pride.

Cara woke with a blinding pain behind her eyes. She recognized nothing. Everything was wrong. Across the way, a tall, unusual chair stood before a glowing hearth.

Something occupied it. A massive shaggy head lolled against a pale shoulder. One arm hung limp nearly to the floor, its fingers casting long, grotesque shadows in the flickering light.

Cara's breath caught in her throat. A ghost! The room was haunted! The beastly creature sputtered, snorted and spat its foul breath past slack-jawed lips.

Fearing the creature was a demon, another glimpse at the other side, she almost screamed. She slapped her hand over her mouth. No ghost snored!

It was not a ghost. It was a sleeping man, snoring very loudly with every breath taken. Cara slid off the bed, tiptoed to the chair. It was Gordie Mckenna! He was naked and reeked of rye whiskey!

She stuck her fingers in his great mass of tousled hair, gripped it as if she would rend him bald in one stroke and yanked his head up right. "You drunken sot, how dare you sleep in my chamber!"

Gordie Mckenna's reflexes were dulled by the spirits he'd consumed. Still, his limp arm flashed up and took hold of her wrist.

"What the bloody hell!"

"What are you doing here? Where are your clothes, you heathen? You've no right to be here...like this!" To make her point clear, Cara yanked harder on his hair, and his grip didn't stop her.

"Yeow! That's enough of that!" Gordie roared, jerked upright by the hard pull of her determined hands. He untangled his other arm from the coil of his plaid and set to the task of breaking her grips. She evaded him, darting round to the back of his chair. The next pull nearly rent him hairless.

"You'll go, you bounder!" Cara declared. "This chamber's been given over to me. Your mother said so!"

Turning out of the chair, Gordie knocked it over, clumsily banging his shins as he stumbled round it. It took two attempts to catch hold of her. He snared her waist between his grasping fingers. Cara slammed against his torso. Her grip on his hair intensified.

"You'll let go, lassie, or be prepared to suffer the consequences," Gordie warned.

Bare feet kicked at him, then tangled in her night rail. Gordie hoisted her higher, pinching her backside with a force that would have sent any of his sisters running in tears to their mother. Lady Cara was undaunted.

"Put me down and leave this chamber!"

"Woman, stop pulling my hair!" Gordie slapped her bottom hard; then he gripped her waist and tossed her onto the bed. Flight dislodged her grip. She bounced and scrambled upright instantly, yelping, tangling in her own hair and hems, her hands like the claws of a cat, ready for battle.

"Get out, you naked savage!"

"Be quiet! You'll shout down the entire house!" It was certain her screeching had woken the dogs in their pens. The din of barking and howling echoed through the now-silent night.

"I'll bring down the roof if you don't leave my room!" Cara shouted, undaunted by his order. "And find yer kilt, before you go, mon!"

"This is my room, woman!" Gordie roared over her screeching. "Dinna yell at me, and I'll wear what I bloody well please! 'Tis my bed your knees are on. Shut up, I said!"

"'Tis no your room. 'Tis one of your rooms." Cara jumped off the bed on the opposite side from him. "I'm no stupid! Your mother told me to sleep here. But if you want this bed, fine! I'll go elsewhere. 'Tis too big of a house to shout over who sleeps in which room! I thought you were a ghost like the others in this room. I don't like this room. 'Tis haunted.''

Not a word she said made one bit of sense to Gordie as he rubbed his fingers across his abused scalp. What did she babble about? His scowl deepened. "Say that again."

"I'll go to another chamber."

"Not that. The other. What did my mother tell you?"

"That I was to sleep here. 'Tis quite unnecessary. I was most comfortable in Rose's chambers. But she said since we are man and wife 'tis my duty to sleep in your quarters. You may have your bed. Where do I go?"

As direct a question Gordie hadn't ever heard. Did she not know anything, not even an inkling of what it meant to be husband and wife? No, clearly she did not. She stood between him and the fire in the grate, not realizing how the light turned her gown invisible. Gordie opted for telling her the obvious.

"You sleep to the same bed as I."

That revelation made Cara scowl very, very deeply. "You mean together?" She frantically tried to piece together Rose's words of instruction. Oh, why was her brain so fuddled? "That's preposterous! I could never sleep in the same bed as you. Why, you're a man."

Gordie just stared at her, his fingers massaging the patches of torn scalp.

Recovering her aplomb, Cara thought to turn the attack back to him. "Pray tell what were you doing in the chair?"

"Sleeping, until you attacked me," Gordie snapped.

"How was I supposed to know it was you? You scared the life out of me! Nobody told me this keep has ghosts."

"I'm telling you. We don't have any ghosts."

"Oh."

Cara struck a finger to her mouth, frowning as she worried the nail, her eyes downcast. Better that she stared at the floor than at him, for God's sake! He hadn't a stitch on and didn't seem to give a damn! It was obvious being a wife was going to take some adjusting. Trying to regain her composure, Cara nervously stared about the room. Sharing a room with Rose had been a pleasant experience. So different from being the lone and solitary creature she'd always been.

"Well, then, you should avail yourself to the bed, sir. Certainly it would be more comfortable than stretching your body between chairs." Did her voice sound normal?

"I had good reason for making the choice I did." Gordie folded his arms across his chest, watching her make a circuit round the room, compulsively picking up his discards, folding and neatening as she wandered. She stopped at a window, leaned over the sill and listened to the dogs' random howling.

Abruptly, she changed subjects again. "I am used to sleeping alone, but with Mimms close by. He is howling outside. He doesn't like to be penned. I will go bring him inside."

"No, you will not," Gordie countered.

"I canna sleep without him."

"And I could not rest in peace were he in the room."

"He does not attack without reasonable cause."

"My answer remains the same. No."

Cara fiddled with a trinket on a tabletop, then looked anxiously to the windows. "I could go and quiet him."

"We are used to howling dogs. He will quiet sooner when his caterwauling does not bring someone to him. Return to the bed, Lady Cara, and go back to sleep."

"Are you going to sleep in the chairs?"

"That is my intention."

"I'm littler. I'll take the chairs if you prefer to have the bed."

Exasperated by her questions and suggestions, Gordie righted the fallen chair, snatched his pillow from the floor and heaved it to the top of the bed. "We'll both take the bed. You can have that side."

He opted for the side closest to the door. Cara worried the corner of her lip, frowning. That was her preferred side. He threw back the top sheet and stretched out. He propped his hand under his head and looked directly at her. "Come to bed, Lady Cara."

"I won't sleep now. I'm wide awake. I will go for a walk down by the sea."

"There's no sea at Mount Kenna."

"I meant the lake. 'Tis nearly the same thing."

"You have been wandering in the hills at night since you came here?"

Cara edged round the bed to the opposite side from him, doing her best not to face him directly. "No. The portcullis is never open. I have found no gate like we had at Dunluce. But I like walking at night."

"Sorely Boy allowed that?"

"Allowed?" Cara's head shot up and she blushed. "He did not care what I did, day or night."

"The cliffs near Dunluce are dangerous. Surely your governess didn't approve of your wanderings."

"What is a governess? Dunluce had no such thing."

"A tiring woman who looks after a maiden."

"Oh. There was only me and old Brenna. She never had time to leave the kitchens. Besides, it was forbidden."

"What was forbidden?"

"The north tower."

"That makes no sense. What was forbidden in the north tower?"

"Entering it."

"Why?"

"Why?" Cara's mouth impatiently tightened into a small knot. "Because that is where I lived. My grandfather forbid everyone from entering my tower. My lord, will you dress?"

"Dress? No. Quit changing the subject and come to bed. What of Dunluce's servants?" Gordie couldn't keep the incredulous tone out of his voice. Hadn't Grace O'Malley implied as much? But then, he hadn't dwelled on any of those thoughts. It had not seemed likely he'd ever see the Mulvaine again.

Cara's chin rose. "I don't need servants. I've always taken care of myself. I have always slept alone, too."

"Alone? What about when you were sick?"

"I have never been sick."

That statement made Gordie wonder if she knew what sick was. But she had nursed him. And there had been something terribly wrong about that at the time. He couldn't begin to imagine what kind of life she'd led, alone in a drafty tower, wandering about the desolate cliffs with no one to caution or advise her. He patted the empty expanse of the bed. "Come to bed, Lady Cara."

"If you will cover yourself, I will."

"I offend you?"

Cara's blush could not have deepened any more. "Nay. It's...it's...well, other than the time that I nursed you, I have had no cause to see an unclothed person. You are...very... handsome." Cara added the last hastily.

Gordie chuckled and drew part of a sheet up to his waist. "There, does that help?"

She nodded, swallowing nervously as she came to the far corner of the big bed. She sat very carefully, shooting him a quick, wary look. "'Twasn't your legs that were tempting my eyes to stray." The words were said before she had time to think. Clearing her throat, she tried to make the best of it, saying. "It's the fine down of hair that covers your chest that intrigues my eyes. It always did, even when you were sorest sick."

"It does? Tell me, what does my fine, hairy chest tempt you to do?"

Appalled at what she'd said, Cara shook her head. "I don't know. It is very...oh...manly. I can only think of when we were dancing and how easy it was to touch you."

"Ah." Gordie turned onto his back, threading his fingers behind his head. "I would welcome your touch, Cara."

"You don't mind? Truly?"

"I would not mind at all."

Hesitantly Cara moved onto the bed, but she stopped herself just at the point of laying her hand to the solid ridge of muscle banding his chest. "No. 'Tis silly of me. We're no dancing now."

Obviously it was too much of a gap for her to bridge alone. Gordie held the gaze of her eyes with his, unclasped his hands and reached carefully for her. "Ah, Cara, you fear much. I won't hurt you."

She sat still as a statue as his hands touched her arms. Lace slid against her skin. That touch alone was so exquisite that Cara caught her breath. She could not drag her gaze from his.

"I want to kiss you, Cara. Come closer to me."

Agonizingly slow, he drew her against the heated flesh of his chest. She splayed her hands then, marveling at the softness of skin and hair, at the firmness of muscle below. "Oh, you are such a lovely man."

Gordie thought he was probably the ugliest fool ever born, but he wasn't telling her that. She settled against him without the slightest sign of hesitation, and he raised his head just enough to capture her lips. Her mouth was sweet and moist, the fullness of her lips a temptation to taste. His tongue toyed at their joining, parting gently, seeking entrance.

Caught up in this newest experience, Cara yielded, jolting at the hot thrust of his tongue within her.

It was a pagan delight. Utterly primitive. She had no experience to guide her, but she would not have refused him anything.

What his hot, burning mouth made her feel was welcome. His strong arms holding her made her feel safe, truly safe for perhaps the first time in her life.

He kept on kissing her, pulling away for a moment, no more, to kiss her cheek, her eyes, then always back to her mouth. Her lips felt swollen, hot and burned against his. Where his wandering hands stroked the silk against her skin, she burned. Little fires erupted everywhere.

"Cara." He whispered her name with such longing, she gasped. "I want to feel your body next to mine. Take off your night rail."

In her heated, nearly mindless state, the request seemed perfectly logical. Her gown chaffed her, prevented her from feeling the true warmth and texture of his exquisite skin. She had never forgot how she'd felt when she had woken, naked in his arms. Cara pulled away, sitting to her knees beside him.

The soft ribbon on her gown came easily free. But then she stopped, hands clutching the loosened ribbon tight.

"What is it?" Gordie raised himself on the prop of one elbow.

Cara sought a sensible answer. "I will be cold."

"Nay." Gordie pried the ties from her hands, spreading the neckline so that it widened across her shoulders. "You will not be cold."

"I will be uncomfortable."

"You will like the feeling in a little while."

"Why?"

"Because it feels good to have your skin free, to be touched like this." His fingers strayed across her shoulders, lowering the gown farther. The curves of her breasts appeared, firm and full.

"I will be ashamed."

"There is no shame between a husband and wife, Cara Mulvaine. As you have the right to see my body this night, I have the right to see yours."

"Why?" Cara asked in a shaken voice as he deliberately drew both shoulders of her gown away from her arms.

"For the purpose of completing our union. The marriage must be consummated."

"Consummated?" Cara pondered that word aloud. "You mean we must finish the marriage."

"Has no one explained mating to you?"

Mating. Cara kept her thoughts to herself this time. Mating. Had that ever been explained? She searched her entire store of learned knowledge and all she could come up with were the cryptic words Rose Mckenna had tossed at her that very day. "You must think me totally ignorant, but I have accomplished some learning in my years."

"Have you?" Gordie inquired mildly, continuing to draw the gown away from her skin. "You bring to me the skills of a chatelaine? You will keep my house running smoothly, see that meals are ever ready, guests cared for, children birthed and nursed and raised through childhood's traumas with ease?"

Cara took one deep and extremely tentative breath. "I am not sure the skills I have would include those duties, my lord. I have been given a scholarly mission. I can transcribe from five languages and complete diagrams and adequate copies of illuminated script."

Nervously Cara shifted to her knees. She didn't know what made her chatter like a magpie, but she couldn't stop the rush of words. "I am certain I could manage the nursing through illness. The other duties I have never performed. You have healthy sons, my lord. Do you have daughters, as well?"

Taken aback by the mention of his natural sons, Gordie's brow flattened over his narrowed eyes. Her skin was quite flawless in the moonlight, pale and smooth, her dusky peaked breasts more perfectly formed than he'd imagined. She remained as she was, kneeling before him. She made no move to modestly cover her breasts or to shield the dark triangle at the apex of her thighs. Gordie leaned back on one elbow, allowing his hand to traverse the outer edge of her arm then dropped to her firm thigh, stroking down to the blunt angle of her knee.

"I have no daughters that I know of," Gordie said, finally answering her question. "I take it you have no objections to my sons remaining within the house."

"Should I object?" Cara asked. "I have been told that men cherish their sons."

"Aye. I will admit I am proud of the boys. However, they are not my heirs, and that is the reason my father forced this marriage upon the two of us. You will be expected to breed a true son to the Kenna."

"Breed a true son?" Cara worried the corner of her mouth, hardly able to think for the hand that continued to rove over the bones of her knee. "Oh! You mean to birth a son as Mary birthed our Lord Jesus."

Gordie smiled at her inference. "With one slight difference." Gordie drew her closer to his body. "We shall not rely upon the Holy Spirit. It is a task I will enjoy doing myself. You are perfectly formed, Cara."

"I am?" Her lashes lowered, a dark fringe shading her highly colored cheeks. "I think perhaps you had too much ale, my lord. I have always been a very plain person, unremarkable in any way."

The shy, downcast look had dissolved completely when her eyes returned to meet his again. Gordie gazed at her wide-open eyes. Those large gray orbs were set a bit farther apart than normal. Had they been brown, he would have likened her to a doe. Her small face was more delicate than that. Childlike, innocent. But her expression showed she was wary of him.

"Come here." He patted the bedding at his side. Cara hesitated, then nodded and moved. Gordie let his arm sweep round her back and drew her closer to him.

There was something about that strong arm. The curve fit beneath Cara's shoulder and the firm contour of his forearm rested in the hollow between Cara's ribs and hip. His warm palm settled on her belly, his fingers restlessly stroking, teasing her. Then her hips grazed his. She couldn't have been more aware of him, ever.

She couldn't find any reason to object to the contact. He exuded warmth, safety, security. She liked the touch of him.

"So you read Latin, do you?" Gordie searched for something to say, reminding himself that he must go slowly to not alarm her. She was skittish.

"Aye, and Greek, French, Italian and some German."

"Not English?"

"No. My grandfather forbid everything English at Dunluce." Cara shuddered deliciously as his hand boldly stroked up her back, his fingers tangling in the drape of her hair. His mouth hovered over hers, his breath warming her lips.

"Are you frightened of me, Cara?"

Chapter Nineteen

Cara couldn't answer. Her heart pounded in her ears. Her tongue twisted in her mouth, unable to form a coherent word. She jerked as his head came forward, bending so that his lips tasted the wild pulse throbbing in her throat.

Gordie's mouth traveled upward to her trembling chin. "So brave," he whispered against her lips. "So scared, too."

"I'm no afraid of you." Cara swallowed the lump that strangled her, speaking against his lips.

"You do not lie well, Mulvaine." Gordie sampled the sweet taste of her mouth, reeling with the intoxicating potency of her yielding lips. She liked kissing, he remembered. He swept his arm down her body, gathering her, turning her so that her back pressed against the bedding.

"Oh!" she exclaimed, startled by the overwhelming heat of his body covering and pressing down on her.

Small hands clutched very tightly to Gordie's shoulders. He liked the feel of her.

"What do you?"

"Bedding you, Mulvaine."

"We sleep, m'lord?"

"My name is Gordie."

Cara fixed her gaze to a plastered wall where a tapestry depicted a hunting scene. Its simple lines and colors had a childish touch to them, as if a very young hand had plied the needle. She could not make out whether the animals were wolves or red deer.

Sensing her distancing, Gordie knew he had his work cut out to bring her mind into the play her body accepted. He kissed her, deeply, soft lips stroking against the other, his tongue playing with the warm heat within her. She moved, twisting beneath the press of his chest, her breasts stroking and teasing him.

Abruptly she pulled her mouth away and went still as a statue. Her eyes had a glazed, unfocused look to them. The unusual expression was fleeting, passed in the blink of an eye and was gone.

"What is it?" Gordie demanded.

Cara's eyes shifted back to his hovering face and Gordie felt gooseflesh rise on her skin beneath his hands. Her fingers suddenly gripped his shoulders with hard, tightening pressure.

"My lord, you must take care," Cara whispered.

The vision was quite sudden and sharp, catching her completely unaware. Since she'd left Dunluce, she thought her gift of second sight had deserted her. She saw trouble, dark sorrow and pain, but not the cause of the reason for it. Not thinking, Cara tightened her grip upon his shoulders as if to hold him to her, safe.

"Care of what?" Gordie glanced sideways, caught by an impression of danger.

The room was bathed in shadows and moonlight. All was quiet without. Even the last howling dog had settled for the night. He half imagined her beast would come crashing through the door, teeth bared and yellow eyes flashing.

Gordie turned his head slowly and studied the puzzling expression on her face. Her widened eyes triggered an uneasy memory. He couldn't fathom it. If pressed, his description would have to be malevolent shadow, danger, the sort that preceded hackles rising on his neck. Something—what, he couldn't imagine—passed before his eyes, between his body and hers and left a chill tugging at his skin.

"You are in grave danger, my lord." Cara shivered, her words urgent. Someone hated him deeply, wished him evil this very moment.

"What?" Gordie shook away the niggling prickles. He strained his eyes, looking at each possession of his in the chamber. Trunks, chests and wardrobes harbored no villains. Nor did any shadowy corner. "Nonsense, there is no danger here whatsoever. Come here. There is no reason for you to shiver from the cold.''

Gordie pulled her to him. He shook off the odd, unnatural feeling. When he had gut feelings in the heat of battle, he still waged war with cold, precise determination. He didn't believe in ghosts and premonitions. Obviously, she did.

Cara watched his hand rise above her head to smooth away the tangling hair on her brow. His palm touched her forehead like a benediction and rode down the curves and planes of her cheek and jaw. The broad bones of his wrist passed before her eyes. It was ringed with a strong, purplish aura, which formed a shackle that reminded her of the irons that she'd freed with magic from his limbs.

He clucked her chin, then shifted and propped his head on his left hand, staring at her most intently. The purple band did not bind his left extremity.

"What is wrong?"

"Are you still a king's man?" she asked baldly.

"Did I tell you that I was?"

"Once, when you told me I would suffer for holding you prisoner.''

"You're a bold one to remind me of that." Gordie's eyes hardened only slightly. "Aye, I remain Jamie's man. My sword is pledged to him and the future of Scotland. The day will come that James will mount the throne of England.''

He expected her to draw away. She didn't. In truth, their faces were so close his breath fanned her forehead. She smelled of roses.

Reading his mind, for his thoughts that very moment were as clear as a bell, Cara settled closer against his warmth and said, "It feels nice to lie here with you.''

"Safe?" Gordie growled. She shouldn't be feeling safe at all. Not with what he was feeling. Was he going to be tormented by lust eternally? Christ, she wasn't even beautiful, but every time he touched her, he wanted her.

"No. Not safe," Cara corrected, because that was the answer he wanted to hear.

"Good." Gordie trailed one finger lower, drawing a line between her breasts. She shivered, and the soft mounds puckered, drawing the nipples into hard little nubs.

She lay perfectly still, breathless, as he roved that one, gentle finger around one pinked aureole, then turned his gaze and his touch to the one closest to his mouth. A shiver swept down her belly, tensing all her muscles. Gordie lowered his head, his mouth open, soft breath warming the trembling orb.

"What...do...you?" Cara stuttered as his lips closed upon her. She gasped as he drew the nipple deep within his mouth, then shuddered deeply as his fingers traveled across the long expanse of her belly to settle at the nest of heat throbbing between her thighs. "My lord!"

"My name is Gordie," he reminded her very firmly, then ignored her protests and fluttering hands.

"Perhaps we should try to sleep," Cara suggested lamely.

"A useless cause." Gordie raised his head, intent upon seeing her reaction. High color flushed her cheeks. Her mouth trembled deliciously. How could he possibly resist?

A kiss bloomed between them. This time as his tongue thrust inside her mouth, Gordie sought to teach her passion and raise her consciousness of desire. His hand slid between her slick thighs, finding and separating her nether lips.

Her moan echoed in his mouth, her hips tensed against his probe. The soft, inner flesh of her thighs tightened over his hand. He hardened his kiss, tasting her, his tongue delving deep to touch and tease, his fingers caressing the nub of her sex with intent to incite a riot within her.

Abruptly he took away the prop of his other hand from his own head and grasped a fistful of her hair, tugging on it so that she could not pull away. He wanted her accessible. He wanted to be buried in her, up to the hilt of his throbbing shaft.

Breathless and tense, Cara swallowed convulsively as he drew up from her, shifting, moving his shoulders and lower body over her. She caught hold of her hair, quickly, pulling it free from under her. Gordie took the length from her hand, twisting it around his wrist.

"Your hair is like a cloak of sable. It is quite the longest I have ever seen." With a knot of it binding his wrist, he let the balance spill onto her belly, spread his palm open in it and rubbed the silken tresses across her skin.

"My lord," Cara whispered.

"You will wear it loose each night for me, hmm?"

"For you?" Cara asked dumbfounded.

"Aye, only for me." A towering sense of possession was overtaking him. Gordie's eyes glittered and a smile dimpled his cheeks. He drew her hair across her breasts and let it drape over her hips, fingering the sharp bones that pressed her taut skin across her belly. The color was identical to that of her woman's curls, but the texture was unbelievably different.

He remembered the sight of it fanning outward as he'd spun her in a wild fling. So she wasn't beautiful. She had incredible eyes and hair. Her body was everything it should be: soft, firm, resilient. He shut his eyes and drew a deep, controlling breath.

Cara sensed the struggle within him, but could not put a name to it.

"Open your legs to me, Cara." His voice was thick and husky with desire.

"My legs, m'lord?" Cara's heart hammered inside her chest. The words came out a shaken tumble.

"Aye," Gordie whispered hoarsely, aching to touch and stroke her. He wanted her badly, yet wanted her compliance and acceptance, as well.

Cara closed her eyes and listened, her senses keening, stretching to the limit. His heart hammered deep within his chest, so loud it was like the war drum she'd heard when the Kenna ghosts had burst inside the room.

Shuddering with the tension roiling like oncoming waves at her, Cara opened her trembling legs to the hand poised over her.

"Ah, sweetling, do not be afraid."

Gordie slipped easily into the seeping wetness. She was ready for him, glistening and aroused just by kisses. Concentrating on the exploration of his fingertips, he closed his eyes to probe the throbbing heat of her. Unerringly, he found her entrance and pressed one thick finger inside her. She shuddered, her flesh encasing him, her walls tightening rhythmically. He heard her gasp and smiled to reassure her.

Startled, Cara turned her face and searched quickly round the dark room. The candles gutted, deep in their waxy beds. The moon slanted at a lower angle, approaching setting.

Gordie felt her mental distancing and brought his hand back to her face, to control her retreat. Holding her chin, staring at her, he waited for her darting eyes to return his look. It took a definite tug on her chin to effect the return of her attention.

"Cara."

"My lord?"

"Stay with me."

Cara swallowed. Gordie loomed above her, his eyes focused upon hers and his thoughts completely inscrutable.

"Open your mouth."

"My mouth?" Cara blinked at the order, for it was an order.

"Aye." His eyes hooded, his finger touched her lips, tracing the upper curve, rounding the deep fullness that Cara so rarely ever allowed to show. "I want to taste you as I enter you."

"How can you do that?" Cara said blankly, not following his directions and oblivious to his intentions. He dropped his head slowly, intent upon the nervous darting of her tongue betwixt her lips. Gordie caught the movement, fascinated by it.

A shiver twisted deep inside her. His hips nestled between her raised thighs, tugging the skin taut where she gripped him. His tongue slid inside. Lips parted, she accepted his kiss. Gordie pressed his advantage, delving deep within the soft sweet cavity. Every tremor that swept down torched another flame to his desire.

His shaft waited at her portal, throbbing, aching to enter the dark cavity and sheath itself inside her. The resistance of her flesh tormented him. He knew for certain that she was a virgin, as well as knew full well his entry would pain her.

He had only meant to kiss her, teach her that he expected more from a kiss than a chaste peck upon the lips. They were not children.

It had gone far beyond the point of no return.

Cara yielded her mouth, accepted the press of his body against her. She wasn't afraid. This was what was meant to be. She knew and accepted it.

His hands went wildly down her body, making her skin sensitive to his touch. Like Almoy's magic fires, she erupted, burning, flaming with a molten heat she had never guessed existed. One touch led to another, each more bold, more flagrant, more intimate. All of Cara's barriers melted in the fire.

When his lips touched her throat, she shuddered, but she cried out when he kissed her breasts and lost her mind when he drew the rosy peak deep inside his heated mouth. Her fingers clasped his arms and stroked upward to grip the hard curves of his shoulders.

His rough-haired knee pressed at the juncture of her thighs. Deep within her, the core of her body awakened to the heat of a furnace. She was blind to protest as his fingers parted her, stroked and petted a warm spring loose. She had no concept of how they would fit together or what the end was to this wonderful, magical world of sensation.

He gave her no warning against the stroke of pain, but took her cry into his mouth as he plunged deep within her flesh. He filled her, totally, his manhood pulsing inside her, burning, hurting, but not killing.

The fire burned out of control, a conflagration. Cara thought she would die from its consuming heat and the utter pleasure of it. He should have been crushing her, but he wasn't. He should have been hurting her, but the pain dissipated so rapidly, replaced by some wild, uncontrollable need, that she couldn't think. She could only feel.

He had no idea of how starved she was for his touch, for the simple human need to be close to another, to be held and loved, accepted and made whole with another.

All the years and the loneliness melted, faded in the union of his body to hers. Cara's spirit lifted, rising from the imprisoning depths of her body to break free, pounding within her like a wild horse shaking the earth. She spiraled skyward out of earthly bounds, caught in a net of all-encompassing desire.

Brilliant lights glowed round him as he moved within her. Strong and violet, his aura pulsed with his life force. She felt her soul and spirit meld into his. The union matched what their physical bodies maintained.

No spell or incantation had ever transformed or touched her so thoroughly. The end came with shattering exhaustion, a little death falling over both of them. Dying, dying to live again, Cara accepted the collapse of his body into hers.

Her breathing was sharp, far from normal. His was as ragged as a winded horse. Their joined bodies trembled and shook.

"Lord Almighty!" Gordie's words came from a muffled gasp against her shoulder. Unable to lift his chest or return any power or strength to his arms, he could not imagine what had happened to him. He was beyond sensation.

Cara knew that and felt what he was feeling. The power, the depth of their union had shaken him.

All that mattered to her was that she was no longer alone, nor ever would be so again.

She closed her eyes, accepting that one gift as all she was due in a lifetime, and fell into sleep with his weight cradled on her.

Chapter Twenty

Dawn brought her awake at the first cock crow. Their entwined bodies had shifted apart. Gordie was spread-eagle, his face turned into a soft down pillow.

Cara slipped out from the coverlet and saw the blood staining her thighs, staining the sheeting. A portion of her regretted the telling stain upon such pristine linen, gifts from the laird and lady. But another part of her saw the blood as vindication, pagan, as old as time itself. It proved that she had never lain with another man.

As Cara washed, she sorted her jumbled thoughts. Rational thought explained nothing that had passed during the night. Her feelings remained strong and focused. She must rely on them. Whatever the source of safety within Gordon Mckenna's arms was, it was of monumental import to her. One she had never experienced.

She knew his father was terribly mistaken. Gordie Mckenna would not keep her as his wife.

Her unfocused eyes saw the village church forty days hence, empty. No wedding would take place.

The sudden intuition did not sadden Cara. It freed her. Forty days was no life sentence. She could endure Gordie's contempt. The gift of union with his soul and body made all the rest to follow worth any sacrifice.

As the Mulvaine rose from the bed, Gordie stirred out of his deep and heavy sleep. His eyes opened to gray dawn, to a room of shadow rather than dark and to the blinding pain of a head thick from overindulgence.

His eyes closed as he mentally ran an inventory on the numerous aches rampant within his body: a vile stomach, a pounding brain, a jaw that throbbed and that toe, that blasted rotten toe! If that wasn't enough to jar his wits, his rod stiffened like forged steel.

Muttering a curse, he rolled onto his side.

Standing naked at his washbasin, a slender woman performed her morning ablutions.

A second curse worked its way round Gordie's grimly pursed lips. Lord Almighty, he remembered. He was leg shackled.

The Mulvaine washed her skin. That sheet of black hair shifted from shoulder to shoulder, following the tilt of her head as she plied a dripping cloth across her body.

Unaware of his gaze upon her, she continued, finishing by parting her hair into sections and weaving a single twisting braid.

The increasing light revealed details Gordie had not noticed in the dark. Her legs were shapely, well formed. Her hips flared with womanly maturity not overfleshed, but solid and firmly muscled. The sight of her hardened his focus back to his throbbing loins.

Damn, he deducted, she's too skinny! Not that his rod cared one whit for logic. No, it did not. It fixed upon the intimate revelation of a woman at her toilette. Because she braided to her left shoulder, her face was turned away from his, but her body was in three-quarters view, her slender arm raised above the firm globe of her breast. That one rosy peak showed the intensity of his passion; the nipple stood hard and thrusting outward, the flesh around it abraded by his beard and mouth. Ah, but she tasted wonderful, he remembered.

A spasm tightened Gordie's scrotum, making the ache more significant. He closed his eyes, but the impression of her sloping waist and the lean curve of her belly remained behind his eyes to torment him.

Lord! Gordie exhaled through gritted teeth. Even with his eyes closed, he could feel the tightness of her sheath when he'd penetrated her. That sensation brought another groan out of his throat.

He had bedded the wench! He had sworn to himself he wouldn't. A glance at the bride's sheet confirmed his memory of firm, muscled thighs gripping his hips. He could attest to the strength of her legs. She had matched him, stroke for stroke, thrust for thrust.

What had happened to the little gray mouse? Gone, gone forever was the gray mouse. It had only been a delusion of his fevered mind. *So what,* he thought to himself. *So her eyes and her mouth are worthy of note, and without her plain clothes, her body was sufficient. Had he felt more than the usual pleasure in joining with her? No, no more, no less. Well, maybe more.*

He couldn't put his finger upon anything this morning. A second glance to the rumpled sheeting confirmed irrevocably that he had done his duty, consummated the match. She had come to his bed a virgin. Well, he hadn't expected that.

It was a complication, not an obstruction.

Gordie pressed his fingers into his aching brow. Had he been gentle with her? He could not remember. The residue of ale and potent whiskey obliterated finer details, leaving behind fuzzy impressions. Hadn't he sat on the window ledge most of the night? Had he spelled out her expected duties as chatelaine of his household? He hadn't the foggiest idea of what he had or hadn't done.

As Cara's fingers pressed downward toward the tail of her braid, she felt his eyes upon her. She hoped to be dressed before he woke. A flush spread up her body, heating it. She should have dressed first, at least donned her shift before braiding her hair. It was too late now. She took a bit of ribbon and wound it through the last of the braid, carefully tying so the braid would stay secure.

Finished, Cara let the braid spill free. Still, she kept her face averted. What was she to say? Her heart hammered at the thought of facing him.

He had been inside her body, her mouth, her... Every portion of her had been touched, handled, caressed.

Cara closed her eyes. The sensation returned of his mouth, hot upon her skin. Oh, her body ached in so many private places. Was any that had transpired possible?

"Do you sit and stare out the window forever?" Gordie asked in a tense, husky voice. The light was even stronger now.

"No, m'lord," Cara answered in a firm, clear voice. She wasn't weaker; she was stronger because of the night. She was no longer a maid, she was a woman. She had less reason to fear a man than ever before.

"Come to bed. 'Tis early yet."

It was on the tip of Cara's tongue to say she had plenty of duties to perform and rising early would see them better done. She held her tongue, rising instead, turning to confront him. Meeting the direct focus of his gaze was not as hard as she had suspected it would be. He wasn't looking at her eyes. Her blush deepened. She could feel the heat of his gaze as it swept down her person.

Gordie scowled deeply. He remembered waking from the dead and likening her to a painting. She was very much the same as that painting of a golden-haired goddess rising from the sea, only her hair was Celtic black. A more appealing color to his eyes by far. His hand patted the empty bed beside him.

What precisely the meaning of his gesture was, Cara did not know. By his eyes, she suspected he wanted to touch her again. His eyes had a look of serious hunger to them.

"Come," he repeated, patting the space beside him. Then his arm raised in a gesture of welcome. It was that opening that Cara focused upon. For within the circle of his arm she had found a peace unlike any she'd felt before. But that had been in the night. There were edges to the darkness now—soft shadows and light focusing in stripes upon the plastered walls of the chamber.

The distance between them felt as wide as the sea of water separating Ireland and Scotland.

"Come here, Cara."

A fragmentary vision took hold within Cara's mind. His raised arm opened an oasis to her. She felt again that overwhelming feeling of security that had struck her in the night. His strength was a refuge. Inside it she need not be strong of her own accord. All her barriers could be loosened, released, if not forever, for the little while that his arms surrounded her.

Protection, security, safety... all hers for the cost of closing a distance and slipping within the bonds of his touch.

Was she to question that? She read his aura in the shadowy light, saw its benevolent purplish glow, rose-tipped, vital and alive. He was a good man, better than any she'd ever known.

A pang of actual pain twisted inside her. She could liken it only to the pain that had assaulted her when the Mckenna had meant to separate her from Mimms when leaving Dunluce. Would this hurt be greater when the days of the trial ended and she was sent from Castle Kenna? Or was this pain inside her like the pain of the body? Was it a pain that would lessen in time?

Again, darker memories asserted themselves. Flashes swept through her mind. A dripping quill in her hand, ink splotches upon parchment and crude childish letters, recitations and verses committed to memory, and beatings for flaws. A cane, a strap, sometimes a riding whip in her grandfather's hand descended over and over again. Sorely cursed her, reviled and hated her from the moment she'd entered his life. Down through the years she had hardened against physical pain. The day came that he could not make her cry or weep, nor even bring smarting tears to her eyes.

Was this new ache inside her of that nature? The cause of it was Gordon Mckenna, this she knew. Could she grow immune to this pain in time?

She heard the ropes beneath the bed give. Raising her lowered lashes, she found her handfasted husband standing before her. "You hesitate to obey me, Cara Mulvaine. Have I harmed you during the night? Are you in pain?"

"No, m'lord, I am well this morn."

His large hands rose from his sides, making somewhat convulsive movements, clenching and unclenching, then both gripped her shoulders. "What is it that troubles you, then? From this morning and those here after, your troubles are mine."

With the wall of his wide chest before her, words had no import. Cara's eyes sought some safe portion of his body to look at. Anything would do, else she meet the hard, hungry inspection of his eyes. What did he see when he looked at her in such a vulnerable state? Never had she been so aware of her own body. It sought to escape the grip of his restraining arms and cuddle in that warm pit of his chest. "I canna say what troubles me, my lord. I dinna ken what it is. Would you hold me again?"

"Hold you?" Her response conflicted with what Gordie thought she was about to do. She had the look of someone poised for flight. His intent had been to halt escape. Now she confused him more by asking him to hold her. Hold her! God in heaven, he wanted more than holding!

He swept his arm beneath her knees and lifted her, striding unevenly back to his bed. "Be warned, Cara Mulvaine, my intent goes beyond a reassuring hug."

Laid upon the crumpled sheeting, Cara scooted over, giving him room to join her. "It does?"

"Aye, it does," Gordie answered quickly. Her skin retained the moisture of her ablutions and the heady scent of fragrant soap. Gordie's head dipped to kiss the rosy aureole of the breast that peeked at him while she'd braided her hair. The other was just as sweet and firm, a taut button, hard against his tongue.

His hands slid beneath her shoulders, fingers spreading against the back of her skull to cradle her head as his mouth descended upon her lips. His hips nestled between her thighs, his hard member nudging at the soft contour of her belly.

A sigh of wonderment escaped Cara's mouth as he kissed her. This touching and mingling of separate bodies into one, she concluded, must have been the meaning of Rose's obscure lecture the day before. She wondered why, when Sir Almoy had been so insistent that she study and learn all that he could teach, why had he never mentioned the joy of mating?

Gordie's mouth separated from hers to trace a soft, warm path across her brow. Cara sighed with delight, nuzzling against him, knowing her life had changed forever.

Book Three

ALL THE QUEEN'S MEN

"There are things the Lord hates, yes, seven are an abomination To Him; Haughty eyes, a lying tongue and hands that shed innocent blood, a heart that plots wicked schemes, feet that run swiftly to evil, the false witness who utters lies, and he who spreads discord among brothers."

Proverbs of Solomon 6: 16-19

Chapter Twenty-One

The loom defied comprehension. Nearly a month of daily practice had not enhanced Cara's rudimentary skills. Its complicated machinery baffled her. It was a beastly spider's web of colored threads, fitted boards and curious gears. The complex, shifting heddles, impossible-to-thread eyes, battens, shuttlecocks and pedals went beyond her understanding.

It was a monstrous thing with a will of its own.

Yet, every woman in the Kenna household could perch herself on the wide bench and take up exactly where another left off, never skipping a weft. Be the cloth a complicated jacquard or a simple twill, they never missed a beat.

Even ten-year-old Becca was a master of the art. Cara glared at the tangled threads holding the shuttlecock trapped, silently fuming as the young girl slipped under the warp threads and gently, skillfully pulled Cara's knots free.

"It just takes practice, Cara." Becca giggled.

"I think weaving takes more than practice. I think it an art to be born unto. I have no such skills."

"Not true." Becca emerged from under the taut stretch of colored threads, smiling as she reseated herself beside Cara on the bench. She applied her feet to the proper pedals and deftly tossed the unsnarled shuttle between the raised and lowered threads. "Poppa told me that you come from a long line of fine cloth makers. He said that at Graham there are two hundred looms and nearly a thousand skilled weavers. Your superfine wools are much sought after by merchants outside of Scotland. Do you not know that the king's own Stuart plaid is made upon Graham looms?''

"My, you know such a lot." Cara sighed. She had no memory of looms or a prosperous village, nor of any home other than Dunluce, though Grace O'Malley had told her nearly the same thing.

"Becca tells you the truth, Cara," Margie McKenna said as she paused in the turning of her spindle. "Mother also speaks well of Graham weavers. She asked father to go and find out about the wheels they use to make their patterns repeat themselves. That is why he went to Aberdeen when Aunt Claire and Uncle Richard returned home. When he returns he will bring drawings of their new machine."

"Wheels." Cara remembered the wondrous toys of her mentor. She wished she was able to share Almoy's deep fascination for all things mechanical.

"Sir Almoy experimented with many peculiar things with wheels and cogs, flying machines and horseless carts. That was my greatest failing, he claimed. That I had no skills with things that move. It always frustrated me to consider things of an impractical nature. I like the idea of a wheel that would make our work easier."

"Poppa prefers the practical," Becca added.

"I'm not surprised," Cara observed. "Nothing here at Castle Kenna has an impractical use or purpose. I think its time I stop ruining this particular cloth. Becca, I yield to your superior skill."

Jane McKenna put aside her spindle and stood as Cara did, brushing lint from her skirt. The sixteen-year-old had become Cara's shadow, replacing Rose, who couldn't bear to be separated from her Ralph and the prospect of a day's courting. Cara didn't mind Jane's company. The younger girl was tolerant of silences and gaps in conversations.

"Do not worry overmuch about the weaving, Cara. Skill improves with practice."

Cara nodded as she opened the door from the weaving room. The sun was full and the afternoon warm. She quietly longed for a solitary walk in the hills.

"There's a new foal just born in the stables." Jane volunteered a bit of news. "Would you like to see him?"

"Perhaps another time." Cara lifted her skirts to clear a puddle adjoining the raised herb beds. A little farther on, she stopped to pluck weeds from the borage, sniffing deeply of the scented plants. "I know of an excellent cordial that uses borage, mint, gentian and mace. It does wonders for a sour stomach."

"Each year mother plants twice as many herbs as the one before and there is never enough when the season ends," Jane said. "You must give her your recipe. Perhaps she'll grant you permission to make it." Jane carefully spread her apron and knelt beside Cara, their hands making quick work of removing the sprouting weeds. This batch of herbs was mature, nearly ready to be cut and hung to dry.

"It seems a very complicated task to manage all that your mother does so smoothly."

"You are learning. In a few years it will all come most easily to you," Jane said encouragingly. Cara sat back on her heels, gazing round the domain of the Mckenna's wife. Aye, she could learn, but that would not make any difference.

Three women laughed in the washhouse yard, talking as they pegged the laundry upon the tautly stretched lines. Megan flounced her hips when she saw Cara look at her. The servant had her hems hiked and tucked at her waist, revealing her firm, fleshy calves and bare feet. She looked earthy, strong and healthy. Cara swallowed down the tinge of nausea that plagued her this morning. If the bile kept rising in her throat, she would have to beg a potion from Lady Elaina.

That was the one thing she might never learn to like at Castle Kenna. She had always taken what she wanted, be that milk or a scrap of cheese or whatever was necessary. Since becoming a handfasted bride, she had learned that if she did not preface her every request with "Gordie asks I be given," she might as well not ask for anything. That galled her.

"Are you happy, Cara?" Jane asked as she dusted off her hands.

"Happy? Oh, I must be. I am in Scotland," Cara lied.

Jane was none the wiser. The sun rose and set in her brother. All the Mckennas assumed Cara could not help but love him just as dearly. But she didn't. Who could love a man that changed to a cold stone the moment he rose from his bed?

Oh, he made the nights hot enough if he deigned to join her. By day, he avoided her completely. Nor did he ever say what he felt when the exhaustion of passion dropped his sweat-damp head to her shoulder. Outside the entrapment of lust, nothing was shared between them.

The days had not been easy.

Then there was Megan. Cara had never known a mean-spirited woman before. In her whole life she had given the trait of vindictive spite to the male of her species. Gordie's leman gave new meaning to the word *cruel.*

Cara left Jane in the garden and returned to Gordie's hall. She gathered her threads and mending and sat near the north window working neat, precise stitches into the deliberate cuts made in her second best everyday gown. She had learned by experience never to send her things to be washed with Gordie's. Each garment she had foolishly allowed to go to the castle's laundry came back to her shredded.

A knock at the open door caught her attention. It was the boy, Kurt, bringing an armload of wood for Gordie's hearth.

"Good morning, Kurt," Cara said to the boy.

"Lady," he mumbled, offering no bow or even a respectful duck of his head.

"Gordie has adequate wood down here, Kurt. Would you mind laying it in the box upstairs?"

"As you wish, lady," the boy said plainly. He trudged up the stairs with his burden. Cara took a deep breath. Had she asked too much? Perhaps he was tired or ill. Her fingers were still while she listened to his step across the upper floor. Then the clatter of the wood being dropped into the box came soon enough. Shortly, the boy came down. "I filled yer tub earlier."

"Thank you, Kurt. That was most thoughtful of you."

His shoulders jerked. He cast her a dismissive look. "And I'm told to remind you that you are to join the laird's table come supper."

"I see." Cara bent her head as she pushed the needle into the fabric. "Has my lord husband no returned then?"

"Dunno," Kurt answered. Cara did not see the snarling curve on his lips. She did feel the malevolence of his stare. It raised hackles on her neck. The fine fabric puckered as she drew the thread too tight. "Did he no come to yer bed last eve?"

The odd question made Cara look up. "You know he took the culled mares to Aberdeen."

Kurt made a face and stared hard at her. "I thought me da was back yesterday noon."

He turned and departed, leaving Cara with questions filling her mind. She watched the swagger of his shoulders, recognizing the blood of the Mckenna's that marked him as a son of Gordon Mckenna. The boy was troubled, a brooder.

Breaking past Kurt's reserve was proving a difficult task. Each evening the whole family came to the Mckenna's hall. Games were played, songs sung, stories told. Cara always brought a coin or set of nut shells and a pebble. The find-the-stone game delighted the other children. Kurt Autry remained apart. He never batted an eyelash over any trick she performed. In that, he was like his father, a skeptic who thought all magic trickery.

It did no good for her to brood. Putting away the irreparable gown, Cara took up a basket and went to the washhouse. There she unpinned Gordie's laundered shirts and small clothes as well as her own, neatly folding each garment before laying it in her basket.

Megan stood blocking the gate with a wicker basket on her hip as Cara prepared to leave. "Well, if it isn't m'lady."

Cara checked behind her to see if Megan spoke to someone else. No one else was about. The servant smoothed her free hand across the soft auburn curls clinging damply to her brow, thrusting out her more than ample and barely covered breasts. "Where do you suppose your lord spent his morning, eh?"

The tilt of Megan's chin showed a darkened mark on her throat. Color flooded Cara's cheeks. She understood the source of such a mark now. "Would you mind moving from the gate, Megan?" Cara requested.

"Aye, Irish. I mind. I mind greatly. I'll no share the mon I love. Ye don't deserve Gordie. He's too good for the likes of you."

"Then why do you hurt him, destroy his things?"

Megan's eyes narrowed, and Cara realized she'd asked the wrong question. "It is no me he blames for his torn shirts and ruined hose and well ye know it. He'll no be keeping a careless, clumsy wench when the trial is up. The clan will no accept ye, either."

Megan wasn't saying anything Cara hadn't already foreseen for herself. Cara shifted the basket and met Megan's hateful glare with a calm, unemotional expression that gave nothing away. "I also have the right of choice...to refuse the Mckenna. Now, move out of my way."

"What a fool ye be. Ye haven't a choice. If ye were wise, ye would leave now. The portcullis is open. None will stop ye if ye just walk out."

Cara sought patience and bit her tongue. "Now why would I want to do that?"

"Because if ye don't, I'll put a curse on ye!" Megan made a crude hex sign. "Be gone, Mulvaine!"

"Think you a witch?" Cara asked, holding within the laugh that threatened to burst out.

"I have powers. The laird's mine. I'll no give him up. Be gone, bitch!"

"Gladly, if you'll just move your wide arse out of the gate." Cara's eyes narrowed. "Get out of my way."

"Ye'll be sorry!" Megan swung round and stomped inside the washhouse.

Cara wanted to laugh; then she really wanted to howl. She would be gone quick enough; the jealous woman didn't know the half of it. She shifted the basket to her hip and exited the gate.

Megan fled to the cluster of other servants in the yard. As Cara passed through the gate into the bailey, two made a sign in her direction to ward off the evil eye.

Now, what have I done? Cara flushed to the roots of her hair, knowing the Scots could be as foolish as the Irish. Rose came storming across the bailey, back from her ride with Ralph Stewart.

"Ach, Cara, let me give you a hand. Are you busy with wifely duties this day?" Rose forced a smile as she took one handle of the basket.

Cara took one look at Rose's face and knew the girl was shamming. "Hello, Rose. Have you enjoyed your ride with Ralph?"

"It was splendid," Rose said through her teeth. "Do you know that you change the subject when asked a question, Cara?"

"No, I most certainly do not." Cara did not know what to say in answer to that, any more than she knew what to say when a rival bared a passion mark on her neck and implied Gordie bedded her. What she knew was that she felt hurt and angry.

She did not want to talk about such things with empty-headed Rose.

"Why isn't Megan carrying this basket for you? The laundry is her work."

"Megan!" Cara spat the name out in disgust. "I'll no be asking her to touch any thing of mine!"

Rose grinned to hear the possessive declaration sprout from Cara's lips. "Good for you! That woman is such a bitch! Cara, did you ever tell Gordie we both think Megan cut your wedding gown?"

"There's another," Cara responded, but this time her voice was carefully lowered. She might risk saying what was on her mind, but no one other than Rose was going to hear her say it. "You may not know it, sister Rose, but no one hereabouts tells yer brother anything!"

"Oh, my," Rose exclaimed, "you are in rare form this afternoon. What has happened?"

Outside Gordie's tower, Cara lowered the basket to the ground. She glared at the soft clouds scattered over the sky and longed to get free of the castle walls. "Not a thing! I hate to say this, but I think the moment has come that I am homesick for Dunluce."

Rose lifted the latch on the heavy door and pushed it open to Gordie's hall. "From the little you've said of Dunluce, I wouldn't think that was a place you'd grow homesick for."

"Perhaps." Cara hoisted the basket again and hauled it inside the shadowed hall. "What I miss is my horse and my freedom and my mentor, Sir Almoy. I thought I was a prisoner there, but now I see that I was not."

"This sounds like a tired woman talking." Rose left the door standing open so that more daylight could enter the tower hall. She hurried to the shutters and opened them, as well. Bright sun sparkled through the mullioned windows and dappled on the polished floor. "Oh, my! Cara, what have you done?"

Cara turned to look at the hall, trying to see it through Rose's eyes. "Do you think Gordie will like it?"

"He'd better." Rose approvingly surveyed the room. It sparkled of polish and shine from its sober ribbon fold panels to the priceless Venetian chandelier hung from the center beam. "But you know how men are . . . impossible to please."

"It took me all morning to arrange it so."

"So when did you find time to scrub and polish the floor? Honestly, Cara. No wonder you are out of sorts. What you need is a nap."

Cara bent to a basket near the hearth that she had filled with dried herbs and flowers. Rose admired the touches of heather scattered about in unlikely places. Cara had even woven a wreath of grapevines and hung it to the wall where Gordie's armor was stored.

"Oh, I want so much to have my own home to make so welcome. You've done a fine job of making this tower homey."

"But do you think Gordie will like it?"

"He'd better," Rose declared again, vowing to make certain Gordie knew of Cara's efforts and was suitably grateful, thinking to herself that at least her brother could be prompted into showing some regard—unlike her Ralph. And why shouldn't Gordie be grateful, when Cara was such a sweet thing, wearing her heart on her sleeve? Anyone could see that the girl simply adored Gordie. Rose sighed deeply and said a prayer that her own marriage would be half as content.

"I have the perfect addition. A woven mat for the door so that loutish brother of mine will wipe his feet and not track a mess on your hard work. I'll bring it to you anon."

"Oh, no, Rose. You must keep it for your own house."

"Nonsense! I can give you whatever I want. And you'll accept it, too! No arguing. Now I want you to go upstairs and take a nap. You've shadows under yer eyes and you're as wan as a ghost. Are you feeling all right?"

"I'm fine, Rose."

"Certain? Mayhaps yer monthlies are coming."

"'Tis time, I suppose," Cara answered listlessly. No topic was sacred in the Kenna household. Even Laird Mckenna had asked Cara this morning if she'd had her flow. Not that such a thing was any business of his. She had been saved from answering by Lady Elaine who had roundly confronted her inquisitive husband and told him to shush and not ask Cara such questions. "I think I will lie down. I am tired."

"Well, of course you are. Everything looks splendid, Cara, but I will say again, you have no need to work yourself to a frazzle. You mustn't take on so much at one time. Men don't often appreciate all our efforts. You will rest now, won't you?"

"Oh, aye, I will." Cara nodded. She was tired—very, very tired. "I think I will just see to the water for a bath."

"You'll do no such thing." Rose turned to the fire herself, moving the large pot over the hearth on its iron hook.

"Rose, don't get your gown dirty touching that." Cara rushed to tend to the fire herself. She laid kindling over the coals and fanned them. Within a few minutes a wisp of smoke rose and a flame burst out of the dry slivers. She watched the flame lick upward on the kindling.

"Here now, you promised me you would rest, Cara. Come on, enough work for today."

"I will. I'll just set a log on the fire once it's going good, then I'll take my nap."

"All this trouble for a bath. You could come over to my room and have one drawn in a minute."

"I would have to ask Gordie's permission to go there," Cara replied.

"No, you don't." Rose stiffened.

"Oh, but I do." Cara reached for a large piece of wood and laid it on the kindling. "I'm a handfasted woman, Rose. Those are the terms given me. What I have is what Gordie grants me."

Rose was at an impasse with those words and knew it. "Well, it needn't be taken so literally," she argued. "I can invite you to share what I have."

"Aye, and I thank you for your kindness. I will remain here and heat my water by and by. And do not fear, I will take that nap."

Rose's pretty brow furrowed with a frown. Something was wrong. Cara wasn't the same Cara as she had been in the days before the handfasting.

Rose tapped her foot impatiently under the hidden folds of her gown. She had more than half a mind to find that bounder and set him on his ear, starting with his leman who still slept under the castle roof. But having just come from a battle of wills with her betrothed, the prospect of confronting her autocratic brother lacked appeal. She needed to regroup and select her battles with care.

"Well, if I stay here we'll chatter the whole afternoon away and you'll never get any rest. Go and heat your water here, but I had better not hear that you are toting buckets from the well. Is that clear, Cara?"

"Kurt filled the tub afore he brought Gordie's wood." Cara stood up then, brushing smudges from her skirt. She did take the bucket of ash to hand and followed Rose downstairs with it.

"Set it here, Cara." Rose insisted Cara take the bucket no farther than the outer door. "I'll send a boy to fetch it. You go rest."

"Fine. I will." Cara put the bucket on the flagstones by the stoop and bid Rose good day. She stood in the open door, gazing over the high wall after Rose had gone up to the manor.

Usually the bailey yard bustled with activity. The Mckenna's vassals did their arms practice there. Today the men had gone hunting, so the inner ward was quiet for a change. The dogs in the nearby pens, however, were making a racket. Cara heard Mimms' unmistakable howl of complaint. It galled her that her dog must remain chained. Each time she had asked Gordie if she could free Mimms, he had said no.

The barking and growling was louder than normal. Cara went to investigate and found a handler had been bitten and Mimms was the guilty animal. He was quite out of sorts, straining at the chain that held him fastened to an iron ring fitted to the castle wall. He snarled and snapped at the knot of handlers intent upon subduing him.

One swung a stick at Mimms' head.

"Hold!" Cara shouted, rushing inside the pens. "Don't you dare hit my dog!"

"The cur bit me!"

"For the love of God, I'd bite you, too, if you came at me with a stick!" Cara ducked under the raised club, throwing her arms round Mimms' neck to soothe and protect him.

"What's going on here?" Gordie demanded as he dropped from the saddle of his horse. He'd heard the racket of the wolfhound down in the village and had come charging back to the castle expecting to find his best hunters with their throats torn out and the wolfhound killing every man in the keep.

Instead he found the collies riled and stretching their leads to the fullest extension of the leathers, snapping to get at the woman that had invaded their domain. "Jocko, what goes here?"

"I was only tryin' t' feed the beast," Jock exclaimed, displaying his wound. His forearm was badly mangled and blood ran down his fingers.

"He beat Mimms," Cara accused, pointing past the trainer to the stick that now lay in the dirt.

"Come out of the pens, Cara," Gordie ordered. He knew what had the collies howling in a frenzy. One bitch was in heat, but not ready to be put to stud. It certainly didn't do for a woman to go walking amid the animals whose noses could detect the most delicate scents. "I said, come away."

The wolfhound snarled more viciously than ever. Gordie's eyes narrowed. Cara stood, her hand fixed to Mimms' collar, staying him, shushing the animal even as her eyes defied Gordie's.

"I'll no tolerate the mistreating of my animal, Gordie Mckenna." Cara squared off, prepared to defend Mimms with her life, if need be.

Gordie passed his horse's reins to a trainer and waved a dismissive hand to the balance of the lookers. All departed from the commotion of howling dogs.

Cara watched the men retreat, then she pointed to the stick that lay in the dirt between her and Gordie. "He hit Mimms with that stick."

"Mistress, wolfhound or no wolfhound, if you do not come away from the pens now, that stick is going to see service upon your fine legs."

He meant what he said. Cara ordered Mimms to quiet, and released his collar. She straightened her shoulders and walked out of the dog pens, avoiding the snap of several muzzles of the shaggy dogs the Mckennas favored. The collies were as beautiful as Mimms was ugly, but they didn't have half the appeal.

She gave Gordie Mckenna a wide berth, never taking her eyes from his as she got around him. In fact, she chose to back into the bailey yard so that her eyes did not break from his. Gordie stalked out of the dog pens.

"It isn't right to keep Mimms chained. He's never hurt anyone here until that man beat him. He needs to run and exercise—and he has a great appetite," Cara argued.

"He's a wild, untrained vicious animal," Gordie growled. It was as low and as dangerous a warning as Cara had ever heard him issue. "There's children all about this castle. That beast is going to stay tethered to that chain and you'll no go near him again."

Cara quit retreating. "What did you say?"

"Don't cock your head at me and pretend you no heard what I said."

Cara had heard him all right. Every soul in Castle Kenna should have heard him.

"I'm no deaf. You needn't shout at me." He was the Mckenna's heir and his word was law where she was concerned. Not even his father would overrule him when it came to her. Cara took her eyes from his face and looked past the wooden gate into the pen where Mimms mournfully whined for her to come back to him. His loving, baleful gaze tore at her heart. His tail thumped in the dust and his tongue lolled out of his mouth. At one sound of distress from her, the dog would give his all to break the chain that held him fast. Cara swallowed the taste of defeat in her mouth.

Without looking back at Gordie, she swirled her skirts around and ran across the bailey to the arched door of the tower. Inside, she put her weight to the heavy oak and shoved it shut. A fit of temper made her lift the bar and drop it into place. If her dog was to be kept prisoner, then she might as well be one, too.

She stood back, dusting her hands, relishing the satisfaction such rebellion had brought her in the past. The north tower of Dunluce had a heavy door and a stout bar to make it impregnable. When she was little she'd had no way to keep her grandfather out. That was why she had taken to searching the hidden passages and obscure nooks. Years of beatings had taken place before she'd gained the strength to bar a door.

She wasn't done gloating before the consequences of barring Gordie Mckenna from his hearth and home came to her. His tower was no defensive keep. It had low windows, mullioned glass and inset shutters that could easily be smashed to pieces if he really wanted to get inside. She hadn't the right to lock him out.

Cara paced from corner to corner, wringing her hands, worrying her lip. She hadn't the right. No, she'd never had any rights, not at Dunluce and not here at Castle Kenna. But she had taken them at Dunluce. She would take them at Castle Kenna, too. Gordie Mckenna be damned.

Gordie wasn't surprised when the Mulvaine turned on her heels and fled from him. She was damned smart to get a head start but damned stupid to slam the door in his face. When he heard the bar drop into place, he froze outside his own quar-

ters absolutely rigid. Not that the barred door was any imped-
iment. He could break the damn thing down if he wanted. Hell,
he could walk twelve feet to the left, reach up to the window
ledge and haul himself inside.

Then the shutters slammed and the bolts that held them fast
were shoved into their slots.

Gordie cocked his head, listening to the sounds inside his
tower. She was running up the steps. Then bang, bang, bang,
she slammed the upper shutters closed. All of them.

"Cara!" Gordie shouted.

His voice echoed up the hollow walls to Ulrich's quarters on
the third and fourth level of the tower. Silence. "Cara."

Nothing. He walked out of the archway and stood back, letting his gaze travel to the top of the crenellated tower seventy
feet off the ground. The bailey wall stood twenty-five feet high.
A century ago it had been reinforced by a matching outer wall.
The interior cavity, for the most part, was filled with earth, except where stores of arms were placed and stairwells and bar-
racks were needed.

He made up his mind then that he couldn't allow her to get
away with barring the door to him. He returned to the arch,
turning to Ulrich's open door, trudging up the steep stairs to the
top.

Ulrich's chamber was not near as comfortable as Gordie's.
His cousin spent little time at Castle Kenna. The room on the
third level of the tower contained a simple trestle, benches and
a low, uncurtained bed. Ulrich groaned when Gordie's shadow
fell across his face.

"Go away. I'm a man in pain."

"The hell you say. Get yer lazy ass out of that bed and help
me lift the quarter door."

"Gordie? Hell, mon, I thought you stayed in the village to
dice with Ralph." Ulrich winced at the sound of wood scraping on the floor. He sat up bleary-eyed to find Gordie shoving
his table aside. Then he dropped to his knee to lift the iron ring
from the slot cut into the oak floor. "What are you doing?"

"What does it look like I'm doing?"

"Opening the trap. Why? Are you locked out?"

"So I am," Gordie snarled. The section of hinged wood was
heavily reinforced. His arms flexed as he lifted, then came up
to his feet.

"I told ya there'd be the devil t' pay if we stayed drinking all night in Aberdeen." Ulrich rubbed his hands over his face and stroked back his hair from his brow.

"Shut yer face, Ulrich."

"Couldn't you have gone through the window?"

"Not without breaking the glass."

"Oh," Ulrich muttered. "She locked you out, then?"

"Aye," Gordie grumbled, none to happy with that. "Close this after I've dropped down. And, Ulrich—"

"Aye?"

"Take yerself over to the hall for the next hour. I want my privacy."

"Well, now, I don't know."

"I do."

Ulrich lifted a questioning brow. "Maybe you ought to think about this."

"Out," Gordie repeated. "And don't come back."

"See if I go drinking with you again!" Ulrich was on his feet. By the time Ulrich reached him, Gordie dangled by his hands from the floor joists.

"Close it." Gordie hissed his final order.

"Maybe it would be more interesting to watch," Ulrich teased. The glare Gordie fixed him with backed Ulrich away. He closed the trapdoor with very little sound. Gordie did listen as the table was shoved back into place. Then he dropped fifteen feet to his bedchamber floor.

Cara jumped away from the washstand the moment she'd heard voices on the floor above. Her eyes fastened to the ceiling, searching until she saw the trapdoor raise out of a coffer.

"Oh, no!" she whispered when a pair of recognizable boots appeared.

She scrambled to her side of the bed and lurched to grab her dressing gown to fasten over her shift. To her horror, Gordie's knees and hips, then his whole body dangled through the trapdoor. She gasped when he fell through the air. He grunted in pain on impact, falling slightly forward, unable to take a single step for the bolt of pain shooting up his leg.

Cara thrust her arms in her robe, her shaking hands seeking the tie belt when Gordie's angry gaze fixed upon her. "My lord!"

"Dinna 'my lord' me." Gordie straightened fully, facing her, making a huge effort to wipe his expression free of pain.

"Oh, dear." Cara knew she should run before he laid a hand upon her. But she saw the pain he tried valiantly to erase from his features.

Instead of running the other way, she ran to him, slipping her arm round his waist to help steady him. "You've hurt your foot anew."

Gordie had, but he was damned if he would admit it. What was a little pain? He was a warrior. He was the next Mckenna.

Cara drew his arm round her shoulder, giving him her body to lean upon, and helped him limp to the side of the bed. He sat heavily. She knelt at his feet, her quick fingers unfastening his laces. She peeled the soft boot off his foot.

"Oh, that's bad." Cara clucked her tongue. "Why have you let it fester this long? Are you daft, mon? It is rotting yer leg off." Cara saw how grimly his lips were pursed, and knew he suffered.

"It's just a damned toe, not me whole leg."

"Sit here, my lord. I can relieve some of the pain."

"Can you? You've caused it."

Gordie wanted to throw her across his lap and beat the daylights out of her for being such an idiot. He couldn't even do that to restore his male ego. She bolted to her feet and filled a basin with steaming water from the large pot she had heating over the fire.

"Why the devil do women think hot water is the cure for everything?" Gordie snapped as Cara set the basin of steaming water before him.

Cara shrugged, making a face as she tried to think of a suitable answer. "Some injuries need ice to soothe, but there is no ice this time of year."

Gordie didn't argue further; he put his foot in the hot water and nearly fainted from the shock. His wife bustled about, intent upon some other cruelty. She returned with numerous supplies—a needle from her sewing, a burning candle, a glass filled to the very rim with whiskey and a clean towel. Gordie fought with the swimming spots dancing before his eyes.

"What's that for?" he demanded as she knelt before him and set her supplies round about her knees.

"Oh, this is for you." Cara handed him the fine crystal glass, another treasure Gordie had acquired in Venice. The amber liquid splashed over his fingers. If he drank all that was in the glass, he'd be in fine shape, drunk as a lord on an empty belly.

It would lessen the ache pulsing within his injured foot. He put the rim to his lips and gulped. It was potent.

Cara carefully shifted so that her back was presented to him and hopefully, his view of his badly mangled toe was limited.

"This won't hurt," she promised, and lifted his foot from the bath, patting it dry with the towel. The needle was red-hot and she carefully picked it up, holding it fast between folds of the towel. Then before he could divine what she was doing, she pierced the nail of his great toe.

"Mille Murdher!" Gordie's Gaelic curse exploded like a bellow from a raging bull.

Cara leaped away from his legs. The basin of water tipped and spilled. Gordie bolted onto one foot, shouting down the roof with foul curses, clutching his bad toe. "Blood and fury. You've killed me!"

Hustling to the safety of the opposite side of the bed, Cara warily waited for him to calm. His dancing about sent spurts of blood in all directions. Actually, that was good. The more blood and fluid that escaped from the injury, the sooner it would stop hurting.

"Och? The mischief is upon us! I've been mortally wounded!" Gordie roared. He hobbled to the high-back chair before his fire and sank down onto the seat, gripping his foot with both hands. "You stabbed me!"

"Aye."

Cara twisted the towel round her hands. Then she saw the lovely glass broken into many pieces on the floor. What was left of the whiskey pooled around it. Water ran down the seams of the oak floor. So much for her morning's labor. She fetched the basin and knelt to wipe up the mess, wringing out the toweling as it soaked up the water and whiskey. She carefully picked up each sliver of broken glass.

"Give me a clean linen, will you?"

Cara swung round to look at the man all crumpled and hunched in his fine chair, and felt a pulling on her heartstrings for the injured little-boy look that was all about him. Gladly, she fetched him a clean linen, then rinsed the basin, filled it with fresh hot water and brought him that and a cake of scented soap, as well. He flashed her a killing look from eyes that were bloodshot. His mouth twisted in a grimace. Cara looked at his foot and saw the hugely swollen toe had gone down considerably.

Gordie groaned. The towel twisted round his foot like a loose bandage. He closed his eyes and leaned his head against the backrest of his chair. In a minute or so, his mouth relaxed slightly.

"Would you allow me to bind it and pack it in a poultice?" Cara asked.

"No. You've tortured me quite enough for one day, mistress," Gordie snapped. "Bring me my boot and a clean stocking if you can find one in the jumbled heaps you made of my things."

Cara knew exactly where his stockings were. Perhaps the order of his things had been changed. After all, she hadn't known where he'd kept anything, but she had been most careful in her sorting, folding and repacking. When she came to him with clean stockings, he had set the basin on the floor and returned his foot to the hot water. So, he'd decided to use his head, she thought.

Gordie's eyes opened to find her standing before him in her short shift, her robe still untied and flapping about her sides. Her legs were bare, exposed. They were nice legs. He tried to compose his thoughts, but her bare legs distracted him.

He cleared his throat. "Explain to me what your purpose was of barring me from my own quarters."

Cara handed him the stockings. She shook her head, then looked up at the coffered ceiling. "'Twas a foolish thing to do. I have always lived in a tower. I forgot this one had stairs without."

"I should beat you."

"Oh, aye, you should. I deserve it. Shall I go and get you a stick?"

"Be damned," Gordie growled. "When I want a stick to beat you, I'll damn well fetch it myself. Go on, bind the foot with your poultice and evil medicines. Then take the bar off the door and fetch me something to eat before I faint from the lack of decent food in my belly. I was all night riding from Aberdeen."

"You were?" she asked. "You no came home last eve?"

"Hell," he growled cantankerously. "I just got here to find that dog attacking my men and my bed barred from me."

Cara's head cocked sideways, considering his words. He spoke the truth. In her mind's eye she saw him riding through the night. Damn Megan, she thought. Had she listened to her own true voice, jealousy wouldn't have made Cara act so foolishly.

She was quick about making a suitable poultice to draw the rest of the poison, and then wrapped the injury carefully in a sturdy linen binding, which she covered with a stocking. When she finished, Gordie silently commended her on her skill. The throbbing pain had ended. He had been out of sorts and in pain since the toe had been crushed all of three weeks now.

She brought her stool and pillow to him and propped his heel on them.

"I'll fetch you a meal quick, my lord."

Gordie caught her trailing robe and stopped her just after she'd made a hasty curtsey to him. "You'll no go running out of here with your robe flapping round yer legs."

"Oh." Cara had completely forgotten how she was dressed. "Oh!"

She colored brightly, conscious once again of her state of undress. It hadn't mattered in the past hour. Gordie released her robe and she took it off, hastily pulling her gray wool gown over her head. It was badly soiled from her energetic scrubbing, but it would do until she had a chance to bathe.

Gordie saw that she never took her laces out completely. "Come here."

Cara hurriedly drew one set of laces together at her right side. She cast a sideways glance at her husband and approached him. He took up the other laces that made the bodice of her gown fit her chest and waist when they were drawn secure.

"You need new clothes," he observed. "No one wears gowns that lace up the sides anymore. 'Tis not the fashion. Ladies at court wear stomachers and binders and undergowns of lace and lawn."

"That is nice." Cara stood still while his fingers neatly tightened the fabric around her. "But I've no need to be fashionable. I'm no going to court."

"No, you are not, but it wouldn't hurt for you to have some other color to wear than gray. And wool is fine for winter garments, but there are all sorts of other cloths that are pleasant to look at and feel against one's skin."

"How does your foot feel?" Cara changed the subject. His hand lingered at her side, his thumb intent upon stroking the nub of her breast.

"What foot?" Gordie asked, not distracted from the ripe fullness of her breasts that the tightened fabric revealed. Despite the wool and the simple cotton covering of her shift, he could feel her nipple harden and thrust itself against the press of his thumb.

"I'll go fetch yer food." Cara felt mesmerized, unable to galvanize her body into motion. She shouldn't stand there and let him handle her, should she? It was broad daylight.

"Aye. Go fetch my food." Gordie dropped his hand to the armrest of the chair. Cara stood there a moment more, then she quickly gathered the soiled toweling and the basin, and put them away.

"I'll be quick," she promised.

Gordie watched her go, then closed his eyes and tried to gather his wits. What the devil was he doing? He hadn't the foggiest idea. Whiskey made him foolish.

He dozed a little, waking when Cara settled a laden tray on the gate-legged table at his side. She had found quite a lot; a half a game hen, a loaf of rye and potted cheese, berry tarts and a pitcher of ale. Gordie shifted in the chair, drew the table closer and set to eating. A moment later he looked up at Cara.

"Don't hover over me like a servant. Sit down, eat with me."

"I ate at noon, my lord, with your sisters."

"You prefer their company to mine? Sit, I said. Try this leg. The meat will do you good. You're too thin by half."

Cara perched stiffly on the second chair. She spread a napkin over her lap and took the hen's leg he held out to her. After she'd taken a bite, she said, "I'm not thin."

Gordie tilted his head in study of her, trying to imagine what she'd look like if she were fleshed out like his sister Rose. In comparison to any of his sisters, Cara Mulvaine appeared delicate and frail.

Gordie pulled off the wing and passed that to her next. "Eat it," he commanded, expecting to be obeyed. Cara nibbled at the piece. She wasn't hungry. She was sleepy. He had dropped in and ruined her nap. Now she'd probably never get a rest. She laid the bones on the side of the tray and wiped her fingers clean.

The cauldron over the fire steamed, the water ready to heat her drawn tub. Cara regarded the tub longingly, but schooled herself to wait. "Did you sell all the mares, my lord?"

"Gordie. My name is Gordie. You overdo the 'my lord.' I expect it will be decades before I'm the Mckenna. Yes, I had good luck selling the four mares. It's what we Kennas are known best for—our livestock."

"Jane tells me there is a new foal."

"Aye, a fine one. He's blessed with fine hooves and ankles, a star on his forehead and a coat as red as my father's beard. My own charger sired him. Would you like to go and see him?"

Cara was torn by that indulgent offer. "Oh, aye, I would, my lord, but . . ." She colored to the roots of her hair and cast another glance to the steaming pot on the fire. If she didn't put another log on the fire, the pot would cool and she'd have wasted the fire and the heating.

"But what?" Gordie glanced where she had, seeing the blackened pot hanging on the swing iron over his hearth. The water was steaming. "What's the water for?"

"A bath, sir." Cara couldn't make herself say his name. It was just too familiar and, right that moment, she felt too awkward.

"Ah, I see." Gordie understood. Her shy blushes told him more than anything else did. She certainly wasn't one to offer much information with anything she said. Was it possible he was mistaken and that she'd barred the door out of modesty, to bathe undisturbed? He didn't think so. "Well, go on then. Take your bath."

Cara blinked. "With you here?"

"My lady, a bath in my presence will reveal nothing new."

Cara just sat there looking at him blankly; then her eyes widened. "Oh, no, I don't think so. You will have to go downstairs."

"I canna. There is this foot that impedes me." Gordie's open hand indicated the propped foot. "And, my lady, may I remind you that it was my sense of propriety that induced you not to run from here in your shift only a few minutes ago. You hadn't given a thought to your state of dress from the moment I dropped in to visit you."

"That's because you hurt yourself."

"So I did." Gordie grinned. He leaned back and patted his full and satisfied belly and forced a deep yawn. "You've been a good, attentive wife, caring for my injury, seeing that my belly is full and sated. I quite feel like a nap."

"Shall I help you to the bed?"

"No, I'll be fine right here." Gordie yawned again, drained the last of his ale and settled peacefully where he was.

Thwarted, Cara busied herself with cleaning up the tray and removing it downstairs. Obviously, he wasn't granting her privacy. She worried her lip, looked at his composed, peaceful face. Then she made up her mind. He was right. What did it matter?

She tiptoed about, pouring steaming water into the cold tub. *God, make him sleep for an hour,* Cara prayed as she untied her shift and let it drop to the floor at her feet.

She stepped into the tub, shivering deliciously at the temperature. It wasn't icy cold as if fresh out of the well, but it wasn't steaming hot, either. The round tub wasn't all that large, adequate for washing clothes, but as a bathtub it lacked dimension.

She made quite a picture in her little tub, Gordie thought as he watched through slitted eyes. She stuck up arms or legs and lathered them one by one, turned and twisted and bubbled, then simply relaxed, untroubled by any serious thought. Like a child, he thought.

There were two dimples at the base of her spine. Her rounded hips were lovely, perfect above those well-formed, strong legs. How much more watching he could take before he pounced on her, he didn't know.

A fine film of sweat damped his upper lip, making him stroke his finger across his mustache and wipe his mouth. He dropped his hand to his tunic, drawing the laces out, and shrugged off the garment.

"Cara." He spoke at last, the pressure in his loins making his voice husky and thick.

"My lord?" Cara turned to the sound of his voice. Her hair clung to her back, slick and wet. She drew a towel before her breasts, her lips parted and full.

"Come here," Gordie beckoned, silently imploring God to make her come to him willingly. He wasn't sure he could chase or catch her if she bolted like a deer flushed from the woods.

"Did I wake you?" she whispered.

"Nay." Gordie moved his hands wide, willing her to come to him. "Come here, Cara Mulvaine. I ache to hold you against me."

It seemed so incongruous, but there was his chest exposed and his arms open wide in welcome. Cara hesitantly moistened her lips, then padded on wet feet across the room to him. Gordie reached up and took the linen from her hands, discarding it to the floor. His fingers touched her breast, sliding down the damp curve, his palm flattening on her belly.

"My sweet Lord, but you are an exquisite creature, Cara Mulvaine. Sweet, soft and compliant," Gordie whispered, his voice hoarse with need. "What great sacrifice did I ever make in my life to be blessed with this treasure?"

Cara hadn't the foggiest idea of what he was talking about. His hand dropped lower on her belly and his palm cupped her; his broad fingers found, touched and separated the sensitive core of her womanhood. His crystal-blue eyes held her imprisoned just as surely as if he'd tied and bound her. Again she moistened her lips, unable to speak a word, fighting to draw her breath into her chest.

"My lord." Cara ached for his touch to deepen.

"Aye, it is sweet, isn't it? Come." Gordie stood and unfastened the belt that held his kilt bound to his hips. It fell with a clank to the floor. He was hard and throbbing, near to bursting with need. Still, he held her away from his body, looking at her, reveling in the beauty of her perfect form and shape. He twisted her hair into a damp turn off her shoulder and drew her against his body. He cradled her head with his own, smiling at the wonderful view his height gave him over her shoulder. It was impossible to resist letting his hands explore what his eyes had been so blessed to see.

"Do you know you have dimples here, perfect twin dimples in the best place a woman can be given them?"

"No, my lord." Cara shivered as his hands cupped her bottom cheeks and drew her hips against his. He was hot and hard, his manhood thrusting against her belly.

"Touch me, Cara," Gordie implored, lowering his head to taste her lips.

"May I, my lord?"

"Aye. I command it. Anything you wish to do, I will savor." His lips burned against hers. He gripped her buttocks and drew her hard against his chest, feeling the quiver of her belly as their stomachs met. Gordie drew her upward, gripping her thighs, separating them.

The sudden lift startled Cara. She threw her arms round his shoulders, catching hold as he lifted her off her feet. His tongue thrust deep inside her mouth, matched by the sudden quick plunge of his manhood deep inside her.

She was wet and slick from head to toe, slippery from the water of her bath and he was hot and dry and turgid, filling her. Without having to be told, she locked her legs round his hips, holding fast to him with both arms and legs. He broke the kiss with her mouth and reared back, looking at her flushed face, her swollen mouth.

"You are a quick study, my lady." His eyes crinkled in a smile that was pure pleasure to behold. Cara thought he was quite wicked and she blushed.

"My lord, your foot," Cara protested, afraid he would try to walk across the room with them thus entwined.

"To the devil with my foot, my lady. There is more than one way to make love, I promise you."

His mouth descended upon hers again and no further thought of protest occurred to Cara. She was barely conscious of the fact that he pressed her hard against the painted, plastered wall of the tower itself and drove into her. "I canna hold back. Go with me, Cara."

He kissed her, his hands gripping fiercely into the globes of her buttocks. Then the madness of passion swept over the both of them, driving out any thought except need.

His release was explosive, twisting his features as he shouted so loud, the closed shutters vibrated. Cara clung limply to him, caught between his burning body and the cold wall. Beads of sweat trickled between her breasts and twisted down her spine. A pleasured shudder quivered inside her thighs where they clenched fast to his hips.

"Sweet mother of God," Gordie groaned, his forehead pressing into the curve of her shoulder. Inside his great chest, his heart hammered with the ferocity of a war drum. His legs trembled, threatening to buckle at the knees. It took all of his concentrated strength to hold the both of them upright while his lungs bellowed in the sweet-scented air—ripe with their lovemaking.

He kissed her damp throat, stroked her waist and slowly pulled away from her. Their bellies were flattened and sticky. She couldn't stand upon her weakened legs.

Gordie laughed and hoisted her in his arms, gamely limping to his bed.

"Your foot!" Cara tried to stop him from doing such a foolish thing. He merely grinned and shook his hair from his neck and face.

"Ah, yes, my foot." He laughed and came on top of her, parting her thighs again for the exploration of his hand. "I am much too rough for you, my sweet. Why, you're hardly more than a raw virgin and I've battered you into a wall. Let me soothe you."

His mouth caressed her breast, drawing the aching nipple deep inside to stroke and torment it with his tongue. She squirmed deliciously against his hand, her thighs wide, allowing the delving play of his fingers inside her. Gordie revelled in her deep-throated groans, delighted by the little squeaks and squeals of pleasure that escaped from her mouth.

She was slick with his seed. He rubbed the heel of his hand against her pleasure nub then took it between his fingers as he moved to her other breast. His motions were tangent, congruent, the stroke of his tongue in rhythm to his thumb, the pressure matched. She began to twist against the unknown pleasure and tension building inside her, fighting him, not understanding what was coming.

She closed her legs against his hand, trying to stop him. He wouldn't allow that. He left her throbbing breast and stretched her upon the bed, forcing her thighs open with his strong hands. He wanted to taste her, see her, watch her face as she reached completion.

"Oh, no, my lord, please, no!" Cara averred when she realized what he was going to do.

"'Tis only a kiss," Gordie assured her and lifted her to his mouth. He wished the windows were wide open so that he could see everything she felt. Her small hands tugged at his hair, and he shook her off; then they clutched the sheets and kneaded them, helpless as her need built to growing explosion. Then it came with a shuddering scream, utter release as sweet and as strong and exhausting as his own had been.

Cara's slender limbs trembled and her heart slammed in her chest.

Gordie laughed and stretched out beside her, gathering her against his body. "Now, my sweet, I do believe you deserve a rest."

He drew a cover from the foot of the bed, tucking it round her. He kissed her soft, pliant lips, inordinately pleased at knowing the sleepy satisfied slant of her eyes was his doing.

"Ach, ye have the makings of a fine wife, Cara Mulvaine." Gordie smoothed the wet tangle of her hair across the pillow and let it fall onto the floor. That mattered not. He could eat off the floor since she'd taken his quarters to hand.

Her slitted eyes closed and her face relaxed as sleep took her.

Gordie grinned broadly as he gazed at her well kissed mouth. He tugged the soft coverlet down, exposing her breasts. Her nipples, like her mouth, were swollen and tumescent. He touched one hard bud, stroking it idly, intrigued as he always was by the wonder of a woman's body. He would never have guessed that his shy little mouse would be so responsive.

The shy little mouse was, in fact, a little wanton giving him great pleasure in bed. He shrugged. Why resist? It made the handfasting tolerable. He wasn't bound, was he? Did he put his mind to it, he could beat his father at this game and think of a way out of the church vows. If he didn't wind up killing her first when she provoked his temper. Gordie shook his head ruefully. If he tried that, he'd have to answer to the Mulvaine's slavering protector—that dog. He had to do something about the dog.

The beast had showed its true colors, maiming a good man. All that held Gordie back from destroying the animal was the fact that when and if the Mulvaine departed Castle Kenna for good, she could take her foul beast with her. But he would not risk another injury.

He was almost tempted to uncover her completely and idle the rest of the afternoon away playing with her. But he thought better of doing that. She would be sore and achy, tenderly abused. He was not so randy that he would hurt her deliberately.

God, but he could not believe the rambling idiocy of his thoughts. Why couldn't he make up his mind? Did he want her or did he not want her?

In all, Gordie decided he was pleased with her. He patted her hip then rose from the bed. He felt renewed, restored, perhaps even a trifle vindicated for the bashing she'd done of his ego not so very long ago.

Barring his door! Well, she'd not do that again. He'd be willing to wager on that. And if she did, well, he'd found a way to subdue her quite effectively. She was the most easily seducible woman he'd ever encountered.

He rose and dressed and went outdoors where he found Kurt and told the boy to empty the tub and bring Lady Cara fresh water. Gordie stayed close by while that job was completed. Cara slept through it. Gordie filled her black pot with water himself and set it back over the fire to warm. When Kurt brought him fresh wood, he saw that the fire was well laid and a suitable log placed on it.

That done, Gordie went whistling on about his business.

Chapter Twenty-Two

Cara dreamed of Dunluce. Sir Almoy beckoned her inside his scented tower.

"I have discovered the most unusual substance. It is a mysterious element, that when mixed with mercury, sulphur, certain boric salts and alums makes the most curious soft and pliable metal. See!"

He banged a silverlike rod against his worktable. It rang with the sound of true metal, yet bent with the consistency of soaked reeds.

"Curious," Cara remarked, watching Sir Almoy twist the metal rod into a circlet. "What will you do with it?"

"I am not certain." Almoy scowled. "'Tis very light."

"Aye." Cara accepted the one he handed to her and studied it. It was light as straw, but it was metal, but not like copper or silver or gold. "Could you make arrows of it?"

"Bah!" Almoy scoffed at that proposed use. "It has no weight. It wouldn't pierce a paper target. 'Tis useless, but most curious."

"Definitely," she agreed. "What else have you made?"

"Well, the gold eludes me. I cannot understand why God gave me two lifetimes to conduct my experiments, and still the quest eludes me. I thought to have it perfected."

"The transmutation?"

"Aye, of lead to gold. I have concluded it is a foolish quest. I wasted two score and learned nothing."

"That's harsh. Perhaps you forgot some ingredient—a salt or a nitrate."

"Yes, yes, and perhaps I wasn't pure enough within my heart. No, it all goes up in smoke. Here, look." Almoy moved to his workbench where another experiment was already set up. His crucible overflowed. Molten metal spilled onto the table-top. Flames erupted, parchments seared and smoked. A disaster of billowing smoke and hiccuping explosions hurt Cara's ears.

Cara smiled in her sleep. Nothing had changed at Dunluce if Almoy was setting the whole place upon its ear.

Finished with the day's laundry, Megan Autry gathered Eric up from his cradle and took him outside to bask in the day's warm sunshine. The spot she chose was against the sun-flooded west bailey wall, opposite Gordie's east-facing bank of windows.

Humming, she settled to a wood bench and bared her breast so Eric could nurse. He fussed hungrily, anxious to be unswaddled. Megan hummed as she unwound his arms and freed the binding from his chubby legs. It pleased her that her son squalled mightily at the sight of her heavily filled breast. She wanted the boy's cries to enter Gordie's chambers. The baby quieted when she lifted her nipple to his mouth. He clamped down ferociously, suckling hard, for the day had been long and Megan had not fed him between rising and now. She leaned back against the warm stone, smiling as the tingle of her milk letting down swept through her like an orgasm.

Megan stroked the baby's head, watching with hawklike eyes the shuttered windows. Earlier, she'd seen the Mulvaine slam and bang every shutter closed. A more telling and pleasing sight Megan hadn't seen since before the Irish bitch arrived at Castle Kenna.

Megan allowed her eyes to wander over the square tower. A telltale stream of smoke rose from the chimney flue high atop the tower. Megan's smile broadened. She would see the last of the Mulvaine shortly.

Eric had only suckled one breast and wanted to play when Gordie emerged from his keep, strutting like a well-sated cock. Megan smiled at him, and he paused before her long enough to admire Eric's toothless grin and give the babe a pat upon his round cheek. But Eric was not to be distracted from his purpose and grinned as he bit down on the exposed nipple at his mouth. His little hand patted possessively on Megan's full breast and the baby laughed.

So did Gordie before he strutted off. He called to Kurt and dropped a hand on the boy's shoulder and they walked into the stables together, father and son.

"Thas all right, me wee laddie," Megan crooned to the baby, lavishing him with affection. "The day will come that he'll take note of ye, too."

Nor would Gordie put aside either of her sons. He had assumed that Eric was his. Megan saw no reason to dissuade him of that notion. Eric would be a knight, just as Kurt was destined to greater things than a servant in a laird's house.

It wasn't right that the Mckenna's eldest grandson carted buckets and filthy trenchers, soiled cups and the slops at the beck and call of any in Castle Kenna. Megan clutched Eric possessively to her breast and watched the pride of her soul disappear with his father beyond the stable wall. Most likely, Gordie would make the boy muck out his stallion's stall. And Kurt would do it, willingly, without thinking ill of his father, ever.

Though she had no pretenses of her own, for her sons, Megan would do anything. She did not blame Gordie for his son's treatment, she blamed iron-fisted John Mckenna, who would not allow his own flesh and blood be recognized.

The Mckenna thought to usurp the place Kurt was rightly owed by forcing the Irish bitch to Gordie's bed.

That would change. The timid little bitch would run screaming all the way from whence she'd come before this day was through, Megan resolved.

What did it matter if Gordie had taken her maidenhead? The Mulvaine wasn't worthy of a Mckenna. What could her scrawny body give Gordie? Gordie needed sons. Strong healthy sons like Kurt and even little bastard, Eric.

What did it matter if Megan was just a laundry maid? Her sons were fine, healthy boys, one, the very image of his father, both as deserving of knighthood as any male in Scotland.

It was perhaps four o'clock, the sun high and hot. Work had been put aside once the cart the Mckenna brought back from Edinburgh was unloaded. Servant and master alike had found places to rest awhile this day.

Gordie rested in the apartment above the stable with Jeffry and Ulrich sampling a batch of Aberdeen rye. The whiskey burned their throats raw. They pronounced it the finest they'd ever tasted.

Gordie proposed a toast to his handfasted bride. They drank to her health.

Then the whole castle rocked and trembled.

Cara jerked upright. Her ears rang from the deafening sound of an explosion.

Almoy's gunpowder! she thought as smoke and saltpeter singed her nose. The bed drapes were in flames.

It was no dream! Panic struck her. She'd set the room on fire. A hot coal scorched her shoulder as she bolted out of bed and rushed to the windows to throw open the shutters.

Choking on the thick, pungently acrid air, her knees impacted with the stone wall, but reaching forward into the billowing smoke, she found no shutters. They were gone. Cara caught herself before falling, hanging on to the cool stone ledge for dear life as the smoke swelled and rose around her.

She dipped below the rising cloud, gasping for clean air, coughing deeply. She blindly groped for the edges of the window, her hands pricked by shards of splintered wood. She couldn't see a thing. She couldn't hear anything either, but she could feel the heat that licked behind her.

Gordie bolted out of the stables at a dead run, pushing past the crowd of kinsmen that had burst from his father's hall and every quadrant of the castle. Men shouted, women screamed and snatched up their children, fleeing a hail of cinders and ash raining out of the flame-engulfed roof of his tower.

"My God!" Ulrich shouted. He skidded to a halt, realizing that if Gordie hadn't kicked him out of his bed an hour or so ago, he'd have been blown sky-high.

"Cara! Where's Cara?" Gordie grabbed the first dark-haired woman he saw and swung her around before him.

"The Mulvaine?" Ulrich took up the call, lurching into the crowd. "Where's the Mulvaine? Who's seen her?"

Gordie slammed to a stop before the inferno. Tongues of fire billowed out the uppermost windows, blistering the clear blue sky at the top of the tower's crenellated roof. His tower was on fire!

Pandemonium set in as men leaped for buckets, bumping heads and arms, running to the well in the center of the bailey yard. Nothing caused alarm as a fire did. The inferno raged like a hellburner attack.

Another explosion sent the uppermost rafters soaring into the sky. Panic drove everyone for cover.

"Get to the roof of the hall, form lines, get the buckets organized. Jeffry, Ulrich!" Gordie shouted orders. "Clear the children from the yard!"

He ran to the cloud of smoke billowing out the gap where his mullioned windows had once held at bay the elements and given his tower light and beauty. His boots mashed through a pulp of shattered glass.

Behind him, screams and cries proclaimed the agony of injury. He hauled his plaid over his head, shielded his eyes from the raining ash and tried to see up the wall of smoke. His heart stopped dead in his chest. The Mulvaine dangled out a window, thirty feet above his head. Her thick braid hung away from her head, smoldering.

"Cara!" Gordie bellowed. Before him on the lower level, flames and smoke belched from the gaps where windows had once been. "Cara...Mulvaine! Hear me, damn you! Jump. I'll catch you."

Blind from smoke and deaf from the force of the explosions, Cara did not hear or see him.

Dragging his plaid around him, Gordie bolted through the gaping window and sought the stairs. The smoke thickened and billowed downward, tongues of fire licking at the walls and the flooring, consuming everything in its path. The door to his upper chamber dangled from one hinge. Inside, a wall of flame spread outward from the fireplace to the west-facing windows.

He choked, gasping for air, tasting the acrid burn, feeling the heat sucking inside him past the thickened wool protecting his face. Leaping over flames, Gordie found solid wood under his feet. The smoke swirled and thickened. His eyes stung, the heat roasted his skin.

He knew the room by heart, visualizing it in his mind, moving through the burning stench and increasing smoke-black oblivion towards the gutted window.

He found Cara with groping hands, touching bare flesh scorched with heat. She bent double over the window, caught in a panic struggle, half-in, half-out where the air was fit to breathe.

He didn't think. He acted, grabbing her up by the waist, straining to keep his lungs still, to not take any of the noxious killing wind inside his chest. He threw as much of his plaid over her as he could, then he turned and ran, back through the flames, the smoke and the hell.

The old keep's wood made fine tinder. A rain of burning cinders set fires all round the bailey. Everywhere, the confusion of subduing the fire caused more danger.

John Mckenna's voice roared over the melee. "Let it burn, damn it," he swore. "I'll no risk lives for wood and stone. Get away, I said."

He yanked Ulrich back from the flames engulfing the arched doorway of the keep.

"Gordie's gone after the Mulvaine. She's in there!" Ulrich shouted hoarsely.

"Lord Almighty!" The Mckenna roared, but his grip on his stalwart nephew never slackened. Swinging the young man round, John Mckenna drove his fist in Ulrich's jaw and knocked him out cold. "Get this young fool out of my way!"

He threw Ulrich's sinking body at the closest man, tore his plaid from his belt and went into the flames to save his son.

Gordie thanked God for the tub of water and the pocket of air trapped between the collapsing upper floor. He soaked his plaid and wound it round Cara's limp and naked body, filled his lungs and hoisted her over his shoulder.

He knew he was running, evading and escaping the fire. His feet found the steps, but the heat singed, strangled and pressed him back. His lungs strained, bursting and aching.

Only by sheer force of will did he stifle the urges to inhale.

The downward tracking steps flew under his feet, yet he could make no progress through the ever-thickening air. The stone floor leveled underneath him and he fell on the bottom riser.

He had to breathe. His face pressed between Cara's hip and the resisting stone, he took a breath. Smoke spiraled inside his lungs, awakening an old, dread memory of his life being sucked away.

Another wave of heat washed at him. He rolled over, knees to the floor, struggling to get up, to gather Cara. If only she would hold on to him! Wrap her arms around him, help! Grabbing the soaked plaid, he heaved her upward to his shoulder and staggered on his feet.

The door yawed. Shades of Hades separated him from it. The crack of a flaming joist splintering, crashing behind him propelled him headlong into the gray-black archway. He slammed into someone rushing pell-mell at him.

For once, he was damn glad that his father could never leave well enough alone. Choking, coughing, he caught hold of his father's shoulder and spun the Mckenna around, pushing him out ahead of him. And yet, he knew there was a grip just as fierce on him, pulling him out just as determined.

Who pulled who out of the raging inferno might be something they would argue about for the next score of years. Clear of the fire, Gordie's boots and kilt smoldered. No less than six clansmen threw the contents of their buckets on him. A good half of that washed over his father.

"Ya damn fool!" Gordie croaked, enraged as he could be. "Were you trying to kill yerself?"

John Mckenna choked and sputtered. A patch of his hair smoked. He wiped his stinging eyes with wet wool, coughed a mouthful of smoke out of his lungs, too shaken to speak.

Gordie tightened his grip around his bride's legs. His wet plaid clung to her body. Reviving in the swaddling bind of sodden wool, she wiggled like a giant worm on his shoulder.

The Mckenna groused unnecessarily, waving back the men with more buckets of water. "Best see to yer lady's care, then, lad."

Settling the Mulvaine carefully on her feet, Gordie uncovered her head. She clutched at his shoulders, her face blackened, smears of blood staining what was left of Gordie's shirt. Words were beyond her.

Gordie swung his arm under her knees, taking the necessity of supporting herself from her weak, trembling legs. The wet plaid was all she wore. Her arms tightened this time round his neck. Grim-lipped, he marched out of the bailey with his wife in his arms.

* * *

Cara's head pounded ferociously as the Mckenna women hastily dunked her throbbing, aching body in a tub of cold water. Everyone talked at once, jabbering like magpies. The stench of the fire permeated every room, but the manor house, itself, was safe. Cara tolerated being treated like a helpless child.

She ached in too many places to count. Worse, much worse, was the heavy ache in her heart. She had heard Kurt screaming in anguish. He had run to Megan and the baby. Both had been killed in the explosion.

Gordie had given Cara over to his mother and sisters to go to Kurt.

The Mckenna sisters pulled Cara away from the tragedy and here she was, in a tub, being washed and scrubbed by other hands.

"Oh, your hair, your hair, Cara." Rose cried, "It was so beautiful at your wedding, spinning behind you in the fling with Gordie."

Rose scrubbed and scrubbed until the smell of smoke and singed hair no longer clung to Cara's hair and skin. Lady Elaina dabbed a cooling cream across Cara's forehead and on her shoulder. Blisters spotted her back and hips, a score of cuts marked her belly and the palms of her hands, but the most grievous injury had been done to her hair. She was lucky. She was alive, but very shaken.

Cara let the women have their way, rising from the tub when asked, standing still for bowls of cold water to rinse her skin. She tolerated the rubbing of a soft towel, the stroke of a soothing cream and thanked Rose for the gift of a shift to wear. Janie provided her with a soft robe. Slippers of Bonnie's were fitted to her feet.

She thought it odd that not a single one of the Kenna women asked why she'd set the fire. Maybe they did, but her ears rang so badly that she couldn't hear words distinctly.

The last thing she wanted to do was sleep, but Lady Elaina pressed her into Rose's bed and insisted. She gave her a tea that was strong and potent. Cara lay passive with her eyes wide open.

She saw that boy, screaming over his mother's body and the tiny little baby. She could not think of any words of hers that would console him.

Why had she started a fire then not tended it as she should? She had never done anything so stupid before.

Until the rafters between the floors collapsed, John Mckenna kept his men away from the fire in the tower. He had already decided there was no reason to try to put the fire out. The more of it that burned, the easier rebuilding would be.

So it was late that night before the smoldering keep gutted and the bucket brigade monitoring it ceased their work.

The Mckenna and every soldier and servant were blackened with grime. Ulrich dunked his head in the open well and came out shaking. His father, Sir Richard, dragged wet fingers through his steel gray hair and shook his head. "I haven't heard the likes of that since Darnley was blown to kingdom come. It shook all of Edinburgh, threw him and his manservant clear of the building."

John Mckenna hadn't been in Edinburgh when Mary Stuart's husband was killed. Bosworth had been banished for the deed. Mary had eventually been beheaded as the ruthless queen had deserved.

Gordie wiped down his arms and squared his shoulders, looking to the ruin that had been his quarters since he was seventeen and judged a man in his own right. He turned to his father, a haunted look in his eyes. "I had no idea I was hated as much as Darnley."

"What makes you say that?" Mckenna demanded.

"Who else could the bastards have been after?"

Gordie's knowledge of explosives was as vast as the field was these days. He knew the charge was small. A handful of gunpowder, possibly. A twist of cotton could have been the fuse. He knew that explosion had come from the fireplace and that told him the charge had most likely been placed in a hollowed log. A log he might have laid on that fire himself. To heat her bathwater. He could have killed her.

That was all she blathered about: she'd started a fire to heat her water and gone to sleep. Because of her carelessness, people had been killed. Gordie shook his head in grim silence. Cara

Mulvaine hadn't killed anyone. The blast was not of her doing. Gordie would set her straight on that later.

Right now he had questions for his son, as well as for the rest of his servants. They had all been told his wishes regarding his handfasted bride. She was to ask for what she needed. Who had she asked to bring her wood? He knew whom he had asked.

Gordie pondered the question of Darnley's unusual death a long while before he walked outdoors. He stood alone, glaring at the ruins of his home. He knew what his father didn't. The blast hadn't been laid for him. It had been set to kill his bride.

How precisely that made Gordie feel he wasn't certain. It boggled his mind. It angered him with a rage so deep, killing the guilty party would never suffice.

Quite without warning he came to a decision and marched round the back of the stables to where the dogs were kept penned and chained. The collies happily barked their greeting, hoping for a scrap of meat or the stroke of his hand.

Gordie's eyes focused on the chained cur that snarled as he entered what had become its territory.

It bared its fangs and warned dire consequences as Gordie put his knee to the ground before it. He held his hand out of its snapping range, daring the dog to injure him. "Bite me, ya bastard, and I'll slit yer worthless throat."

Mimms growled, holding his aggression, barely. His ears lay flat against his head, his long dangerous teeth revealed in the brutal snarl he had for the man that had taken his mistress from him.

The click of the collar latch unfastening brought Mimms erect on his huge paws. Catching the dog's collar, Gordie drew the beast's snarling muzzle close to his face. "Go and see to your mistress. Mark my words, dog. Do not let any harm befall her."

Gordie released the dog's collar and sat back on his heel. Mimms did not move, preferring to tell how tiresome he found the whole affront of being chained and kept from Cara.

"Go, guard the Mulvaine," Gordie ordered again.

Mimms lurched forward, then stopped and shook himself from neck to ugly tail. Then he loped out of Gordie's sight.

Chapter Twenty-Three

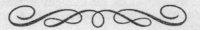

There was a funeral the next morning. Cara stood at her husband's side throughout the ordeal, her head covered by a borrowed veil. She had not a stitch of clothing of her own. Gordie didn't, either. The service was brief and quietly held. Kurt stood rigidly under his father's hand, as stoic as the Mckenna who said the words of the ceremony.

It hadn't mattered to Cara that she had barely known the woman who had died. Nor had Megan's spite made Cara less generous in offering prayers. It was the happy little baby that seemed the greater tragedy. Cara couldn't hold back the tears that formed in her eyes for the small child. She was completely taken back when Kurt emerged from the graveyard and turned upon her, saying, "'Twas you who killed my mother!"

"Kurt!" Gordie's hand clamped down upon the boy's shoulder. Mimms barred his fangs. Gordie pushed the boy backward, out of the reach of Mimms' protective anger.

"'Tis true, da! 'Tis all her fault. I hate you! I hate you!"

Gordie snatched the boy off his feet so fast, Cara hadn't time to blink.

Then he stomped away from the graveyard next to the plain little kirk in the village with the boy clenched under his arm.

Cara started to rush after them.

"Desist, lady." John Mckenna caught a fast hold on Cara's arm.

"My lord." Cara turned on the Mckenna. "The boy is distraught. He knows not what he says. The fire was my fault."

"Nay, Lady Cara. It was not. You had no part in taking gunpowder from my storeroom."

"Well, the boy didn't, either. What is Gordie going to do to him?"

"That is not your concern," the Mckenna answered. "Kurt is Gordie's son. You be wise to learn today you'll no interfere in the disciplining of a son. Your place is with the women. Go and join them and walk quietly back to my hall."

Cara wanted to scream and pound some sense into the Mckenna. Who could ever do that to a man his size or stubborn ilk? All men were alike, she thought rebelliously. She did as she had been told, joining the sisters in the solemn walk back to the castle proper.

They were, it seemed, expected to return to their usual activities, which Lady Elaina saw to directing immediately. There was no further homage made to a servant of the house, no meal or wake, though the talk in the busy kitchens went round and round about Megan's ways.

Gordie came into the cold kitchen at noon, his cousin Ulrich with him. The cousin tossed a pack upon Cook's table and asked that it be filled for travel. Cara paused in the slicing of a celeriac and looked at her husband. What manner of man was he? The coldness about him permeated the very air. Had that demon claimed his soul so long ago? Had she unwittingly kept a soulless, heartless man alive?

A shiver at the thought swept down her spine, and she couldn't help but cross herself in fear of it.

After that she returned her attention to the root she was slicing, finished the task and that of paring a pail of windfall apples to be set to boil for juice. She washed her hands and dried them, then went out into the yard with Mimms tracking at her heels.

The sky had changed from the bonny sun of the day before. Today, soft, gray clouds covered it from end to end; a feel of mist hung in the air. A feel of a chill, too. The sound of pickaxes, the ring of hammers broke the peace. Carts piled with burned rubble creaked as they were drawn out the portcullis gate.

Cara sat on the outer steps of the great hall. Mimms parked himself at her feet, his big head up and alert to every nuance of sound, every activity within his domain.

His head swiveled to watch the three males emerging from the stable. Two led horses. Cara followed Mimms' inspection and regarded her husband, his cousin and the boy, Kurt. Ulrich clasped Gordie's shoulder and forearm then swung himself up into his saddle. Gordie lifted the boy and placed him on the other horse. Kurt sat with the ill ease of someone unused to horses while his father tightened stirrups and checked the cinches.

Cara's interest in the tableau was not singular. Within minutes, the Mckenna, his wife and two of his daughters emerged from the hall. Gordie finished his words to his son, patted the boy's thigh and slapped the horse's flank to send it trotting after Ulrich.

Only Becca broke away from her family and ran to intercept Kurt. "I will miss you, Kurt."

The boy cast his youngest aunt a long look, holding fast to the reins his father had placed in his small hands. "God be with you, Becca Mckenna."

"And you too, Kurt Autry mac Kenna." Becca stood aside as the horse trotted on. Cara heard Becca's broken sob. The young girl stood there woodenly, watching after the boy, her hand up, waving, but Kurt did not turn back to acknowledge her farewell.

There seemed to be nothing anyone could say. The tension in the yard palpated. Cara took a deep breath and rose to her feet. When Gordie turned and saw the frozen tableau, he glared with a fury that was unmatched. Cara heeded his look, caught her skirts up and whirled about, fleeing inside where it was safer. Behind her, she heard Becca's plaintiff cry. "How could you send Kurt away? How could you be so cruel?"

Then the girl streaked past Cara, pushing away anyone who dared to get in her way. She cried in a loud, wailing, heartbroken sob all the way up the fine stairs. The long gallery echoed with her sorrow until silence was granted the hall by the vicious slamming of a distant door. "Good for you, Becca Mckenna," Cara whispered.

Conversation remained stilted and strained at the evening meal that night. Cara retired to Rose's room. Rose having graciously moved next door with sisters Jane and Margie. After midnight, Gordie joined Cara. Rose's bed was not his own. His length left his feet dangling off the end. He didn't care for his sister's heavily embroidered linens edged with crocheted lace.

He didn't like Cara's grim-lipped silence nor her dog's malevolent, baleful stare.

He dealt with the dog, first, ordering it outside while he held open the door. It paced past him then laid down in the corridor. Gordie slammed the door in its ugly face. Then he rounded on his wife.

"You have something you want to say, lady?"

Cara stood and faced him squarely, her chin up. "I have not said a word, my lord."

"Aye." Gordie struck out his hand, spreading his palm against the wall beside him. "But you communicate without words. Say what you think, so I may give answer to you."

Did he mean that? Cara doubted him. "You have been doubly cruel, my lord."

"Think you so?" Gordie snarled. "Not cruel, nor stern enough by half. You judge before you know the facts."

"The facts, my lord." Cara stood as firm against him as she dared. She feared the beating her confession would cause, but would willingly accept any punishment if it would relieve her soul of its terrible burden of guilt." The fact was, my lord, I set the fire that burned your tower to the ground and killed a woman and her child."

"Nay, woman. You tended a hearth I ordered never allowed to burn out. Megan was the cause of her own death. She coveted your place. She sent her son on a fool's errand. Kurt confessed to me what he had done. He stole powder from my stores, packed it and searched out a hollow log. Inside of that he packed his charge. He laid the log to the top of your basket, knowing that you tend your own fires. He planned to frighten you, to send you running back to Dunluce. But he could have killed you. Killed me.

"Aye, woman, I have sent the boy from my house. He will be fostered in England. I should have done so a year ago, but I tarried making the decision. It was my own selfish pleasure of having him underfoot that kept me from the duty I owed my son. I did not think of his pride or that he chaffed under a bondage no free-born man can withstand. In my own way, I love him. His mother was a convenience to me. I will no hear again you take blame for the fire or Kurt's mother's death."

Cara wasn't certain she could believe him, his tale was so wild. "How could a boy know of gunpowder? You have fought no wars at Kenna in his lifetime nor have you any alchemist in residence.''

Gordie shook his head and took his hand down from the wall. Rose had a low-backed chaise to rest upon. That he sat heavily on, bending his foot to knee to unlace his leggings. "That is my guilt. Last winter when the snow was deep, I sat to the hall. As men are want to do, we talked of wars, of battles on sea and land, of raids and killings and death.''

Cara followed his movements with keen interest as he shifted his feet and worked the other legging free, dropped his boot beside the first. "When I went to England, I went as King James' man, to spy upon the English, to learn everything I could, because the past four years—nay, all the years—of Jamie's life have been dangerous. Elizabeth guards her throne consummately. She is a vain woman, but as wily as a fox. I cannot recount the number of loyal men that have felt the wrath of the queen's ax. What we feared, after Mary's beheading, was the same vengeance worked upon our king, who is the right and only heir to the English throne.

"So, against my father's wishes, I went to England seeking adventure. I was young, strong, bullheaded. I was sent with credentials to Walsingham and there enlisted to spy for the English. A double plot if you may. Do you ken what I am saying?''

Cara nodded. His feet bare, Gordie stretched, looking for comfort in Rose's too-small chair. It evaded him.

"I outfitted a ship, the *Swiftshure*. I trained under Giambelli and accompanied him to Antwerp in '85 where we first used the art of explosions—mortar made of brick and scrap iron—to blow up a bridge. How enormous a bomb is you cannot imagine. Do you know of such things?''

Again, Cara nodded. "Sir Almoy found fireworks most fascinating. Even the smallest charge delighted him. I know that controlling the powder and the oil it weeps is the most dangerous part of it.''

"Who is Sir Almoy?" Gordie fixed her with an inscrutable look unable to discern how she came to know of such things.

"Sir Almoy is Dunluce's wizard," Cara explained.

"Wizard?" Gordie rolled his eyes and mentally asked for patience. "Ach, Cara, first ghosts, now wizards run rampant at Dunluce. Next you'll be telling me trolls and leprechauns kept you company.''

"They most certainly did not. Sir Almoy is as much flesh and blood as you are, my lord. And furthermore, he was a most dedicated instructor and sworn to uphold all truth and light. He is the last preceptor of the Knight's Templar."

"Cara, that is preposterous," Gordie said evenly.

"It is not."

Gordie sighed resignedly. "I canna convince you that there are no living Templars, can I? The last was buried two hundred years ago. I know this. I am a knight, you know."

"Well, a hundred years ago, Almoy was born, more perhaps. You dinna know him. I do. You can ask your father if you doubt me. When the Mckenna came to Dunluce, I refused the marriage because I did not want to leave Sir Almoy. He is a Knight Templar. He wears their patte cross on his tunic and keeps their shield in a place of honor above his hearth. And he has the ring!"

"Have it your way," Gordie agreed to placate her. "He must think himself a Templar if fire intrigues him. All defenders of the Temple are fascinated by raw power."

"Aha!" Cara pointed a finger at him. "I just heard you say that, Gordie Mckenna. Don't think I didn't. Defender of the Temple . . . I'll no forget it, either. Only one of the brotherhood dares say that title. You're a Knight Templar, too." Cara's eyes sparkled, knowing she was onto something.

Gordie folded his arms across his chest, the pose one of stubborn, implacable resistance. "May I remind you that we were talking about the Armada."

"No, we were talking about how a small boy came to know of gunpowder. Go on, you don't deny it, do you?"

Gordie's leveling looks no longer made her snap her mouth tightly closed as they had in the first few days after the handfasting. Despite the urge to be sterner with her, a smile tugged at the corner of his mouth. "Deny that I taught my son the rudiments of working with gunpowder? No, I certainly do not. I admit the fault is mine."

"Ach!" Cara threw up her hands. He frustrated her so badly when he did that! Talked circles round her so that she did not know which way was up. Impulsively, Cara launched herself at him. "You make me lose my wits, Gordie Mckenna!"

Catching both her hands, Gordie neatly turned them into the controlling grip of his left, caught the tie-belt at the waist of her robe and hauled her onto his lap. "What means this, wench? I am attacked."

"If only I could clobber you!" Cara tried to do that, and couldn't. She stilled abruptly. Her face turned somber. "Have it your way, you stubborn old Scot. Mayhaps your vow prevents you to name your order, but I know you are a Knight Templar, in spirit, if nothing else."

"And I have told you, there haven't been any Knights Templar in two hundred years!"

"Then why do you wear their ring?"

"My ring?" Gordie let go of her wrists to turn his hand over and examine his signet. The diamond centered between the calipers and rule winked at him.

"See." Cara touched the face of the signet with one finger. "Tell me you are not part of the brotherhood, a son of the widow."

Gordie went as still as a rock. "Where did you hear those words?"

"Sir Almoy," she answered smugly.

Gordie grunted softly. He stroked her head with a gentle hand, regretting deeply the loss of her beautiful hair.

"Gordie, when you washed up on the shore of Dunluce, 'twas this ring that compelled me to serve you. I knew you were a convict, condemned for life by the Spaniards. The manacles told me that. But this ring told me you were a pledged man, a good and valiant warrior in the service of God."

"There are not five men who know the meaning of this crest. Pray tell me how does a mere woman learn of such things?"

"Sir Almoy knew. 'Tis the same as his Templar's signet save for the vines and roses. He told me that binds the order to the House of Ross. 'Tis they who hold the preceptories and repositories in safekeeping."

"And there aren't a dozen men alive who know that." Gordie scowled.

Cara smiled. "Make that thirteen and one lone woman. Do you tell me now, that you have sent Kurt to someone true and loyal, who will make him into a chivalrous knight?"

"Aye, I have sent him to a friend in Wales."

"Will you ever welcome him home again?"

"That will depend on how he turns out," Gordie answered. "Being fostered is the way of a knight. I was first fostered when younger than he. A knight must earn his spurs. It canna be done tied to his mother's apron strings. Had I severed the ones binding Kurt a year ago, what happened yesterday might never have been. Who is to say? Time will out."

"And Becca. She is very hurt."

"She will come round. Her own fostering commences this winter—that is why she took Kurt's leaving so hard. You may not know it, but Bonnie has only just come home from three years in Edinburgh. Our squires and pages come to us from other houses and several of the younger maids are fostered in my mother's care to learn her way of managing a shire. Kurt will be in the best of hands."

Gordie set Cara back on her own feet and proceeded to undress, loosening the laces on his doublet, removing the garment from his shoulders.

The quiet night settled between them. He stripped down to his hose and garters, washed at the dainty porcelain basin and turned, running a towel across his chest and wet arms.

"The hour is late, Cara."

She knew his meaning, that it was time for bed. Cara put out the candles carefully, making certain each was truly out. Rose kept no fire burning in her small chamber this time of year.

The last thing Gordie did before he climbed into bed was to unsheathe his sword and lay it on the floor in his reach if the need arose during the night. He settled to the bed, swamping it with his overlong arms and legs. Cara's elbows and drawn-up knees poked at his side. He turned his head sideways and looked at her.

"You plan to sleep like that?"

Cara had. She was comfortable. He wasn't. "Is there another way?"

"Hmph!"

"Well?"

"Many. Here, turn over. Put your back against my chest."

That was a very intimate position to try to sleep in. Cara shifted, turning away from him. His warm hand slid round her hip and pulled her back against him, till she was cradled in the curve of his body. He smoothed her hair down her shoulder, out of his face and came to an abrupt end.

After Lady Elaina had repaired the singed ends, her hair was no longer than her shoulder blades. The curl that Rose had guessed was there, had sprung free when the weight of uncut hair was gone forever.

"How is your shoulder?" Gordie asked.

"Fine. Your mother knows her salves and unguents."

"She may, but had I to choose between her skill to save my life, or yours, I would choose you, Mulvaine."

Cara slipped her hands round his firm biceps, holding the muscled flesh between her palms. "My lord, I owe you my life. Thank you for saving me. I was too afraid to jump from that high window."

"I am glad you did not." A shudder passed over Gordie's back. "You could have broken your neck and I would not have been there to catch you."

"Instead you risked your life coming after me." Cara turned her face to his flesh and placed a kiss upon his arm. "Thank you."

"I will always come after you, Cara Mulvaine. I have sworn to protect you. I do not give my oath lightly."

Cara settled her cheek against the prop of his extended arm. She stared into the darkness, listening to his breathing, opening her mind to his presence. The band of benevolent purple still glowed at his wrist.

"Cara," Gordie said against the top of her head.

"My lord?"

"This old knight, Almoy. Do not speak of him to others, hmm?"

"That is the first charge he gives to any who serve him. Dinna worry. I only mention him to you because I know you are a knight who can be trusted." Cara yawned and closed her eyes.

Her breathing evened out. Gordie knew the moment she fell asleep. Her head lolled more heavily against his biceps. He drew her bottom neatly against his loins, cradling her body with his. His hand splayed possessively across her soft belly. The threat against her had shaken him deeply. He had failed to protect her, to keep her safe from all injury.

He rubbed his chin against the top of her head, the whiskers of his now clean-shaven jaw making odd little scraping and tugging sounds. He swallowed, feeling the lump in his throat rise again to strangle him. He closed his eyes and sighed, then kissed the soft, sweetly scented crown of dark hair as he mouthed the soft words, "I love you, Cara Mulvaine."

His throaty voice was swallowed by the heavy draping on his sister's bed. Gordie drew a long breath inside his chest and realized he'd loved her since the moment he'd opened his eyes and seen her lying crumpled on the floor of a dungeon. God's gift to him. Maybe. If so, he'd failed his duty in seeing that her life prospered. It would not happen again.

Odd, but Gordie seemed to know his mind at last. This was what he wanted. The Mulvaine as his wife.

He kissed the soft curve of her shell-like ear and she wiggled a little, burrowing into his arm, her face tucked away and unaccessible. Come morning he would no doubt face her with a furious need. One that would have to be appeased. But for the moment he was content. He fell asleep, certain his handfasted bride was safe in the circle of his arms.

Chapter Twenty-Four

"What word have we from my man in Ulster?"

"Kelly's messages have just arrived," Walsingham answered.

"Not that. Tell of the O'Neill. Has that huge red-bearded oaf secured and pacified Antrim? Out with it, Francis, we would hear your answer."

"The O'Neill remains a law unto himself, Your Majesty. When has he not, since you conveyed his father's earldom upon him? He stands a heartbeat from declaring himself king of Ireland."

"The knave would not dare, no matter how kingly a figure he makes. Such height and pleasing form and that wild spirit that drives a lowly woman to distraction. I can think of no other who dances until the night is over, who holds his head up when the spirits have laid every other low. His tongue is no less glib than Leicester's was or my darling Robin. Tell me, does he have better sense than to be so bold as to declare himself king and invoke my wrath?"

"Bold." The minister grunted, leveling his queen with a telling look. "Kelly renders a better accounting than O'Neill. Tyrone's missives are too full of compliments to Your Majesty's flawless person to make head or tail of the fact under discussion."

"What precisely does he say?"

"Your Majesty, please, the hour is late and my bones, weary. Would you but read his letters yourself, you would have full measure of his adoration to you."

"Ah, Francis, I forget how England has aged you. Go then, be brief. Tell me what this boring Kelly does surmise. I will try to listen."

"You remember when last we discussed the Mac Donnell, a year ago, that the old bastard had died. He left his fortresses to his granddaughter, Cara Mulvaine. She is the woman Kelly has inquired about regarding marriage."

"Mulvaine . . . ah, I vaguely remember the name. What became of it? Has the chit married some suitable scallywag, this officious Kelly perhaps?"

"You did not grant him leave to do so. The girl was also a subject of King James. She was pledged young and Sorely Mac Donnell took offense and kidnapped her from Graham, Scotland.

"Ah . . ." Elizabeth stretched her memory. The hardly relevant information was old, not worth bringing back to mind. "I vaguely remember. James mentioned it in a letter to me some years back. He wanted money and asked to borrow more from me. I refused. I am queen, but I am not made of money. Answer my question. Did Kelly wed and bed the chit?"

"No, Your Majesty. You did not give him permission to do so."

"How odd. Is he a handsome man? His letters are concise, but I cannot place his face. Describe him."

"He is brown-haired, tall enough, though not overly so. He's a good, sturdy man, strong of arm and leg."

"Is he handsome?"

Walsingham cleared his throat. "He is scarred by the pox, Your Majesty."

"Horrid!" The queen shivered. "Give him leave to marry the Irish chit. Who else would have him?"

"It is too late."

"Too late? He has already done so? Without my leave? Send word for him to present himself at once."

"You misunderstand, Your Majesty. He made no move to wed or court the woman. She was ransomed by James and given to a Scot a month ago. That is the body of Kelly's letter. The O'Neill approved the match and restored Glenarm and Dunluce to Sorely's son, James. To wit, James Mac Donnell has taken a second wife, a young widow who will breed him a passel of sons to inherit Dunluce. O'Neill wasn't about to let the properties fall to your crown, and the Scot did not wish to be bothered with them. He gave it away, taking the ransomed bride and only her dower properties as her due.''

"A Scot who gave away properties? Is he mad?''

"Nay, Your Majesty. He is one of the most loyal of James' subjects, the Mckenna himself.''

"Mckenna, Gordie's father?''

"Yes, Your Majesty.''

"He has taken another wife. Why, that randy old devil. Isn't that just like a provincial cur! What has Sir Gordon to say about that?''

"He has said nothing, Your Majesty. The bride was not acquired for the old lord. His wife is a hale woman, much loved and revered within their shire. The bride was ransomed for the Mckenna's heir.''

"Be damned you say. He wouldn't dare. Gordie is my man and has been for a decade.''

"Six years precisely, Your Majesty.''

"Don't presume to correct me! I have not given Sir Gordon leave to marry and should I do so, it wouldn't be to any issue of Sorely Mac Donnell. Where is Drake? You will send for him at once.''

"Your Majesty, Drake and Hawkins are in Portugal.''

"Not Drake, you old fool, Gordie! Send for him immediately.''

"How can I when he resigned his commission and retired from your service? You released him, bid him Godspeed and gave him a fine reward for his service to you, ten thousand ducats of Spanish gold. Even his boat, the *Swiftshure*, has been decommissioned and sits in dry dock awaiting purchase.''

"No, no, no! I remember no release. Perhaps I granted him leave, but that was all. I will not have this! Not at all. Why isn't he in London? You will check his usual haunts. Oh, I can see that scoundrel James plotting and maneuvering in this. How dare he! I will wring his scrawny neck! If the marriage has taken place I will order it annulled. Send for the archbishop. We will just see about this. I know Gordie Mckenna. Why, he'd never settle for a stupid Irish savage for a wife.''

"The girl in question is a Scot, Your Majesty. So, may I remind you, is Gordon Mckenna. He is beyond your control so long as he remains in Scotland. My information is that the wedding was completed in the old traditions of the Kenna clan.

They were handfasted a month ago and the church vows will take place on the thirtieth of June.''

"Why, that's ten days away. It is not too late. No, no, no. I will not have this. First, you will send for Kelly immediately. Send the archbishop to me to instruct, as well. I want that wedding stopped, Francis. Do you hear me?''

Walsingham's tired eyes kept their fix upon his queen. She was a virago when it came to men she favored and looked upon as lovers, more so now than in the past when Dudley had been at hand to soothe and pacify her. It was her age, fifty-eight. Francis made no bones about his own age. He would gladly retire if the queen would settle her debts to him. He kept working because he could not afford the poverty of retirement.

"Don't you dare give me that look, you damned old fool. How could you have let this happen? Why, before I know it my royal personage will be swamped with rebellion. I hate it when they sneak around behind me, marrying this beauty, bedding that one. I will have that girl put in a cage and hung outside of the White Tower seven years longer than the last lovesick fool I so detained. Order it done, Francis. Have her brought here to me, before the church vows are spoken. That will bring Gordie back to court and we will see what temerity he has then. Bah! A pox on the Mckenna for vexing me so.''

"Your Majesty, may I point out that he is not your subject.''

"The devil he isn't. He bent his knee to me and swore to serve me faithfully unto his death. An oath is never foresworn or forgotten. James is vassal unto me and so his vassals are all my servants to bid as I so choose. See that my orders are completed without delay and have Kelly flogged before he is set before me. What a bumbling stupid oaf! I will write to the O'Neill in my own good time.''

Elizabeth stalked off shouting for John Dee and Robin Devereaux, a wake of people jumping to open doors and scuttle after her as she stormed from one end of Windsor to the other.

Long after the queen had departed from Francis Walsingham's office, he sat at his cluttered desk staring deeply into space. As Her Majesty's man, Walsingham had committed many a deed in her name and by her authority for the good of the crown and England. Upon occasion, the capriciousness and petty vanity of the queen vexed him beyond his temper. And other times, it merely appalled him. He was too old for the job. His health was failing. He longed for peace and a restful ending to his curiously complex life.

He had walked an unbelievable tightrope of power for over three decades and doing so, he had cultivated and culled the cream of England to his service. A secret service, a vast network of spies and operatives in the field throughout Europe and the constantly expanding navigable world. Among those men, he viewed Gordon Mckenna as most competent.

Oh, he knew that Mckenna had come to England as James' agent. He had recruited the young Scot anyway. Mary had been queen of Scotland then, a captive of England, and her young son sat upon a throne ruled by a regent. Elizabeth was fifty-three when Mary was beheaded at Fotheringhay. Who precisely Gordie owed direct allegiance to, Walsingham had never quite divined. Sir Gordon had served England well. How well he'd served his own king or the king's doomed mother, Walsingham could only speculate.

The truth was, Elizabeth's only heir was King James of Scotland. The young king would be the next king of England. Walsingham didn't doubt that for one minute. Knowing that and knowing that he wanted to live out his days in peace, he hedged this bet as he had many others before.

He wrote a coded message to Hawthorne. He hand-selected the messenger, John David Conan, to deliver it, informing the young knight that he was to equip himself with the best available horses and take himself immediately to Wales and not spare his animals or himself until the messages had been placed in Elliot Saint Clair, earl of Hawthorne's hands.

"And then, sir?" John David inquired.

"Then, my young pup, then? Damn my eyes, then I don't give a farthing what you do or how long it takes you to return to your post. I am sick to death of upstarts and adventurers. Go, complete the order you've been given."

Chapter Twenty-Five

A feeling of utter, absolute contentment washed through Cara's bones. Gordie's chest pressed sweat damp against her cheek. Beneath her ear, his heart hammered loudly, a heated rhythm that matched the pulse singing through her veins. She sighed and he chuckled. Around them a few bees droned in and out of the sea of purple flowers.

All was so right with Cara's world that she had nearly forgotten her apprehensions of the morrow's wedding.

"What are you thinking?" Gordie asked.

"I am not thinking at all. I am feeling. Can we stay like this forever?"

Gordie's hand stroked down her naked back. "You will get a terrible sunburn right here if you do."

"There?" Cara squirmed deliciously against him. "I don't care. This is exquisite."

"Indeed," Gordie agreed. "Too perfect. Well, wench, what say you? Tomorrow, do you give me your pledge for life? To worship my body with yours forever?"

"Isn't that what I am doing?" Cara asked.

"Yes," Gordie admitted that. "With my body, I thee worship. I am content."

"I have come to understand that you are much more complex than that, my lord."

"So, I cannot fool my little gray mouse. I would never have dreamed you would be so free as to lie with me here amid the heather."

"Have I complained?"

"Nay, you purr like a contented little cat."

"All we needed was a measure of privacy, a difficult thing to obtain in Castle Kenna, my lord."

"Tomorrow I will give the guests ten hours to drink my father's vats dry then bundle every man, jack and woman on their way. We shall have peace and quiet and all the solitude we desire once the vows are said. Does that suit you, my lady?"

"It suits me." Cara kissed a sun-warmed patch of skin at his throat. "You are turning red."

"Me? I am used to the sun. You are as pink as seashells," Gordie said.

"I suppose we ought to get dressed. We've been gone for hours. Someone might come looking for us," said Cara.

"Mimms will give us sufficient warning," Gordie replied.

Cara looked to the rocky hill where Mimms had perched himself as their sentinel. Gordie's hands caught her waist and turned her beneath him. He kissed her deeply, thoroughly, leaving her head dazed and fuzzy.

They had stolen two hours from the crowded, hectic hall. Castle Mckenna was in utter turmoil. The rush to get two marriages ready was only compounded by Rose's hysteria. A bigger case of wedding jitters no bride had ever shown. Gordie had snatched Cara out of the center of the bedlam and brought her here to seduce her. She went willingly.

"I can't get enough of you. I swear, I am a driven man. Have you bewitched me, woman? Cast one of your odious spells over me? My thoughts are not my own. I have fought it, struggled against it, but here I am, drinking your sweet nectar as if it is the staff of life."

Cara blushed at his earnestly spoken words. She didn't know how to respond. He kissed her again and neither one of them heard Mimms' warning bark, at least, not for a little while.

"God's blessed robe!" Gordie bolted upright, startled, casting about for riders coming over the ridges, throwing out his long arm to snatch up a handful of both their clothes.

Cara laughed at his panic. She didn't care if an army came. Who was to gainsay them?

"Cara, get dressed. Don't sit there looking like a moonstruck maid. Oh, for heaven's sake."

Gordie snatched her to him, sorting out her shift and hastily yanking it over her head. She managed the armholes and fastened up her petticoat. Her dress was ordinary and fitted over the rest with gaps and hanging laces. She could hardly manage one task when he was pushing her to do them all at the same time. He jerked a kilt round his waist and fastened a belt, drew a saffron-colored shirt over his shoulders and stood over her, tucking here, tugging there.

They were both a rumpled, crumpled disorderly sight when Ulrich bolted over the hill, shouting curses at the dog that nipped his mount's hooves.

"Damn that blasted animal. He'll unseat me yet. Mulvaine, call him off!"

"Mimms, chase him out of here," Gordie ordered. Mimms sat and grinned hugely at the trio.

"Mimms is laughing at you," Cara said unnecessarily.

"Someday he's going to regret that. I have a very long memory." Gordie turned Cara round to face him, and tugged her laces tight across her bodice.

"Cousin," Ulrich said by way of greeting. "My lady."

"Ulrich, your timing is as horrible as ever. What do you want?" Gordie snarled. Cara cast a shy smile at the other man. He simply sat up there on his horse, grinning foolishly at the both of them.

"Well, my lord?" Cara asked more politely. She wasn't in the least ashamed to have been caught out by Ulrich. The pleasure of sneaking away with Gordie equalled the risk of being thought a wanton. She now knew what a wanton was. A wanton was a woman in love.

Where or how or when the bolt of lightning struck, she didn't know. Every moment with Gordie was to be treasured. Being in his company on this fine summer day became a jewel to hoard a lifetime.

"I was driven from the hall by a termagant, a shrill hysteric, who on the brink of womanhood has fallen to veritable pieces and shattered like glass. Your lady mother begs I find your calm, clear-thinking wife, Gordie, and bring her posthaste to young Lady Rose, who any moment now is likely to poison the hall, jump from the highest parapet or else drive every living soul in Castle Kenna to the sea to drown themselves like lemmings to escape her harridan cries."

"Oh, it can't be all that bad," Cara scolded.

"You see what I mean. There is the face of calm. The tempest surrounds us all, yet Lady Cara keeps her wits and her good sense. Will you come back to the keep?"

"I can see that I am unnecessary," Gordie ruefully declared.

"Oh, yes, you are. Someone has to see that Jamie is happy."

"The king has come?" Gordie snapped to attention.

"The king, an entourage of no less than seventy and the damned Sassenach arrived in force. Your father is besieged and considers surrender before Mckenna blood flows like that which soaked Flodden Field. To wit, since I value my hide most greatly, if you will both not return, I ride to Aberdeen and will not step foot within this shire until after your fourth or fifth child is born, period."

"A promise you will not live up to, you blowhard." Gordie untied his horse from the nearby tree, and set Cara on the saddle, then swung up behind her. "Duty calls," he muttered for her ears only.

"At least we have something to fortify us for the ordeal ahead." Cara looked to the bright side. Gordie leaned across her shoulder as he gathered the reins and planted a kiss on her cheek.

"Ordeal is the precise thought. You will let me know if Rose does not settle down."

"She will be fine, I am certain."

"Well, if not, send word to me. I'll truss and bundle her and cart her over my shoulder and drop her at Ralph's feet before the minister. I'll no be cheated of being rid of her."

Rose really was in a terrible state, crying one minute, laughing the next. The packing of her worldly treasures set off her flood of emotion. Her mother and Lady Claire had thrown up their hands in desperation. The sisters weren't helping. Becca cried pitifully. Margie snarled in a frustrated snit and Jane waxed moonstruck over young King James. Bonnie was the only one trying to calm all the ladies down. She had worn herself to a frazzle.

The evening's meal remained to be served. The house crawled with people. There was hardly room to breathe, the night promised to be long and hot before the morning brought the vows, the feast and the day of celebration.

Cara shooed everyone out of Rose's temporary bedroom, and did what she could for her sister-in-law. When the room emptied, Rose sank to her dainty chair, a picture of utter despondency.

"I just can't do it," Rose declared.

"Do what?" Cara asked mildly. She opened the windows and let the sheers drop across them so they would have air and privacy. Then she took up a brush and eased it through Rose's damp, flame-colored hair.

"Marry and leave this house. I canna bear it. I don't want to go away or live in Edinburgh. It is a city and it isn't at all like here. I will hate it. I will miss Mama. I will die without Poppa around to scold me and laugh with me. I will even hate not having Gordie to yell at or all my sisters borrowing my things. I will be lonely."

"I see." Cara drew out one curl and brushed it smooth and tangle-free. "This is a wonderful home, so full of love for everyone. It must be a very hard decision to make, to agree to leave it just because of a man."

"Precisely." Rose took a deep breath. "I like Ralph. I do. We have known each other since we were children. But Edinburgh? It's a world away."

"Have you been there?"

"A dozen times, but I will have no family there."

"I can understand that."

"How did you do it, Cara? How did you find the courage to come here with Poppa when you didn't know a one of us?"

Cara shrugged her shoulders. "It wasn't my choice. You are lucky. You have picked the man you are to marry."

"But you love Gordie, don't you?"

"Now. Yes, I love him. I didn't know what that meant when I came here. I didn't even know what it meant when we were handfasted together. You are the one who has instructed me on what love is. How it feels, how it sends tremors through you and ties your stomach up in knots. I thought it was indigestion."

That brought a weak smile to Rose's lips. "That's the trouble, now. I don't think I am in love. Oh, forget I said that! You are such a dear, Cara. This is going to be the longest night of my life."

"Well," Cara demurred. "It doesn't have to be. We could go for a walk before the sun sets. It would calm us both down and then when we are tired we'll sleep easier. What do you say to that?"

"Yes, that's a grand idea," Rose said. "I feel absolutely caged. A walk will be a better tonic than any I can think of. We will take Mimms with us. Mother won't object to that."

"I think she will be happy to see you've quieted."

"Ralph is staying with the minister in the village. I have to see him one more time…to be sure about this. Do you suppose we could circle round the village and stop for a little visit on our way back?"

Cara changed her shoes and took up a shawl for her shoulders. "I can't see that that would hurt anything. It might do you good to see him, but we mustn't stay long and Gordie will only let me go if we promise to be back well before dark."

Of the contingent of newly arrived Englishmen, three had grouped together at a trestle in the great hall, surrounded by the ebb and flow of an incredible multitude, but apart from it, as well. Castle Kenna had the look of a house besieged by the queen's annual progress rather than a remote highland outpost staging a wedding.

"This will be a trick to pull off," Thomas Patton said as he surveyed the hall critically.

Hawthorne merely turned his quelling gaze upon the man. Patton shut his mouth and said not a word more. John David stood across the huge chamber presenting a velvet traveling case containing the queen's gift to the lady of the keep. Lady Mckenna appeared suitably impressed when the box was opened and set within the display of wedding gifts.

Sir Conan displayed the penned card bearing Elizabeth's signature where all could see it. The dozen gold plates were not the only ostentatious gift, but they were perfectly matched, a complete set. John David only just realized there were two weddings taking place on the morrow.

Lady Elaina set the plates in two stacks, six to each side of the folded open message of good wishes by the English queen.

Before Sir Conan returned to his fellows, he met the Mckenna, King James of Scotland and a number of soldiers and clansmen related to the family. He did not meet Gordie, whom he knew and would have recognized. Mission accomplished, he secured a glass of stout from a passing, harried servant and joined his companions.

Hawthorne stood now, tall enough to see over most of the multitude. It was coming up shortly on evening. They would have to act quickly when the time came. He already had the lay of the house and had made his plans.

He knew both the brides slept in chambers on the upper floor that faced the west and had wide windows accessible from the roof by rope. Their timing would be crucial, and there was the risk of discovery that already had his blood pumping at an accelerated rate. To snatch the Mulvaine from a house as crowded as this one was, to escape with her and manage to elude the hordes that would surely follow in his wake, lent the necessary adrenaline to hone his senses to a thin, sharp edge.

Hawthorne could think of no other man in England bold enough to do what he was about to do. The fact that the Mulvaine was Gordon Mckenna's bride only heightened his pleasure with the deed. And to take the woman, right out from under King James' nose added another measure to it. It was all he could to do not to laugh outright at the thrill rushing through him at an ever-quickening pace.

His attention was caught by two women coming down the wide stairs. One was a slender, black-haired winsome lass. The other, a ravishing beauty, whose hair gleamed as golden red as polished copper. He staggered at the sight of the second, struck as dumb as a statue for the space of time that the angel floated down the steps. He stood transfixed, as one who had been hit by a thunderbolt.

In a hall where the dress alternated from saffron-dyed cotton shirts, leather jerkins and ridiculous kilts to sumptuous silks, furs and noisy rustling satin, that woman came forth wearing the simplest day gown of homespun wool. A Kenna plaid embraced her shoulders, tied simply in a knot beneath her full and luscious breasts. The earthy colors complimented her fair skin and auburn hair.

The beauty and the dark miss stood apart and separate from the throng, like diamonds in the rough. Neither had a single glance for him, and Hawthorne felt a burn scorch his cheeks. He was also known to stand out in a crowd. In this crowd, his height was commonplace, his arresting looks, ordinary. The clan Mckenna was a particularly tall and handsome lot. That made Hawthorne feel he'd blended into a patterned tapestry, one dark thread among many colorful ones, having no identity apart from the cloth itself.

It wasn't a feeling he relished, not in this case. For the flame-haired beauty was a woman he could covet to himself, forever. His careful plans, his devious plotting and measuring and mentally marking of Castle Kenna's strengths and weakness went up in smoke.

The women were the brides of the morrow's weddings. The wolfhound he'd been warned about padded at the side of the black-haired Mulvaine.

The women halted in their progress, brought up short by Laird Mckenna. "Where do you lassies think you are going?"

"For a walk, my lord." Cara gave her father-in-law a smile and received one of his own in return. There was genuine fondness between them. "It would be just the thing to calm Rose's splintered nerves. I fear this is all a bit daunting to the both of us."

The Mckenna drew both girls under his arms, escorting them to the wide-open doors. "Ach, girls!" he scolded, then held them at his sides, surveying a yard that housed a multitude more of arriving guests, a backup of unsaddled horses waiting their turn to be moved to holding pens. He couldn't imagine where he would put all these people for the night.

There would be many a man sleeping on the ramparts and curling up in blankets under the stars if they slept at all. He looked down at Rose, seeing her swollen eyes, stained nose and a quiver on her lips. He swallowed a lump in his throat and glared furiously straight ahead. How could he part with his darling Rose?

"Aye, maybe a walk will do you both good. Now, mind you, do not go out of sight of the towers."

He kissed both, lingering a trifle longer over his eldest daughter, wishing he could say the words that choked his throat. Instead, he patted her and sent her hurrying after the slender, gray-gowned Cara.

He watched the two girls link arms as they passed under the portcullis; then they turned to the right to cross the fields and skirt the village. Still, he lingered on the steps, ignoring the traffic that passed in and out, surging round about him as men and ladies, servants and children rushed hither and thither.

The Mckenna threaded his way through the milling crowd, greeting some, accepting claps upon his back and shoulders from others. He directed all inside his hall and quit them, following an instinct. He took the stairs up to the battlement, and when he reached the crenellated west wall, he paused and let his gaze wander across the hills.

Before long, he saw the two girls climbing the steep face of Fellows Rise. There, they both sat to a broad rock and faced the sun, surrounded by a waving sea of heather. Cara's dog chased here and there, spooking quail and pheasants out of their hiding places in the heavy gorse.

"My lord, what are you doing here?" Lady Elaina caught his sleeve and tugged urgently. John drew back from the niche between the wall and looked down upon his wife's flushed face. She was out of breath. A tendril or two had slipped from her elegant coif and curled about her brow. Her coloring was high, and she looked radiant and beautiful to him.

"What is it, wife?" he blustered. "Can a mon not stand upon his battery and survey his land?"

"Ach! Yer daft and gone maudlin. The king needs company and his men are devouring every scrap of toast within the house. I need your help."

"Do not tell me you have run out of food?"

"Nay, husband. I have everything well in hand and will order the bounty forth from the roasting spits. But before that is done, I wish you to taste the beef and tell me if it is seasoned enough and will meet the king's pleasure. Can you do that for me, mon?"

The Mckenna smiled and bent to kiss his wife's flushed face. She quivered in the wrap of his brawny arms, allowing his pleasure, but so keyed-up she was—like a taut string about to pop. "Of course, wife. I was only taking a moment from these duties to watch my daughters walk upon the hills."

"Which daughters?"

"Lady Cara and Rose. They are yonder, on Fellows Rise." John pointed to the hill to the west. Elaina followed his hand, shading her eyes from the sun with a raised hand.

"Well, they've gone now. Thank God for Cara. She's a way with Rose I've never had."

John squinted at the bare hill, finding no girls sitting on its peak, no dog bounding round about, stirring up the game. A little farther south there were birds taking flight but the church spire prevented him from seeing what was causing their disturbance. He chuckled, knowing the culprit was most likely that odious dog.

The noise in the hall prevented Hawthorne's capable ears from denoting the details of the Scottish laird's conversation though all three were well within Hawthorne's sight. The Mckenna took both women to arm and walked with them out of the hall.

Hawthorne drained his tankard and set it aside, signaling three men to join him, and shortly followed in the ladies' wake. One glance over his shoulder to John David to communicate without words and Hawthorne received a nod of confirmation from his young aide-de-camp.

"Black," John said cryptically, confirming to Hawthorne that the woman they were seeking was the black-haired wench accompanying the red-haired temptress outside of the castle walls.

"Get my horse, Thomas. Wickham, you will remain here. Mix in with the crew and mind your manners that you do not start anything, no matter how much the Scots provoke you. We will meet due south of Rosslyn Chapel in two days' time."

Immediately after they emerged from the portcullis gate, Cara steered Rose to the path on the right that skirted the bailey wall and dropped into the open fields behind the village. She had no wish to come upon Gordie on her way out of the castle, fearing he would forbid her to leave. If she happened to come along and find him on their way back, that would be fine. She wanted the walk and she thought Rose really needed to escape the pressures of the house for a little while.

There was plenty of daylight left and the warmth of the summer day still lingered in the air. Hers and Rose's shawls were unnecessary at this point.

Of a singular mind with one another, both she and Rose set out walking at a good pace. Soon they were both laughing at Mimms' idiotic pursuit of hare, partridge and quail while they sat and rested on the top of Fellows Rise.

They could see for miles all round about them and were blessedly far removed from the commotion and confusion within Castle Kenna. Cara watched as Rose slowly unwound and finally relaxed.

After a bit, they took the path down the hill to the road that wound back into the village. It approached the brook and a little woods that was a haven for red deer amid the plowed fields and open pasturelands. That was as far as they went, traveling now alongside of the gurgling water. Cara stopped to catch a drink with her hands.

"Oh, this is wonderful. Why haven't we been doing this every day at this time? The air is so crisp and clear. The grass smells wonderful. I feel so much better."

"See there." Cara laughed as she stood up, shaking the water from her hands, wiping her chin dry. "Not a problem in the world now."

"Thanks to you." Rose linked arms with her. "Can you believe I have been such a ninny?"

"You have good reason." Cara wouldn't judge or criticize. "Perhaps you just needed to think this over one more time. You have given me a thousand reasons why you ought to marry Ralph. Which one do you think is the most important?"

"Oh, I don't know," Rose said, and stared off into the distance. "All I can think of today are the reasons why I shouldn't."

Cara made no comment, turning to look for Mimms. With evening near, the sun had dropped behind the higher mountains and the shadows were long and deep. She cocked an ear at the sound of a bird cawing excitedly and some thrashing in the woods.

"Mimms has caught another." Rose turned round about, facing the woods.

"I don't think so." Cara went completely still. All sound seemed to have hushed. She felt a prickle creep across her neck. Both she and Rose looked at one another and their faces held exactly the same wide-eyed, alarmed expression. "Can you feel it?" Cara whispered.

"Something." Rose didn't know what she sensed.

"It is the banshee." Cara's voice dropped to a low, soft treble. Rose could barely detect the low keening moan in the near distance of the woods.

As one, they turned, facing the north stand of trees. There, obscured by the shadows, a lone warrior sat astride a black steed, his head and body swathed in a black cloak, only the glint of a sheathed sword catching any light.

"Rose." Cara stretched out her hand, grasping Rose's wrist. No spell or incantation to ward away the specter of black death could come to Cara's mind. Their only hope was to run. She jerked upon Rose's wrist, yanking her hard as she turned and galvanized her feet into action.

The village lay not far, only up the rise where the woods fell away. The view was open and clear from there to Kenna's walls.

Rose stumbled, slowing Cara down. Dragging her, Cara's voice froze in her throat. She could run. She couldn't scream. Rose snatched up her hems, freeing her feet. Behind them the unearthly thunder of the horse's hooves bore down upon them.

Rose's scream died on her lips as she chanced a look backward. In her fright, she saw a black-gloved claw coming for her. It snatched her off her feet. Cara's grip upon her wrist ripped viciously away.

"No!" Cara screamed, and turned throwing herself at Rose's legs. Her arms wrapped around Rose's knees.

For a blind moment they were together, fast and secure, their combined weight and struggle unsettling the rider.

Cara never heard or saw the other rider, nor knew what hit her. The separation wrenched painfully. She heard Rose's skirt rip, then its fabric tore out of her hands. The wind rushed from her lungs with incredible force.

A black cloak descended over Cara's head. She impacted facedown over a hard pommel that drove the last of her wind from her chest. Stars came out in the sudden night surrounding her head. They spun dizzily round, circling, spinning, then faded into black oblivion.

Chapter Twenty-Six

Two days of exhausting riding, short harrowing stops to rest horses, relieve the body or feed it, brought Cara to a strangely beautiful chapel outside Edinburgh.

There, within its quiet, ornately beautiful walls, her captor handed her his black cloak and allowed her to collapse in a heap upon the cold stone floor.

Curiously, it was full daylight and there was not a soul about, no priest or worshipers, none save the dusty black-clothed man who had taken her from Kenna. The man was the most stubbornly uncommunicative sod Cara had ever had the misfortune to meet.

Where she huddled on the cold floor against a bank of carved columns, she shivered with her arms wrapped round her knees and willed her nausea to cease. The man's spurs clinked upon the stone as he paced restlessly back and forth before beautiful stained-glass windows. The colors of the morning light were splendid in the church. Dust swam in the sunbeams, and Cara, feeling that they were not alone, raised her eyes to the scrolled, baroque ceiling.

Surrounding them were ancient Celtic faces. The green man grew twining vines out of his mouth that spread upward, meeting and joining with other patterns. In the center of the kirk, where all the light seemed to focus in wondrous splendor, Cara saw a form taking shape in the dust of a hazy sunbeam.

Whether she wished Sir Almoy into being or he was transmuting himself to her aid, Cara would rather have seen Gordie than frail, old Almoy. She shook her head and swallowed the nausea back from where it came. She was hungry, tired and exhausted. It was only natural to be seeing things.

Still, the light turned round about, spinning a whirlwind without the elemental force of air. Sir Almoy's withered long form, his Templar tunic, appeared nearly solid. His trailing white beard, his hands upraised in invocation, even his curious old fashioned sandals took shape before her eyes.

Then the huge doors at the east of the lady's chapel burst wide open. The vision evaporated, and leaves, dust and dirt flew at Cara, making her wince and duck. A coin clattered on the flagstone, spinning to a stop within her reach.

Oblivious to anything else around her, Cara snatched the orb before it finished its rolling spin. It was warm to her touch, as if it had been held close in hand for a long time. She had no chance to examine it before her attention was drawn by the ringing clatter of a destrier's hooves upon the stone floor.

"Put me down, you son of a bitch!" Rose screamed, and pounded her fists against a huge man, sheeted in a knight's full armor. He was as black as coal, save for the narrow patch of skin behind the slits in his helm.

Cara blinked, too stunned to find so much as a squeak of a voice. Rose dropped heavily to the floor of the chapel. A dozen other riders came from without. Two foot soldiers dragged a screeching abbot into the nave.

John David Conan jerked the Mulvaine up from the chapel floor and flung her ahead of him to the railing of the kirk. Hawthorne dismounted, handed his horse over to his squire and dragged the screaming redhead to the chapel rail.

A soldier pressed his sword point into the monk's back, nudging him forward. "Give the words of marriage, Priest, or prepare to meet your maker!"

"You bastard! I'll no stand for this!" Rose swung out at the black knight, her ineffective hands thudding on his armor. The man dug his gauntlet-covered hand in Rose's tangled hair, jerked her harshly against his body and turned her to face the priest.

The frightened man of God looked wildly round about him at the twenty warriors set upon enforcing their leader's marriage. He raised his hands, made the sign of the cross and got on with it.

The protesting woman wasn't the first to come to his altar against her will.

He made short work of the sacrament. Rose Mckenna's outright refusals were countermanded by the black knight. The deed was done. The knight signed the monk's register, forced Rose's hand to the pen and pushed it across the page until her name was laid permanently in the chapel's book. Cara was thrust forward and the pen put into her hand to witness the joining.

"She won't do it, you fool!" Rose jerked her mouth away from Hawthorne's silencing grip and spat at him.

"I will sign my name, Rose." Cara was too dumbfounded to say anything else. She looked to the page and read the near illegible scrawl of Rose's name; above that, the name Elliott Saint Clair, Earl of Hawthorne, was written in Latin. She signed carefully, Cara nea Mulvaine, Lady Mckenna.

The man who had tormented her last two days put his own signature next to hers as the second witness. Sir John David Conan. So he had a name. They all had names. Cara blinked as the priest was tossed a coin for his trouble; then the whole group drew up their horses and clattered up on them.

Cara gasped at the rude way she was dragged off her feet, and winced when her tired, aching bones made contact with saddle leather again. Sir Conan obviously had few words for anyone. He did not apologize for the injury his armor caused her person.

They galloped out of Rosslyn Chapel, skirting the castle that adjoined it and nearby Edinburgh. It was dark when they reached Leith and the docks there. Rose was held under a cloak and gagged as the soldiers made haste to quit the highlands. She had screamed and fought her way across half of Scotland.

Cara had gone passively, knowing that this was what she had seen of her future and Gordie's. She was also an old hand at abduction and knew the futility of fighting the inevitable. Struggle and resistance only made the captors mean. She simply didn't have the heart to fight it. Without Gordie, it didn't matter a bit what happened to her.

In the deep pocket of her dress, the piece of gold lay warm and heavy against her thigh, reminding her that Sir Almoy had almost appeared to her. Sir Conan marched her across a narrow gangplank onto the ship. Another man had opened a hatch. It was dark, but Cara could see the slanted steps that went down into the bowels. She went down, glad for the release of Conan's hard grip upon her arm.

Alone at last, she pulled the coin from her pocket and marveled at the golden glow and light that it emitted in the cup of her palm. "Ah, Sir Almoy, how did you find me?"

Cara stroked her fingers across the characters inscribed in the metal, tracing them, reading them. "Invisibility! Sir Almoy! Gordie won't find me, either!"

There was no answer to her outspoken exclamation. Cara sighed and returned the talisman to her pocket. She shook her head and muttered, "He probably forgot what he was doing, again."

The quiet of the hold was disturbed then. Rose came flying down the steps, landing in a heap at Cara's feet. Cara bent to help her, pulling her up to untie her bound hands and the gag that cut into Rose's mouth.

"Coward! Cur! Son of a cursed dog!" Rose screamed at the hatch cover as it slammed down, enclosing them both in inky blackness. Then the fight went out of her and she collapsed against Cara, weeping.

Cara wrapped her arms around the frightened girl, rocking her, repeating every soothing word or phrase she could remember.

"It's all right, Rose. It's all right. You are fine."

"I'm not!" Rose hiccuped, dragging her aching hands across her eyes, wiping the back of her hand against her mouth over and over again. "Cara . . . Cara . . . he made me marry him!"

"I know." Cara stroked the tangled hair from Rose's brow. "It's going to be all right. Nothing worse could happen to you."

Rose groaned at that and subsided into soft, keening moans. Her grief was so tangible, so unbearable, that Cara simply kept her arms about her, crooning softly, rocking her as one would a distraught babe.

The ship moved into the wind, swiftly leaving the Scottish shore behind. Cara felt the distance increasing. The danger that had passed like a shade before Gordie's face on the night of their handfasting had come full circle.

Book Four

HER MAJESTY'S FOOL

"When the tempest passes, the wicked man is no more; but the just man is established forever."

Proverbs of Solomon 10:25

Chapter Twenty-Seven

*England
July 4, 1590*

As swift as the *Victorious* rode the water, Hawthorne wasn't satisfied with its progress until he put to port at Hornsea. From there, he herded the women ruthlessly westward. At Leeds he procured a room at a stalwart inn aptly named the Cock and Tail.

The innkeeper's table was adequate, his upper rooms clean and airy. The two women looked a fright. Hawthorne ordered a tub and hot water for them and sent John David into the village to purchase whatever women's clothing he could find.

Rose Mckenna still snarled like a wildcat whenever he neared her, but the Mulvaine did a marvelous job of calming Rose's wild, untamable spirit. By morning he was forced to separate them, sending the Mckenna woman with the majority of his men to guard her on the journey to Llanwst, deep in North Wales.

From Leeds he also purchased fresh horses that morning. He set the Mulvaine astride a stalwart mare, mounted a gelding and with only John David and Thomas as her other escorts, set out upon the winding road moving south.

It wasn't until midday, when they had stopped to water the horses and stretch their legs that the black-haired beauty turned her incredible eyes upon Elliot Saint Clair. He hadn't paid her much notice, for the truth was, beside fiery Rose, the Mulvaine was a most ordinary and simple woman. But then, Elliot surmised silently, she had not gazed at him directly since the journey had begun. Now she did.

Those cool gray orbs had the width and intensity of a child's innocent stare, but it was more than that, more than size alone, that riveted his attention to her. She was compelling, and emanated some power he could not put his finger upon.

"Where are you taking me, Lord Hawthorne?" Her voice, a clear contralto, contained a husky depth that denoted passion. No will-of-the-wisp woman there. He shifted, chewing upon a nourishing strip of jerky.

"Conan, didn't you tell her?"

Undaunted, Cara repeated. "Please, sir, I would know your purpose. Are you my husband's enemy? Have you debts unpaid by him? What is your reason for taking me from my home?"

Oh, there were hundreds of possible reasons he could have given her to cloud the facts. But the facts were simple. "I have no quarrel with Gordon Mckenna, lady. I merely do the duty given me by my queen. Your presence was commanded at Windsor."

Cara knew that was a lie and she hated the man for denying her the truth. She was of no importance to any Englishman, much less the queen. She stared at him, holding in check her anger. It was Gordie who was in danger. "If your English queen has need of me, then what purpose have you served by destroying Rose Mckenna's life?"

The tall man met her stare with a growing smile upon his face that reminded Cara of the sly, devilish grin Gordie sometimes showed when he was set upon stalking and bedding her. She had come to think of that particular look as one that meant *to hell with everything*.

"Because," he answered lightly, "I fancy her."

The queen had moved to Nonsuch prior to going on progress. Windsor Castle was a huge vacant shell when Cara arrived. She was given a small, unpleasant room in the upper levels. Too tired from the bone-breaking pace that Hawthorne had set, Cara didn't give a fig about her quarters. It had a bed, and there she collapsed.

Cara slept nearly round the clock. She was woken finally by Hawthorne himself. "You will get up, Mistress Mulvaine. I have ordered you a bath at no little cost or effort to provide. There are also suitable garments for you to wear this day. Jen, here, will assist you. In one hour, we travel to Nonsuch. Wake up, I said."

Cara opened her eyes, struggling mentally to separate dream from reality. Sir Almoy had invited her to join him in the working of another spell. Cara hadn't wanted to assist him and would have preferred dreaming of Gordie, reliving the nights in his arms. She woke to find her nemesis, Hawthorne, towering over her like a black giant. Did he never wear any other color?

"Did you hear what I said, Mulvaine?" Hawthorne caught her wrist and drew her upright. She was boneless, weak and pale. Something fell from her hand and thunked onto the coverlet.

Forced upright so quickly, Cara had no defense for the wash of nausea that immediately surged through her. She caught her left hand to her mouth, jerking herself free from the odious man, and scrambled for the chamber pot.

Hawthorne was confused at first by her illness, then his eyes narrowed. The wench was breeding, was she? He should have guessed. So that was the reason Gordon Mckenna was forced to take her as his wife. It made sense to him then. She simply wasn't the type of woman who appealed to a worldly, experienced man. She had no appeal whatsoever in her current wretched condition.

He started to leave, but then the coin that had fallen from her hand caught his eye. It wasn't a coin at all he realized when he'd picked it up and held it in his hands, examining it. It was a talisman, a charm, incised on one side with miniscule characters, on the other with an all-seeing eye, calipers, rule and crossbones. His blood ran cold. He spun about to the woman rising from the corner of the chamber, wiping her face with a damp towel that Jen had handed her.

"Where did you get this?" he demanded.

Cara looked at the disk Hawthorne held before her eyes. Her shift-covered shoulders moved in a helpless gesture. "'Tis not my chamber, my lord Hawthorne. I have only occupied it to rest and you know better than I, all I have with me are the clothes upon my back."

Hawthorne turned the talisman round about, glaring at it, then back at her. There was something about her that just wasn't right. Again her eyes confounded him, and for a startling, breathless moment he saw not her, but a white-haired, bearded wizard wearing the Temple's cross emblazoned across his chest.

"Mother of God!" Hawthorne exclaimed, and tossed the coin to her.

It spun in a high arch between them, spinning end over end, glinting with the light of pure gold. Then it dropped into her hand and held its valiant color a second more. After the wholly natural blinking of his eye, the foolish orb appeared ordinary lead. The short hairs on the back of Hawthorne's neck prickled in a wave that ran clear over the top of his head.

Cara smiled at the warm pulsing object in her hand, then returned her gaze to the man before her. Hawthorne could not believe the innocent, guileless face she presented him. He would not believe that ruse again.

"Do you know who I am, mistress?"

"Aye, you are the earl of Hawthorne."

"I am Elliott Saint Clair, lady. Knight of the order of St. John, Protector of the Temple. I am a son of the widow. Who is your mentor?"

Cara tilted her head, hearing from this odd, huge and powerful man the coded words known only to true initiates of the secret Order of the Templar. "Sir Almoy of Dunluce, my lord."

"Almoy of Ireland?" He drew a sharp breath.

"Aye," Cara nodded.

"There is no repository of the Temple at Dunluce."

"You are correct, my lord. Almoy was last preceptor at Mussenden Temple. It fell to ruin and Almoy repaired to a private tower in Dunluce many years ago."

"God's blood." The knight swore a terrible oath before he came to his senses. "Be he an old man, white of hair and beard to his waist?"

"Aye." Cara wondered how he knew that. "You know of him?"

"Aye," Hawthorne said sharply. "What of his repository, his papers, his books, the Temple's knowledge? Does that also remain at Dunluce?"

Sweet blood of Christ, he prayed fervently, *not at Dunluce!*

"Nay," Cara replied. "Arrangements had been made for his comfort in his declining years. Restorations at Mussenden had been completed, enough that he returned to the preceptory to live out his days. 'Twas my last duty to him before I left Ireland, to see him settled and in good care. He has possession of all his treasured notes and the book of Solomon secure within his rooms. The Irish respect that.''

But the English didn't! Hawthorne swore. Then his eyes narrowed even farther. "The book of Solomon, you say? This knight Almoy has a copy of that?''

Cara did not see the significance of that question. "Every alchemist must have one or they can accomplish nothing, my lord.''

"Right you are there, mistress.'' Hawthorne came to his senses at last. "See to your toilette, my lady. I will grant you another hour's respite to see to your belly. Do see that she eats something mild but filling, Jen. I will return in two hours' time.''

The servant's eyes were agog with what she'd witnessed. The dialect spoken between Lord Hawthorne and the woman he'd brought to the queen's court was unknown to her. But she had seen plenty. And everyone who worked in the queen's household knew the way of making oneself better. Information was as good as a coin when it was passed to the right person. When it came to magic and things beyond the ken of mere mortals, John Dee paid the best coin. Jen knew magic when she saw it and knew lead could not change into gold by any other means.

Hawthorne paced his apartment, agitated and uneasy. "What in the name of all creation made me so blind?''

He knew the answer to that and it chaffed him. He hadn't looked twice at Cara Mulvaine. All he'd been able to focus his eyes and his thoughts upon was the flame of Rose Mckenna. Lust had brought him to this end.

Had he not been so blinded, he would have known by looking at the Mulvaine that she was special, gifted with a power, a conduit to another level of being. A link, possibly between the old Celtic spirits and gods and the present mystery and magic of the universe. Hawthorne was no dabbler in the art, but he was foresworn to protect all knowledge and to guard that with his life. It was the one special charge of the vast Saint Clair family and their duty before all other duties, God before king and country.

He ended his pacing, holding every muscle in his body at a pause and focused his thoughts, his energies upon the deed he'd committed.

He did not fear the wrath of the Mckenna any more than he feared the wrath of petty tyrants such as Elizabeth or her undeclared heir, James of Scotland. As the sword arm of *Continuum,* he was beyond reproach. As a son born of the Saint Clairs, he held higher rank and privilege than Gordon Mckenna. Even his taking to wife an unwilling daughter of the clan Mckenna could be smoothed over, given time and the proper inducements. He would have to conquer Rose before that could be done, but he doubted not that he could be won to her heart.

The Mulvaine was now a more critical piece on the queen's chessboard. What was Walsingham up to? If only he knew. Gordie would come to London. Hawthorne doubted not that truth. In the meanwhile, Hawthorne must see that the Mulvaine was protected—and that she had no discourse with John Dee.

They went by river to Nonsuch, King Henry's summer lodge built on the River Thames, away from the hustle and bustle of city life and the noxious odors of Londontown, out in the countryside where hunting was pleasant.

Disembarking on Hawthorne's arm, Cara swept the grounds with open eyes. She had been much in awe of all she'd seen on the small journey. She had never seen bridges that spanned great rivers or houses and palaces crowded together to make a city.

The houses in London were stacked up like pigeon coops on her grandfather's roof. One narrow little house after another rose five and six stories into the sky. All manner of transport had been within sight, from huge wagons pulled by sweating horses to little jaunty carts ferrying loads of passengers, foot traffic of every sort and variety, beggars and hustlers rubbing shoulders with fine ladies and gentlemen taking a stroll.

There were parks and wondrous buildings, cathedrals like she'd never seen in her life. Oh, she was agog with wonder long before they reached the quiet countryside where old men fished for the day's meal or barefoot boys herded cattle with a staff in their hand.

Then they came to Nonsuch. Cara gathered her skirts to manage them as she walked and accepted the offered support of Lord Hawthorne's arm.

There appeared to have been some outdoor fete previously. A grandstand draped in bunting was erected on the lawn, and many servants hurried in the waning morning hours to right the disorder of the night before.

Within the complex, servants tiptoed about, for the gentry slept late, as did Her Majesty the queen. Hawthorne saw Cara settled in a receiving room and went to pay his respects and announce his presence.

Cara smoothed down the tightly fitted stomacher encircling her chest and waist. Her underdress was of deep brown fustian. It was devoid of ornamentation but so full, she felt like a battleship awash in a sea of petticoats. The maidservant, Jen, had insisted she wear five of the ruffled undergarments to give the necessary fullness to her skirt. The bodice was modest, for a white chemise was worn beneath the gown, and that fitted to her throat and was enclosed with a stiff collar that made her keep her chin firmly up.

She picked at the sleeves, then touched the center of her chest where the stomacher flattened her breasts. The talisman tucked there felt warm as soft candlewax.

So, she ordered her thoughts, she was to meet the harlot. What would her grandfather give to be in her place? She knew what he would do. He would fasten his gnarled fingers about Elizabeth's neck, taking the hated harlot with him into hell. Cara blinked at the thought, and knew she would do no such thing. She prayed she could acquit herself well enough that no shame came upon her beloved Gordie's name. All the hate of Dunluce was done. It was the past.

It was a long time that she sat there, waiting for Hawthorne to return. Finally he did come and several others with him, men like he, handsome, youthful and virile. He introduced Cara to all of them, but other than the slender tall man he called Essex, she could not sort out their names. She found it confusing when titles were mixed with Christian and surnames. Essex was called Robin, but his name was Robert Devereaux. They began to walk her through a warren of rooms.

Nonsuch was like Kenna the night of her handfasting, filled with people all waiting for something to happen.

The queen perched upon a chaise in her private chambers with a dozen ladies attending her. Countless servants rushed hither and thither laying steaming plates upon a table at her side.

Though it was well past the noon hour, Elizabeth was having her breakfast. And she wasn't dressed. Cara's mouth dropped open in shock to find the woman entertaining in her shift. A yellow satin, heavily embroidered polonaise gaped between her vast bosom, which was uncorseted and belied her true age. Were it not for her lawn shift, she would have been bare bosomed. That didn't stop her from extending a regal hand to the four men escorting Cara to her presence.

"Robin! Darling, come and kiss my hand. Where have you been, scamp?"

"Perishing from the dullness of life outside of your presence, my queen," Essex said, and bowed perfectly before her, putting his knee all the way to the floor before taking her jeweled hand and kissing it. "Am I forgiven for deserting you?"

"No, of course, you aren't. You shall have to make it up to me and that will cost you dearly. Is that Raleigh with you?"

"Your Majesty." The sparkling-eyed Sir Walter bowed with more flourish than Essex and, were it possible, his compliments to her person were more outlandish. Cara had never heard the like and wondered if Gordie did the same when he was in the presence of this queen.

"Hawthorne," Her Majesty said last, nodding coolly to the black knight. Cara sensed his tension. He held back, why, she couldn't guess. Yet he also kissed the queen's hand, bowing low and speaking endearingly. Then the queen turned to an older man called Walsingham and smiled like a cat that had just swallowed a bit of a mouse.

"Taste that, Nora." Elizabeth waved a bejeweled hand at a plate of eggs that one lady held before her. The woman, Nora, dutifully took a fork to hand. "Well, Francis, so this is the Mulvaine? What do you think of her?"

Cara felt all eyes in the room turn in her direction. Walsingham held her attention. He was known to her by reputation. His agents had murdered her uncle James' wife and four sons. Upon his order, her grandmother Mac Donnell was locked in a cage hung outside the wall of Dublin Prison and slowly starved to death. Uncles and cousins had died. It hadn't mattered their age or gender, infant or adult—be they seed of Sorely Mac Donnell, they had been marked for death.

Francis Walsingham cleared his throat and shifted in his chair, glad for the queen's generosity this morning that had earlier caused her to offer him a chair. His bones ached. He blinked his eyes and looked beyond the tall young men to the small brown person behind Hawthorne. He blinked his rheumy eyes and glanced quickly up at Elliot. His face was masked and somber.

Again, Walsingham fitted his eyes to Cara Mulvaine. Wearily, he rubbed his fingers into the yellowed sockets. "My eyes would fail me now, Your Majesty. I fear I was up too late reading the missives from Drake and Hawkins. All is not as we planned in Portugal. The Mulvaine looks as I expected her to look—insignificant."

Elizabeth had to agree. "What is there to remark about the chit except her brown and offensive-to-my-royal-eye trappings? She won't do at all, will she, Robin?"

Relieved to hear that, Robert Devereaux exhaled. Privately, he thought Cara Mulvaine sweet and lovely, but his heart was pledged in a secret marriage unbeknownst to the queen. The Mulvaine wasn't the woman for him, not even if she came with all of troublesome Ireland and Scotland to her name. She didn't, and he was relieved Elizabeth found nothing of more interest to her.

"Nora, take the girl off and have Constance give her some duties to perform. And, Hawthorne, do something about her clothes. She looks like a hedgehog. Brown is a depressing color, fit only for Papist priests. John, come and present yourself. What took you so long in Antwerp?"

Lord Hawthorne snapped his heels as he saluted the queen and withdrew, taking Cara from her presence. When they were two rooms down the corridor, he looked down at Cara and discovered her solemn little face was lit by a great smile. He drew a handkerchief from his doublet and mopped his brow. The tension between her and Walsingham had been electric, charged like lightning. All the old one had done was dig his fingers in his eyes and moan about Portugal.

"What is it that makes you smile, mistress?"

"Oh?" Cara hardly noticed Hawthorne as she concentrated intently upon the warm talisman laying between her breasts, shielding her with its charmed cloak of protection. "I must be relieved, my lord. Who was the other man with us? I did not get his name.''

"Dee, John Dee." Hawthorne turned to a stairwell. He allowed Cara to precede him, checking behind them to see if anyone observed their progress.

"Who is Lady Constance?"

"Mistress of the queen's wardrobe."

"Does she have so many clothes that there must be attendants for them, as well? Is that what I will have to do? When will you take me back to Gordie, my lord? And what of Rose? What have you done with her?"

"Quiet, lady." Hawthorne stopped her at the foot of the steps. They were alone for the moment with not even one servant hovering on any of the landings. "Listen to me, Mulvaine. You must tread carefully in this palace and guard your tongue with diligent care. Keep all your thoughts and opinions to yourself. I will do what I can to gain your release from Her Majesty's service, but until I have that, you are by duty her subject to command."

"May I assume correctly that you regret the deed?" Cara asked him.

"You may." His answer was sharp and curt.

"Then I forgive you for it, Lord Hawthorne. I will add you to my prayers."

Lord Hawthorne had already found himself brought short by her direct words and questions, but to be summarily forgiven for abducting her left him speechless. Without further ado, he took her to Lady Constance.

Nonsuch was small by royal standards. There was not adequate space within it to house all who traveled with the queen's entourage. Lady Constance kept apartments in the nearby village. It was a small, crowded house where no less than twenty other members of the court kept their own belongings and actually had pallets that passed for beds.

Lady Constance was fifty years old if she was a day, and she put her fisted hands on her hips and shouted at Lord Hawthorne. "Where the devil will I put her? Find me a scrap of space to lay out one more pallet? I am walking on people as it is!"

Cara had never heard a woman yell at a lord the way the queen's woman did. Huge Hawthorne, who had boldly kidnapped her and stolen Rose from under her father's nose, grinned as sheepishly as a naughty boy. "'Tis the queen's request, Lady *C*, not mine. Do what you can, if you please."

"What I can do... is box your ears, you huge ugly man."

Cara blinked and watched Hawthorne retreat. First, the queen had called all these men to her feet like a pack of puppies. Now, this woman, whose only duty for England was to sort the queen's trunks of underwear, laid another low with a few choice words.

Cara marveled that Hawthorne had not raised his hand and slapped Lady Constance for her outspokenness. It seemed the way of things was different in England.

That got her to thinking as the days went on when she was called upon to pack and unpack Her Majesty's gowns, robes, shoes and headpieces. Perhaps men and women were not exactly as she had always assumed they were. Certainly, her grandfather had ruled Dunluce with an iron hand. Knowing what she did of the clan Mckenna, she had never once witnessed any of their women and girls being beaten out of hand as she had been.

The more Cara watched and listened, the more she learned. Why, ladies of the court regularly tore a piece of hide off the men, so to speak. Their tongues were as cutting as knife blades. It wasn't just the men who became their victims. From the queen down, there was a pecking order than ran through her household like that in a henhouse.

One day, a lady in a gown so beautiful it took Cara's breath away, came bursting into Lady Constance's apartment, ripping her sleeves from their fastenings.

"Oh, that nasty old cow!" she railed breathlessly to the two women who accompanied her.

"What's happened now?" Lady Constance demanded.

"'Tis the queen again," said the other plaintively. "She declares my gown too fine for my station and demands I give it to her at once."

Lady Constance scowled over the sumptuously embroidered Turkish silk. There were so many topaz and sapphire jewels adorning the bodice that the gown shimmered with a life of its own.

"Well, she can have it, damn her eyes!" the other said.

"She'll never get into it," the one unhooking the stomacher declared.

"She's a sagging old cow, Henriette. She's just jealous of your beauty and your youth."

"I've a mind to poison her," the first declared sniffing. Yet she relinquished the gown to Lady Constance to be added to the queen's wardrobe. Cara was given the task of putting it away.

When she had a moment of quiet to call her own, Cara let her mind go backward to Dunluce. Not to the east tower where Almoy had cosseted her, but to her grandfather's hall, where she had been so unwanted. What had made him so cruel and hateful to her? She could not bear to see anyone suffer pain, and always wanted to comfort others.

"Cara, Cara! Stop daydreaming and come pack this skirt with tissue and mind that you do not wrinkle the silk. We must hurry. The queen leaves Nonsuch on the morrow. Don't dawdle."

Cara was glad there was always work at hand. She didn't like court. Lady Constance's crowded house made her sick, the tempers of the courtiers made her wary. She wished Gordie would come for her. But would he? Handfasting her had never really been his choice.

Oh, he had come round in the weeks after the explosion had destroyed his quarters. He was certainly more solicitous of her after that. He had given Mimms his freedom and often took interest in her. But was his interest solely limited to the pleasures their bodies could share? Cara didn't fool herself that he cared beyond that level.

Worse, she feared for him. That horrible vision she'd seen of someone hurting, hating and endangering him, now nagged at her relentlessly. Half of her willed him to come for her. The other half wanted him to stay far, far away from England and danger.

She learned one more thing of import at the queen's court. It was that despite her belief that the joining of bodies was a special, holy thing between a husband and a wife, it was not a rare bond.

The queen's adventurers stalked receptions day and night in pursuit of ladies who would lift their skirts. Those same faithless men dallied with the queen and reaped quantities of unbelievable praise upon Her Majesty's head, but their lust was expended generously among the women of the queen's court.

Cara saw a devious game played in utmost earnest. The queen gave her ear to men whose devotion exceeded all boundaries. She played her favorites against the others like game pieces on a chessboard. Ambitious women sought to be aligned with the men who held the most prestigious positions.

Because the queen talked lustily and flirted outrageously, duels were often fought. The loser—as well as the winner—was like as not to wind up cooling their heels in the Tower of London. Cara witnessed Raleigh lose his temper and cut Essex's cheek in swordplay. Both were sent to the tower, and it was two weeks before Her Majesty relented and allowed them to return.

Cara found out later that only Raleigh had served his term. Essex had gone across England to his home and stayed there the decreed time. He came back, as happy as a lark, the best of friends with Raleigh, their intense rivalry an undercurrent that continued to flow. The court laughed and thought nothing of this.

The progress moved again and again to Cara's dismay, for she could not imagine how Gordie would ever find her if they kept moving so much.

In the town of Horsham the citizenry had gone to great lengths to prepare for Her Majesty's visit. Children had prepared a pageant and the townsmen a fair, displaying all manner of goods and produce for Her Majesty's inspection.

The woman was truly regal when she advanced upon her populace and met them within their shires. She made the most of her looks by appearing in overwhelming splendor, which the common people thought her most wonderful trait. No one seemed to notice that the queen was an old, haggard and hateful woman. She was Elizabeth Regina, Glorianna.

In private she was another person completely: mean, petty, vain, unreasonably jealous and destructive of any who crossed her.

Cara was again summoned to her presence.

"We have received a letter regarding your person, Cara Mulvaine. I would like for you to read it to me and then tell me what precisely you would like to have done about it."

Elizabeth handed to Cara a creased parchment, which Cara dutifully unfolded and spread open. She scanned it, recognizing the separate letters, for the alphabet was the same in Latin, French and Italian, but there was little sense in her trying to make heads or tails of the English words.

"Your majesty—" Cara made certain she dipped a curtsey to the queen "—I canna read English."

"You cannot read?" The queen leaned closer and her long fingered hand stretched across the paper Cara held. Her forefinger pointed to the words, Cara Mulvaine. "What is that?"

"I believe it is my name, Your Majesty."

"So it is. But you cannot read English? Are you a lackwit?"

"No, Your Majesty, I do not think I am." It was the wrong thing to say. Cara knew that immediately.

"Impertinent strumpet! Take her to the tower until she learns to read Greek!"

This was too much. Cara shook off the first set of hands that grabbed at her. "I can read Greek very well, Your Majesty! I can write translations from Latin to French, parse verbs and correct both pronunciation and grammar in Italian. Also, I am skilled in the mystical forms of numbers and can interpret the theorems of Pythagorus, and should you need a tissane or a poultice to cure the running sores on your legs, I could make one that might cure you."

"What say you?" The queen sat back, her eyes as wide as saucers and her mouth a round cipher of surprise.

"That is correct, my lady queen. I am not unschooled or unlettered, nor ignorant."

"John, come here. Take this girl and test her. Give me a full report on her skills and claims by this evening. Do you lie and brag to save your neck, I will have you flogged, then locked in Little Ease for one day's time."

Cara went willingly with the man named John Dee. He was of some import to the queen, but other than the one time she first had been summoned to the queen's presence she had neither seen nor heard of him.

Chapter Twenty-Eight

The village of Horsham had quarters only for the queen.

Dee had a splendid tent and retinue of servants. One accompanied them from the queen's presence. Umlaff was a huge man who spoke not at all, but by his very silence made Cara uneasy.

Cara hesitated as the servant drew back the tent flap. She wished she knew where Hawthorne was. He wasn't at court and she had misplaced her talisman in the hurry to pack and move to another little town.

"Come, Mulvaine, don't be shy. I don't actually eat little girls," John Dee scolded.

Cara ducked her head beneath Umlaff's arm and entered. The servant let the flap fall and remained outside. It took time for her eyes to adjust to the gloom within. The interior was hung with Persian rugs and layers of fine, priceless rugs carpeted the earth floor.

Cara stood away from the walls, feeling the fabric billow with the morning wind. Why had she popped out those words to the queen? What had come over her? She didn't know. All she could think of was Gordie and how much she missed him.

She turned to study the man the queen had ordered to test her. He was small of stature, dark-skinned and his eyes glittered above a hawklike nose. His black beard followed the lines of his jaw. He was certainly not handsome, as most all of the queen's men were. His pointed ears and penetrating stare made Cara liken him to a fox.

"You read Greek, you say?" Dee opened a low trunk and sorted through his papers. He had a table in the center of the tent, too tall for sitting to a meal. The top of it was clean and smoothly polished except in the center, where an object sat under a black silk drape.

"Yes, I do," Cara said, and shuddered. Troubling sensations emanated and throbbed throughout this dark pit. By the time the ordinary-looking man turned about with his crackling parchments in hand, Cara knew who he was. The Welshman was a black magician, a cabalist. Reluctantly she took the parchments to hand.

The first was written in crude Greek and was only a partial rendering of the eighteenth chapter of the *Key of Solomon*. She scanned the fragment, then turned to the second parchment. That was in Latin, the twenty-third psalm. Agitated, she handed both pages back to Dee and met his intense inspection with a resolute gaze of her own.

"The bottom testament states in Latin, 'Yea though I walk through the valley of the shadow of death, I shall fear no evil.' It is a common prayer taught to all clerics and still ascribed to the book of prayer in the queen's own service."

"And the first, Mistress Mulvaine?"

"Is a fragment only from the *Key of Solomon*. A portion of chapter eighteen. It begins with the words, 'of Earth, of Air, of Water and by Fire, against poison which hath been drunk, against all kinds of infirmities and necessities, against binding, sortilege and sorcery, against all terror and fear, and wheresoever thou shalt find thyself, if armed with them, thou shalt be in safety all the days of thy life.'"

"Are thou so armed, Mistress Mulvaine?"

"Sir Dee, I am but a simple maid who boasted badly. It went against my grain to be thought ignorant."

"What is this *Key of Solomon*?"

"Words of wisdom, sir. Who embodies more knowledge than he?"

"You couch your words most carefully. However, you did not read either text—you recited them from memory. In the case of the Key, your memory perfected the crudeness of the copier's hand. Where did you have opportunity to commit such texts to memory? You have seen the book, held it in your hands. Who instructed you?"

"I come from Ireland, sir. All books are treasured there."

"This is most curious." Dee returned his papers to the trunk. As he closed the trunk and keyed a lock to it, Cara saw the curious design of a pentacle. It read, *Chaigidel*. His guides were the shells, the faceless ones, as evil and as putrefied as their master, Beelzebub. She was in the presence of an evil, corrupted man.

Swallowing down her fear, Cara asked, "Have I passed your test, Master Dee? May I return to my duties?"

"Nay, wench." He moved to his upright table. He took the black silk from the one object centered there, revealing a large black crystal, set upon a curious base. He passed his hands over it, warming the air, stirring the currents. "Come closer, Mulvaine. Care you to glimpse your future?"

The polished orb began to pulsate, taking its life from the currents and the mystical words he chanted. It shed green light upon the polished table and illuminated the object supporting it. A human skull.

Abruptly, Dee's head shot upright and his eyes shone evilly at her. "You are breeding. A child grows in your belly."

"No!" Cara backed away. He snatched up her hand, imprisoning it upon the table between them so that she could not draw away.

"You must take care, little mother."

"Nay, you speak false!" Cara refused to believe anything he told her.

"Nay, 'tis true. See. Look into the glass. Aye, it is there. A man's seed is well seated within you."

So compelling were his words that Cara looked into the crystal ball. Stormlike clouds convoluted upon themselves, clearing to the deep center of the orb. There, in startling clarity, sunlight washed a meadow. Gordie's cloak spread upon the heather. His broad, sinewy back rippled with their mating, a scene as old as time, as primal as the earth itself.

"No!" Cara cried out, jerking her wrist in Dee's hardened grip.

"You hide your nature well." Dee's gaze swept downward, noting the heaving of her breasts. "Who would think to look at you that beneath your plain garments, there lies a wanton."

His black gaze scorched her.

"Let me go!"

"Don't be frightened," he crooned as his fingers drew out the pins that held her hair. Cara twisted away from his touch, disgusted by him.

Dee spread the loosened curls upon her shoulders. "How quickly your face changes, Mistress Mulvaine. Your hair becomes a lion's mane when it is freed of confinement. I see your origins in your piquant, elfin face. You are a Celt, the same as I. A beauty from the ages past, and you are breeding. What a boon that is!''

Trembling in the trap of his power, Cara shuddered as his hand passed down the stiffened fabric of her stomacher. Had she been naked before him, his touch wouldn't have shamed any less. Her breasts suffered the harsh compression of his hand, then he stroked lower, pausing for a long, dreadful moment over the life growing in her womb.

"Aye, I can feel it now. A male child is most special and unique. This one has his own life force. He is very strong, powerful."

Abruptly the magus released her. "You may go now. I will tell the queen that she may spare the effort of flogging a stupidly vain girl. That may save your skin for other pleasures, but I think a spell in Little Ease might make you more amenable to my needs. I will summon you when your fate is decided."

Cara stumbled out into the light, blinded by summer's glare. She wound her way though the crowds and stalls of Horsham, seeking the only solace she knew to find, the tiny cramped quarters of Lady Constance's traveling cart. There she huddled with her arms tight around her knees, her head buried. She listened to the sounds in her head, the flux and flow within her body.

There was another fast, small beat that she had not noticed before. Gordie's child.

Whatever was she to do?

Chapter Twenty-Nine

Hawthorne had nearly killed a horse driving it from Llanwst to London. He was only gone from the queen's progress a week, no more. In his absence, all hell broke loose.

Scorching, unbearable heat tormented the dog days of August. Storm clouds gathered, yet rain refused to fall. Summer lightning set Horsham's grandstand ablaze in the middle of the celebration to honor the queen. That caused a panic of retreat and evacuation. The fire spread quickly through dry, trampled fields and engulfed the whole town.

The progress ended abruptly. The queen was in foul temper, tongue lashing anyone who came within her range. Even her darling Robin smarted and sulked, riding far to the outside of her Royal Horse Guard as they approached the outskirts of London.

London brooded, fearing another onset of plague. Conditions, everyone said, were ripe for it. August's unusual heat, coupled by the damp, humid air without relief of rain and general malaise, had shortened tempers to the breaking point.

Threading his way through the endless baggage train, around worn-out horses bearing weary gallants and wilted ladies, Hawthorne could not find Cara Mulvaine. He had a sinking feeling. A terrible sinking feeling.

He sought out the ladies with duties in the queen's wardrobe. One gave him the first confirmation of bad news that Lady Constance had collapsed in Horsham and retired to the coast to regain her health.

"Into whose care was the Mulvaine entrusted?" he asked.

"Who?" The three simpering overheated ladies wagged fans at their faces.

Perched upon a jaunty cart in the harsh sun, their painted faces seemed to melt. They looked affright, like harpies. When, Hawthorne wondered to himself, did the lush beauties of Her Majesty's court shed their appeal to him? He could not fathom that answer. It did his spirit good to remember the clear skin, lightly covered with freckles that enhanced, not detracted, from Rose Mckenna's beauty.

"We know of no one of that name, Lord Hawthorne."

"The little Scottish lass," he prompted impatiently. *Didn't anyone ever notice the woman and remember her?* "Nora, you were at Nonsuch the morning I presented her."

"Oh, the little Irish lass, you mean. Ask Isabella. Perhaps she knows. I haven't seen her for days."

"Do you think she's run off?" the silliest of the three speculated.

"No, she would not have run off," Hawthorne said with good authority. "She is a lady, not a servant."

"Why are you so testy? It isn't as if you ever paid attention to her, Elliott. Don't be such a bore."

The queen's train fanned out in all directions once they'd crossed London Bridge, some to Windsor, most to their own quarters within the city.

Hawthorne continued his search. Isabella didn't know. Essex couldn't be found. The queen retired to Windsor, exhausted.

There was only one person Hawthorne could think of who might give him a straight answer. That is, if the worst he suspected had come to pass. He went to the privy council to waylay Walsingham.

Hawthorne cooled his heels a long time. Drake and Hawkins were closeted with both Cecil and Walsingham giving reports of their efforts to harry Phillipe of Spain via Portugal. Hawthorne paced and sat and paced again. Night fell, stars littered the sky. Torches and lanterns were lit all around Windsor.

Finally the sea captains emerged from the privy chamber. Walsingham came slowly after, his cap upon his stringy-haired, balding head, limping with the shuffle-footed gait of one crippled by gout.

"Sir." Hawthorne blocked his egress, drawing the older man up short.

"Hawthorne, I thought you'd departed hours ago. It's late. I'm more tired than I can ever think of being. I will see you tomorrow. Come at ten. You may have the first minutes of my day."

"Sir, the business that concerns me will not wait until the morrow."

"Unless the Spanish are at Gravesend and storming the city at dawn, it will keep."

"I must know what became of Cara Mulvaine. Was she sent back to Scotland?"

"Why, no, she wasn't. A warrant was issued for her arrest. She is in the Tower of London at the queen's perogative."

"Who asked for the warrant? Was it the queen who ordered it?"

"Nay, she has little interest in the chit. 'Twas John Dee who made a charge."

"Charged her? With what?"

"Witchcraft and plotting to murder Her Majesty. A sly poison had been instilled in the queen's clothing, causing sores to develop on her legs. She has retired to her bed and treatment."

"For the love of..." Elliott's voice trailed off, "Lord Walsingham, the queen has been plagued by sores for years. They are caused by her bulging veins and riding. Every progress ends with such for as long as I can remember."

"'Twas Dee who brought the charges. I know not how or from whence he got his evidence. I have not had time to look into the matter. Her Majesty will recover if it is God's wish. Good night, Saint Clair."

Hawthorne had no choice then but to go to see Sir Owen Hopton, lieutenant of the tower.

Chapter Thirty

Gordie stood with his back to the window. The sun brought little cheer through the grimy panes of the Hart's common room. The hour was late and Gordie had wasted another day futilely prowling London. Two months ago he had written an impassioned plea to the queen, begging her assistance in the matter of the abduction of two women. His letter preceded his arrival in London by six weeks' time.

Elizabeth had been on one of her tiresome progresses, this time winding her way to the seaside through the districts south of London. Her answer had come roundabout via Scotland and forwarded by his father to Gordie in London. Ulrich had only just placed the sealed document in his hands.

It was to reading her flowery script that Gordie taxed his eyes in the dimming light.

> "My most dearest Captain Mckenna,
> 'Twas with great surprise that I read your letter. You had not shown a propensity to remain my servant since given leave of my presence June past. How time has flown... without a word from you to ease the ache in my heart your departure created. I have asked of myself, how had I offended you? Did you not swear to love and honor me in all things? How fickle is a man's heart. How careless and intransient. While I, poor lowly woman that I am, must tread the weary steps of duty, never erring from that which I have sworn to do. Such is the duty of a woman born to serve a kingdom. I ask little. A word now and then would suffice.
> You ask a great favor of me. That I grant you leave to

marry. What do you tell me of this person, Cara Mulvaine? Is she winsome? A beauty unmatched in all your travels? Are you so taken with her that no other woman of good house, nay, good standing with our person would not suffice? Does she come from a loyal family? Are her lands what you covet? Is her dowry so great that it lures your heart from England's greater path of glory?

Were the answer to all these questions to rank in the woman's favor, I would beseech you, bring her to me that I may see this treasure you covet above all others. Present her to me. I will give you my answer then. Regarding the sister you much love and regrettably have lost, I offer my deepest, most heartfelt sympathies. We have no word of her crossing the border into England.

Elizabeth, Regina.

Gordie tossed the stiff parchment to the cluttered table. Ulrich picked it up and read it through. When he finished, he met Gordie's glare and asked, "Did you no write to the queen telling her of Rose's kidnapping? Weren't yer questions most carefully worded to gain information regarding Rose?"

"Exactly," Gordie answered, his mood becoming fouler by the second. "I included one simply worded sentence telling of my father's selecting a bride for me. I stated no more than Cara's name."

"Then the queen has her."

"Aye." Gordie sat to the common table in the inn. "And most likely corrupts her."

The trail from Scotland had been a misery. A dozen mysterious riders had taken off in every direction by pairs on the 29th of June. It had been a nightmare, following blind leads, dead ends and purposely crossed tracks. Until they came to Leith.

There, a ship had departed in the dark of night. Many riders had boarded it. Some villagers swore they heard a woman screaming. But no one could name the ship except to describe it as a goodly made craft with a fine draft, a swept prow and seven sails on its masts. It had discharged no cargo nor taken on any supplies. The soldiers had come with their own horses and departed with same. Half of the people of Leith swore the ship was English, the others claimed it was not.

So here Gordie rotted in a tavern on the waterfront in London, not that far down the wharf from Traitor's Gate. Every day, every night, Gordie prowled the docks, mixed among the sailors and asked if the ship they worked upon had been in Leith on the first of July.

The futility of his search, his helplessness, chaffed and burned. Gordie's temper was on a short fuse. He had half a mind to blow up Windsor, next St. Paul's and then the newly completed Great Storehouse within the tower. One monument at a time, he could reduce Elizabeth's grand city to rubble.

"Someone must know something," Ulrich said. "Perhaps it's time to make more direct inquiries. Go to court, Gordie. There would be those who know. Use your friends. What of Drake? Hawkins? Raleigh?"

"I think that is exactly what the queen wants me to do. I would play right into her hands. She is obsessive about the subject of marriage. Remember the fate of Catherine Grey?"

Ulrich nodded, for ill-fated lovers, Catherine Grey and the earl of Herford had crossed the queen's wrath in the early days of her reign and their secret marriage declared invalid. "To this day, Herford's heir remains a bastard, unentitled to his father's name and lands."

"That is here in England, and neither I nor Cara stand in any proximity to the throne."

"Isn't Owen Hopton lieutenant?"

"I believe he is."

"What of the plague? Talk is that it grows more virulent by the day. Won't Hopkins take his prisoners to the country if the outbreaks continue? It would be an easy task to rescue Cara if she were being transported elsewhere."

"Bite your tongue, Ulrich."

"'Tis a better idea than the mayhem you consider. I know your methods, Gordie."

"Shut yer face, Ulrich. Leave off and give me peace." Ordering a fresh pitcher of ale, which the barkeep brought speedily, he vowed to get roaring drunk.

The tavern was crowded, trafficked by many a seaman. Late in the evening two nobles sauntered in, staggering from drink. Francis Drake threw himself down at the first bench, propped his feet upon the table and shouted for ale.

"Damn my eyes," said the tall, slender man who had accompanied the famous captain. "Mckenna, what are you doing here?"

Both Gordie and Ulrich raised their bleary eyes to the gentleman. Gordie saw nothing but red, and Essex, the queen's favorite.

"Good God, man!" Essex slapped him on the back so hard, Gordie sprawled across the table. "We thought you dead, again. What took you so long in coming to London? The queen declared you would be here a month ago."

"Did she now." Gordie rose to his feet, a dangerous glint in his eye. "And, why, mon, would she think that? Does she hold something of mine? Something that I might value and demand returned to my keeping?"

"Hold, Mckenna." Essex made the mistake of setting his hands to Gordie's wide shoulders to steady him. Gordie's fist sent Essex reeling backward into Drake.

"What the bloody hell? Mckenna, are your wits addled?" Drake bounded to his feet, shoving Robin Devereaux aside as the drunken Scot took a battle stance. Drake had plenty of his men in the tavern. They favored the Hart. Ten of his lads lurched to their feet. He held up a staying hand and tried to placate Gordie. "The brew here has addled your brain, Mckenna."

Robin wiped his mouth and got his feet back under him. He was no coward. "You want to brawl, so be it."

"Now what's this all about?" Drake put himself between the two men. Ulrich clenched his arms around Gordie's chest, holding him back, possibly also holding him up.

"A woman's at the bottom of it," Drake surmised without surprise. Few women could resist Devereaux or Mckenna.

"Right you are," Gordie declared in a deadly voice, and launched himself once again. "My wife, damn yer eyes."

This time there was no holding him back. Ulrich threw up his hands, muttered what the hell and went to his cousin's aid. After all, alone the odds were twelve to one. Gordie needed his help this time.

The brawl was long enough in duration to wreck every table and bench in the common room. The tavern keeper only just managed to save the clay pitchers he'd filled for the *Revenge*'s crew. The ale, instead going down their gullets, ran under their feet. He ducked under his bar and stayed there while bodies flew and furnishings were smashed to smithereens. He was oblivious to the fight, busy tallying the bill for damages that Drake would pay.

When quiet finally came, it was an odd quiet, punctuated by groans and moans and the sound of retching. Jonas poked his head over the bar. The two Scots stood amid the rubble, the last two men on their battered feet. He ducked back beneath the solid oak countertop and crossed himself out of superstitious habit. The damn heathens were wild animals when they were drunk!

"Hell and damn, man, what in the name of God has gotten into you?" Drake moaned as he struggled to his knees. Essex was in worse shape, blood gushing from his nose, one eye closed solid, his clothes half-torn from his body.

Gordie Mckenna stood like a raging bull, blind with fury, and stomped to the bar, slammed his bloody fist upon it and demanded another drink. Jonas popped up with a whole pitcher and slammed it on the counter. Gordie upended the clay vessel and drank till he quenched his thirst. Then Jonas watched in wild-eyed horror as the Scot toppled over on his back, out cold.

"I'll be damned," Ulrich muttered through swollen lips. "He never did that before."

"Ulllll," Essex slurred. "I'll have that drink, Drake. You shaid yew were buying."

"Jonas, another pitcher if you will."

They passed the pitcher between the three of them, since the rest of the crew, including Gordie, were flat on their backs. When Ulrich had rinsed his mouth and spat out the residue, he poured the remainder on Gordie's face. Gordie's eyes fluttered, then he shook his head, groaned and subsided into the heap.

"Wherz yer roomz?" Devereaux groaned.

"Upstairs," Ulrich managed. What he couldn't manage was finding the strength to lift Gordie from the pile of human wreckage.

"I'll help you tuck him in." Devereaux staggered to his feet.

"Get yer stinkin' English hands offa me," Gordie growled when he realized who was hoisting him from the floor. It wasn't in him to lay on any more punches.

"Shut yer gob, Gordie," Ulrich muttered. Between him and Essex, they managed to drag Gordie up the stairs and heave him onto a bed.

"I'd like to say I didn't know what this was about," Robin said as he collapsed across Gordie's legs.

"I wouldn't advise you stay there, mon," Ulrich softly warned. "The laird can kick like a horse."

"I know," Devereaux groaned. He accepted the offer of Ulrich's hand and changed seats. Ulrich thought he should leave and said so.

"Can't. Got a matter of conscience. I know where the Mulvaine is."

"You what?" Gordie's bloodshot eyes opened.

"Hit me again, Mckenna, and I won't tell you."

"Slit his lying throat, Ulrich."

"She's behind Traitor's Gate, Mckenna. Will you listen to me, or are you stupid as well as foxed?"

It took everything Gordie had in him to rise from flat upon his back, but he did it. He dunked his head in the cold basin of water, shook the excess from his hair and rubbed down his face. Then he turned and glared at Essex.

"Say it again. Where the hell is my wife?"

"Six hundred feet east of where you stand. In Cradle Tower."

"What the hell is she doing there?" Gordie roared.

"Whiling away her time, waiting trial or acquittal, what else? I have a plan, you idiot. If you will but listen to me."

"On whose order was she detained?"

"Some trumped-up hocus pocus of Dee's. The man's gone over the top. He always was an odd egg. Now he's berserk. She can be gotten out. Owen is a reasonable man, and there is nothing he hates worse than seeing an innocent woman tortured."

"Tortured!" Gordie screamed. Ulrich got hold of him before he could start delivering blows again.

"Christ! I'm not against you, man," Robin shouted. "I'm trying to help. Hawthorne is doing everything he can to see that no further harm befalls her."

"What's Hawthorne got to do with this?"

"Walsingham sent Hawthorne to Scotland to get her."

"I might have known."

Gordie sat down then, too weak, too heartsick to think. Betrayed by his best friend, Hawthorne, Elliott Saint Clair. Lord God in heaven, they were both sworn knights of the same sacred order, Defenders of the Temple, knights of St. John's

Hospitallers. Gordie had fostered in the charge of the earl of
Hawthorne; Elliott's father had trained him to be a knight.
He'd pledged his own son, Kurt, to Saint Clair's good hands.

Worse was the pain that tore his heart in two. When had Cara
Mulvaine become his one obsession? He gripped his throbbing
head with both hands, as if it would fall off his shoulders if he
didn't.

Robin's voice droned above him, making little dent in Gordie's pain-filled thoughts. If he hadn't been such a fool, such
an arrogant swine, he'd have married Cara straight out. Elizabeth wouldn't have touched them if their vows were sanc-
tioned by her Protestant church. This was God's punishment
to him. Finally Gordie raised his head.

"Well?" Devereaux asked.

"Well, what?" Gordie responded stupidly.

"Do you want to try to do it?" Gordie hadn't the foggiest
idea what the man blathered about. He looked at Ulrich, who
gave him a curt nod of his head.

"All right," Gordie agreed blindly.

"Good enough." Robin straightened his clothes and limped
out the door.

When Devereaux was gone, Gordie asked, "What did he
offer?"

"Damn little, himself. He thinks we can bribe Cara's way out
of captivity. The risk is all ours. One question, cousin. Can the
man be trusted?"

"As far as you can throw him."

"What about Hawthorne?"

"I'm going to kill him. But Cara comes first, then Rose.
After that, I'll settle accounts with Hawthorne."

"Then we'd best make our own plan."

Chapter Thirty-One

Little Ease was meant to punish a man. The stone held the temperature of winter ice. A heavy iron door blocked out the light, trapped in the fetid air and kept whomever so unlucky to be imprisoned within it well contained.

It was a sunken niche, cut out of an ancient Norman wall. Its flooring was of the same hewn rock as its walls. Cara didn't think it had been exorcised in four hundred years. Oddly enough, it held no ghosts. She thought that was because no man forced to dwell inside its limited proportions could bear haunting its cramped confines for eternity.

She subsided to the floor, each wall close about her. There was no room to stand or sit, much less to stretch out or lie flat completely. Her eyes took time to adjust to the dark. There was no more horrible place elsewhere, not even the Tower of London. She curled her body on her side, closed her eyes and dreamed of Gordie.

A day, the queen had said, a day in Little Ease. Dee came with the written warrant this very morning. The queen was ever reluctant to see her orders completed. So Cara languished nearly a week in the Cradle Tower, awaiting her punishment. It was morning now.

Tomorrow she would be released. To console herself and pretend she was in less danger, she imagined she was back at Dunluce, deliberately hiding Gordie in the dungeons to keep him safe and alive.

Actually, she slept a while. She was tired. The journey from Horsham to London had tired her greatly. John Dee's tiresome company hour after hour in the Cradle Tower she would have preferred to do without. The pompous little man was quite full of himself and his acquired wisdom. He claimed he wanted true knowledge, the ways of all things, the secrets of life and creation, the means of communicating with all spirits, powers and beings.

As if any man could have or understand it all.

Cara shook her head, amazed by his conceit.

The cell grew foul and fetid as the hours lengthened. She had no means to judge the time. Then, when it seemed she actually might give in to the terror of Little Ease, the door opened and Sir Owen reached in himself to help her out.

She could not straighten out her spine. Her legs would not support her. Worse, she was feeling the cold of the sunken Norman stones. It penetrated right through her.

"My lady." Lord Hawthorne swept a cloak around her and lifted her gently into his brawny arms.

"Thank you," Cara whispered. "I think I would have fallen."

"You may bring her this way," Sir Owen brusquely ordered. Lord Hawthorne did not hesitate to take Cara up a winding staircase into the light.

Shielding her eyes against the blasted sun, Cara exclaimed, "Why 'tis afternoon, Sir Owen, you made me tarry longer than the required day."

"Nay, Lady Cara," Sir Owen corrected, "'tis just noon of the same day."

"Oh."

Cara made a little protest to Lord Hawthorne, claiming that she might walk a bit now. He wouldn't let her. Shortly, the knight carried her into the chamber where she had spent the past five days in the Cradle Tower. The furnishings there were similar to Dunluce. In fact, the room had reminded her much of her north tower, except it was smaller. Hawthorne gently eased her down upon a cushioned chair, tucking the wool around her like she was a child.

"I would have a few minutes with her, if you please."

The lieutenant had a curious expression, but he nodded his head and withdrew. There was the sound of the door locking, then silence.

"I came as quickly as I could. What happened in Horsham?"

Cara stretched her neck and remained seated. "It was most odd, my lord. I woke one morning and could not find my talisman. The next I knew, the queen accused me of being a lack-wit. She handed me a letter and bid me read it. I truly wanted to because I think it was written by Gordie, but I do not know English. Then she ordered me to prison until such time as I learned Greek. I was impertinent, I suppose, because I informed Her Majesty that I can read and translate Greek. She charged John Dee with testing me. He is a necromancer, sir, an evil man."

"Aye, did I not bid you to mind your tongue?"

"You did. Had I obeyed you, I would not be here."

"Had I not been used for a fool, you would not be here, mistress. Take heart, I am working on the queen to secure your release."

At those words, instead of gratitude and hope, the young woman shrank even more within herself. Hawthorne dropped to his knee, taking her hands between his own. Her fingers lacked all body heat. "What is it, Lady Cara?"

Cara looked at this huge man kneeling before her and blinked in astonishment. "Do get up, Lord Hawthorne. I am most undeserving of your solicitation."

"Nay, my lady, 'tis I who owe you much recompense. Do not despair. I will get you out of here."

"But to what avail?" Cara's huge gray eyes regarded him with solemn steadiness. "Where would I go? What would I do? At least here, I have a roof over my head. I would not know how to survive on my own in London."

"I will return you to Castle Kenna. You have my solemn word on that."

"You do not understand," Cara said, shaking her head. "Gordie will not want me. The Mckenna forced our union. Now that Gordie is free of me, there will be no marriage. I do not meet his clan's approval."

"Why do you say that, mistress? What of the child?"

At that question, Cara pushed aside the blanket and stood to her feet, a bit unsteadily at first, then, finding she wasn't so cramped, she walked to the vertical slit in the outer wall. Through it, she could see sunshine and hazy sky, and could feel just the lightest touch of the day's heated air. That only made the cold, dark tower a more miserable prison.

"The child has his own fate, my lord," Cara said with grave acceptance.

Confused, Hawthorne rose and walked up behind her, turning her round about so that he could study her placid, calm face. He expected hysterics, tears, volumes of blame heaped upon his head. How else could such a gentle soul react when faced with imprisonment in the tower? There was nothing predictable about the Mulvaine. Holding her shoulders in the grips of his huge hands, he searched her face for some trace of emotion. She was as cold as her delicate skin.

"What is it that you do not want to tell me? You hold back. I swear to you, Mulvaine, I will do everything in my power to get you free of here."

"But, my lord, it is not in your power, and there in you make your mistake. We each have our fates for which we were born. I see that now. My thanks to you for making what could have been a greater trial less a misery. You must go now. I have things I must do."

"What things?" Hawthorne demanded.

Cara's shoulders lifted, then sank in defeat. She pointed to the single lantern provided her. It sat on the chamber's one rude table where a prisoner might write or eat a meal. Upon it rested a small leather-bound case.

Looking to where she pointed, Hawthorne strode across the room, turned the lock on the case and laid it open.

Within were implements: a pen knife, quills, seven flasks of colored inks and two sets of fine parchments well cut and trimmed, stacked side by side. "Quills and parchment?" A deep scowl creased Hawthorne's brow as he lifted the knife and turned it so that the delicate gold symbols etched on it could be discerned in the light. "What do you with these?"

"They are not mine." Cara shuddered involuntarily. "But I am to use them."

"For what purpose?"

"I am challenged by Master Dee to make whatever pentacles I can to protect myself and my unborn babe from his power."

"You will do no such thing!" Hawthorne slammed the lid shut. He faced Cara, towering over her, intimidating by both size and demeanor. "You will not! By what foolishness do you think you can protect yourself from a man of Dee's learned power? You will be clay in his hands. All he wants from you is the location of the last preceptory and access to your mentor, Sir Almoy. Under no circumstances will you give Dee proof that you have seen such things as pentacles, esoteric books or insight into his obsession with the cabala."

"But, my lord Hawthorne, I canna lie to him. He has means of knowing what I think, what happens within me."

"Nonsense! You will hold against him until I secure your release."

"My lord, you are as powerless as I am."

"Nay, Mulvaine, I am not. You would be correct to say I am not one of the adept. When I was a youth, my size and thoughts were fit only for skills learned on a battlefield. I had no use for higher learning, despite my father's desire that I should do so. A man's gift might be to understand his limitations, and I know my own. You and Master Dee have guides that enlighten you, but you have chosen the true path while ambition and greed rules him. Clear your mind and meditate upon what the world would lose if Dee comes into possession of the most sacred documents ever penned. You will give nothing to him."

"Oh." Too astonished to say any more, Cara looked at Lord Hawthorne's rough and serious face. He was a good man, in his heart, a very good man, indeed.

"So, I have shaken your complacency at last, mistress. Good. Then I will bid you Godspeed and when we next meet, I hope to bring you better news. Should I not do so shortly, do not despair."

He chucked his knuckle under her pointed chin and smiled in what Cara thought was a most peculiar manner as if he bore her some special fondness. Then he bowed very deeply and graciously to her and, taking the locked case into his hands, departed.

Long after Hawthorne's departure, Cara paced the cell, thinking deeply. Her courage did not increase simply because Hawthorne insisted it should. If anything, his visit had only driven her fear deeper. Her child needed protection. Did she have the skill to cast a spell that would protect her babe? She had only glimpsed a fragment of John Dee's dark powers and it had overwhelmed her.

She knew the words, the chants, all that was necessary to cast any spell. That was not enough. Try as she might, she could not repeat what she had done in the bowels of Dunluce. Aye, she'd cast a powerful spell to save Gordie's life; she'd summoned an angel to give him back his will to live; she'd exorcised the demon who had coveted Gordie's soul. Magic such as that required special settings and the release from all distractions and impure thoughts.

To do such for herself was an impossible thing. It was selfish. She had no companion to accompany her. Without Mimms to guard her body when the spell was cast and the elements warred, her soul would be lost forever. Not even for the child could she accomplish such a thing. The child was not yet a breathing being. He was part of her and thus vulnerable to evil.

Cara rose and tended the fire, laying several fagots upon it to burn away the gloom. She would bide her time and wait. Perhaps on the morrow, she could ask Sir Owen to bring her a cat for company.

Chapter Thirty-Two

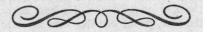

John Dee was also a patient man. While he bid his own good time before confronting the Mulvaine and squeezing the last dram of knowledge from her simple head, he spent his hours pursuing a mystery.

This particular mystery had confounded him for years, become his obsession so to speak. It cropped up now and again, like an elusive half thought in the stream of consciousness.

Dee's home, outside the confusion and hubbub of London, was seated in quiet parklike grounds. He had a wall built around it for privacy. Within those confines, he allowed ten mastiffs to roam freely. They were ever alert to trespassers and uninvited guests.

Within the house, which was not grand by royal standards, his collections were housed. Dee had in his possession the most elaborate library of his times. He had works of Cicero, copies of the *"Prieure"* documents of Rene d'Anjou and an unimaginable quantity of Leonardo da Vinci's original texts. Like the fragment he had put in the girl's hand to test her skills, he had partials of many, many esoteric documents, spells, incantations and treatises.

The mystery that Dee pondered centered round the most powerful order of knights the world had ever known. The Knights Templar. To all outward appearances, those ascetic warrior-monks all disappeared from the face of the earth more than two hundred years before his time. In France there had been wholesale burning of them as heretics.

Dee was convinced that the Order of the Templars had not been extinguished in 1314 by Philip of France. Instead, his readings and searchings proved otherwise. The powerful order had gone to ground. They existed in secret society wherein only a handful of unbreakable men remained entrusted with the esoteric knowledge taken from the Holy Land while they were the ruling force. They had also taken an unbelievable quantity of wealth. For two hundred years the Templars had, in essence, ruled the whole of Europe and controlled the Mediterranean east.

In his reading and years of searching, Dee had found many references to the *Key of Solomon*. He had uncovered many fragments of the text, proof positive that the book had once been well circulated, copied and passed on to other enlightened ones. He had references to it from so many different sources out of different lands, from different epochs, that he was positive it existed, somewhere.

To stumble across a guileless girl who could quote from memory verse and chapter, had shaken him. Through Cara Mulvaine he would have the book in its entirety, all its spells and incantations, all its names of God, for therein lay the key of wisdom that none since Solomon had known or invoked.

And with that knowledge he would hold the power of the entire universe within his hands.

Dee moved from the chair where he had gathered his thoughts and looked down upon the charts spread across his largest worktable. They were astrological charts, showing the movement of the stars, the planets and their risings and powers of the moon and the sun. Once again he lifted the natal chart he had prepared, checking his calculations.

The Mulvaine's child would be born on the winter solstice. That day when the night was the longest of the year. It was a powerful omen, auspicious for a male child to be born when the powers of darkness were at their zenith.

Dee could think of only two uses for such a soul. To be a sacrifice to a greater power while still innocent and uncorrupt, or to become his companion, his apprentice and finally a sorcerer to rival Merlin. The latter would be a long, tedious route to the power John Dee wanted. Indeed, if he could get his hands upon a complete text of the *Key of Solomon*, what need would he have of an apprentice?

And with his having the *Key*, then the child would become an even greater sacrifice.

If his intuition, his consummate studies and all his empirical deductions were correct, the mystery of the disappearance of the Knights Templar was about to be solved.

Taking the natal chart to hand, he rolled it and tied the cylinder with a piece of silk cord. He placed it inside his pack and went on to other business. The Mulvaine would keep until he was prepared to confront her.

Chapter Thirty-Three

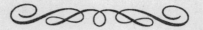

"Nothing," Ulrich declared. "I have been able to accomplish nothing. The day has been a complete waste."

"Not entirely." Gordie leaned against the stucco wall at his back. The smell of fish lingered in the air and that had brought an influx of cats prowling round the barrels Gordie had stacked outside the innkeeper's back door.

"Gads, that's ripe." Ulrich backed away.

"Think so? Good." Gordie went to the cistern and scrubbed his neck and arms, wiping wet hands across his face. "So," he said as he straightened and fixed Ulrich with a steely gaze, "you had no luck bribing your way inside the tower."

"None."

"Well, you shall have to go again tomorrow. I have a better plan than the one Robin suggested. It is too risky to run a rope from the heights. We cannot assume that Cara has the strength to traverse it from end to end. No, we shall just have to transport her out another way."

Ulrich looked at the barrels that the stray cats had decided weren't worthy of further investigation. "Now, listen, Gordie, if you are thinking to blow up the whole damned place, perhaps I should remind you that the woman you wish to rescue is within it. And we don't know where Rose is. There is no word of her whereabouts."

"Cara's in the Cradle Tower," Gordie said tonelessly.

"How do you know?"

"I just do. Don't ask me why."

The size of the purse Hawthorne dropped on the table before the woman was impressive enough to make her complacent smirk lighten. "Well, boy-o. What is it ye need done, then?"

"I need your ship and your crew waiting at Gravesend."

"Ha!" Her blunt laugh was harsh. "That will be the day! I'd as soon step up to the harlot's gibbet and put the noose round my own neck."

"It's no trick. I am acting in this matter alone. My ship will be there, to use as a decoy if necessary. I will also have the *Revenge* nearby. We are couching our bets, madame. If that is not sufficient to sway you, give me your price."

Grace O'Malley leaned back and looked the young adventurer up and down assessingly. He was a great big man, of Celtic origins most likely, judging by his black hair, the violet color of his eyes and the skin that stretched so tautly across his bones, without spare flesh anywhere upon his lithe, pantherish body.

"I am already engaged that eve."

"Madame, I am not prepared to dicker. State your price. You will be there at my service, or you will be nowhere. I will see to that."

"Do ye threaten me, boy-o?"

"Let me put it to you this way. My influence is not hindered by the borders of England, and though you may take me for an Englishman, I am a Scot, first and last. Beyond that, my services are with the future of England, Scotland and Ireland. Do you take my drift?"

O'Malley snorted and folded her arms cross her broad chest. "That whelp James again!" She rolled her eyes expressively. "Suppose I tell ye that I have already been asked to be at Gravesend, by another Scot and one I like a damn sight more than I care for ye."

"Say that again," Hawthorne roared, then caught himself and lowered his voice to a suitable level for a clandestine meeting in a very public and unsavory part of London. "Who is it?"

"Would ye be knowing a man named Mckenna?"

"Oh, lord." Hawthorne dropped to the bench opposite O'Malley. He signaled to a bar maid to bring him a whiskey and bolted it in one shot. "What is he planning to do?"

"How should I know? Looks to me, boy-o, as if ye have got a problem on yer hands. I'll be at Gravesend. This is a show I wouldn't miss for the world."

"Damn yer eyes, O'Malley. You could have told me that in the first place," Hawthorne growled as he grasped the purse between them. O'Malley slapped her hand over his, holding his wrist to the table.

"I wouldn't, boy-o," she cautioned. "I've a single bore pistol aimed at yer family jewels beneath the table, and though I wouldn't mind reducing ye to a eunuch, well, the truth is, lad, these guns make a bloody mess at this close range."

"You wouldn't dare." Hawthorne's eyes narrowed to slits, his temper barely held in check.

"Oh," Grace slowly drew back the hammer upon her pistol. It fitted into place with an audible click. "I dare, boy-o. Yes, indeed I do."

"I will ask you only once again, Mistress Mulvaine. Where is the *Key of Solomon* hidden in Dunluce?"

"And I have told you, Master Dee. There is no *Key of Solomon* at Dunluce."

"Don't play games with me! If the damned book is not in Dunluce, then at what Irish hovel is it kept?"

"I would not know of such things."

"Perhaps I have not convinced you how determined I am to have the book, Mistress Mulvaine." John Dee circled round behind the pillory, pausing at Cara's back to spread his hands out the pillory tree to where her wrists were tied. Cara turned her head enough so that she could keep part of him within view of her peripheral vision. "I have given you a choice, offered you great honors. I could..."

He trailed his hand across her bared shoulders, raising hackles on her spine as he lifted her hair and stroked downward across her exposed back. "I could be induced to sponsoring you at court in a favored position. Why, think of the feel of silk upon your skin. Hmm? What say you, Mulvaine?"

Cara said nothing. She had grown incredibly stronger in the days since coming to the Tower of London. Not in body, but in spirit. "I would refuse, Mr. Dee. Like your hand, silk makes my skin crawl."

"You have no liking for jewels, furs, splendid gowns?" His words dripped with scorn. "Why, with better clothes, you could rival the queen, hmm? The bones are there, your face has its own piquant charm. Those eyes . . . that mouth of yours is like a peach waiting to be kissed, tasted sweetly and savored long."

"Indeed?" Cara returned her gaze to the shadowy corner. Dee rounded the pillory to meet her gaze fully. Lust shined from his eyes and made his ordinary looks repellant. Worms and slugs infested his blood. He had to talk of lust to make himself a man. He enjoyed another's pain. Cara mentally dismissed him.

"So you are not moved by position or promise of earthly goods. What of your child, Mulvaine? Will your infant be as stoic to suffering as you are? What of birthing a babe upon a straw pallet? How will you feel when the umbilicus is cut and the boy is handed over to me? I have a special use for him. Do you know of it?"

Cara knew Dee astutely recognized her mental distancing. He would not allow her that comfort, and took her chin in his hand, forcing her gaze back to his powerful, opaque eyes.

"I know of it!" Cara snapped defiantly.

"Then your gifts have told you when the child will be born? I have cast your natal chart. I know of every event of your life, your quirks and foibles, your wants and desires and the outcome of your resistance to me. The boy will be born on the winter solstice, that day when darkness rules the earth. I will take him from you when your blood still covers him and use him as an offering to the most powerful spirit of Beelzebub. What think you now, Mistress Mulvaine?"

"There will be no child come winter solstice, Master Dee." She looked beyond him, preferring to see a different future than the one he predicted. "Your cruelties will destroy him long ere winter comes."

"I think not." Dee nodded to Umlaff, who waited patiently behind the pillory. Cara jerked at the sound of leather striking the floor. It was done to frighten her. She met Dee's rigid, unfeeling gaze.

"You cannot have it both ways, Mr. Dee. If you destroy the mother, you harm the child, as well. Will your evil guides accept a stillborn babe?"

"Damn you!" Dee exploded. He drew his hand back and slapped her in the face. "Give her ten and see that you don't break her skin! Do it, I said!"

Cara remembered not to bite her lip as the strap abraded her tender skin. Umlaff knew his craft and reveled in it. He had selected a strap that was wide enough not to cut her, but he did not spare his effort in laying it across her bared skin. She heard his grunts, his wind sucking in his huge chest before each blow. He cut ten agonizing tracks across her skin. For the first time in her life, she blessed her grandfather's cruelty. The Mac Donnell's hatred had made her strong. That she did not shriek and blubber in terror, made Dee even more furious.

"You think I haven't the will of yours! You are mistaken, Mulvaine. This was a lessoning. I will have the *Key of Solomon* and the gold and wealth and knowledge of the last Templar Priory. Do you press me with your stubborn nature, I will see that your body is broken into a thousand pieces. But I'll not let you die. Nay, wench. You'll linger to suffer. You will change your mind when the child quickens."

Meeting his gaze, Cara held her chin up and slowly shook her head. "Nay, Master Dee. This child will never quicken. The day is long past when it should have. You will not have my child."

"Think you not." Dee paused and took from his doublet her talisman and held it up before the lanterns. It glowed with the sheen of freshly poured ingot. "I have this. Recognize it? Time, Mulvaine, is on my side. And each day that you refuse me, doubles your pain. Ten lashes today, tomorrow twenty. Forty the morrow after. Do not think I will have mercy on you. You are strong and brave now, but you will weaken, little by little. Tomorrow you will scream and beg for the punishment to stop. You have yet to taste the rack or Skeffington's Irons. This is merely a taste of what is to come—so that you may know your future is the one I grant you. You will change your mind, and shortly."

He flipped her talisman toward her and the golden color held as it arched through the air. It landed upon her wrinkled hem and turned to dross. He laughed in triumph, glad that his vile touch had defiled the charm. Cara hung her head, more defeated by that than by his beating.

Returned to her cell in the Cradle Tower, Cara stood on tiptoe to gaze out across the rooftops of London. Night had come and the city radiated heat. The Thames cast up a foul and fetid smell from its waters, which ran not a hundred feet away.

A single candle illuminated her cell. It was fitted upon a holder on the table. The evening meal was a hunk of meat, a slice of cheese and bread. It never varied, for to get better fare, one had to pay for victuals.

Cara took her shawl from the chair back and drew it across her shoulders. Despite the heat, the stuffy room retained a humid wetness because of the river just beyond the wall. She ate for the sake of the child, folding the bread about the meat and cheese, chewing with deliberate slowness, thinking.

She did not doubt Dee's promise to double his punishments on the morrow.

Her only worry was that she might break and tell him what he wished to know. The child was most precious to her. She wanted it more than she had wanted anything in her life. A child of Gordie's to love, to cradle in her arms. But envisioning it eluded her. Betraying Almoy was the child's only means to survive. Cara could not do that.

Her only hope was Hawthorne, and it had been three days since she'd last seen him.

This night, she could not seem to stop the shivers that racked her bones. The tower was getting to her. It was the dungeons that had made her cold. The haunting screams of tortured men echoed throughout its hollow chambers. The smell of fear permeated it. The evil that resided in the Tower of London's dungeons was a frightening malevolent spirit, well fed upon pain, sorrow and hopeless suffering. It was a terrible place. She had no wish to return.

What choice did she have? None, except to give ancient Sir Almoy's treasures away to the most evil man alive.

Umlaff had let her keep the talisman. Cara took it from the pocket of her skirt, holding its lifeless form in her palm. Dee's defiling touch had drained its power to dross.

Rising, she took it to the embers that remained of her fire. She stirred them with a dry faggot, uncovering seven red coals, heaping them one upon the other. She leaned carefully over the glowing coals and fanned with her breath, gently, adding the chips and scraps of wood from her supply.

A bright flame caught and twisted upward, granting the gloom a faint light. Cara broke the last stick apart and laid that on top. Then she dropped the talisman on the miniscule fire and held her hands above it, intoning softly, "Accursed be he who taketh the Name of God in Vain! Accursed be he who useth knowledge unto an evil end, be he accursed in this world and in the world to come. Amen. Be he accursed in the Name which he has blasphemed!''

She sat back upon her heels and watched as the fire grew brighter and brighter, consuming every scrap of fuel. Then the metal glowed, red as the burning coals, and the talisman turned quicksilver and ran in little rivulets onto the ashes.

White smoke twisted upward. The strong odor of incense filled Cara's nostrils. She gazed at the lingering cloud, watching its shifting forms.

"Ah, Almoy, what am I to do?" Cara wondered softly aloud.

There was no immediate answer and she consoled herself, saying that maybe come morning her mentor would have sent her a sign.

There was a commotion outside her chamber, which did not alarm Cara duly. The Cradle Tower was connected by the Long Gallery to other towers and cells.

The light from the little fire faded. She drew her shawl around her as her cell door was unlocked, then opened. A wave of despair washed over her as she imagined Dee returning to gloat over her. But it was only the crooked man with the sweetwagon come to gather the slops. He was a harmless sort, addled in his mind. She returned her focus to the fire.

Gordie pushed the heavy door almost shut and turned with the creaking wagon inside the cell. He found Cara kneeling with her back to him, stirring a tiny fire. He dropped the tongue of the wagon and strode across to her.

"Cara!"

Cara swung round on her knees, startled by the voice she'd heard. She looked for Gordie and found only the huge, twisted form of the tower servant reaching for her with his filthy hands.

"Cara!" Gordie caught her shoulders, snatching her to her feet. His appearance frightened her so, a scream almost escaped her lips. "'Tis me!" He jerked her against his body, straightening automatically.

"Gordie!" Cara squeaked, so startled, her scream died in a gasp. He dragged her against him, his arms crushing her, then his mouth covered hers and any sound she might have made was lost. His kiss bloomed stark with need and hunger.

"Oh, Gordie," Cara whispered against his mouth, her hands frantic as they pushed back the hood that covered his head. She gripped his head and gazed at him, filling her sight with his face, and kissed him again in hunger and desperation.

A long, sweet moment passed before either of them broke apart to speak again. "Oh, you shouldn't be here!" Cara whispered. "'Tis so dangerous and evil! You must go, quickly. Leave before someone catches you."

"Hush." Gordie put his hand across her mouth, silencing the torrent of silly, unnecessary words. "I'm taking you out of here." He lifted her in his arms and moved quickly to the wagon.

"What?" Cara gasped as he removed the wood lid from one barrel. "No! Gordie!"

"Now, listen here, woman!" Gordie drew her against him. His hold was harsh and dangerous now. The hand clamped over her mouth silenced her every sound. "Not another word from you! I have everything in hand and must be quick about it. You will do exactly as I say. No questions! Understand?"

Cara searched across his face. She nodded against his hand. He lifted her and stuffed her none too gently inside the dry barrel.

Banging the lid on top, he set two pegs to hold it in place then resumed his disguise and twisted gait and hauled the creaking wagon with its two barrels out into the gallery walk.

The guard shut and locked the door, keeping his nose, at the smell reeking from the barrels, turned the other way.

"These barrels are full!" Gordie announced, and the heavy creak of the wooden wheels attested to that.

"Well, you know what to do with that, then." The guard wagged him off, following to lock the gates after the cart and crippled man lumbered out. The guard set himself back at his post, on a stool outside the Cradle Tower gate.

The night burned hot and fetid, stiflingly so. He watched with interest as the twisted man hoisted one barrel onto his sweetwagon. "Better not drop it! I'll beat your arse if you spill it here where I have to smell the stench all night!"

Gordie gave a rude laugh for the guard's benefit, wiped his nose on his sleeve and took up the barrel with Cara in it. He staggered on purpose and behaved as if the weight of the cask was too much to carry. The barrel thudded onto the wooden cart, already loaded with barrels. He grunted, flexed his shoulder with the hump affixed to it, then shoved the barrel into place. There were eight all together and seven had the stench of their true contents fouling the air.

"Wull, thas the lot for this trip!" He tugged his forelock to the guard then lumbered heavily onto the cart, took up the reins and clucked to the broken-down pair of dray horses. "Giddy'up, Light'n'!"

The guard laughed as Lightning plodded from the courtyard at a turtle's pace. The horse and cart trundled to the water gate in the bowels of the prison. Ulrich manned a barge outside the gate, a long pole in his hands.

Gordie waited impatiently while two sentries unlocked the gate and swung it open. Ulrich loosened his lines and poled the boat inside the black arch, ducking under the iron grate.

Together they worked in grunting silence transferring the heavy barrels onto the barge. Gordie let one of the first spill upon the steps and that caused the guards to holler and shout and back away. When the last was loaded, he tugged at his hair and climbed onto the barge, taking up the other pole.

"We be back later, gents." Ulrich saluted. "'Tis a fine sweet night, eh, mate?"

"Ugh!" Gordie grunted and put his back to the pole, pushing away from the Tower's dock. The boat lumbered into the current of the Thames, its heavy cargo causing the craft to glide sluggishly upon the water.

All along the wharfs of the Tower, ships crowded the docks. All of London was out-of-doors this night, with everyone who could manage it, trying to get a breath of air. The wind wasn't favorable. Even the river ran sluggish.

The two Scots plied their long poles, moving slowly under London Bridge, past fine houses and the crowded city. Downriver, the residences thinned out, until at last, they came to the countryside. In a little turn, Gordie searched for the boat he'd hired. He spied the crew hulking in the shadows under a clutch of elms. Not a breeze stirred the leaves.

Working together without unnecessary words, Gordie and Ulrich poled the barge closer to the skiff. Gordie's shoulders were on fire then from the exertion of the hard work. He unpegged the dry barrel with a sigh and removed its lid.

Cara could not move. The barrel had been as bad a prison as Little Ease. Worse, it stunk so vilely, she was ill. Gordie roughly took hold of her shoulders and pulled her out in a tangle of petticoat and skirt. The stench outside the barrel was worse than anything Cara had ever had the horror to smell in her life. Gordie smelled, too. His hands were filthy, and grime was splattered all over him.

That didn't stop him from hugging her as if she were the most precious thing he'd ever touched. A smirk plastered across his filthy face as he said, "We're even now, Mulvaine.... The dungeon of Dunluce for the sewer out of the Tower of London."

Then he kissed her sputtering lips.

Cara's sensitive belly knotted dismally. She gagged and said, "You son of a bitch," and pushed him away. Then she lambasted him with her fist. "Don't you dare touch me!"

For a second after her fist impacted on his jaw, Gordie was stunned. But he wasn't senseless. "You'll wash up," he promised and threw a black cloak around her, drawing it close and tight around her arms. Then he tossed her over his shoulder and stepped out of the barge and into the skiff. Ulrich was already at the helm and the crew had the oars in their hands. "Give it yer best stroke, lads. We've a timetable to meet."

The oars cut into the water. Gordie set Cara aside, between two of the burly straining men. He stood in the prow, striking a flint, tossing what he held across the water to the floor of the drifting barge.

"Pull!" Ulrich shouted.

Gordie leaped to the center of the skiff, catching Cara in his arms and pummeling her to the floor of the boat. Before she could scream or kick the hell out of him, his body crushed hers and his hand covered her mouth and cut off her air. She fought him, furious at his horrible treatment of her; then the shadowy night erupted with an explosion.

The skiff rocked dangerously and every man ducked. Behind them the barge turned into a splintered inferno that plumed and rolled across the water then sank into hissing steam before silence returned.

It was a deafening silence. One that competed with the loud hammering of Cara's heart, the stroke of the oars and the grunts of the crew. Gordie chuckled and slowly eased his weight from Cara's soft body. He kept his hand across her mouth, even when she bit him. Her eyes were huge with fearful terror.

"Careful, lassie," Gordie cautioned when her wiggling beneath him touched his manhood. God, but he wanted her! She groaned something obscene against his palm and again tried to bite his hand. Oh, she was in a furious snit, she was. He grinned, feeling more like a pirate than he ever had in his whole life.

The boat moved on toward Gravesend.

After a little while, when Cara's furious struggles had quieted, Gordie shifted to sit in the prow facing east and drew Cara tight against his chest, his arms surrounding her. She laid heavily against him, weeping in almost silent misery. Gordie trailed his hands in the cold water, rinsing them, then touched her chin and lifted it to his gaze.

"Don't be frightened, sweetling. 'Tis only a little farther."

Cara shook her head and ducked it beneath his chin, not caring what he smelled like anymore. He wrapped his arms round her shoulders, content to hold her.

Ahead, the river flowed round a sharp bend. Gordie fixed his gaze to search for O'Malley's *Avenger*. It would be waiting just a little closer to Gravesend. Drake's warship, the *Revenge*, as well.

But neither of those alerted ships came out from hiding beyond the point. Instead, a fully rigged carrack glided into view and it sat blocking further passage downriver. Across its broadside a full deck of upper and lower cannons pointed at them.

Drake's four stalwart crewmen drew up their oars and looked at Gordie first, then back at Ulrich where he leaned against the tiller.

"What the devil?" Gordie exclaimed softly. There was no question that the crew of the carrack had spotted them. "That's the *Victorious*, isn't it?"

"Aye, sir," Jenkins replied, holding his dripping oar aloft as the skiff shifted round sideways, its prow facing north.

"What the hell is Hawthorne doing here?" Ulrich asked. They didn't have a long wait to find out. One gun exploded on the upper deck and a cannonball soared across the water, falling short of the skiff, but dousing them with a spout of water.

"Ahoy, Mckenna!" Hawthorne stood at the lower rail, cupping his hands to his mouth to assist his shout across the water.

"What do you want, Saint Clair?"

"The Mulvaine, if you please. I'm sending a boat to get her. Do cooperate, or I guarantee you, I'll blow the lot of you out of the water."

"No! My lord Hawthorne, you cannot!" Cara threw her arms across Gordie's chest, as if she could shield and protect him from a cannon's barrage.

As the skiff drifted closer to the huge gray ship of Elliott Saint Clair, Gordie pressed Cara's arms away from his chest and stood in the prow of the little boat. A skiff from the ship rowed out from beneath its shadow, cutting quickly across the distance.

"The woman in question, Hawthorne, happens to be my wife."

Hawthorne gritted his teeth and fought a wave of pain that sent shards through his brain.

"Go on," Dee coached him, and jabbed a pistol deep against his kidney. "You're doing just fine, Hawthorne. Continue."

"She's too valuable for a highlander, Mckenna. I've a better use for her, now that you have done me the favor of releasing her from the queen's perogative. We won't be staying in England so you needn't fear about her languishing away in the queen's prison."

"You traitor!" Gordie howled a furious oath.

"Steady," Ulrich cautioned Gordie.

The other boat came up to their side.

Gordie looked down at his wife, his jaw painfully clenched, and what he saw in her shadowy face were those impossible-to-forget eyes. What she saw was beyond his ken, and a cold feeling washed down his spine, one that could only be equated to raw, utter terror.

The four Scotsmen in the other skiff had grim faces as they confronted their countryman. "Forgive us, Mckenna. We've got no choice."

Neither did Gordie. Cara resisted the draw of his arms as he pulled her to her feet. His hold was gentle, but she knew he was surrendering her, nonetheless. She clung to his hands refusing to be bartered.

"It's all right, Cara. If I could get you out of the Tower, I'll get you away from Hawthorne. What the devil does he want from you?"

The betrayal was simply too much for Cara. She had trusted Hawthorne, even to refusing to name him to Dee under the threat of punishment. "I would rather die here," Cara whispered.

"No." Gordie shook his head, refusing to consider such a thing. Then he clutched her to him, kissed her, lifted her into his arms and swung her over the side to the other boat. "I love you, Cara. I'll come for you. I don't care how far away he takes you. I'll find you."

As the long boat stroked away, he stood in the skiff, his hands cupped to his mouth, calling, "You are all that matters to me, Cara Mulvaine. Do you hear me?"

"Aye." Cara huddled in the black cloak, shivering, tears streaking down her face.

"Damn you, Hawthorne, you're a dead man!"

"Damn your own soul, Mckenna." A voice laughed back wildly. Cara jerked about, looking to the deck of the ship. It wasn't Hawthorne who was laughing. The wild voice coming across the water belonged to John Dee. All too quickly she was being hauled on board the *Victorious*, pushed and lifted and dragged against her will.

Dee caught her wrist and hauled her up against him. "Had a little adventure, did you, Mulvaine? Did he take time to plow your belly, hmm? I see by your distraught face that he did not. My, and the smell of the Scot is a foul odor indeed. Here, don't be shy."

Dee jerked her against the lower deck rail where Gordie could have full view of her. Dee caught Cara's hair in his fist and twisted her head back against his hard shoulder. He threw her cloak to the deck and tore his hand down her simple bodice, exposing her throat and her breasts.

"A lovely woman beneath, wouldn't you say, Mckenna? Firm and delicate in all the right places. I shall enjoy using her and perhaps, when I've finished with her, I will reward Hawthorne and his crew and let them have what is left of her."

"Curse your evil eyes, Dee!" Gordie roared.

"Welcome to hell, Mckenna. Blow him out of the water, now!"

Dee's order was instantly obeyed. Eight cannons blasted, then a second volley fired. Cara covered her ears and screamed and screamed and screamed.

Chapter Thirty-Four

"That takes care of that." Dee tossed Cara inside the captain's cabin and dusted off his hands. She caught herself and clutched her torn garments to her. Then she saw Hawthorne. He was a battered bloody mess under the crushing feet of Dee's servant, Umlaff.

"Now, Mr. Templeton. Your orders are to set sail for Antwerp. Do so quickly. My friend Umlaff is not a patient man. I cannot say how long I can keep his juices under control. How much more blood do you think yon Hawthorne can stand to lose?"

The first mate of the *Victorious* ground his jaw close together and wheeled about, stalking back to the helm to order the ship set on course and sailed where Dee would have it.

"Boy-o, this is a fine kettle of fish you've got us into." Grace O'Malley declared as the six-man crew of the English skiff dropped like wet kelp on the decking of the *Revenge*. "Your friend Drake there was hell-bent on detaining me. Not that he can, mind you."

O'Malley swung round to the man in question, who was not all that steady upon his dashing feet. The pride of England Drake might be, but he was laid low now.

"Hell!" Drake moaned. "What kind of vermin do you consort with, Mckenna? She's damn near plundered my warship!"

"Now, I wouldn't say we've gone that far." O'Malley laughed. "Just evened the score a bit, Lord Admiral Drake. Well, boy-o?"

She returned her attention to the Mckenna, waiting his deliverance of the belly full of water he'd ingested. The other five were coming about. She sighed. Gordie would take his damn good time coming to grips with things—that was a man for you! She cupped her hands to her mouth and shouted over the rail to her crew standing by on the *Avenger*. "Get after them!" Then, turning back to the flustered crew of the *Revenge,* she smiled and raked her wild black hair back across her shoulders. "Well, don't just stand there, laddies. Battle stations!"

"Damn you, this is my ship!" Drake roared.

"Oh, shut yer face," Grace snapped. "You're in no condition to give orders to anyone. That's the price you pay for brawling when you go ashore. Restraint, Captain Drake, that's the name of the game. Restraint. Tess, go an' see if there's a beefsteak to slap over that blind eye of his."

Gordie choked out the last of the water from his lungs and staggered to his feet. He lurched to the rail, squinting in the distance where the *Victorious* had a damn good lead and was entering more open waters past Gravesend.

O'Malley's adepts had their sails trimmed, and the *Avenger* was slipping away, taking the lead in pursuit.

"I'd like to know what this is all about," Drake rumbled, then hollered for his men to get into the riggings and set the sails.

"That son of a bitch Hawthorne has taken my wife. He's got John Dee on the *Victorious,* escorting him to Antwerp."

"Hawthorne? Consorting with Dee?" Drake asked, surprised. "That's an odd match. Thought he couldn't stand the fellow." Drake looked around, puzzled. "Robin, get hold of yourself and make an accounting. Didn't you tell me this morning Hawthorne was taken into custody?"

Robert Devereaux emerged from behind a pile of ropes, staggering unsteadily, a wet rag held against his head. O'Malley thugs had taken them all by surprise, swarming over the sides of the English warship like vermin crawling out of the denizens. "I think that's what I said. The queen ordered him held in the Devil's Tower to rot until he repents a lifetime."

"So what's he doing captaining his boat?" Gordie swung round his face, as puzzled as anyone else.

"Dee's gone mad," Devereaux surmised, and it took great effort for him to manage that in his condition. The Irish had fists as heavy as the Scots. "He was ranting to Her Majesty all night long about having found some key to a temple's treasure and the philosopher's stone. If you ask me, the man's barely got a grip on reality, and that is slipping daily."

"Must be all those sulphur fumes he's breathed." Drake dunked his head in a barrel of rainwater to clear his brain. He came out shaking like a puppy.

Gordie had gone as still as a statue at Devereaux's words. He closed his eyes, discovering at last what this was all about. Of course Dee wanted Cara; he wanted her knowledge of the Templar's last preceptor—Almoy. He had Hawthorne, too. Curse the damned bloody traitor!

Drake shouldered aside the Irish thugs who had overpowered him and his crew. "Dicken, get a load of iron up here and throw these Irish savages in the brig. We'll deal with them later. You!" He pointed a long finger at Grace O'Malley. "Get your unlucky hide off my deck. Get below, woman! That's an order."

"Oh, stuff it in your nightshirt, you pompous ass." Grace caught a trailing rigging and deftly hoisted her body up to the first yardarm. There, she tucked her skirts about her knees and settled to watch the chase. As the *Revenge* swept past Gravesend, the wind came up and filled its sails. "Go on!" Grace cheered as her ship leaned into the wind, tacked and struck out across open water, decreasing the *Victorious*'s lead. "Ahoy, Drake! The *Victorious* shows its colors. They've raised the Jolly Roger."

Drake studied his own filling sails, pulled the wheel hard to port to take advantage of the wind. "All hands, ready about!" he shouted.

"Ready, Cap'n!" A dozen men and one female aloft responded. Gordie gripped the quarterdeck rail and held fast as Drake spun the wheel hard. Cutting across the wind, the sails flapped then snapped, and men scrambled like monkeys to fasten sheets, cranking the winches to draw in the lines. The maneuver complete, the *Revenge* leaped forward in the water, leaning as hard against the wind as Drake dared to push the wheel. He locked it into place with a wood pin and stepped back, rubbing a knuckle into his battered eye.

Gordie had been calculating the whole time and now he stood back, as well, his eyes on the horizon. Beneath a heavy bank of low clouds the sun was making its presence known. "If you can draw alongside of her, I can put a shot straight through the mainsail," he said.

"What then, we board her?" Drake asked. "Cutlasses high."

"Forget it, boy-o." Grace called down from above them. "The *Victorious* stalls. Her mainmast just broke. Someone's sabotaged her."

"I'll be damned," Gordie and Drake both said in one voice as they looked. Sure enough, the ship had lost its mainsail. The mast went heeling over, shattered in two.

"Press on. Stay on course. Get ready to board. All hands on deck!"

"You presumptuous English!" O'Malley scoffed. "Your quarry lies ten leagues away and you lick your chops thinking you can taste victory. My mates will see to it."

Lord Hawthorne was in terrible shape. Cara dipped a cloth in the basin of water and gingerly touched his right eye. He did his best not to flinch, but she could see that it was taking all his concentration. He had little of that left and she thought his brain was concussed. She had never seen a man who had taken a worse beating. Not even the sea had gobbled up Gordie as badly.

But it had him now. She choked down a sob as she ripped the last of her petticoat into strips. Hawthorne groaned as she set his arm inside a makeshift sling. She had most of his more serious injuries bandaged.

He had stores of medicines in his cupboards, including thick salves that staunched all but the most major bleeding.

"I don't deserve your kindness," he mumbled through swollen bloody lips. Cara wondered how many of his teeth were loose. Another sob threatened. She held it in by biting down on her lip. The thought overwhelmed her that at least Hawthorne lived, because Gordie didn't.

"Please don't cry," Hawthorne groaned. "I cannot stand this if you do."

"I'm not crying." Cara dashed tears from her eyes, forcing her concentration on the injured man before her. Gently she smoothed the coarse black hair from his brow and tried to fix a brave smile on her face. Then the crack came.

It wasn't an explosion like a cannon shooting. It was a crack like wood splintering. The whole ship pitched, and she was

thrown across Hawthorne's legs and he into the walls supporting his bunk. They both howled with the agony of unexpected
impact. The ship stalled, lurched, then listed horribly.

"What is it?" Cara screamed in alarm. It was still dark and
the night had been horribly long. The splintering sound went
on and on, yawning, stretching out, joined by other sounds:
shouts, screams and a thunderous clap that shuddered aft to
stern.

Once the awful sound ceased its tearing and reverberating,
the ship leaned dangerously starboard. Hawthorne moaned, his
mass of injuries jarred. Cara hastily got herself off of him, and
did what she could to help him straighten himself. Then the
horror struck her. Water gushed in the porthole beside the
bunk.

"We've fallen over in the water!" she cried. "Hawthorne!"

"Calm, *bella*." He struggled against the press of gravity.
Cara ducked as unstowed baggage bounced across the cabin.

"Oh, dear God, we're going to die!" she screamed, shaken,
terrified.

"Shut the portal! The window!" Hawthorne pointed to the
small orifice. Cara jumped to do that, stumbling, twisting on
her skirts. She crawled to it, slammed the glass frame shut and
forced the lock tight against the swell of the water.

"What happened?"

Hawthorne had a pretty good idea what had happened. The
mainmast must have gone. He could hear the sound of axes
chopping and subsided to the awkward juncture of bed and
wall. "Lost a mast. Not to worry. The crew knows what to do."

"They do?" Cara looked around blindly. It was so dark.
Dee's things were scattered everywhere. One of his trunks
spilled open. She was certain his horrible crystal and skull
floated just beyond her in the puddle of seawater. "It's evil. I
can feel it," she said, pointing to Dee's trunk.

"Come here." Hawthorne stretched his left hand to her.
"There's naught we can do. The crew will fix it. You'll be safe."

"No, no I won't." Cara scrambled across the oddly slanted
space. Hawthorne offered her his hand and she took it. She was
so frightened. "I'll hurt you," she protested as he drew her
against his side.

"Nay, you'll help me. Can you load a pistol, Cara Mulvaine?"

"I've never touched one," she whispered.

"If I tell you what to do, will you do it?"

"Aye," she answered solemnly.

"Good. While the boat's in this angle you can open the hatch. Feel for it there, underneath the mattress."

"Where?" Cara felt about blindly underneath them. She found a slot and a brass hasp and, lifting it, found the hatch. She moved off the bed and braced herself against the tilted floor. Hawthorne moved deeper into the oddly raised corner. Cara lifted the hatch and felt inside its dark confines.

"My pistols are in a case. There will be a soft sack, as well. Bring that out, too."

"I've got it." Cara snared the two items. She felt something else, something very soft. Since she was grabbing everything, the cloth followed.

Hawthorne squinted and chuckled. "I might have known you'd find that, too."

"What is it?" Cara said as she tried to straighten up. It was impossible to do so with the boat listing so badly. Someone screamed like a demon on the deck and the thuds of the axes kept pounding into the wood, thudding inside the dim cabin.

"A rather blowsy dress, if memory serves me correct." Hawthorne relaxed when she let the hatch fall back into place. He resettled his aching body in the niche. Everything hurt dreadfully. The listing wasn't helping.

"A dress?" Cara exclaimed, tugging the last of the rich silk from beneath the wood. She set the gun case and the sack down and spread out the garment. It was all in one piece, which was more than she could say for her tattered and mangled brown. "What color is this, blue?"

"Azure, I believe."

"Why, Hawthorne, wherever did you get it?" Cara marveled. The cloth was pale and delicate, nothing like heavy wool or stiff linen. How she could be distracted by something so beautiful when her heart was sorrowing for Gordie she didn't know. Unless it was that her soul could only take so much pain.

"I don't remember," he mumbled. Cara clutched the gown to her torn bodice and ran her hand down it, pressing it to her stomach.

"May I please borrow it?"

"Be my guest," Hawthorne answered, but he was fast sinking into oblivion. He didn't want to do that. He had troubles enough without losing consciousness. He had to stay awake long enough to protect the Mulvaine. He'd be damned if he'd watch Dee abuse her again.

Somehow the girl braced herself against the base of the bunk and stood erect enough to discard her torn gown. All that was actually left of it were its plain brown skirts and the tatters of her chemise, which she had tried to keep fitted to her shoulders.

Hawthorne dragged a stinging breath through his broken nose and kept his eyes focused on the woman, but she kept fading in and out of his blurred sight. She had sacrificed her petticoat to bandage him. He wondered if Gordie knew what a superbly splendid woman she was. She smoothed her hands across the bosom and down her belly, then shook the wrinkled skirts.

"I shall look a fright in daylight, my lord, but at least I will be properly clothed. Now, you were going to instruct me in the means of loading a pistol."

The ship shuddered from stem to stern as the mast was finally cut away and heaved overboard. Immediately the list altered. The ship rocked in the waves at the whim of the sea.

Hawthorne winced as his right side collided with the hard bunk once more. Cara moved to straighten the mattress.

"Leave go of that. Listen to me. You must be quick. Do exactly as I say."

Cara sensed his urgency. Perhaps John Dee and that awful man that had hurt Hawthorne would return. She concentrated and did exactly what he told her to do. There were two pistols. Hawthorne propped his shoulders against the wall and stuck the first under the tangle of blankets at his left hand and repeated his step by step directions on how to load the second. She handed the armed gun to him.

"Now, my lord? What next?"

"We wait," Hawthorne admitted. He swallowed painfully and fixed his gaze to the cabin door. There was all manner of noise about, men tramping back and forth on the deck, Dee's hysterics above the din. "Can you look out the porthole, Cara?"

"Aye." Cara found standing much easier now that the ship was upright. She moved to the tiny portal and wiped the sheen of seawater clinging to its inside with her hand. "I don't see anything...no...wait...there's a ship. Ah!"

She gasped out loud. "'Tis O'Malley's black *Avenger*." And just as she said that, the *Victorious*'s starboard guns cut loose, one right after the other. Cara ducked away from the port-hole, screaming, covering her ears.

"Mulvaine!" Hawthorne croaked loudly.

"Oh, no! Oh, no!" Cara bolted back and forth, at the point of utter hysteria.

"Stop that!" Hawthorne shouted brutally. "Come here, damn you!"

Cara fled to him because he was the only thing safe in the entire world. Gordie was gone. She howled underneath the compression of Hawthorne's arm, terrified as the guns on the other side of the ship erupted.

Hawthorne pressed her against his chest, absorbing the noise and hysteria of her cries. He could do nothing to calm her tremors or ease the fear that sent her burrowing nearly beneath him. He braced his back against the wall in anticipation of returning volleys and listened as his crew scrambled to reload and commence firing again.

"Cara, promise me one thing. If I do not make it out of this mess I have brought us both into and you do, will you tell Rose that I love her?"

"You do?"

"Aye, with all my heart and soul."

Both the *Revenge* and the *Avenger* circled the *Victorious*, which was dead in the water. Dee ground his teeth and hit the first mate with a wenchpin for the misfiring.

"The boats are out of range," Umlaff told him.

"They are ships, not boats, you stupid oaf. Damn their eyes. Go and get me the woman. By God, I'll have some concessions out of these stupid Scots and vermin Irish. Fetch my whip when you bring her topside. Tie her to the mizzenmast. We'll see just how far they want to play their game to stop me!"

"If you do that, there will be no blood sacrifice on the solstice," Umlaff countered.

"Are you so stupid to think there aren't others born that same hour? Go and get her I said."

Hawthorne's first mate, Templeton, pushed himself to his feet, blood trickling down his neck, and he looked to the mutinous faces of Hawthorne's crew. Events had gotten far out of hand. Hawthorne couldn't defend himself, much less the Mulvaine. Not a Scot was going to tolerate a wee woman being lashed. He nodded once and every man who saw the look in his eye found a makeshift weapon to take to hand. The two who had cut the broken mast from the ship gripped their axes and moved closer to the quarterdeck.

"Load those guns again, damn your eyes." Dee whipped his pistol about in his left hand, the only sword on the ship dangling from his right. He'd forced Hawthorne's men to throw their arms overboard when he'd taken the ship. He hadn't much practice in using either pistol or sword, but he was hell to account to with a whip. Now he wished he hadn't left that below, coiled on Hawthorne's massive mahogany desk. The ship was in shambles. But he would force either Drake or that bitch O'Malley to surrender their ship to him.

"I said, load the bloody cannons."

Gordie checked his instruments one more time. He bent over the breech, closing it, then cranked the swivel two degrees higher.

"What do you think?" Ulrich asked.

"I think Hawthorne better say his prayers." Gordie looked down the sight once more. "Stand clear on deck," he shouted.

"Hold yer fire, boy-o. Look to the *Victorious*. Be that mutiny or not?" Grace ranted excitedly from the yardarm.

"What?" Gordie bolted to his feet. Both he and Ulrich and every man on the lower deck shot to the portside to see what was happening on the *Victorious*. The reports of small arms firing, three pistol shots, came in quick succession.

Then, what appeared to be every man on board the *Victorious* swarmed up to the quarterdeck and engaged in a war of fists and fury.

"Ready about!" Drake shouted down the deck and the *Revenge* heaved over, swinging toward the damaged craft. "Prepare to board. Get the grappling hooks. All hands on deck!"

Grace O'Malley's ship completed the same maneuver from the other side. She dropped out of Drake's riggings, grinning broadly and brandishing both cutlass and pistol. Pointing the end of the blade at Drake's throat, she warned, "Release my crew, ya bastard, or I'll slit you from stem to stern."

"Save yer histrionics for the Scots, O'Malley. I'll let you cut off Hawthorne's balls."

"You will, laddie?" she said with bloodthirsty interest. "Now there's a proposition I can hardly refuse. And he such a big, strapping lad."

"You'll have to wait yer turn for that," Gordie promised, arming himself and taking hold of a rope to be one of the first to swing over into the fray.

Whatever mayhem was happening on board the broken vessel, both O'Malley and Drake thought it wiser to let the blood be let first, then board when things had calmed.

"Ahoy, *Victorious,* this is Drake. Lay down your weapons and prepare to be boarded. Surrender and your lives are spared."

Matthew Templeton straightened his shoulders, squinting though the hazy glow of dawn, laden with smoke and mist. "That's enough, mates. Tie the bastard to the mizzen, Bates. Drop yer weapons."

The thunk of wood dropping to the deck sounded round the twenty or so men who had beaten Dee to a pulp and pinned him to a mizzen. They made no move as the grappling hooks were thrown over their sides and the two ships drew upside.

From the riggings of the *Revenge,* Gordie was among the first to swing himself over the side.

"Where's Hawthorne?" he demanded.

As one, the crew of the *Victorious* met his glare. They were none of them sure if Hawthorne lived. There had been too many pistol shots, two from his quarters below.

In a blind haze Gordie pressed to the quarterdeck, yanking open the galley door, leaping down it. He landed with pantherlike grace and rushed to the captain's cabin. The door was blocked. Ulrich came after him.

"I'll have to break the damn door down!" Gordie snarled.

He reached for a bench to use for a battering ram. Kicking hadn't budged it. Ulrich lent his strength to the battering. The door splintered before it budged an inch. Ramming it one more time, the upper half shattered and fell away.

"Hawthorne!" Gordie roared. Murderous blood surged through his veins. With one last pound, he kicked whatever it was that blocked the door, out of his way. Winded, he gripped his cutlass to one hand, fitted his pistol firmly in his grip and stepped inside the dim cabin.

Were it not for the fact that its furnishings were fitted to the floors and walls, the cabin could not have been in worse shambles. Hawthorne was perched upon a narrow bunk and, curled in his arms, as pretty as you please, was none other than Gordie's wife, Cara Mulvaine.

Ulrich stumbled over the dead body that had blocked the door. The man was a massive creature, a mountain of flesh and bone. He had flattened backward across the threshold, a bore through the center of his forehead.

"Hawthorne, get the hell out of that bed and stand up and face me like a man!"

"Hold on there, boy-o! That one's mine! Drake promised me his balls!"

Cara was crying so hard, she didn't hear Gordie's order. Grace's shriek didn't register, either. She clung to Hawthorne's inert body and cried out the sorrow of her soul, a grief that had laid on her shoulders for years and years and years.

"I said get up, mon!" Gordie fired his pistol through the exterior wall, blowing a splatter of wood out a new porthole.

"No! No! No!" Cara shrieked, turning round, placing her body before Hawthorne's. He'd protected her life, she'd give hers for him. But then her jaw sagged at what she saw. For there, looming before her like another Kenna ghost come to haunt her forever, stood Gordon Mckenna.

She felt a faint fluttering in her belly, a movement so soft and frail, it was like a butterfly's caress. "Ah, Gordie, you look so real, so solid."

Astounded, Gordie watched her pass her hand across blue silk over her belly. Still she blocked his view of Hawthorne. "Get away from him, Cara! Now, I said! Obey me, woman!"

"Gordie, you've come to haunt this ship?" Cara questioned her eyes, her sanity, as well. He looked so real, so furious. Then she stood and bolted for his arms, wanting to touch him one last time.

He had not an embrace to give her. He thrust her aside for Ulrich to catch and contain. Gordie moved closer to the bunk, his eyes adjusting to the lack of light. He slapped the flat of his sword across the sole of Hawthorne's boot. Up close he could see well enough. Hawthorne was unconscious or dead, he didn't know which. He could hardly recognize the huge man half lying, half sitting upon his bed in a crushed welter of blood-splattered linens. Hardly an inch of his exposed skin was whole and unabraded. There wasn't much left of the handsome face.

Gordon Mckenna turned round and swore viciously, ending his tirade with the words, "You can have his balls, O'Malley, if you got the stomach to cut what's left of them off."

At what point Cara realized Gordie was no apparition, she didn't know. But the man who slapped steel to boot leather wasn't a ghost.

Cara snatched her hand from Ulrich's grip and leaped between Gordie and Hawthorne. "Nobody touches Hawthorne, do you hear me! He saved my life. You aren't going to touch him!"

"I'm backing the lady up," Matthew Templeton said as he shouldered inside his captain's quarters. Other members of the loyal crew were there to back him, as well.

"Go against me in this, Templeton, and you'll be singing a tune for the maiden." Gordie threatened Scotland's version of the guillotine. "Hawthorne, this crew and this ship are under arrest, in the name of James the Sixth, King of Scotland."

"Then you'll have to arrest me, too!" Cara declared.

"You!"

Gordie finally turned his attention to his wife. His eyes nearly rolled inside his head when he realized what she was wearing—a silk gown that was suitable only for a bordello. It clung to her body like a soft glove, enfolding a form that had changed considerably since he'd last seen it. What, dear lord, he asked himself, had happened to her breasts, her hips? Was his worst fear that she had rutted her way to the top of the queen's court now realized?

That was the last straw!

In a blind rage, Gordie snatched her hand from her side and yanked her along with him as he strode from Hawthorne's cabin.

"Gordie!" Cara hollered out, protesting. She might as well have saved her breath.

Topside, a milling crowd of the crews of three ships were every last one of them shouting at one another, trying to sort out what the problems were, who was at fault, who was guilty and who was innocent. Charge and countercharge bellowed into the close air. Gordie ignored the shout by Frances Drake to account for himself and bring his wife into the fray for her testimony.

No one, Gordie swore violently, no one else was going to see his wife dressed like that! No one except him! He got as far as the rail before Cara balked.

"Now just one damn minute!" she roared in a voice that should have been heard all the way back to Gravesend.

Where she got the strength to bring Gordie's momentum to a dead halt, he would never know, but somehow she got her hand fixed upon a rail on the *Victorious*'s deck and held on for dear life. "Cease, I said!"

A stroke of lightning cracked out of the sea and shot into the tumbling clouds overrunning the sky. Not three seconds later a bolt of thunder shook the ship and every man and woman had hackles standing on their necks. They all turned to gape at Cara Mulvaine. Including Gordie.

"What did you say?" He rounded on her, shaken by the volume of her voice and the lightning and thunder that had punctuated it.

"I've had it!" Cara declared. "That's all I'm going to stand and I'll be damned if I will take any more!"

The strange lightning and thunder rumbled over her head and swept across the ship's deck, giving power to her words.

"That is the last time anyone is taking me anywhere against my will!" Cara lowered her voice, but even then it rang out true and clear. Every soul on deck heard her.

The sea had suddenly gone still, silently roiling like a tempest about to brew into a violent, shattering storm. "I will not be abducted again, Gordon Mckenna. Do you understand me? Do you?"

Since the lightning decided to rack his ears and rattle every spar and timber in sight, Gordie guessed he did understand her. "Cara." Words failed him, "Cara, do you know what kind of hell this has put me through?"

"Do you know what kind of hell I've been put through, Gordon Mckenna?"

The elements weren't backing him up. Thunder rolled again after she subsided, her question lingering on the breathless air.

Everyone of the Irish looked to the heavens and crossed themselves automatically.

Gordie looked at her, really looked at her. He didn't see what he wanted to see this time, but saw instead the soft, vulnerable girl who had worn her timid heart upon her sleeve.

"Cara." His voice softened. "I don't know how to say what I feel. I failed you. I only ever planned to keep you safe, here." He laid his hand on his chest, covering his heart. "Here, within the sweep of my arms. That's where you belong. That's all that matters to me. Come to me. Let me take you home."

He spread his arms wide, inviting her, words unable to express his meaning any clearer than his most heartfelt gesture.

Tears welled in Cara's eyes. She had thought there wasn't a dram left within her. Surely in the past hours she had flooded the sea with tears. Tears wasted because she thought she had lost him forever.

She fled to him, throwing herself in the wrap of his arms, home at last as they turned round about her and clenched her to his hard, hurting chest.

O'Malley was the first to clear her throat and roughly declare, "Drake, you sot, we're in for a hell of a blow. Cut your lines and see to your sails, else we'll be scuttling yer ship, too. Mates, the *Avenger* needs a trim. All hands back on deck."

Drake gave Essex a shove to send him stumbling toward the *Revenge*'s deck. "I hate it when that woman betters me at my own game."

But in spite of the muttering and grumbling on just about every side, every man and woman of the three crews cast a glance back at the entwined lovers and granted them a benevolent smile and a moment's reprieve.

"Templeton, cut yer lines and drop yer sails," Drake directed. "We'll lash a cable to the bow and take the *Victorious* under tow."

It was a long time before either Gordie or Cara came up for air. Their kiss was soul binding. It didn't matter where they were or who witnessed the need and passion surging through their reunion.

A thunderbolt crescendoing finally brought Gordie to his senses. He raised his head and looked about him dazedly, and found the only person in plain sight was his cousin Ulrich. That lout had parked his oafish body in a nearby coil of rope, just sitting there, grinning and watching.

"What are you grinning at?" Gordie demanded sourly.

"Not much, cousin. Didn't you tell me this past spring, you'd know you were in love when a thunderbolt hit you?"

"Aye!" Gordie set Cara aside in the tuck of his arm.

"Well, Mckenna. You've been struck. So many times, yer hair is standing right on end." Ulrich grinned.

Unconsciously, Gordie ran his fingers through his wild hair, smoothing it, feeling the crackle of static spark off the friction of his hand. "So I have," he admitted. He caught Cara's chin and tilted her face upward so that he could gaze at her. "I'm in love with you, Cara Mulvaine. Will you marry me and put me out of my misery?"

"I fear I must, this time, my lord Mckenna," Cara answered in a softer voice. "I'm rather great with child."

"What?" Gordie turned her in his arm, searching her face, astounded. "Are you certain? When? How?"

Cara blushed, stood on tiptoe and whispered something too private to share with nosy Ulrich in Gordie's ear. "Do you no remember the day we made love in the glen with Mimms guarding us?"

"I knew that!" Gordie blushed to the roots of his hair, then he laughed. "Let's heave over to the *Revenge* and get Drake to say the words."

"Oh, no." Cara refused. "This time, Mckenna, the only one speaking the words is going to be a churchman. And I want to be married in the same kirk where Rose got married. It's a special place—wonderful and sacred."

"Where Rose what?" Both Gordie and Ulrich shouted at the same time.

"Oh, no!" Cara folded her arms across her chest and the wind picked up suddenly, sending her wild hair flying about her face. "You're not going to intimidate me ever again with that voice of yours, Gordie Mckenna! Or you either, Ulrich! You can roar at me till the heavens open and I'll roar right back!"

"Is that so, wench?" Gordie leaned ominously close to her face. Cara stood her ground, not flinching, not even when their noses touched. "All right, then." Gordie softened his voice, turning it sugary, convincing. "Where, pray tell me did my sister Rose get married?"

"At the Lady's Chapel at Rosslyn Castle. I'll marry you there and nowhere else."

"And who, dearest handfasted wife, did my sister deign to marry? Would you be sharing that information with me, then?"

Unflinchingly, Cara looked him straight in the eye and said, "Hawthorne."

"I'll kill the bastard," Gordie declared.

"No, you won't," Cara countered right back at him. "He's your brother, now. My brother, too. You'll be doing him no further harm, Gordon Mckenna."

"When?" was all Gordie said.

"The first day of July. It was all done right and proper with a priest and witnesses. I signed the register and I know it's a valid marriage. He's a good man, Mckenna. One of the very best."

"He's a dead man," Ulrich injected, "when the Mckenna gets his hands on him."

"Well, we shall just have to see that our lord Mckenna does not get his hands upon Lord Hawthorne," Cara said unequivocally.

Then she looked about her on the lower deck of the disabled ship and saw that John Dee had been securely tied to the mizzenmast.

"That rascal." She shook her head, confounded by the fact that he hadn't been thrown bodily overboard. Hawthorne's crew had paid him back full measure, but she could tell in a glance that Dee lived and wasn't going to die anytime soon.

"Gordie, I have something that must be done."

"What is it?"

"Come with me."

Cara returned to Hawthorne's cabin. Drake's surgeon was there, as well as Templeton and another mate called Bates. Between the three of them, they had Hawthorne's bed back in order and the man more properly bandaged, cleaned up and laid on his unlashed stomach in bed. But there hadn't been time to straighten the cabin itself.

Cara cast her knowing gaze about. She looked at the spilled trunks and the parchment trash, the tablets, books, omens and evil talismans. "All of this must be thrown overboard," Cara ordered. "The trunks must be weighted with stone, locked and sunk to the bottom of the sea."

"Why?" Gordie asked.

"It's evil." Cara kicked aside a black silk cloth and revealed Dee's hellish skull and black crystal. "It's black magic, desecrated by blood sacrifices. Dee was going to take our son and sacrifice him, Gordie. Do not touch anything with your bare hands. You, either, Ulrich. A gentleman of Hawthorne's ilk must have gloves about. Here." Cara seemed to know exactly which cubby to open. She withdrew three pair of gloves, one for each of them. "Put these on first."

"I wonder who that was?" Gordie regarded the hollowed skull.

"'Tis better not to know," Cara answered. She donned the gloves quicker than the others and set her mind to doing the task that must be done. She bent and took the black crystal between her hands, then solemnly marched out of the room, bearing it straight to the aft deck rail.

"What do you?" Dee shouted when he saw what she had in her hands.

"Ending your madness, Master Dee." Cara met his gaze fearlessly now.

All about her, the sea seemed to be breaking upon some terrible violence. The storm was bearing down upon the convoy of ships.

"No!" Dee's scream rent the air. Cara stared at him, then held the globe aloft. It began to pulse with its terrible life, its odd green light shining forth, seeking a soul to command to do its will.

Dee's shrieks were like that of a man twisted by possession.

"Be gone, Satan. Get thee back to hell!"

She dropped the orb and it fell like the solid stone that it was, splashing into the sea and disappearing from sight forever.

Gordie stood at the door of the galley, frozen there by the sight of his wife being washed in an unearthly, heathen glow. Dee had thrashed about and now slumped against his bonds. He looked old, withered, shrunken upon himself.

Cara dusted off her gloved hands. "No more, Master Dee," she said softly, as if she were alone and there was no one to hear her speak. "The powers and the dominions will always set someone like me in the way of someone like you. Take heed that you do not ever get what you wish. The wisdom of Solomon and the key of the universe is more than man can hold in his limited brain."

"Cara, come away from the rail," Gordie softly called to her. She drew off the gloves that had touched the evil thing, tossed them into the sea then ran to Gordie and was swept up in his arms.

"We will let Ulrich and Templeton restore Hawthorne's cabin to order. The first mate has most graciously given us leave to rest in his quarters. Your wishes will be carried out to the letter. All of Master Dee's possessions will be packed inside his trunks, weighted with stone ballast and sunk to the bottom of the sea.''

"By wind, by fire, by earth, by water, in the name of God Almighty, amen,'' Cara said most solemnly.

"Amen,'' Gordie concurred. Then he lifted her up into his arms and carried her below. "As you command, my little one.''

"I have another command, my lord Mckenna.'' Cara settled her arms round his broad shoulders and gazed deeply into the sparkling blue of his eyes.

"Don't let a little success go to your head, mistress,'' Gordie advised. "I won't tolerate a termagant.''

"Then just kiss me, my lord, and I promise you, I will most sweetly do you bidding from that moment on.''

Epilogue

The night was icy and cold as the wind howled round Castle Kenna, rattling panes in the windows and the shutters all along the north walls. Snow swept in flurries across the barren courtyard and piled high on the ledges and the roofs.

Before the fire in the great hall, the men of the house sat whiling away their time. Talk was subdued. Laird Mckenna paced anxiously back and forth before the hearth. At the end of one circuit he stopped and glared at the hound lying across his rug. The beast raised a back paw and scratched at his fleas, then yawned and let his great head sink back onto his paws.

"The damn thing is roasting its brains," Mckenna observed.

"Assuming it has any." Gordie ran his fingers across the strings of his harp, tapping out an idle tune.

"Mimms," he called to the animal.

It raised its head and fixed its blind eyes upon him, that huge pink tongue lolling out of his mouth.

"I still find it hard to believe you did not destroy the creature," Gordie admitted to his father.

"How could I when I know what he means to Cara?" The Mckenna bent and scratched the dog's ruff. "He was nearly dead when I found him in the woods by the village. But he lives."

"Don't torment the beast." Ulrich tossed it a bone from the clutter piled on the trestle.

Mimms found the bone, took it between his paws and gnawed it greedily.

John Mckenna paced back the opposite way, stopping this time when he came face-to-face with the tall, black-haired man who leaned negligently against the outer wall and silently stared up at the empty gallery. The patch over his right eye made his dark face more sinister and harsh.

Unable to think of any way to break through the man's deep reserve, the Mckenna said, "It's going to be a long night."

The earl of Hawthorne shot the Mckenna a killing look and said nothing.

Suppressing the urge to have at the lout one more time, the laird snorted, about-faced and paced back the way he had come. His fool of a nephew, Ulrich, pretended that nothing was amiss in the house.

"Longer than usual, what with the storm trapping us all indoors before dusk."

"Shut up, Ulrich!" Both John and Gordie Mckenna growled.

Miffed, Ulrich dropped into a chair. Hawthorne's face turned toward him. Ulrich held up both his hands, palms open, and shrugged, unable to do more to affect the uneasy peace that kept Hawthorne and Mckenna from killing one another.

Mimms' ears perked up. He stood abruptly, tipping over a stool. Then he added his voice to the rising howl of the storm.

Hackles rose on Gordie's neck. "Not the banshee," he whispered as he rose to his feet.

"Poppa, Gordie, Ulrich, Elliott, come! 'Tis here. 'Tis here!" Rose came running down the stairs, nearly tripping in her excitement. She grabbed her brother's hand and pushed him toward the stairs. Then she whirled again and ran into the hall, caught hold of her husband's hand, urging him to come, as well. "Nay, Elliott, ye must come. Cara's asked for ye."

"Well, it's about time!" John Mckenna exclaimed as he hurried up the steps after his son.

Behind him, Ulrich said, "I guess this just proves what fakers and charlatans magicians really are. Winter solstice, my eye. This is the thirteenth of January."

"Fourteenth," Hawthorne corrected, marking the hour past midnight.

He paused in the gallery to take hold of Rose's hand and bring it to his lips. Rose held back with him, letting her father and cousin advance into the bedchamber. Hawthorne's one good eye beseeched her for the truth.

"Tsk! Elliot," Rose said sincerely. "If you give my father a little more time, he'll be coming around, too. My sister Jane always had a crush on Ralph. Poppa will be happy once their banns are read.''

''Will he?'' Hawthorne said, not convinced.

Rose kissed him and whispered softly. '''Tis a beautiful, perfect babe. Dinna fear it. Cara has long since forgiven you.''

Lady Cara might have, but by everyone else's standards, Hawthorne was the vilest bounder ever born. All within Castle Kenna feared something most horrible had gone wrong, for Christmas, the winter solstice, had come and passed and no predicted son with it.

Hawthorne doubted he'd ever forget the mad lights glistening in Dee's dark eyes when the magus had stated how exactly he'd planned to sacrifice the infant minutes after its birth.

''Come.'' Rose pulled him forward. ''Come, look, you'll see. 'Tis a wondrous babe.'' Rose brought her husband inside the birthing room.

Cara lay on a large, comfortable bed in a cushion of warm quilts. In her arms was a tiny, red-faced bundle.

''Why, 'tis the most beautiful babe I've ever seen!'' John Mckenna leaned across the bed opposite his son, falling in love in an instant with the tiny round face that looked up at him with such wonder in its eyes. ''Look at that hair. 'Tis as red as Gordie's was.''

''Ach, John, let your son look at the babe,'' Elaina Mckenna scolded.

''Do you think so?'' Cara asked hesitantly, her focus only on her husband's reaction as she unfolded the flannel that wrapped the babe so that all could see the plump arms and legs and sweet little face crowned with a cap of auburn hair. Gordie sank to his knee at Cara's side.

But it wasn't the reddish hair that each man in the room stared at. It was the babe's perfectly naked body. Every man in the room exclaimed in one astonished voice. '''Tis a boy!''

''Why, so it is.'' Cara chuckled at the sight of Gordie's wry and instantaneous smile.

''A son,'' Gordie echoed, taking the tiny bundle into his hands.

''And we shall name him Graham, if it pleases you, my lord husband,'' Cara requested softly.

''Aye, he pleases me, my love. You please me, as well. Thank you. I love you, Cara.'' Gordie held the babe secure against his warm chest and bent close to press a kiss upon Cara's lips. Standing, he turned to present his son to his family.

Still dumbfounded, he looked across the sea of heads crowding to croon to young Graham. As shocked as anyone else in the chamber, Hawthorne met Gordie's gaze.

The earl's hard face softened for the babe, but fixed into its rigid, shuttered mask for the babe's father. Gordie cleared his throat. "Cara has another wish, imparted to me before this ordeal began, Hawthorne. She requests you stand as my son's godfather. I can think of no other to whom I would commend the soul of my child. Will you swear for Graham at the christening, mon?"

A pleased light glinted in the depth of Hawthorne's single eye. He answered firmly, "Aye."

Rose stood on tiptoe and kissed his cheek. "I told ye so!" she whispered for his ears alone.

Last to enter the chamber was the wolfhound. Using his nose to find the woman he served, Mimms wound around legs and boots and came to rest his head on the bed, snuffling at the baby's blanket.

"Here, now, none o' that." Gordie settled the baby within the flannel where Mimms could take the infant's scent. "He's too young to run with you, old boy. You'll be waiting a year or two for that. Besides, I shall always claim the right of first protector to my family, but you may stand as my second."

* * * * *

Author Note

Dunluce Castle stands in ruins today. In 1588 the octogenarian Sorely Boy McDonnell sheltered the five survivors of the shipwreck *Girona*. His contemporary, Grace O'Malley, lived on Clare Island off the coast of Ireland and pirated the open seas. The earl of Tyrone, Hugh O'Neill, was taken from Ireland as a boy-hostage, and fostered in England so that Irish could be educated out of him. He returned to Ireland and spent his life fighting English rule. Robin Devereaux was charged with subduing the Irish when the O'Neill controlled more than half of Ireland. It is said by some historians that O'Neill and Essex met in the ancient tradition of single combat. The two parted, their armies retreated. Essex returned to England and shortly afterward lost favor with Queen Elizabeth. She ordered him imprisoned in the Devil's Tower, which to this day is called Devereaux Tower. He was beheaded on her orders in 1602.

To this day, theories abound regarding the mysterious Knights Templar, but no one truly knows where their wealth and vast collections of knowledge disappeared to in 1314. The order of St. John's Hospitalers adopted the title Defender of the Temple shortly after 1314 and Templar properties in England, Scotland and Ireland were held in trust by the Order of St. John for centuries after.

Harlequin® Historical

MORE ROMANCE, MORE PASSION, MORE ADVENTURE...MORE PAGES!

Bigger books from Harlequin Historicals. Pick one up today and see the difference a Harlequin Historical can make.

White Gold by Curtiss Ann Matlock—January 1995—A young widow partners up with a sheep rancher in this exciting Western.

Sweet Surrender by Julie Tetel—February 1995—An unlikely couple discover hidden treasure in the next *Northpoint* book.

All That Matters by Elizabeth Mayne—March 1995—A medieval about the magic between a young woman and her Highland rescuer.

The Heart's Wager by Gayle Wilson—April 1995—An ex-soldier and a member of the demi-monde unite to rescue an abducted duke.

Longer stories by some of your favorite authors. Watch for them in 1995 wherever Harlequin Historicals are sold.

HHBB95-1

HARLEQUIN®

PRESENTS
RELUCTANT BRIDEGROOMS

Two beautiful brides, two unforgettable romances...
two men running for their lives....

My Lady Love, by Paula Marshall, introduces
Charles, Viscount Halstead, who lost his memory
and found himself employed as a stableboy by the
untouchable Nell Tallboys, Countess Malplaquet.
But Nell didn't consider Charles untouchable—
not at all!

Darling Amazon, by Sylvia Andrew, is the story of
a spurious engagement between Julia Marchant
and Hugo, marquess of Rostherne—an engagement
that gets out of hand and just may lead Hugo to
the altar after all!

Enjoy two madcap Regency weddings this May,
wherever Harlequin books are sold.

REG5

From author Susan Paul

This spring, don't miss the first book in this exciting new series from
a newcomer to Harlequin Historicals—**Susan Paul**

THE BRIDE'S PORTION
April 1995

The unforgettable story of an honorable knight forced to wed
the daughter of his enemy in order to free himself from
her father's tyranny.

Be sure to keep an eye out for this upcoming series
filled with the splendor and pageantry of Medieval times
wherever Harlequin Historicals are sold!

BRP-1

Harlequin® Historical

Gayle Wilson

**The talented new author from
Harlequin Historicals brings you
the next title in her series set amid the
sophistication and intrigue
of Regency London**

THE HEART'S WAGER
April 1995
The compelling story of an ex-soldier and a casino dealer who must
face great dangers to rescue his best friend from certain death!

Don't miss this delightful tale!

And you can still order THE HEART'S DESIRE
from the address below.

To order your copy of THE HEART'S DESIRE (HH #211), please send your name,
address, zip or postal code along with a check or money order (please do not
send cash) for $3.99 for each book ordered ($4.50 in Canada), plus 75¢ postage and
handling ($1.00 in Canada), payable to Harlequin Books, to:

In the U.S.	In Canada
3010 Walden Avenue	P. O. Box 609
P. O. Box 1369	Fort Erie, Ontario
Buffalo, NY 14269-1369	L2A 5X3

Please specify book title(s) with your order.
Canadian residents add applicable federal and provincial taxes.

Harlequin® Historical

Claire Delacroix's UNICORN TRILOGY

The series began with UNICORN BRIDE,
a story that *Romantic Times* described as
"...a fascinating blend of fantasy and romance."

Now you can follow the Pereille family's ongoing quest
in the author's April 1995 release:

PEARL BEYOND PRICE

And if you missed UNICORN BRIDE, it's not too late
to order the book from the address below.